GAIA'S CHILDREN

May

Also by Paul Kieniewicz

Immortality Machine

GAIA'S CHILDREN

Paul Kieniewicz

Matador
9 Priory Busines Park
Wistow Road
Kibworth Beauchamp
Leicester LE8 0RX, UK
Tel: 0116 279 2299
Email: books@troubador.co.uk
Web: www.troubador.co.uk/matador

ISBN 978 1 78088 086 0

British Library Cataloguing in Publication Data.
A catalogue record for this book is available from the British Library.

Jacket Note
Earth image © NASA
Cover Art: © Johanna Kieniewicz and Jon Reades

Typeset in 11pt Aldine by Troubador Publishing Ltd, Leicester, UK

Matador is an imprint of Troubador Publishing Ltd

Printed and bound in the UK by TJ International, Padstow, Cornwall

MIX
Paper from
responsible sources
FSC® C013056

ACKNOWLEDGEMENTS

I am most grateful to my wife Amber, who edited various drafts of the manuscript and kept her sanity throughout its creation. Thanks also to my manuscript readers: Adam Archibald, Charles Ashton, Annie Ashton, Rachel Ashton, Natalia Kieniewicz and Amanda Still for their valuable feedback. A special thanks to Stephan Harding for reading an early draft and for encouraging me to publish the story. The cover art was generously provided by Johanna Kieniewicz and Jon Reades.

I am indebted to James Lovelock for his writings on the Gaia Theory, Stephan Harding for "Animate Earth", David Abram for his work on deep ecology and to Shaun Ellis for his work with wolves. The discussions between David Bohm and J. Krishnamurti on the nature of psychological time played a major role in developing lupan psychology.

The St. Francis Wolf Sanctuary in Montgomery, Texas, founded thirty years ago by Jean LeFevre, allowed me to interact and communicate with wolves. Thank-you Jean, for your wolves and for your insights.

ONE

It was the perfect day to die.

Scott Maguire climbed into his glider. He looked long at the mountains, a collage of purple and gold that shimmered through the sultry air. They beckoned him. Come lie with me, die here. You won't find a better resting place. Behind the range rose the angular peak of Mona Gowan where he'd often walked, years ago when it was still safe to roam the countryside.

He attached his seat belt, fumbled with controls he knew well but today looked unfamiliar. Two men in overalls leaned on the nose sharing their impressions of the World Cup. When would they find the winch and attach it so he could escape? The tall fence, surmounted by barb wire coils, still enclosed him like a prison. Through it he made out the wasteland of blackened tree stumps and a couple of bombed-out houses. Smoke rising from a yellow plume to the north made the air hazy. The battle of the day or a wildfire? It wasn't a farmer burning his rubbish.

He took a sip of water from his flask, swilled it in his mouth and swallowed cautiously. His throat was raw. The swelling under his chin reminded him that he was infected. His clock was ticking toward its appointed end.

The plane jerked, telling him that the winch was attached. So it's up, up and away. The cable tightened on the sailplane, pulled it briskly along the runway and then free. Scott drew the stick toward his chest, watched the plane's nose tilt up. A flawless takeoff for his flight out of the world. If he held to his plan and

1

didn't wax nostalgic about the gift of life. Life – a gift? He laughed, loud enough to hear himself above the whistling air but could not dispel a growing numbness. If he was about to die of Plague why not go out with a bang rather than in bed? Or in jail? After all, his dream was over.

Unfortunately he wasn't dreaming when he woke up the previous morning to find the police at his door. Someone had tipped them off to his less-than-legal activities. At first he kept his cool, gave detailed answers to their questions, but when they kept at him like pit-bulls he grew angry. After an intense discussion he persuaded them that they could find him at any time. They took his passport and left.

Did he have to end his life? He did, unless he wanted to die in jail, disgraced and branded as a traitor with his name raked over by tabloids. Dad and Mum would be bereaved, but they would get over it. For years they hadn't even tried to stay in touch. Living in Sweden they might not hear about his death for another month. Joan would hate him for it. Though they'd broken up five years ago she still wrote him sentimental emails. He'd sent her a delayed text that he was ending his life and why.

At the edge of a forest the plane caught an air wave that sent him a hundred meters up. The yellowing ground retreated, waving him good-bye. Steadying the plane he made a second run at the forest, gained some lift then turned the glider's nose toward a prominent line of mountains. At that altitude he'd make at least twenty miles, to reach less populated parts of Aberdeenshire.

Through the smoky haze he made out more trees, stretches of healthy pines then acres of stumps that hadn't borne a leaf for years. They were soon replaced by homesteads, each consisting of a stone cottage, vegetable patch, a few farm animals and an electrified twelve-foot fence. Most had a lookout tower with an armed guard. Before global warming kicked in, sheep and cattle roamed a pastoral landscape. You could walk for miles and no one bothered you. Then the high oil prices and exotic diseases drove the farms out of business. People escaping from crime-ridden cities or flooded-out homes filled the vacuum; built their private fortresses.

The smoke plume originated in a large homestead, now no more than a bombed-out shell surrounded by several craters. He made out several people standing nearby, no doubt weeping at the devastation. Electric fences and armed guards might deter wandering climate refugees but they only attracted city bounders by advertising that here was something worth raiding. When bounders came, they came with shoulder rocket-launchers. Each day a new raid figured in the news. The Scottish army, spread thin in the Highlands, often came too late to help individual homesteads.

And there it was – three covered lorries, a tank and a bulldozer all on their carriers creeping along a mountain road, except that they were heading toward Braemar, in the wrong direction. They hadn't come to help out the locals. This was a demolition crew bound for the Braemar refugee camp. President Christie was making good on his election promise to secure Scotland's borders and clean up illegal camps.

I'll be gone by that time. My work is finished. I gave a few people a decent life but in the end it didn't do a damn bit of good. My clients will soon be locked up in internment camps. I can't fight a tank with a tooth pick.

He tried to steady his hands, but they kept shaking. *I never thought I'd be afraid to die, but I will not die in jail. Better make an end of it in the heather and hope that at least one quality paper will run a sympathetic headline, like: Fake Visa Lawyer Crashes in Highlands. Human Rights Groups Praise Lawyer. Death is the ending, Scott. There's no afterlife. It's like going to sleep one last time.*

The sailplane crossed into a small glen where it caught a weak slope lift allowing him to skim over the hill and down into the next glen. More homesteads, and he was headed for a high fence and its metal watchtower. He yanked the stick, lifted the glider's nose, only barely enough to clear the structures. *I can't crash among those bastards.* Several shots echoed from the hills. A guard in the closest tower had decided to open fire. He crouched lower in his seat, banked the plane away. The shooting ceased.

'Idiot,' he screamed. 'You think I'm a bounder coming to steal your bloody cabbages?'

Not enough lift. The skirmish left him drifting into heather and scrubby forest. Losing altitude. The ground rushed at him with finality. *Not here – I can't die here.* He held the stick steady. If he stayed on course a lucky thermal near the distant tree line might still rescue him. As the gnarled trees rose to meet him he braced for impact. Then he felt a gentle tug from rising air. The ground rolled out of sight and was replaced by blue sky. The plane cleared the crest of the hill.

He was in a narrow valley with several homesteads and a meandering stream along whose banks stood a small settlement. He could tell it was a refugee camp from the motley collage of whitewashed cobb houses with thatched roofs, Italian-style villas and wooden sheds with tar-papered roofs. Smoke seeping from stove pipes formed a white pall over the valley. He made out several lines of flapping laundry strung across mud-caked streets and small children playing there. Farther up the hill several wind generators turned slowly. There were no watchtowers or security fences other than a wolf-fence that snaked up hill and down valley. Where was he? He knew all major refugee camps but couldn't place this one. Intrigued, he banked to the right and circled over it. A stand of mature olive trees suggested they'd been planted twenty years earlier, which would make this one of the first camps. How had it survived government edicts that had closed so many others?

His eye was drawn to several faint lines that crisscrossed the glen, not respecting fences, houses and man-made boundaries, apparently painted on the ground, punctuated by standing stones and small stone circles. The web appeared to converge on a nearby hill. Close to its summit were several thatched domes like huge haystacks, and small patches of cultivated land.

'Impossible,' he muttered. 'What the hell is that doing there?'

The hill had all the features of a lupan colony, an active one judging by the smoke seeping from the domes. Most colonies had been eliminated years ago, the lupans shot or taken to government reservations. Why had this one escaped sentence? He made out small dark figures walking between the dens. They appeared to walk and run like humans, but he was sure that they weren't.

He'd seen lupans close up in a primate research facility. As expected they wore no clothes. Their arms and legs, sticklike as if after a long fast, appeared abnormally long. Sores on the hands and feet only emphasized their miserable state. Most characteristic were their ochre leathery skin, golden eyes and long black hair. Born of human parents, they should elicit at least the sympathy you felt for handicapped children, except that they were a species apart. Their hungry golden eyes sized you up the way a leopard might before it pounced on you. Like most people, he felt that lupans were a mockery of the human race and of everything he valued; nothing but grief to families cursed to bear them. They had less ability to bond than a canary. He tried to talk to them, but they responded with clicks, whistles and a deep throated moaning like the baying of wolves. Lupans were able to retain at most ten common nouns. If they were destined to take over the world from humans, they represented no evolutionary advance.

In a field near the dens several lupans milled about as if they didn't know which way to go. Maybe they were lost and needed to be helped out. He'd give them something to remember. He turned the sailplane's nose around, pushed the stick forward and let the plane drop. As he closed in, the squirming things ran for their lives, hair flying in every direction. Their high-pitched yelps echoed faintly as they hit the ground. He forced a smile.

'Count yourselves lucky,' he shouted through the window. 'At least you'll live long after the rest of us are gone.'

It's over. We're the last generation, and we're headed for a final exit.

He crossed over a forest that covered several hills all the way to the horizon. If he went down there, only a few lupans might

5

see him. A large thermal lifted his plane a few hundred feet. He circled the valley and returned to the lupan hill – one more run over the forest and then a straight shot to his resting place. Something moved him to delay, to take a last look at the glen. Hadn't he been there before? Its southern slope rose through several cultivated fields to a white, two-storied cottage. A small fence with hanging cloth flags surrounded the property. No watchtowers either. Whoever lived there counted on luck to keep bounders away, and flapping cloths to discourage wolves. In the adjoining meadow a lorry's cab painted with graffiti was half buried in the grass. Its empty windows stared into the sky like the sockets of a human skull.

He'd seen a picture of the graffiti cab before. In his office. This was Koppiemaul Cottage, with Koppiemaul Refugee Camp at the bottom of the glen. A few years back, the woman from the cottage barged into his office. A tall figure with long white hair, she demanded, in a mongrel accent somewhere between Glaswegian and Polish, that he obtain settlement visas for several undocumented women in her camp. More to get her out of his office, he promised to help. He managed to finagle two visas. Two women would be given a chance to integrate into society instead of living like hunted animals. What about the others? Koppiemaul camp wouldn't survive for long. The tank and dozer would be there after they finished with Braemar, shoot up the place, pack the terrified refugees into vans and drive them off to internment camps.

He drifted as low as he dared over the camp for a closer look at the residents. Dark-skinned children playing in the streets waved to him. He waved back. With his other hand he pulled the stick to gain altitude. The plane's nose barely responded. He tugged harder, banked slightly left. The hill with the lupan dens rushed at him. Damn, I'm going too fast now. His body braced for impact, but it did not come. Carried on a weak thermal, the plane missed the hilltop, skimmed the grassy field and headed for the trees. Like statues, the lupans watched him approach but this time did not move out of the way. He leaned on the stick but it hardly moved. A hand stronger than his held it still. He could only sit helpless and watch the spindly trees rush at him with finality. All thoughts died inside him.

A tree grabbed the plane. His body jerked sideways; slammed against the seatbelts. A belt caught him under the chin and tightened on his throat. The sky was replaced by tree branches. Coming out of nowhere they smashed into the cockpit. One struck his face. He tasted its bitter sap. He was falling again, out of the trees. His head jerked back. Time stopped. He was floating in slow motion. Cool air brushed his face. So here I am, dying. Isn't that what I wanted? But if I'm dying, why am I so alive, like I've got all the time in the world?

Silence enveloped him, final as a grave. He was still tied into his chair, tilted at a slight angle. Wave after wave of pain coursed through him. He spluttered, wheezed but each breath cost him a painful stab.

Several bony faces with wrinkled skin and long hair looked down at him, muscular male figures, and bare breasted females. Their golden eyes looked him over as if figuring out how to cook him for dinner.

'Damn my bad luck,' he muttered, 'I've screwed up badly. Kill me. Just finish me off.'

A male figure with stringy hair thrust his wrinkled face up close. His breath stank of rotten meat. Like a dog he sniffed Scott all over, cracked a smile or what might be one. Lifting up his head he let out a loud howl. The others joined in with a chorus of clicks and whistles.

TWO

Linella's outdoor table had a pine surface with knife nicks and oil stains dating back to her grandmother. Hundreds of people had dined there: homeless Glaswegians, illegal immigrants and refugees. Every village child celebrated their birthday there. Though she had no idea who would show up, each evening she laid out a spread of homemade pasta, olives from her trees, sun dried tomatoes, apples and figs from the camp and dandelion wine. She arranged freshly cut flowers in a vase, poured herself a glass of wine from her cellar, and waited. Her boys usually drifted in, often with a stray kid from the village or a nearby homestead. Women from the camp regularly materialized out of the heather and stayed long into the night. She never put away leftovers because lupans usually cleaned them up. After sunset they emerged from the shadows, stood wordlessly at the table and ate in front of her. After scooping leftovers into cardboard boxes, they clicked loudly to express their appreciation.

She drained her glass, poured herself another and looked around to make sure everything was there. She smoothed the napkins. Her hands felt better when they were doing something to pass the time. Would the new refugees show up? She always felt better about unknown guests after sharing a meal with them. The smell of roasted vegetables carried on a warm breeze indicated that the newcomers had other plans.

She'd been cutting flowers for her weekly delivery, when the rusty lorry appeared round the corner. It spluttered and gasped as it bumped along her access road, looking for a place to expire, its back crammed full of dark skinned people and furniture. She stood in the middle of the road, her feet planted like tree roots, and did not move until it rumbled to a stop, barely a yard away. There were at least four families, including three children under two. A tall bearded man with a lean face, clambered out, offered her a cigarette. He stuck one in his mouth when she refused.

'I'm Roberto.' He waved his cigarette at the lorry. 'My family. We're from Corsica.'

'I see.'

'You've got a nice place,' he said looking around.

'You're on my property. Put out your fag.'

Roberto tossed the cigarette on the ground. 'Have it your way.'

He related a familiar story, that the army had closed the camp where they'd been living for five years. They took to the road ahead of the tanks. Someone told them that the woman at Koppiemaul was friendly toward refugees. Could they stay with her a few nights?

Should they? The cab contained a well-loaded gun rack. Roberto had a duplicitous look about him. He might be desperate enough to take over the cottage and call it his own. The men in the back of the pickup looked capable of any crime. The women didn't make eye contact. Like all refugees who landed on her doorstep they were scared, unable to kindle an ember of hope. The children's grimy faces were smudged from crying. She needed to decide on the spot. She knew that she didn't always make smart choices.

'You can stay. Put your tents up by the graffiti cab,' she said. 'Your guns must be left with me. You'll get them back when you leave.'

Roberto returned a caustic smile. 'We're worth more to you armed. I don't see many guards protecting you. Are you going to call the police when the bounders come?'

'That's none of your business. The guns stay with me, or you can go somewhere else. Your choice.'

'Fine. We'll leave the guns. I only say that we could protect you if we kept them.'

'I don't need your protection. All guns go over by the door.'

Roberto talked to his people in Italian. After considerable grumbling they agreed to hand over their weapons and accept her hospitality. She rarely had trouble with her guests, but this time she felt some disquiet. After they drove off to set up camp, she phoned the village.

Arjan listened to her description of the Corsicans and let out a sarcastic laugh. 'Why do you always take in complete strangers?'

'Because I'm crazy. Arjan, I couldn't help it. When people appear on my doorstep, they're my responsibility. It's the way I am. I can't send them off into a war zone. Not if I can give those women a few peaceful nights.'

'But these are dangerous times. You know absolutely nothing about them.'

'I didn't know anything about your family either when I took you in. Look at how well that turned out. Trust me, Arjan. I'm very intuitive about people. So far I've never had any trouble with my guests. I think that this lot will turn out okay.'

'You'll attract vigilantes is what you'll do.'

'Arjan, I need your help, not your commentary.'

'Fine. We're ready to help you if anything goes wrong, but don't say I didn't warn you.'

She needed to stay home, and so she sent Andrew off in her jeep to deliver flowers to the neighbours. Lately their support was wavering. They told her that *her refugees* would attract the army's unwelcome attention. The only way to keep them on her side was to send regular flower deliveries, along with Andrew who could repair any software problem.

Later he called her about the sailplane. It circled soundlessly like a vulture covering the cottage, the village and the lupan colony. For several months there hadn't been any military reconnaissance. She believed that the government had lost interest in Koppiemaul. Any plane that entered the glen awoke her concern for the refugees. Pictures of the village and the lupan colony might already be all over the web. After the plane disappeared over the hill she sat alone in the garden to gather her thoughts.

Her life had changed thirty years earlier, the morning she climbed the fence to investigate a large marquee in her neighbour's field. The hand-sewn patches and the chimney sticking through the canvas roof all pointed to climate refugees. The tent was packed with several families. On the run from war and famine, they came to Scotland looking for a home. Many of the women had been gang raped. Most were pregnant. She offered them her field to build their houses.

Sandria's baby, Asra, was the first to be born. She had ochre, leathery skin, stringy black hair and a long, thin nose. Most peculiar were the large eyes, bright golden with a penetrating look. She ran a constant fever. Sandria applied cold compresses and wrapped her in wet blankets but nothing worked. Asra did not want to be held by her mother or anyone else for that matter. Autistic, Linella thought, noting that she responded adversely to touch. The second child was born to Lina; also golden-eyed. Then came Zia, Amber, Zariya and Ali. With each birth fear spread among expectant mothers that their children would have similar deformities. Local doctors were equally puzzled. They remarked that throughout the country similar children were being born, most often to climate refugees but occasionally to locals. Researchers muttered something about the effects of a virus or a solar flare, but no one really knew what was going on.

They still didn't know. They called the children *homo lupus* because they preferred wolf milk, and enjoyed the company of wolves.

Josh appeared from the house, poured himself some wine and sat down.

'We have some new neighbours,' Linella said.

Josh rolled his blue eyes. 'I saw them. Are they okay?'

'I suppose so. They're human.'

'They look like bandits. Mum, sometimes I really wonder about you.'

'I couldn't turn them away. They've been evicted from their camp. They're only here for a few days. Arjan and Elijah are on call if there's any trouble. I think you can relax.'

Josh heaped pasta high on his plate. He gulped down more wine, grimaced slightly. He'd never developed a taste for dandelion wine, but drank it anyway.

'What's on your mind?' Linella said.

'Last night's riot in Aberdeen.'

'Which one? Weren't there a dozen?'

'You didn't see the pictures?'

'You know I don't watch the news.'

'A bunch of yobs smashed up a block of shops on Union Street. They're pissed off about the refugees and want something done about them.'

'I wish they'd leave us alone. We're not harming anyone.'

'Mum, sometimes you don't get it. Here you are taking in more refugees, while the army is out there closing the camps. It's not a smart thing to do. Before long the tanks will be out here looking around, and yes, they'll find that we have a good looking camp at the bottom of the hill.'

She slammed down her glass, so hard that wine splattered on the table. 'Let them try. There's only one access road, and that's my road.'

'I don't think we can stop them.'

'We'll see. You're always seeing things so dark. Is the army coming up the road or did I perhaps miss them? The government is completely broke. No one has the money to round up thousands of refugees – or the wolf-children, not to mention feed them and house them. My women are not doing anyone any harm.'

'Mum's going to pack a machine gun and stand them down. I'll teach you to use one.' Andrew had just appeared. His latest

12

getup of camouflage pants and the shaved head still unnerved her. She told herself that his military look was a passing phase, but what if it wasn't?

She let out an angry snort. 'Just wait. You haven't seen me when someone goes after my women.'

Andrew scratched his stubble. 'I know an Italian who has access to rocket launchers. We could recruit some guys from the village. By the time the army shows up, we'll have a top-notch army ready.'

'I don't want any of your fucking weapons. There are enough of them down in the village. I don't know anyone who for all their machine guns feels any safer.'

'How will you stop the government if you don't have guns? They'll just mow you down and take what they want. That's the way it's always been. We're all ducks waiting to be picked off.'

'You want to fight a war with the government?'

Andrew pulled up a chair. 'At least we should have a watchtower.'

'You want to stand up there, wear a uniform and play soldier.'

'I want to know ahead of time if the army's coming. Before they drive up and knock at our door. What do you have against towers anyway?'

'I don't want towers, and I don't want guns. Understand?'

She hoped it would end the discussion. Talking about weapons always evoked the memory of her sister Jane, gunned down in front of her in Glasgow. No weapon could have protected her.

Andrew loaded up a dinner plate and sat down. Josh ate his pasta in silence. He maintained a dreamy look, not wanting to engage with her. She realized that in snapping at him she'd made him withdraw. 'Okay Josh,' she said. 'What's on your mind?'

Josh pushed his curly, red hair away from his face. 'I don't think you want to listen to me.'

'I'm listening. Talk to me.'

'Look, I'm not making things up. You always say that I have

dark thoughts. Like for the hell of it. You never think I know anything worthwhile.'

'I'm sorry if I hurt you. I get very protective when it comes to the women and the wolf-children. I'll try to listen.'

'The butcher – you know, Colin. He said that convoys were heading this way. The worst bit is that he was so glad about it. Everyone wants the army to come in and clear out the wolfies. They know who I am and where I live. They call me a lupie. I'm sick of it.'

Lupie lover! Lupie lover! The shouts still rang in her ears, children's taunts that used to follow her down the street. Shopkeepers she once regarded as friends, turned against her after they found out that she hosted refugees and protected lupans. She swallowed a mouthful. The cold pasta slid down her throat; tasted like sawdust.

Some of the local attitudes were understandable. Lupans survived by poaching livestock, had no concept of property and viewed the entire world as belonging to them. High fences didn't keep them out. Their nocturnal raids weren't restricted to cows and sheep, but included harvested grain, tools and anything not locked up. 'Worse than tinkers,' was the general comment about town. More than lupans' behaviour, their physical appearance unnerved people: their witch-like golden eyes, their silence, and that though they might look like anorexic humans with long hair, they broke a basic taboo by walking naked. People were more afraid of what they might do than what they did. They didn't belong in the Scottish countryside living side by side with people. The zoo was where they belonged. People who shot lupans, mistaking them for deer, were rarely prosecuted.

But they are our children – children of our women. Why can't people see that? She knew why. Lupans tended to be born to refugees from Africa and the Middle East, and not to Scottish women. Even the lupans' mothers were estranged. Their children never bonded with them; only with each other. Or with wolves. If a child wandered off to join others like it, the mother might initially grieve, but usually felt released from a heavy burden. Very few maintained contact with their children.

'People are scared,' Josh said.

'There's a lot to be afraid of,' Andrew drawled. 'The Plague, bounders and incompetent cops. The sea's still rising. Everyone's moving to Scotland. People blame refugees for taking their jobs, gun-running and even the Plague.'

'Okay, I've had enough of dark news,' Linella said. 'I know it's all bad out there, but I can't change global warming. I can only change things here, in my glen.' She held up her hand to silence the protesting looks. 'I know you think that I want to shut out the world. I don't have time for problems I can't do anything about. I can only take care of the women.'

Josh nodded at the hill with the lupan dens on the far side of the valley. The standing stone on its summit was silhouetted against the evening sky.

'Who'll protect the wolfies?' Josh said.

Linella shook her head. 'I hope we'll never face that one.'

She drained her wine, pushed away her plate, still half-loaded with pasta. 'You guys finish this. I have things to do.'

She retreated into the kitchen. From the living room came the sounds of small explosions and mortar fire. George was lying on the couch with a computer helmet on his head. His glazed eyes followed a war game. With a flick of his eyebrow he gunned down rows of aliens. She yanked off his helmet to reveal his magenta mohawk. 'Go get some dinner.'

George looked up in surprise. 'Why does no one ever call me?'

'How can you hear me above that rubbish?'

She stacked dishes, still unwashed since yesterday. Usually domestic work calmed her agitation, but this time it set her teeth on edge. Josh's news reminded her of a recent nightmare. She was walking among piles of dead bodies in the middle of a burning village. She was supposed to meet a wolf-child but she couldn't remember its name.

She slammed a dinner plate into the drainer. 'But they are my children. I won't let anything happen to them.'

If an army raid was imminent, Brigadier Johnson would

know. He had helped her before but she hadn't spoken to him for almost a year. Since their last fight he no longer came around. He told her that he'd been transferred but she suspected a lie, and that he wanted to keep his distance. He liked her well enough; enjoyed having sex with her, but just wasn't interested in pursuing an intimate relationship.

They met four years earlier, soon after Stan left her. The army was conducting helicopter raids on the hill. Soldiers bundled any lupan they came across into a copter. Soon the lupans learned how to disappear into the forest upon sighting the helicopters. Officially, lupans were being taken to government centres for their own health and protection, so they'd be cared for by *experts*. Actually the locals, tired of lupans raiding their farms and vegetable plots, wanted lupans out of the way. Captivity for lupans usually meant a quick death. Though they were immune to the Plague they died from the common cold or flu. Few survived for more than two years in captivity.

Linella stormed every government agency looking for help and finally located Johnson. The first official who actually listened to her, he asked her questions and offered to help. When he came out to Koppiemaul she served up her best meal and offered him vintage champagne. His official demeanour quickly faded. He found her beautiful. Said he admired her fiery spirit. The next morning when they woke up together in her bed, he told her that the wolf-children would be left alone. The raids stopped. For several years it appeared that the government forgot about the colony.

She picked up her phone. It was an antique with a handset as heavy as steel and an old fashioned dial that whirred and clicked. Miraculously it still worked. A robotic voice instructed her to leave a message. 'Hello Brian, this is Linella. I haven't talked to you for a while. Been thinking about you. Hope you're in the neighbourhood. Need to talk to you. Call me when you can. Bye.'

She sipped her wine looking through the kitchen window out at the table. Her sons sat relaxed, their chairs tilted back. Laughing. The sun had set over the western range and shadows grew in the garden. Andrew rolled a cigarette. He passed the tobacco and paper to Josh. George complained that the others had eaten all the pasta. So that was the worst complaint he could muster? Lately they'd stopped moaning about wanting some city life or moving to England to live with Stan.

She was about to turn from the window when a dark figure appeared in the garden – a tall woman in a black robe, out of breath as if she'd been running all the way up the hill.

Andrew told her, 'She's in the house.'

Sandria stepped into the kitchen. She had an oval face with a dark complexion, large dark eyes, a brow covered with lines wrought by suffering. 'I thank God that I've found you. You must come.'

'What's happened, Sandria?'

'A plane has crashed on the hill. The pilot's wounded. The wolf-children have taken him.'

'Is he critical?'

'He's dying. Can you come and help?'

'Have you told Eisa?'

'Yes, but they won't let him see the pilot. Rami stopped Eisa outside the den, and threatened him. Please come. I think they'll let you in.'

'I can wrap his leg in a bandage, but we really need Eisa.'

'You must try to persuade them to let Eisa through.'

'I'm on my way.' Linella grabbed a head-light.

'We're going up to the colony,' she shouted to the boys, still sitting about the table.

'Oh no,' George said. 'She's still trying to adopt a wolfie.'

'More to the point keep an eye on our new guests. Call Arjan if there's any trouble.'

'So you really aren't sure of them?' Josh said.

'Just mind yourselves. I'll be back soon.'

THREE

The sun is already half hidden behind a distant hill when Blue
Sky climbs the earthwork to the standing stone on its summit. He
is one of the eldest and most respected in the colony, well-known
for his ability to keep up with the wolves during their hunt. His
large brow is more wrinkled than most males and exudes a calm
that could quench any gale. His black hair, always combed, hangs
halfway down his shoulders. 'Blue Sky' is only of his many names
for he is also called Tallest, Cloud Brow or Old Ash. Only the
Elder People refer to him by his birth name, 'Rami', a name that
conveys nothing to him anymore.

He leans into the standing stone, listens to the Earth's
heartbeat. When he was younger it used to be too faint to make
out but on this day the beat is so loud that anyone should be able
to hear it. Even the mothers in the village might hear a low hum,
a continuous vibration reminiscent of a swarm of bees on a
summer day. If they paused long enough in their daily bustle to
listen.

His eyes are drawn to the forest, to the gash in the trees where
the giant bird crashed. Its remains are there: the wing of twisted
metal and paper half-buried in the grass, the white tail hanging in
the branches. It was no normal bird but a toy of metal and wood.
Its arrival awoke in him an excitement he hadn't felt for a long
time, that something had changed in the order of things. The sky
had opened and brought the People a gift.

Who is he? If he's a messenger from Sky, he's a very unusual

18

one. Should be named Lone Man because of his solitary eyes. When his bird circled the hill, it fluttered in pain, looking for a place to die. Twice it swooped down like a falcon. Saplings playing outside, seeing a predator about to devour them ran for shelter. The third time the bird approached the hill, so low that it lacked all power to rise. The Earth pulled the bird down so that it impaled itself on a tree. Such an event hadn't happened before. Was the Earth stronger than it used to be, capable of capturing mechanical birds? Or had the plane landed where it needed to, to bring the man to the People?

What if he is the one, long-expected, who will heal the wounding of the People's birth?

Returning to the den he finds Lone Man on the heather bed. His frail body appears elusive as a shadow. He struggles to breathe, cries out in pain, tries to move a leg but the effort reduces him to tears. His voice consists of single guttural words, each sounding like a bird's cry. Blue Sky senses the man's frustration. That he wants to die. His eyes dart from object to object, like a captured animal about to be slaughtered. When he finally deigns to look at Blue Sky, he grimaces as if tasting something disagreeable and quickly turns his head away. His faint breathing draws a pittance of life from the air. Pale as a corpse he heaves, coughs and produces bloody phlegm.

Blue Sky allows his awareness to merge with the man. Among adults merging awareness is as natural as breathing. Blue Sky often tried to merge with Elder People but found their minds occupied with restless thinking, too lonely to be capable of merging. Lone Man may be different. Blue Sky closes all distances that separate him from the pilot, but just as his mind is about to merge with him, he encounters a patch of darkness. Instead of a warm presence there's nothing. As if the man isn't really there. Is his body an illusion, a reflection in a pool of water that disappears when you touch it? The man's pain-ridden body appears real but his feelings are too confused to understand.

Moreover his spirit clings tenuously to life and needs to be strengthened, led back from the netherworld where it has strayed.

The warm breath on his shoulder tells him that Beauty Woman is nearby. Tied to her back, Starlet has fallen asleep. Beauty Woman has a slight body that moves with the grace of a deer. Her clear eyes can penetrate any illusion; she was recently named Beauty Woman, because people feel beautiful in her presence. Blue Sky merges his awareness with her. Looking through her eyes he knows that she's in awe of the wounded man. She views him not as the victim of a cruel accident, but rather a child who is about to be born; a very special child sent to the People.

She kneels beside him. She strokes his head. With the power in her body she calms him the way she'd calm a flustered child. He twitches, withdraws fearfully; appears to be repulsed by her – normal behaviour for one whose spirit has wandered so far that his body is left to fend for itself.

– What is he? – Blue Sky asks.

– A messenger. That's what we'll call him

– What's his message?

– He'll tell us. If he lives.

– Where's he from?

She points to the sky.

– Yes, that's obvious. Is he one of the Insect People?

Long ago Insect People attacked the colony. Monstrous mechanical insects swooped down on the hill and disgorged Insect Men armed with lethal stings. They resembled Elder People except that they wore identical spotted clothes and their bodies emitted an unwholesome smell. They shouted angrily, burned dens and laid waste to the gardens. People soon recognized approaching danger and scattered into the forest before the insects landed. Those who stayed behind were taken away.

After the raids stopped, Blue Sky pondered why they had happened. If Earth and Sky are in a perfect relationship surely Sky would not allow such dangerous insects to fly and to inflict grievous harm. Perhaps the Earth-Sky relationship needed to be strengthened. A vision came to the People of a web that must be laid out on the Earth, pathways marked by stone that would allow Earth to draw Sky into its embrace. So began the great labour of carving the stones and laying them out across the land. They were arranged in stone circles and aligned with rising and setting points of prominent stars. The Earth's voice, audible even inside the den, tells him that the great labour has been fruitful.

– He's not from the Insect People – Beauty Woman remarks.

– Could he be the one we've been waiting for?

– If he lives. Yes, he may be the first man to take the Dark Path. To be like us.

Starlet whimpers, struggles on Beauty Woman's back. She slings the baby to her front and offers her breast. The Messenger looks away as if disgusted. Surely he should regard feeding as normal. Unless he never was a child, knew nothing of food but grew to manhood like a shadow without bone or blood, growing during the day only to fade at sunset.

The child ceases whimpering; falls asleep at the breast. In the silence they hear steps approaching from far off. Blue Sky recognizes Dark Woman's faltering step and Cottage Woman's determined stride.

– They want to take him away.

– They must not. He belongs with us. We must help his spirit find its way back.

– Living among us will unsettle him.

– Not if Dark Woman takes care of him.

Blue Sky doesn't like the proposal. Dark Woman, still wounded by her child's birth, might inhibit his healing. She remains in the colony mainly because she still wants her child back or at least to see her. She does not understand that the child she remembers no longer exists. She remembers Young One, a squalling baby suckled by grey wolves and who is still the subject of stories beloved by saplings. She's no longer a child. Wolfborn

21

is wise among the People. As a wolf, she runs with the pack and answers to no one's summons.

– Better to keep him away from all his kind – Blue Sky says. – He and Dark Woman could develop a troubled relationship.

FOUR

The pain that racked Scott's body intensified to where he longed to pass out, but the wrinkled faces with golden eyes didn't go away. Their hands pawed him, pulled at his arms and legs until he yelled out. At least that made them let go. He felt them carry him through the woods, and then dump him on some wiry bushes. He couldn't move even an arm or leg without a painful stab. He gasped. His body needed air badly but each breath he took provoked a painful coughing spasm.

If only the wrinkled faces that leered down would go away. Their clicks and whistles set his teeth on edge. A sea of naked bodies competed for a front seat. Let them fight each other. Even better if one of them knifed him and put an end to his agony. At last he faded out. After several turbulent spells between waking and dreaming, he found himself alone on his back. He gasped for air, but the swelling under his chin only allowed a trickle. *This is what dying feels like. But why do I have to die here – among lupans?*

When his eyes grew accustomed to the dim twilight, he saw that he was in a dim windowless space. Above him rose a smooth domelike ceiling of tree trunks and branches encased in dried mud and straw. The walls appeared to move with the rise and fall of his chest. Either the den was breathing or he was more delirious than he thought. Its flowing curves with little recesses and protruding walls were what you'd expect to see inside an animal that had swallowed you alive. Jars and pots were squirreled away on shelves. The clay stove and chimney in the centre of the

23

room morphed into a twisted tree-trunk with gnarly growths. Flames licked its base. Was the tree on fire? No, he was looking through a small opening in the stove at a glowing log. Its heat soothed him, allowed him to forget his pain. As long as he didn't move. After a few minutes he noticed a male lupan sitting on the floor on the far side of the den, tall and thin as a yogi after a long fast. The penetrating eyes studied him, not missing any movement, his every cough and splutter. He felt that his inmost thoughts were laid bare.

'Kill me. For God's sake just kill me,' Scott said, regretting it immediately for a chest spasm seized him, so strong he thought it would never let go. The lupan's stare continued to dissect him like a piece of meat.

A female lupan appeared beside the male, naked except for a metal belt of dangling stones on her hips. A small baby tied to her back looked out at him curiously. Her hair was swept away to reveal an oval face with high cheekbones and a creased brow. Her golden eyes met Scott's, but they appeared to inquire gently rather than strip-search him. What did she want? *I don't have anything for you, madam. Let me die.* He closed his eyes so he wouldn't have to face her probing stare. Her fingers touched his brow. Their heat scalded him, making his jerk aside. Of course, lupans had higher body temperatures than humans. She touched him again; this time the heat felt more soothing so he did not pull away. She massaged his brow gently, emitted a low whistle and smacked her lips as if in inviting him to kiss her. *Kiss a lupan? I'd rather kiss the grim reaper.*

He opened his eyes. 'Get me a doctor. Doctor! Understand?'

I've really fucked up, crashing here among these Neanderthals. Not killing myself properly. How did I do it? He raised himself on an elbow, turned to the female. 'Kill me now. Please. Finish me off for God's sake.'

Her golden eyes didn't respond. If she understood him she didn't show it.

She stroked his brow as before, tentatively as if asking his permission to continue. Despite the warmth of her hand he forced himself to remain quiet while her long fingers massaged his scalp, seeking out tender spots. The heat spread throughout his head, and to the rest of his body. The tightness in his chest relaxed to where he could breathe more easily. He closed his eyes, hoping he'd fall asleep. As his breathing deepened he realized that his mouth was so parched that he could drink a lake.

'Water,' he said. Apparently lupans could repeat a few simple nouns. Was 'water' in her vocabulary?

From the abrupt way her hand withdrew, he felt he had said something to offend her. Opening his lips, he pointed at his mouth. She understood the gesture because she walked over to the stove and returned with a bowl of warm brown liquid. He dipped in a finger. The broth was fragrant and earthy, like nothing he'd ever tasted. He pushed the bowl away. Lupans' bodies could probably tolerate berries and mushrooms that were poisonous to people. She put aside the bowl, gazed at him in silence. What did she want now? Whatever it was he was too tired to figure it out.

'Leave me alone.' He rolled over, turning his back to her. He heard faint rustling as she moved about. When he looked again, both lupans were gone.

The reeds covering the doorway rustled and a lupan boy and girl appeared. With clicking sounds they giggled and jostled each other. The boy slung the girl over his shoulder and headed for a dark corner while she kicked and laughed but only pretended to struggle, until she gave him a sharp bite on the arm that made him drop her onto the heather. Sucking his arm he left her there, headed for the door but before reaching it he almost tripped over Scott. Immediately both were at his side their wrinkled faces thrust within inches of his. He decided not to talk to them; they wouldn't understand anyway. They looked at each other; from their changing expressions he sensed a rapid communication. Smiling, the girl grabbed Scott's hair and tugged.

'Let go,' he shouted. The force of his words impressed her because she sprang away, the boy too. From the far side of the den they watched him, poised to run for the door if he turned hostile. Having made his point, that he wasn't a toy, he closed his eyes. When would they go away? For a while he heard nothing and thought they'd gone, but then heard them croon and whistle to each other. Looking around he found them in a dark corner, lying on top of each other, exploring each other's bodies and emitting embarrassed giggles. *God, why did I have to end up among perverts?*

He must have dozed off, because the next he knew the den was crowded again. The adult lupans were back. Beside him stood a small dark-skinned woman in a black dress and head scarf, and a tall fair-headed woman in jeans who was screaming at the lupans in a Polish accent, 'The man is hurt. He must come with me.'

She had the reddish complexion of someone who worked on a farm, a broad forehead, and high cheek bones. Though her smooth forehead suggested she was no older than forty, her wrinkled hands with gnarled fingers indicated an older age.

The male lupan folded his thin arms. Standing with his feet firmly planted, he wasn't about to be moved.

Her hand-gestures emphasized each word that she spoke. 'He's coming with me, Rami. Down to the village.'

Sometimes Rami didn't get it, not even when Linella stuck her face within six inches of his and yelled. Zia fiddled with her necklace and kept shifting her weight carelessly from one leg to the other. From Rami's agitated eyes Linella knew that she had his attention. He might not have understood a word, but he read her body well enough to know what she wanted. 'That man is hurt,' she said. 'He must come with me. He needs a doctor.'

The wounded pilot appeared familiar. From his noticeable paunch and his balding head, the hair well-trimmed about the neck, she was sure she'd seen him before, behind an office desk. His clenched jaw indicated he was trying not to cry out; the grey eyes had an empty, lifeless look.

'Get me away from them,' he said barely able to whisper.

'Who are you?'

'Maguire.'

Scott Maguire? That's it. She recalled how she had walked into his office. Barely looking at her, he asked politely what he could do for her. She told him bluntly that she wanted him to save the lives of several women arrested and locked up in Aviemore Detention Centre. At first he'd railed and blustered at her, saying she was asking the impossible. When she stood her ground, he smiled and told her that he admired what she was doing. If only there were more people like her. Later she called to thank him for the visas, and asked if she could meet him socially, but he told her he was too busy.

Perhaps he still didn't want to see her because he kept turning his head to avoid eye contact. When he tilted it back she noticed a lump under his chin, a typical Plague symptom. What should she do? Bringing Maguire into the village could put everyone at risk. No one there had been diagnosed with Plague and she wanted it to stay that way. Though the disease wasn't passed on by human touch, rodents and fleas, both in abundance in the village, could spread it. She would have to quarantine him. In her own cottage if she wanted to chance it.

Rami spread out his hands in what could be a gesture of helplessness but he showed no sign of yielding.

'Do you understand?' Linella said.

Rami moved his head sideways. Usually that meant, 'Yes.'

Linella took Scott's hand. He didn't resist when she lifted his hand toward her chest, to make her point to Rami. With lupans, gestures often succeeded where words failed. She said, 'The man must come with me.'

Zia jerked Scott's hand away from Linella and then planted herself like a tree between them. She was quite clear that Scott was not going anywhere. End of discussion.

Taking Sandria's hand Linella presented her to Rami. 'Can Sandria look after him?'

Rami's domelike face did not react. Either he hadn't

27

understood, or disagreed. Among lupans, silence often indicated dissent.

He's going to have to stay here, she thought. He's not going to like it. What does he really want? Someone to put him out of his misery? He hated lupans, grimaced at them as if they were the scum of the earth. If she wanted to talk to him, she would have to be left alone with him.

'Everyone out!' Linella said. With a sweeping gesture she sent Sandria out of the den first and then pushed Rami and Zia through the door. Once they had gone she returned to Scott. 'I'm sorry. I'm doing what I can for you, but you don't make it easy.'

Scott smiled faintly. 'Don't bother.'

'We don't have time for this. I'll ask you one last time, do you want to be left here to die?'

'I'd rather not. But I'm prepared.' He paused to catch his breath, and then said. 'Just do one thing. Get someone to hide the wreck. The police will be looking for it. I don't want anyone to find it.'

'Why not?'

'Never mind.'

'Are you on the run?'

'You don't need to know.'

He took several breaths, wheezed and spluttered as if trying to cough out his lungs. 'One more thing. I don't want to die here among those freaks.'

'Really?' Linella snapped. 'Do you imagine they're going to carve you up for Sunday roast? You'll be better treated than in hospitals.'

'Right.'

'You need to respect things you don't understand. Just because we don't understand their language, because they don't wear clothes or use high-tech wrist-coms is no reason to demean them.'

'Okay. Save me the lecture.'

'You have to let me look at you.'

Scott shrugged. 'I'm infected. You want to risk it?'

'Touching you won't give me the Plague. Do you want my help or not?'

'As you wish. Look, I'm not trying to be a jerk,' Scott added observing her remoteness. 'I'm tired of fighting the system, fighting tanks, the lot of it. I'm about to die no matter what you do. The cops are after me. They'll arrest you if they find out that you've hidden me. Best for you to forget you saw me.'

'What have you done?'

Scott shrugged, closed his eyes. 'No more than you would do.'

'Forged visas?'

'It's not important.'

'The refugees are very grateful to you. Around here you're a hero.'

He shrugged. 'It won't make any difference in the end. They're fucked. So am I. Just get me out of here.'

'You really don't like wolf-children.'

'Do you? I'm sorry for them, like I'm sorry for spastics. But I don't get the fuckers.'

'They have language of their own. If you'd shut up you might hear them using it.'

'And you understand it?'

'Sometimes.'

'Good for you.'

'They want you here. I don't know why. I want to move you down to the village to see a doctor, but I have to get permission. You might have to stay here a few days until I sort it all.'

'I guess I'm stuck with them.'

'Sandria is here a lot of the time. You'll have her for company.' Scott nodded.

'Why are you being such an arsehole?'

He closed his eyes. 'Sorry, ma'am. It's nothing personal. I'm dog tired. Go ahead and look at me.'

Before touching him again she rinsed her hands with boiling

water, using the heather for a quick surgical scrub. Scott winced when she touched his left leg. From the way it lay she knew it was broken. His wheezing suggested a punctured lung. He probably had a cracked rib or two. Luckily she saw no dark patches on his chest that might indicate internal bleeding. Judging by the swollen glands under his neck and under his arms, the Plague was well-advanced. He might not have more than a month left.

Outside the den she found Sandria sitting alone on a large rock. Rami and Zia stood together gazing up at the stars.

'I heard you talking,' Sandria said. 'I'll keep an eye on him.'

'He's infected. Are you okay about that?'

'You think I care what happens to me? Linella, I lost my baby. The worst thing has already happened. I don't worry about dying.'

Rami and Zia didn't react when Linella walked up to them.

'I need your help.'

Zia looked straight into Linella's face – a sign that she wanted to communicate.

Using gestures, Linella tried to explain that the plane's wreckage must be removed, but the lupans only stared back. From their bemused faces she suspected that they had no idea what she wanted of them.

She pointed to the den. 'Why must the man stay?'

Zia moved her head from side to side. Pursing her lips she said one word, slowly and with great effort, 'Messenger.'

'What?'

'Mess – ger,' Zia repeated.

Zia only knew a handful of nouns, such as 'wolf, man, woman, fire or soup.' Where had she learned an unusual word like 'messenger?' Did Zia regard Maguire as a gift from heaven?

'So – he's a messenger,' Linella said.

Zia nodded.

'Man from village' Linella gestured with her arms. 'Eisa will come.'

Rami stiffened, glared back at Linella. Refusal – there was no other way to interpret the look. They didn't want anyone to interfere with the pilot. Linella pointed to Sandria, and to the den. 'Sandria — and the man, together.' She crossed her hands to indicate togetherness, or union.

Zia whistled and clicked, added a croaking sound that sounded like a laugh.

'I didn't say they're going to have sex,' Linella said. 'He's dying, so sex is a bad idea. I'll be back tomorrow with medicine.'

FIVE

Moonlight provided enough light for Linella to make her way back down the path. The gusting wind rustled the dry gorse bushes and combed the long grass. It tore at her clothes and pushed her against the hill, forcing her to pause to regain balance. Above the dim landscape several wind turbines stood like sentinels, their blades a whirling blur. Upon rounding a corner she saw the dark village houses, the occasional window lit by flickering candlelight. People rarely used electricity at night. For years the camp survived by keeping a low profile, and residents wanted it to stay that way.

She couldn't stop thinking about Maguire, wondering why Rami and Zia were so interested in him. What did they see in him? Surely they were empathic enough to detect his outright racism, and that he was a human derelict. Though he was dying as surely as night follows day, she couldn't muster any sympathy. What do you tell someone who has no hope and is resentful to be alive? She could only bring him medicine, perform first aid and leave him for Sandria to sort out. As for taking him down to the village, where he might have human company for his final days? It was too risky. Even though the Plague hadn't appeared in the village, one day there would be a first victim.

She crossed the wolf-fence through a breach where the posts had fallen over. The villagers were in no hurry to repair it as no wolf had ever been sighted in the village for years. Perhaps wolves respected an unwritten treaty that obligated them to stay out of the way. Nevertheless the villagers repaired their fences before the winter months, just in case a hungry or demented wolf came looking for an extra meal.

She had almost reached the village before she decided not to wait until morning, but to see Eisa immediately. A night owl, he didn't go to bed until four in the morning. At that late hour would he misinterpret her visit? Years back they had a passionate affair that lasted several months. She spent many nights in his cottage but soon realized that Eisa would never settle for one woman and that, except for sex, they shared very little. Somehow they never understood each other's emotional language. Eisa's whitewashed cottage stood at the end of the village street, its narrow windows lit up by a dim light.

She knocked on the rough pine door. Eisa stirred inside. Through the window she glimpsed his moving shadow. Shuffling steps approached and then his head, covered in long grey hair, appeared in the doorway. He had a thin, hungry face with a hooked nose and a chin covered with four day-old stubble. His faded dressing-gown, tied at the waist, was parted to show a hairy chest.

'Linella Sienkiewicz! At this hour it had better be good.'

'I have to talk to you.'

Eisa yawned. 'What's happening?'

'I'm sorry to wake you, but I've just come from the colony. I checked out the pilot.'

'Let me guess. You want me to have a fist fight with Rami so that he'll let me into his den?'

'No. I need some medicine. The pilot has a fractured leg, a punctured lung, a couple of cracked ribs. He may have internal bleeding. And the Plague. He's at least a month into it. So, Doctor Habash, what do you think it sounds like?'

'Come on in.' Eisa held the door wide.

The small room contained a cast-iron kitchen stove, a small sink by the window, a large double bed in one corner, a dining-table piled with dirty dishes, his work table cluttered with papers and wall-shelves crammed with hundreds of medicine bottles. He turned on a bare bulb that dangled from the ceiling and nodded for her to sit in a soft chair that was about to disgorge its stuffing. Linella landed on some bare springs and scooted about to find a comfortable spot. Eisa picked up a tobacco pouch and cigarette paper. His dark eyes looked hollow, staring at her but thinking of other things. 'I'm sorry. I haven't been sleeping much these days. Some new projects have been keeping me up. You doing okay?'

'Couldn't be better.'

He laughed showing his stained teeth. 'Then you're the only one in the glen who is. Maybe the only one in this lousy world.'

'It's because I don't watch the news.'

'Ignore the news and it will visit you anyway.'

'In that case, I prefer to wait.'

'So, he has the Plague. That's really interesting. He might make a good test case.'

'What do you mean?'

Eisa smiled. 'There's a lot about Plague we don't understand.'

'Are you worried that he'll infect us?'

'No, there's no danger to you or Sandria.'

'As long as we keep our hands clean, and don't lie down with fleas?'

'Fleas won't infect you either.'

'I'm not following. I thought that fleas were one of the main carriers.'

Eisa rolled a cigarette. 'Have you ever wondered why no one in the village has been infected?'

'Eisa, we all wonder that.'

'We've beaten the statistical odds. You find the Plague everywhere. Why not here? That's the question that keeps me up at night.'

'You do look rough.'

'I've come up with some intriguing results. What do I do with them? I can't publish them, but I can't keep them to myself either.'

'Can you explain them to a woman who doesn't understand science?'

Eisa lit his cigarette. 'I'm pretty sure that everyone in this glen is immune to the Plague.'

It was an incredible assertion. She'd heard that some people were immune, but no one knew why. There was no cure for the Plague. The best antiviral drugs delayed death, but only by a few months.

'You're saying we're immune?'

Eisa took a long drag. 'We're in a unique situation in that we live in close contact with lupans – you and Sandria on a regular basis; others by giving birth or by rocking the wee buggers till they spit on us. Everyone knows lupans are immune to the Plague. They die of the flu, of measles or even the common cold, but they don't die of Plague. If I'm right, their immunity can be passed on to anyone who is in close contact with them. He offered Linella the tobacco pouch, but she shook her head. He smiled. 'Oh, the irony, the irony! While the Plague decimates the human race, the cure to the disease is right in front of us – the despicable lupans. Go kiss a wolf-child. You'll feel better.' Eisa rattled with laughter. 'But it doesn't do, at least culturally speaking it doesn't.'

'Why has no one else stumbled onto this?'

'Because people are stupid. Their prejudices blind them to the obvious. A couple of recent papers out of Georgia set me in this direction. Georgians have always been the leaders in phage therapy – using bacteria to fight bacteria. Unlike antibiotics that kill every bug in your body, bacterio-phages are specific. They attack only one or two bacteria. Phage treatment has been around for over a hundred years but it never caught on. Antibiotics were, more effective and cheaper for fighting infections. Well, you see what antibiotics gave us. Superbugs that no antibiotic can touch. Like the Plague.'

'Okay Eisa. To the point. Where do the wolf-children come in?'

35

'Give me a minute to get there, Sienkiewicz. Wolf-children are immune, and no one knows why. According to my lab tests, there's an ingredient in lupan blood, and I think it's a phage, that attacks the Plague Virus Complex.'

'Have you told anyone about this?'

Eisa lifted up a finger. 'Not so fast. There's more to the story. The cure is not just in lupan blood, but in their bodies. They are total carriers of the phage – and it can be transmitted to me, to you, by sweat, a kiss or having sex with them. Any close contact can transfer lupan immunity to us.'

Linella's head spun. She wasn't sure she understood the science, but the conclusion screamed at her. 'Well, when are you going to shout this from your rooftop? People out there are dying. By the thousands.'

Eisa's remote look hardly changed. 'I know.'

'So?'

'It's not that simple.' He tilted back his head and let out a thin stream of smoke. 'I don't want to be the one to make the great announcement. I don't have much faith in the human race. When people's backs are against the wall they turn nasty. They're better at killing each other than anything else. Think about it. The moment the word gets out that lupans carry the phage, every wolf child will be rounded up and stuck in a laboratory. They'll be reduced to lab animals. Experimented on and destroyed. Or they'll be enslaved. Every rich person will keep a lupan in his cellar, for insurance against the Plague. The children are our future. We have to protect them, and pay the price, however high.'

'That is downright idiotic! No, you listen to me,' Linella screamed. She pushed Eisa away as he began to protest. 'Thousands of people out there are dying of this disease. Are you trying to tell me that you'll let them die? Will you sit on this discovery, because you're afraid about what it might do to the wolf-children?'

'In a crisis wouldn't you protect your children first?'

'I'd no idea that you were so attached to them that you'd let people die.'

36

Eisa gave her a hard look. 'Now you listen to me. We're not only talking about wolf-children, but about us – our men and women. Everyone in this village. Before I tell anyone about this – let's call it what it is, my hypothesis, I want something in return – our security, and the security of our children. Because they are our children. I will not sell them out.'

'You really believe that they'll be destroyed if you release this information?'

Eisa nodded. 'They're being destroyed today. This will be the icing on the cake. I won't be part of it.'

'So – what will you do?'

'I'm not sure yet. Give me some time.'

'Meanwhile hospitals are overrun with victims. How long are they supposed to wait for your cure?'

'There's more.'

'I think I've had enough of your science for one night.'

'You've got to hear me out, because it has to do with the children. About the birth of a new species.'

'Use that word and I'll kill you. They are our children. No one else's.'

'Don't get so upset. The fact is that the children don't interbreed with us. There's never been a lupan-human child. Technically that makes them a separate species. Ever wonder how they came about?'

'Didn't a solar flare or something cause some genetic mutations?'

Eisa let out a dry laugh. 'That's the old tabloid story. Probably wrong, because it doesn't explain why wolf-children were born first to climate refugees. The latest idea is that their mothers were infected by a virus.'

'Like the flu?'

'Will you shut up for a minute. This virus was sophisticated enough to splice itself into the women's DNA. Rewrite the genetic code of their ovas. Babies that were subsequently born were lupans. A new species.'

'What virus are you talking about?'

Eisa smiled. 'They've been looking for it for a while. This year a French team discovered a desert flea with the same DNA strands that are unique to wolf-children. Do you see the implications?' Eisa's eyes gleamed with excitement. Linella wished she could follow his reasoning but her head had turned to mush.

'I'm trying to understand, but I'm no scientist.'

Eisa grasped her hand. 'Sienkiewicz, this is important. Go back to what we know. Wolf-children originated with climate refugees, Israelis, Arabs, Kenyans, Ethiopians, and Italians: all running from dry, desolate countries. The French team believe that the women carried a virus transmitted to them by desert fleas. Fleas that multiplied as a result of global warming. They nested in camels, horses, wildlife and women's hair. Why did the virus appear and how did it end up being carried by fleas?'

'Eisa, you can't possibly be asking me. I can barely follow all this stuff.'

'The Earth created it. Unless the virus came from outer space it originated in the Earth.'

'Okay – I could have told you that. Isn't it obvious?'

'Sure, the Earth is obvious. Volcanoes spew out gases, living plants and animals bubble away in the oceans and new life is created deep down in underwater geysers. Yes, it's all obvious, but someone has to put different ideas together. That's how discoveries are made. Back in the late-twentieth-century a bloke called Lovelock suggested we have to look at the Earth as one vast living system, a system he called Gaia, that regulates the Earth's environment to make it hospitable to life. If it weren't for the presence of life, we wouldn't even have oceans today. Our planet would be a desert, like Mars. Our biosphere has given us not only oceans and a breathable atmosphere, but for a billion years has kept the Earth's temperature pleasant enough for the likes of us.

'He also pointed out that the human race was waging war on Gaia. By burning the rain forests and pumping greenhouse gases into the atmosphere we were interfering with the Earth's life processes the way a virus attacks a healthy body. It's a pretty close analogy. The Earth views the human race as a disease, a threat to all life. What do you or I do when threatened by a disease? Our immune systems kick in and increase our body temperature to kill off the virus. This is what the Earth is doing, raising its temperature to decrease our numbers so that we won't have such a deadly effect on her. Follow me?'

'It's a pretty shitty way to look at people.'

'People are shitty. We're no longer in the driver's seat. Gaia is steering our ship, and it's headed for the rocks. Time was, eighty years ago when we had a chance to avoid this disaster, but we didn't take it. We didn't have the balls to make the hard choices to cut our carbon emissions. Maybe we had the balls, but we couldn't do it because for millions of years we've been programmed to put our family and our tribe first. To hell with others. This tribalism kept us alive for millions of years. Saw us through many crises, but finally that same tribal isolationism was our undoing. When faced with problems on a global scale, we're like deer caught in a spotlight. Can't figure out which foot to move.'

'All my life the media has been saying that we're fucked,' Linella said. 'I'm hearing nothing new tonight.'

Eisa put his hand on her arm to restrain her. 'But something new is happening. Gaia has one last use for us – to be the host for a new race. To bring it to birth. Somewhere in the depths of the ocean, God only knows where, Gaia produced the messenger virus that created the lupans. With higher body temperatures they'll survive in places that today we can't tolerate. Curiously, they're also immune to the Black Plague. Not too interested in technology. Maybe that's what will save them in the end. Unlike us they won't have such a devastating effect on the planet. To put it bluntly, evolution, and Gaia are on their side.

'As long as we protect them, remain close to them, we have a chance to survive. If we don't, Gaia has no further use for us. I wouldn't want to interfere with the lupans' welfare; do anything that might harm them. Sharing my biological theories about the

Plague could be the worst thing for them. I doubt our village would survive such a revelation either. We're here only because we've kept quiet, below everyone's radar. I hope you understand.'

Linella felt a chill creep over her. Eisa's words wormed their way into her. Made her feel small and inadequate. She struggled for a comeback, but she had to admit that in large measure Eisa was right.

'I guess I understand. I just hate it all.'

'So do I. But I know where my loyalties lie. I have to take care of this camp. Our people.'

'Talk about being isolationist. It's exactly the attitude you just complained about.'

'Maybe it is. I don't know what else to do. I can't worry about stupid human beings. Let them hack each other to bits or die of Plague. I can only take care of this camp.'

Linella pulled herself out of the sagging chair. She felt a detached sense of numbness. 'I'm exhausted. I need to lie down or I'll fall down.'

'What about the pilot? Didn't you come here to talk about him?'

'He needs medical help. I've told you what I think is wrong with him. If we could at least make him comfortable for the last month of his life, it would be something.'

Eisa closed his eyes. 'Let me have a think. Come in the morning and I'll have a package for you. Didn't I show you how to set broken bones and splint them?'

'Only twenty times.'

'Fine. Meanwhile I'd rather you and Sandria kept your contact with him to a minimum.'

'Aren't we supposed to be immune?'

'If I'm right. But what if I'm not? I can't risk it. Tell Sandria to stay away from him. No sex for one.'

'That's most unlikely.'

Eisa sucked on his cigarette stub, staring at her as he blew out the smoke.

'You're fantastic when you're all fired up. I miss you. You've a bit of a walk up the hill. Don't you want to spend the night here?'

'Thank you but I've too much on my mind.'

'You like your wounded pilot, don't you? I can hear it in your voice. There – I saw that look in your eyes.'

'Don't be daft. He's an arsehole and hates wolf-children. Besides, I know nothing about him.'

'He's a man, and you get lonely at night. That's how it is. I've watched you, the way you stare at every man who comes into the glen. Maybe that pilot is the one.'

'Stick to your medicine, doctor, because you know nothing about women.'

Maybe she should have stayed with Eisa, she thought as she climbed the hill toward the yellow lights of her cottage. It had been a long dry spell since Brian went away and, while she hadn't missed having a man around to complicate her life, she fantasized about a one night stand. But for her, a one night stand was never for only one night. It inevitably produced heartache. She was never content with just sex, but wanted relationship, something no man had been able to provide.

It wouldn't be Eisa. Too much separated them: an entire scientific lexicon, and now this Plague cure. Thinking about it stoked her anger and helplessness. Something had to be done, but what? She saw herself thoughtlessly blurting out the cure to an outsider. Because the cure represented hope for millions of people. She'd have to watch what she said. If Eisa was correct, the lives of the wolf-children were at stake.

She looked back at the lupan colony, a featureless shadow against the grey sky, without any artificial lighting except for a tiny flicker of an outdoor fire. A howl broke into her thoughts followed immediately by a chorus of yelps. Those were not hunting calls, but greetings such as, 'Good evening. What's going on?' The pack was gathering on the hill for a meeting with the lupans. Hopefully their howls wouldn't give the pilot a heart attack.

41

The living room lights blinded her as she walked in. Andrew was half asleep on one couch. George was watching a football game on the wall-screen, and Josh sat up in an armchair, a book reader in his lap and electronic plants in his ears. He pulled out the plants when he saw her.

'Isn't it time to shut it down for the night?' she said.

'Mum, you have messages,' Josh said, adding with a smirk. 'Your old friend the Brigadier called you three times. Wants you to call back tonight.'

'Thanks. Keep the noise down while I'm on the phone.'

She passed into the study where she picked up her handset. She couldn't wait until morning to respond. Johnson could be just returning her call, or something more sinister might be afoot. Taking a deep breath she dialled his number.

'Yes.' His gravelly voice echoed in the phone.

'Brian, it's Linella. I hope I didn't wake you. What's up?'

'Can you turn on your video?'

'I don't use it.'

'Don't have a wrist-com either?'

'You know I hate them.'

'It would have saved me the trouble of calling you three times. Will you be home the next few days?'

'I don't see why not.'

'I need to stop by and see you. How about next Thursday.'

'Thursday's fine. Brian, what's going on? I can tell from your voice that something's happening.'

'I don't want you to worry about anything. I'm sorry I've been out of touch. Been really busy down South. You wouldn't believe what's going on down in Perthshire and Edinburgh. It's a war zone. Up here you don't have problems. Anyway I'll be up in your area soon. I just want to reconnect with you.'

His business-like tone told her that he wouldn't say more that night. Something was happening, and it had to do with Josh's rumours.

'Thursday night then. Bye.' She put down the receiver.

SIX

Beauty Woman looks on while Cottage Woman fills a glass vial with coloured liquid, attaches a needle to it and thrusts it into the Messenger's leg. He gasps in pain. What sort of healing is this? To hurt the man and pollute his body with poison? After removing the needle, Cottage Woman positions the leg on a long board. This doesn't hurt him as much, but that's because his spirit, weakened by the poison, has withdrawn and left him barely conscious. She binds the leg to the board. Presumably to discourage him from walking. The entire process appears both complicated and unnecessary.

Beauty Woman touches Cottage Woman's arm, offers to demonstrate an easier way to advance healing but Cottage Woman pulls away, indicating that she wants to be left alone. She speaks gently to the Messenger in comforting words. Closing his eyes he mutters, 'Thank you.' She lingers beside him, her hand on his chest. Her hesitant body says that she'd like to stay with him longer but feels that she can't. Turning to Beauty Woman she asks her to take care of him. Protect him from an unspecified threat. Beauty Woman takes Cottage Woman's hands and holds them still, a gesture that appears to reassure her.

A metallic roar shatters the stillness, a tortured scream no animal could make, only a machine built to cut and destroy. The scream rises to an unbearable pitch. Pain and unbearable suffering are woven into the sound. The forest goes into a nervous flutter. The trees strain with anxiety, their branches and leaves atremble.

Cottage Woman tries to tell her that everything is fine, but words are too weak to dispel the storm. Saplings run for the cover of their dens. Flustered birds fly away, anywhere as long as they're far from the noise. It comes from a cutting machine. At the forest edge, village men are clearing away the fragments of the metallic bird. One man has climbed the tree where the bird impaled itself to attack its branches with the cutting jaws. One by one the branches are gnawed from the trunk and come crashing down. Then the bird's body, freed from the tree's embrace, slides to the ground.

The machine cuts off but its echo lives on, reverberates from trees to the hills. Relieved, the forest lets out a deep sigh. Relaxes. The village men don't notice. They stand laughing as if nothing terrible happened, unaware of the distress they caused. They drag the bird's broken wings into the forest.

They've barely left when a cloud of mechanical birds, each the size of a sparrow, appears over the forest. Like real birds they gather and separate rhythmically, soar into the sky where they have a full view of the land, and then swoop down to examine their prey. They circle ever closer. One bird hovers so near that she can distinguish its metallic fluttering wings, the cold eyes, angry because it hasn't found what it wants. It would as soon kill her to appease its fury but Blue Sky interposes himself to protect her. Responding to his power the bird drifts away and rejoins the others. After several passes they regroup and fly off over the forest.

A gigantic insect descends from the clouds and sends everyone running again for their dens. Its wingless body, supported by two whirring circles is large enough to contain Insect People, the kind who long ago attacked the colony and abducted many people. Several multicoloured eyes on its underside scan the dens. From far in the forest comes the howling of anxious wolves. They have an acute sense for approaching danger. Long ago their warnings alerted the People to run for shelter from the Insect People, ahead of their landing.

Blue Sky takes her hand to reassure her. – It doesn't want us. It's looking for him.

Inside the den, the Messenger twists as if his life is about to be taken from him. The insect's drone evidently terrifies him. He'd run off if his broken body would let him. Beauty Woman tries to calm him down but he shouts back barely recognizing her. Finally he collapses into the bed, and lies there, his eyes staring at the ceiling. Fear holds him in its grasp until the insect leaves.

Beauty Woman listens to the distant baying, feels its anxiety seep into her body.

– They're afraid – she says. – We need to bring them here. Reassure them.

– Rather, they'll demand that we repel those insects instead of attracting them.

Soon after sunset distant wolf calls indicate that the pack is on its way and so Blue Sky summons a meeting in a small clearing near the forest edge. The wind has grown strong enough to stir the branches of the largest trees. He feels privileged to stand close to such untameable power. Its fingers tear at the long grass at his feet, sweeping it into long waves; it moans and whistles through the branches. The birches all bend low in unison, their branches and leaves fluttering. Thousands of airborne voices scream so loudly that no one else can be heard.

Saplings are always the first to arrive. While others sit in a circle, they gather twigs in the fire pit and bring fire from a den. At first the wind blows out the fire before they reach the pit but after several tries the fire pit is alight. Once the flames are steady, the saplings dance around the fire, jumping over it with their arms spread out to catch the wind. All saplings dream of flying like birds.

Outside the circle, Dark Woman, also known also as Sandria, frowns in the shelter of an overhanging oak. Anxiety consumes her from the inside. She's obsessed with her child, Wolfborn, hoping she will appear that night. But she won't. She's in the forest, taking care of a new brood while the others go hunting.

Before long several pairs of gleaming eyes appear among the trees. The Protector enters the circle followed by several others. His massive shape moves with deliberation, his head turns from side to side, taking in each person. He nuzzles two saplings whose smells he doesn't recognize, appears to approve of them and looks around to ask who called the conference. Out of respect, no one looks at him directly. Pressing himself against Blue Sky, he allows himself to be stroked.

Mother follows the Protector, greets Beauty Woman with a murmur, then Blue Sky. Beauty Woman hugs the large wolf and lays her head on Mother's neck.

From her perch on Beauty Woman's back, Starlet begins to whimper. Her hungry sounds excite several wolves who scurry to her side. Among them is nurse, a large wolf with a pendulous abdomen, who recently raised four new pups. Beauty Woman slings the baby from her back for feeding. Before long the baby is lying against a row of teats and sucking noisily.

Blue Sky presents the Protector with a small piece from the Messenger's shirt.

The wolf recognizes the smell. His low growl indicates that he doesn't like it. Neither do the others. Why must the People shelter the man instead of killing him? Why not make a clean finish to an obvious threat?

Blue Sky holds the cloth against his face to tell the wolves that he wants the Messenger to remain with the People. He is a gift of the Sky; not a threat. The Messenger may be able to save the People and the pack from Insects.

The Protector isn't reassured. The Messenger is an unknown. Dangerous, unless shown to be otherwise. Where is he anyway?

The Messenger isn't strong enough to meet the pack. Not yet. But they'll meet him soon.

The Protector rouses Mother. She's resting with her head against Beauty Woman and would rather be left alone, but he drags her to her feet. Demands that she respond.

Mother wags her head from side to side thoughtfully. Something that day isn't right. An unnamed threat hangs in the air. All the trees tell her so. Insect People have returned. The forest no longer feels safe, a place of refuge. The threat demands a response.

Blue Sky remains still to show the wolves that he is not afraid, certainly not of Insect People.

It's a language the wolves should understand but Mother looks away, unconvinced.

The Protector laughs. He doesn't accept hollow reassurances. Blue Sky is naïve. The world is dangerous and always has been. A wolf must either hunt or be hunted. It's the way things are.

Not with us, Beauty Woman tells Mother with a swift look.

Mother's frown deepens. How will the People protect themselves? Whenever Insects appear, the People run for the shelter of trees. Their bodies don't have the strength to resist Insect Men. Never have. Which is why they need wolves to look after them.

The Protector's sarcasm is replaced by a cold, determined look as when he closes in on a kill. He'll do what it takes to keep the pack healthy and safe. He won't allow the children suckled by wolf-milk to come to any harm. Isn't protection the basis for their friendship? If Insect People threaten, the pack stands ready to defend them.

He licks Blue Sky's face; shows his teeth. His red tongue hangs out, asking if the conference is over. Hasn't everything been done and said? For several nights the pack hasn't hunted. What better night than tonight? Moonlight and a strong wind will unnerve and fluster deer, making them an easy catch. The young wolves, bored by all the talk are already wandering off and yelping for attention. They want to know when the fun will start.

The Protector trots off with Mother. The others run close behind. Soon the hunting howls multiply, each wolf altering its call to create the impression of many more wolves than there really are. Blue Sky adds his voice to the chorus, wishing the pack success that night. They gather near the forest edge till everyone is there and then run off into the trees.

Sitting up in his bed Scott tried to activate his wrist-com. For days he'd had no news from the outside world. For all he knew an army could be out there looking for him. There was nothing wrong with most of the com's functions, but he had no reception on any news channels. The screen remained fuzzy and the sound was reduced to unintelligible crackling.

Reluctantly he admitted that he felt better. The tightness in his chest was gone. Had the gentle touch of the lupan woman helped him? Supposedly some dogs could stop your bleeding by licking you. More likely Linella's painkillers had kicked in and sedated him. He hoped she'd come back soon. For the past couple of days Sandria had been aloof. She barely responded when he spoke. He no longer objected to Rami and Zia's company, but conversation with them was strictly limited to grunts and whistles.

A medley of yelping jerked him awake. They'd never been this close, almost pawing at his door. He struggled to stand up but his splinted leg collapsed under him. Here he was, alone wounded and helpless. He could cry out for help but would anyone come? If wolves found him he was finished. His body screamed that it wanted to live; not to be mauled to death by wild animals. Even death from Plague, described variously as slow drowning or suffocation seemed more welcome. Though he could move his splinted leg without great discomfort, it had no strength to support him. If the wolves rushed him he'd make a super effort to run. He might not get far, but he'd go down fighting.

Footsteps approached, the grassy curtain over the door was swept aside and a female lupan walked in. He knew he'd never seen her before because she was an albino, with white skin and well-combed white hair. Her large golden eyes told him she was lupan but he couldn't tell her gender, because her breasts were small enough to be male and unlike with other lupans, a loin cloth across her waist hid her genitals. Though she wore no jewellery her soft skin suggested she was female. Halting a few feet away she scrutinized him with a look that didn't miss any detail no matter how insignificant. What did she want? She produced a low whistle that could mean astonishment, disgust or anything.

'What do you want?' he said.

A gleam in her eye silenced him. She was there as a judge, to decide what should be done with him. He felt small, too confused to speak in his defence. She knew her power and wouldn't be shy about wielding it. He forgot about the wolves. No wolf could possibly do him any harm without her consent. A look from her would send it scampering off.

Feeling suddenly exhausted he closed his eyes and began to drift off. He'd only been asleep for a moment when a nearby movement brought him back. Instead of the albino lupan, Sandria stood over him.

He raised himself on one elbow. 'Where's she gone?'

'Who?'

'The albino. She was here a minute ago.'

'There's no one else here.'

'She was standing right where you are.'

'Maybe you saw Dream Woman – she's the only albino around. She's a bit of a recluse; only comes out at night.'

'Dream Woman? Yeah, that sounds just like her. How do you know her name?'

'She told me. She speaks more than most of them. She's not from around here.'

'Weren't all these lupans born in the refugee camp?'

'Most were. We have some strays. The children are able to find each other, even over large distances.'

'What's this camp doing here? I thought all lupans in Scotland had been rounded up long ago.'

Sandria looked away evasively. 'I can't tell you. You might ask Linella.'

'Why Linella?'

'She deals with government agencies.'

After stoking the fire until it blazed she stirred a rusty pot on the stove. Her hijab slipped onto her shoulders to reveal black hair highlighted with silver strands. With a nervous movement she drew it away from her face and then tightened the belt about her waist. He wondered if she was flirting with him.

'Do you want some soup?' she said

'Lupan soup?'

'Soup.'

'Is it safe?'

'What do you think? Am I going to poison you?

'I'm only asking. I don't know anything about lupan food.'

'I eat it. If you want to get better you have to eat.'

'Thanks.' Taking the bowl he looked it over curiously. It was of unglazed clay with a pattern carved into the side that suggested leaves. The soup had a musty smell of mushrooms, contained vegetable chunks and some unidentified meat. After forcing down several bites he felt warm and full.

While he ate Sandria sat on a small stool near the stove, looking away from him and withdrawn as if she'd received some bad news.

'Something bothering you?' he said.

'I wanted to see my daughter tonight.'

'She lives here?'

Sandria's glare made him realize his mistake. *Of course you idiot, Sandria has a lupan child.*

'I'm sorry,' he said. 'It must be very hard for you.'

'How so?'

'I don't know. Well, I've heard that a lot of mothers who have lupan children find it all very difficult.'

'More difficult than you can imagine.'

'Where is she?'

Sandria closed her eyes. 'Out there with the wolves. She lives with them, howls like them and runs with them. Just think about it. How do you expect me to feel?'

'I've never understood lupans' attraction for wolves.'

Sandria glared back. Again he realized he had said the wrong thing.

'I'm sorry. I don't know anything about lupans. How did she end up with wolves?'

'At three months she started feeding from a wolf nurse. Don't tell me you've never heard such stories?'

'Only what I read in the tabloids, so I don't know what to believe. Are you saying that you brought Asra to some wolves for feeding?'

Sandria nodded. 'Linella did. I remember that day. I was so tired of finger feeding Asra, dipping a finger into broth so she could lick it. She wouldn't feed any other way. She was so thin. Inconsolable. Linella took her so I could get some rest. She climbed the hill with Asra because she heard the wolves nearby. Wolf howls were the only sound that calmed my baby. Near the forest, a wolf pack surrounded them. They wouldn't release Linella until she allowed Asra to feed from a wolf nurse. It was all so strange that no one believed her. We thought she'd made it up.'

'Wow. What a story.'

'It would have ended there except that the wolves began to kidnap our babies. I remember the horrible morning when I found Asra's cot turned over and my baby gone. Lina's was also missing. The men searched the camp but found only wolf tracks. The next two days were the longest days of my life. While the men were out searching, I waited – alone. We finally found the babies at the edge of the wood, asleep and well fed. Their necks had little bite marks where the wolves had carried them.'

Scott's head spun. The story seemed unreal, like something out of Grimm's fairy tales but Sandria's seriousness convinced him that she wasn't making it up. 'After the next kidnappings, we knew we had to take the babies to the wolves for feeding. So our relationship with them began. As long as the babies fed, the wolves didn't steal them. As soon as the children could walk, they wandered off into the woods to be with wolves. We did what we could to contain them. We built a special house for them, surrounded it by a tall fence. Linella and I took care of the babies there. They were happy enough to be together but they still wanted to get out. When their howling became unbearable we walked them to the woods to find the wolves. Finally they went off on their own anyway, sometimes for days.'

'You weren't afraid the wolves would hurt them?'

Sandria shrugged. 'They never have.' Her voice grew thick as if she was about to burst into tears. 'Our children are wild, more like wolves than like us – don't you see?'

'And Asra?'

Sandria wiped away a tear. 'I can't talk about her.'

'It must be hard for you to stay with me,' he said to change the subject to one less painful.

She looked away. 'I'd be here anyway.'

'Why do they want to keep me?'

Sandria shrugged. 'They think you're some sort of messenger.'

'A messenger? Whose messenger?'

Sandria waved her arms. 'From the air. From the spirits of the woods. I don't know.'

Scott laughed. 'So, I'm some sort of god. That's really interesting.'

Sandria stared at him coldly.

'Have I upset you?' he asked.

'You're so arrogant. I can't stand that about you.'

'I can assure you that I'm a lawyer who happened to crash here. End of story. I'm no messenger. But I'm not surprised they might think I'm a god. Primitive people can't tell advanced technology apart from magic. Why shouldn't they think that I'm a god fallen from the sky?'

'They don't have gods.'

'No gods?'

Sandria tightened her lips. He had upset her again. Obviously she didn't take to his sense of humour.

The doorway rustled and Zia entered. She uttered a short click. Scott assumed it meant, 'Good Evening. How are you?' He made a similar sound back. She didn't catch his attempt at sarcasm because she smiled, as if she appreciated his effort at communication.

'Where's Asra?' Sandria said.

Zia returned an impassive stare.

'You understand me. Where was she tonight?'

Zia reached out gingerly to stroke Sandria's shoulder but she moved away. 'Not now. I don't want to be touched.'

For a minute the two faced each other in a contest of wills. Tears started in Sandria's eyes. She collapsed on the floor, her head between her hands.

Zia knelt beside Scott and looked into his face. Her eyes were so still that he could not imagine a thought arising in her. She appeared to be looking through him, studying him from the inside, aware of his confusion and his fear.

'Now, you just leave me alone,' he said, uncomfortable under her intense stare.

With her supple fingers she stroked his leg slowly, rested her hand on the break where the pain was localized. She looked up as if asking him how he felt.

'Yes, it hurts,' he said.

She nodded.

Why do I have to stay here in a lupan den eating lupan swill? I need to find my own people.

She uttered a soft click as if responding to his thoughts. Her gentle eyes asked him a question. If her click meant anything, it was the lupan equivalent of, 'Why?'

'It's too complicated,' he said. 'I want to be left alone.'

Zia turned her eyes away but continued to stroke his leg.

'Why do you hate wolf-children?' Sandria said.

'For the same reason most people do. They're Neanderthals. If they were handicapped or retarded children, I'd feel sorry for them, because I'd feel that they're ours. Only unfortunate. But lupans aren't unfortunate. They don't belong to us except by

53

accident of birth. They're a mockery of everything human. Look at their eyes, their nakedness, their smell, their juvenile sex and all that howling. Don't get me started or I'll be sick. Not even their mothers can stand to be around them. You must be about the only one who cares about the fate of your lupan daughter. And now, while we die from Plague, famine, war or scalding temperatures, their numbers multiply. It doesn't make me feel better about them.'

He winced as Zia's fingers dug into a tender part of his leg. She was so focused on treating him she didn't appear to follow his words. He hoped not.

'Does she understand me?'

'I don't think so.' Sandria stoked the fire with strong jabs of the poker.

'I'm sorry if I offended you. You asked me why I don't like them. I told you.'

'I'm not offended,' she said in a cold voice. 'I'm sorry for you.'

SEVEN

Once a week Linella caught up with the news. Before falling asleep, she took out a handheld screen whose scratched surface flickered so much no one else could read it. She flipped through the channels for anything noteworthy. Outside the glen the world was disintegrating. Wars over food and water, mass starvation and the ever-advancing Plague were the order of the day. Viewing atrocities she could do nothing about left her feeling more numb than horrified.

When the news depressed her she would calm her nerves by working in her flower garden. Years ago she had dug up an acre of bland grass around the cottage and planted dahlias, chrysanthemums, lilies, asters and daisies along with hawthorn hedgerows to keep out the blustery wind. Global warming meant milder winters, but Atlantic gales still blew in frequently and flattened any standing crop. Homesteaders cursed the wind; lupans danced in it. She had adapted to its constant presence.

Every week she loaded flower bunches into her creaky Land Rover, put Lisa the black collie in the back and sputtered off to the neighbours. She budgeted at least an hour for each visit, the tea and biscuits and latest rumours around the glen. From Mrs. Law who kept the pig farm across the glen, and who supplied Linella with meat, Linella first heard confirmation of Josh's news. The army was on the move; two Braemar camps had been shut down and the Findhorn camp had been served a warrant. Who would be next? Mrs. Law knew everything noteworthy in the three counties. She confirmed each rumour with her extensive network of contacts. Unlike the media, she was never wrong.

'Ye should be thinkin' aboot aw that,' Mrs. Law said with a slow nod, meaning that she was of two minds about Linella's refugees. 'They're heedin' oor way, and I'm a fierd aboot Koppiemaul. I ken that yer people are nice folk. Not armed like aw the others, but these days we dinna like refugees.'

After dinner Linella pulled the pickled venison heart from the refrigerator, prepared the short-crust pastry for tarte latin, selected her best canned beets, relishes and chutneys from the underground larder, setting the table with dishes she knew Johnson liked best. She unwrapped her handmade beeswax candles and fitted them into an assortment of bronze and ceramic candle-holders – all purchased from charity shops. She cut a cornucopia of dahlias, making sure that his favourite red variety dominated the display.

Why am I doing this? She wondered as she cut the flowers. It's how I used to greet him when we were together. It doesn't feel right. The preparations all appeared futile. Years ago she had used her body and her table to bring him to her side but those days were over. At dinner-time the boys wondered about her nervous silence but didn't ask her what was happening. They knew when she wanted to be left alone.

She sat with her digital pad at the kitchen table, a glass of dandelion wine in front of her while she answered correspondence – a good way to help the time pass. Ten o'clock approached; she finally accepted that he wasn't coming. She tossed the pad into a basket of odds and ends, crammed the hors d'oevres into plastic containers and threw them into the refrigerator. The flower arrangement stared back at her. Should she divide it up and spread the flowers about the cottage, or take them down to the village? She barely finished clearing the table when his cruiser roared up the driveway, all four headlights blazing. Josh and George, still wearing their gaming helmets ran to the window to see who it was.

'It's an army four by four,' George said with a smirk. 'Propane powered.'

'It's probably Brian Johnson. Let me deal with him.'

'Here we go again,' Josh muttered, jamming his helmet on tighter. 'Why do you get involved with all those idiots? None of them are worth having.'

Johnson climbed down from his car, stretched his arms and tilted back his head and shoulders to loosen them. He smiled upon seeing her at the door. With a tired step he walked up to her, his head bowed as if not sure how to greet her. A tall man, he had a cleanly shaved head with a thoughtful forehead, a long curved nose and a red bushy moustache. His broad shoulders created an impression of massiveness, of someone not easily influenced. Since she last saw him his paunch had grown more visible through his loose-fitting khakis.

'Well, look at her, the cottage mistress at the door,' he said, a wry smile emerging underneath his moustache.

'You're looking fine,' she said. 'It's been a while.' She stepped forward to embrace him but he moved out of the way. He was either eager to come in or didn't want to be touched.

'Can you believe it? I'm here again. I've missed Koppiemaul.'

'I've missed you too, Brian. Is there a reason this cottage mistress can't get a hug?'

She wrapped her arms about him and drew him in close. He stiffened at first, but then relaxed into her. She tried to give him a full kiss on the lips. His lips parted and their tongues met, but he pulled away and kissed her on the cheek instead.

'Hey, I don't have the Plague,' she said.

'Ah, but I might.'

'Seriously?'

'Just joking. It's good to see you again, sweetie.'

'Come on in. The champagne's chilled.'

'Is that an invitation to spend the night? You know I don't drive on champagne.'

'That depends on you.'

'How about a cup of herb tea? I'll think about the champs later.'

She led him through the living room toward the kitchen. 'Oh look at them,' Johnson said with a nod at Josh and George, sitting on the couch, their glazed eyes absorbed in their games.

'How are you doing?' Johnson said.

George lifted his helmet partway, 'I'm fine. And you?'

'Very busy. How's the veg this year?'

'Not bad,' George said and pulled on his helmet to continue his game.

'Very good,' Johnson drawled. 'Can we go into the kitchen?'

'Sure,' Linella said, crestfallen. His remote manner suggested that he hadn't come socially, but to tell her some upsetting news.

She put the kettle on the hob; took two mugs from her shelf. She held up a small jar of tea-leaves. 'I have some real, Spanish tea.'

'Really. How did you manage that?'

'My refugees have their sources. Classified of course.'

'These days it's worth more than cocaine. I'll take it.'

With trembling hands she measured the tea into a teapot. She took several deep breaths to calm her disquiet but only felt tenser.

'So, what's up?' she said.

Johnson sank into the kitchen chair. His lined face looked tired; his jowls sagged as if weighed down by concerns. He shook his head silently, but said nothing.

She put his cup in front of him. 'Something's going on.'

He stirred in a teaspoon of sugar. 'Something's always going on. These are difficult times. Watched the news lately?'

'You know I can't keep up with all the mayhem. I've enough trouble down here.'

'That's a big mistake. You need to be glued to the news station every day. You can try and forget about the world, Linella, but it doesn't forget about you. It's dangerous to isolate yourself.'

'What am I missing? Wars? Murders? Statistics about Plague casualties? Tell me, Brian, what am I missing?'

58

Johnson nodded, his lips breaking into a smile. 'Still the same Linella. One of a kind. There'll never be another.'

'Okay then – am I missing something I should know about?'

Johnson lifted his arms in a gesture of helplessness. 'Maybe. The country has changed a lot since the day you first walked into my office. Then, we had refugees trickling into the country. Lupan colonies were appearing here and there. We had no idea what those lupans were, or what to do with them. Things are different today. The level of violence is unreal. Thirty years ago unarmed policemen settled knife fights in Glasgow. These days the army is called in to deal with heavily armed gangs. The water's rising fast. The country is inundated by refugees and lupans. We're a lifeboat that's dangerously swamped. About to sink.'

'Complaining about immigrants and lupans has been a national pastime since the dawn of time. Tell me something I don't already know.'

'You've got to listen to me. What you may not know is that things are very tense. The racism is as extreme as I've ever seen it. Before you say anything, let me say that I believe it's unjustified. But that doesn't make those sentiments less real. We could handle it all if it weren't for the Plague. Last year it claimed a million people in the UK alone. The latest vaccines are slowing it down, but you know the story of vaccines. It's only a matter of time until a super-strain appears that can't be stopped.'

'Hmm.'

Only two days earlier Eisa told her there was a cure for the Plague. Now was her opening if she wanted to tell Johnson about it. Even as she considered speaking, she recalled Eisa's warning. She fiddled with her teaspoon, aware of Johnson's penetrating look.

'So, things out there are bad. I already know that.'

Johnson scratched his day-old stubble. 'You've a lot of enemies, people who want to shut down your camp; dispose of the lupans.'

'Right. I have enemies.'

'People blame refugees for all the violence, gun-trafficking and even the Plague. If you walked up Union Street and told anyone who you are and what you do, they'd kill you. A month ago, bounders attacked two refugee camps in the highlands and set them on fire. They had commandeered a tank. We had to engage them in battle before we restored order.'

'I saw it in the news. Brian – what can I possibly do about such situations?'

'They could happen here.'

'I'll deal with bounders when I see them.'

Johnson frowned. 'Did you hear about Christie's new decree?'

'No. Should I have?'

'He wants to solve his re-election problems by shutting down the camps and moving all undocumented immigrants to detention centres.'

'Stick them all in prison?'

'It'll save their lives. Also take a lot of guns out of circulation.'

'You seem to like his idea.'

Johnson took a sip of tea. 'I don't like it but I don't see an alternative. In the long run it's the best thing for everyone. Pick your poison. I'm concerned for you. Armed vigilantes are closing in, Linella. It's only a matter of time before you'll face some very nasty people. You need to get out of the way and let the government do its job – to protect the refugees. They'll be well treated.'

'Yes they will. Like all others. I've been to Dunvegal Centre. I know the conditions there: the overflowing toilets, Plague in every cell, the rats and the cages where good people are locked up. Even small children. It's a death sentence. Don't talk to me about the government's treatment of refugees.'

Johnson didn't appear to be listening.

Her lips felt dry. She swallowed with difficulty. 'And the lupans? Is it prison for them too?'

'They're totally illegal. They should have been gone long ago. I don't know what will happen to them.'

'What are you saying? Will they get lined up and shot?'

Johnson let out a long sigh. His lips tightened, indicating he wouldn't answer her question. After a long silence he said, 'I don't know what to say.'

'Brian, if there was ever a time when I needed your help, it is now. Please help me.'

'I wish I could,' he said after a long pause. 'This visit is illegal; I could lose my rank for this conversation. If there's any resistance when the army comes, I could be court-marshalled.'

'When the army comes? Are you telling me the army's on its way?'

'They'll be here.'

'When?'

'I can't honestly say. I don't know. Warrants have been served to – what's the chap's name, Almagheri or something like it? We haven't heard back from him. You may have a few weeks left, but not much more. You should tell him that the situation is serious. If he ignores the warrants, the army will come to enforce them. If the refugees escape into the hills, that's their choice, but their houses will be gone when they return. The army has orders to bulldoze them.'

'You seem to know a lot about this operation. Are you in charge of it?'

'Not as far as I know.'

'You fucking bastard. You sold me out. I'll bet that no one knew about our camp or about the lupan colony until you mentioned it in some fucking report. That's why you've kept your distance from me. I have never been so completely and totally betrayed.'

'That's not true.'

'Fuck you.'

'Why do you think I came here? If I didn't care for you, I would have stayed away.'

'Why did you come here? For a bit of sex no doubt. Sorry, those days are over. Find it somewhere else.'

'Linella.' He stood up, kicked back his chair. His eyes searched her, and then looked down at the table, unsure of what to do or to say next. He shrugged. 'I really have to go. One day you'll realize how much you owe me. I helped you because I admired you. These days there aren't many heroes. Everyone is corrupt. It's like the god-damned Plague which has us by the balls. I'm not proud of anything I've done. But you should be.'

'Flattery will get you nowhere.'

'I'm very sorry for what's going on. You don't deserve it. But I'm only the messenger. I can't change anything.'

'You're too cowardly to take a stand.'

Johnson let out a sarcastic laugh. 'Call me names if that makes you feel better. If my superiors crucify me, it won't help your situation. We have to be smart about our choices.'

'I know yours. You've chosen to play it safe. Fuck the children and everyone else. You'll take care of number one. There is a no more tragic sight than a mediocre man.'

'I helped you before. I didn't have to do that.'

'Right.'

Johnson looked out of the kitchen window at the darkening hills. Either he'd run out of things to say, or he was waiting for her to calm down. She could barely see him through her hot tears. To think that she'd given him so much. That she'd even contemplated resuming their relationship. He didn't give a fuck, not about her, not her kids, not anyone.

'Get out,' she said.

Her fury didn't move him any more than it might have moved a mountain. He took a sip of tea then placed the cup gently on the wooden table. He stayed put.

'Why? In God's name tell me, why can't you leave the lupans alone?' Johnson shook his head. 'Turn on the news and you'll understand. This country is at war. It's tearing itself apart. Lupans are one more aggravation that we'd rather not have. They're a constant drain on our resources. People hate them.'

'Supposing ... just suppose for one split second that the wolf-children could save you. What if in some mysterious way they could supply you with the cure to the Plague? What then?' The words were out before she could stop them.

Johnson opened his eyes wide. 'That's a bit of a stretch.'

'What if it's true? Would anything change in your attitude to them if they had the cure for the Plague?'

'I don't think it would make any difference. Feelings about lupans run very deep. People resent them – the way Germans resented Jews last century. I know, it's racism, pure and simple. We need a scapegoat for our problems and lupans are it. You won't change human attitudes by a scientific discovery that the lupans have something positive to offer.'

Linella swallowed hard. In his own words Johnson confirmed what Eisa had said. She closed her eyes, tried to suppress her tears but her sobs only grew louder.

After a few minutes he said, 'I'm sorry. Believe me I'd do something about all this, if I thought it would do any good. The lupans are a difficult problem. What you or I think about them doesn't matter. Their status has always been murky. Unlike UK citizens, they're not entitled to human rights. A month ago three lupans were shot in the mountains near Ullapool. The men responsible were booked by the police, and then released with no charges brought against them. These days there's so much racism, no one wants to stand up for lupans.'

'So the army will just round them up and shoot them?'

'No. They'll take them to special facilities. We don't kill lupans for the heck of it.'

'You're trying to sound so fucking detached, like you have nothing to do with all this. You are so deep in shite. You know the people who could call off the attack. You've done it before.'

'That was then. It's beyond me or anyone else to stop it now. Coming here and telling you is the best I can do.'

'Forgive me if I don't believe you.' She leaned on the kitchen stove, her back to Johnson.

After a minute of silence, he said softly, 'I'm going now.'

She didn't turn around while he shuffled to his feet. As he was about to leave the kitchen he stopped. 'That thing you said, about the lupans having a cure for the virus. Do you believe it?'

'I don't know.'

'Sorry, I just wondered if you were serious.'

'Maybe I was.'

He nodded a "good-bye" and left the room. After the front door slammed, she broke into more sobbing spasms. She clenched her fists and let out a loud cry.

'Mum, are you okay in there?' Josh said from the living room.

She forced out the words. 'I'm fine. Don't worry about me.'

EIGHT

Scott sat outside the den, leaned his back against the wall. When would Sandria return from the village, hopefully with canned food to chase away the earthy aftertaste of lupan swill? And a change of clothes. Meanwhile he was stuck there, unable to move on his own. The confinement of an Aberdeen jail seemed more welcome. At least he'd have guards to talk to.

As hours crept by he watched naked children chase each other in circles. They were often accompanied by large grey dogs. Or were they wolves? He hoped they were dogs. The kids tussled with them, teased them until the animals growled. One of the beasts stopped to give him a long look. The clear, steady eyes displayed an intelligence he hadn't seen in any animal. It was no dog.

In a scene out of National Geographic, female lupans strolled by, naked except for glittering bracelets, earthenware pots on their heads. He found himself admiring their graceful movements, sensual as a dance. A tall female paused close enough for him to smell her musty body odour. Her golden eyes searched him. Aroused by the smell and her raw nakedness, he wondered what she'd do if he made a pass at her, but before he could make up his mind, she walked on.

Several males lazed outside the adjoining den, looking aimlessly into space. Not unlike the Edinburgh unemployed who gathered outside St. Giles Cathedral for someone to drive by with their lorry and offer them work. They didn't even click or whistle to each other.

Uphill from the den a crew laid out the wooden framework for a new den. Another crew used rusty blades that looked a hundred years old to shape beams out of birch trees. While two males worked the blade up and down the tree trunk, others slowly turned the wood, to create a human powered lathe. They were well coordinated though they worked in total silence. How did they do it? Evidently they communicated better than human beings, though he couldn't make out how.

Working with stone was their never ending obsession. A trolley loaded with a four foot granite block struggled up the hill. Five males pulled on ropes while two others pushed. At least they hadn't turned their backs on the wheel. Nevertheless he wondered how so few people had the strength to transport such a large rock. And why the cart hadn't collapsed under its weight.

Didn't they have more important work than to cover the hills with monuments?

So these are the people who will take over from us. Thousands of years of technology, all our culture, music, arts, everything we've built is being tossed away – for this. Here they are: Aborigines, Indians, indigenous people or a cross between all three except that they've no capacity for rational thought or language. Maybe that's why they get along so well with wolves.

How did Sandria stand it, living with creatures she couldn't talk to? What did she see in them? Perhaps her longing for her lupan daughter was stronger than boredom. No wonder she talked incessantly to him; he was the only company she had. He heard all about her cousin Lina, her husband Arjan, and a host of other names that quickly became a blur. About tangled relationships and family squabbles, the stuff of soap operas. The lupan children were often present in her stories, but only as something that had gone wrong. Something not to be talked about.

'I haven't seen anyone come up here except for you and Linella. Do the mothers ever visit their kids?' he asked her earlier that morning.

'No.'

66

'Except for you.'

'Except for me.'

'Why?'

'It hurts them too much.'

Her tense voice made him change the subject.

He caught sight of her climbing the path. Her bulging backpack weighed her down. She made frequent stops to catch her breath. When she reached him she dumped the pack at his feet.

'Thanks for getting me some stuff. Really appreciate it,' he said. 'I'm sorry you had to haul that pack all the way up here.'

'I do it all the time. How are you feeling today?'

'Amazingly well.'

After only five days he was able to lean on the bad leg. Either it hadn't been broken in the first place or Zia's potions and witchery were working. Incredibly the swelling under his neck had subsided to where he could swallow without pain. He checked himself often for new eruptions, but since his arrival, he found none. The Plague was unstoppable so he couldn't hope for a cure. At the best he had a temporary reprieve.

She smiled at him. 'You're looking good. Want to take a walk?'

'Yes, far away from here.'

'Now that's not nice. No one's mistreating you.'

'That's not the point. I don't mind your company but this place is unreal. I don't get lupies. They drive me crazy. I want to be around normal people.'

'Rami and Zia want you to stay.'

'Should I care what my captors want?'

'They're not your captors. They're your healers. Don't you already feel better after that horrible accident? You look like you can almost walk.'

'I guess I'm better.'

'And I want you to stay. I like having you around to talk to. I'm going to miss you very much if you leave. Can't you stay? Just a few more days?'

'I don't mind the interlude, but I don't want to die here of Plague.'

'I'm really sorry about your infection. Is it getting worse?'

'So far, not a whole lot. What's really bad is knowing that I've only a month left. Soon my body will be covered in lumps and the one under my neck will finally strangle me. It's not a nice way to die.'

'Sounds terrible.'

'Do you see why I want out of here?'

Sandria nodded. 'Where would you go?'

'I'm not sure.'

'Would you stay here longer, if by staying you would be cured of the Plague?'

'What?'

'You know that we haven't had a case in this glen.'

'Now that's remarkable. Are you all just plain lucky?'

'Maybe it's in our water. Or our clean air.' She broke off unexpectedly as if not wanting to follow her train of thought. 'I still think you should wait until you're stronger. What have you got to lose? Maybe the Plague symptoms will go away.'

'Sounds like rubbish to me.'

'Let it be rubbish. Fine. How about a short walk about the colony?' she said, to change the subject. 'Exercise your leg a bit.'

'Do you have some crutches?'

'You can lean on me. It's the best I have to offer.'

'You don't mind touching me?'

'Not really.'

Back in the city most people in the streets wore latex gloves and surgical masks to guard against infection, yet here was Sandria offering to hold him with her bare hands. Either she was incredibly brave or had a death wish.

He shrugged. 'Let's try it then.'

He wasn't particularly keen to see the colony, but a walk sounded a lot better than staring at the den's ceiling. Sandria grasped him under his right arm, her other arm about his waist.

He leaned into her enough to take the pressure off his left leg. For her small size she was remarkably strong. They hobbled up the hill together. Strange, how just touching her awoke in him sexual desire. He hadn't touched a woman for months and now that he was stronger, he missed it. Was she interested in him that way – even though he was infected? Several times he caught her looking at him with a look that appeared sexual. The way she tried to keep him in the colony told him that she had to like him enough. She must be plain lonely, living among lupans with no one human to talk to, and no significant relationship that he could determine.

They headed for the earthwork with the stone on its summit. An alley of smaller stones formed an approach. He shook his head in disbelief. Why did the lupans put so much energy into their monuments? Whom did they benefit? Four thousand years earlier Neolithic people, built Stonehenge and other sites because they believed that a capricious deity needed to be propitiated to bring about the return of Spring. Also because an oppressive priestly class wanted to show the commoners who was in charge.

'How many lupans does it take to stick a stone in the ground?' he said.

Her cold look made him regret his sarcasm.

'Why do they do it?'

'Scott, I don't know. It's unlikely we'll ever know. Not unless they tell us. They work so hard at their stonework that I have to believe that it's important to them.'

She nodded at a long line of stones that snaked down the hill from the colony, crossed the creek and led up the hill toward Koppiemaul cottage.

'This is such a throwback to ancient Britain,' he said. 'They're like Neoliths, worshipping the sun and moon. Do they have a religion? Priests?'

'None I know of.'

'Someone has to plan out all that work. Who's the boss around here? Rami?'

Sandria helped him stagger up the hill, a few of steps at a time, before replying. 'They don't have bosses. They're not like us.'

When they reached the summit he noticed that Zia had joined them. She had the severe look of a nurse who caught her patient outside his bed.

'We're just going for a short walk,' Scott said. 'Let's keep moving. I think she wants to come with us.' To Zia, 'I'm not going to escape. You don't have to follow us. I'd rather you didn't.'

Zia rattled her golden bracelet, grinning as if to say, 'Well, I'm coming anyway. Accept it.'

Looking back he saw that the colony consisted of about twenty dens laid out in several lines that converged on the hilltop. Each den was sunk partway into the hill so that it appeared no more obtrusive than a small growth on the hill, its roof covered in green grass. The chimneys poking out through the roofs reached up like the pipes of a cathedral organ. He wondered if they hummed a tune when the wind blew over them.

'Interesting structures,' he said. 'How did they come up with those shapes?'

'I'm not a lupan. What do I know?'

'You were here when they built them.'

'Sure. Our men taught them how to make cobb and how to use a saw, hammer and scrapers, but the children designed their dens. Except for that one.' She pointed at a partially completed stone house close to the forest, looking very alone. Its window holes were empty. An improvised roof of branches and cob had been hastily slapped on. 'That's what's left of our efforts to build a proper house. They sabotaged the builders until they gave up. It was standing empty until Dream Woman settled there. But she's a strange one; doesn't mind living in a house.'

'What do lupans have against houses?'

'They've never liked them. They don't build them anywhere in the world. Houses aren't part of the lupan way.'

'I know. I heard somewhere that the den design seems to be standard. Worldwide. What the hell is going on?'

70

Sandria almost pushed him away. 'Scott, you're asking questions that I can't possibly answer.'

Obviously she hadn't thought much about what many anthropologists found so perplexing. Within one generation, lupans everywhere converged on a design for their homes. They developed a unique culture, not derived from their human parents, while unable to communicate across large distances. Were they born knowing how to build a den the way a swallow knows how to build a nest?

Lupans wore no clothes. All had similar looking body ornaments. They all learned new crafts within a year of each other, no matter whether their colony was located in Russia or the United States. Murder among them was unknown but when attacked by humans they responded with slingshots. Their stones had brought down many a helicopter. Colonies were located usually at the edge of a forest or a wilderness populated by wolves, bears or some other large animal. They invariably developed a close relationship bordering on symbiosis with their animal.

The dome closest to the earthwork, the largest, had a green turf roof without chimneys. Smoke escaped through a large opening in the centre.

'Is that the boss's place?'

'I told you they don't have bosses. That's where they meet.'

'Like church?'

Sandria sighed but otherwise ignored the remark.

Outside the dome several children played in the baked clay. Their thin bodies were well toned; their faces smudged. A female lupan emerged from a den, clicked loudly to the children. They ran up to her, and disappeared inside.

'Is that school time?' Scott said.

'They don't have school. They play like wolf pups.'

She smiled at him to see if her jibe discomfited him.

'I thought that they studied Shakespeare, or at least basic algebra.'

'Maybe they're learning something more important.'

'Like what?'

'Oh – stuff.'

'You mean Stone Age stuff. At this rate it'll take them a few centuries to catch up with us.'

Sandria's grip tightened on his shoulder. 'You're so determined not to understand them.'

'Show me something that's not out of the Stone Age. They haul their stupid stones all over the place. No one can figure out why. They grind corn with pieces of granite, run around naked and they can hardly talk; unless those clicks are what you'd call a language. Like people thousands of years ago, they follow wolves about the forest. What don't I understand?'

'They have other interests.'

'Yes, hauling stones.'

Sandria turned away. He realized he'd upset her. 'I'm sorry,' he said. 'Thanks for taking care of me, and for helping me walk. I do appreciate you. I'll try not to be an arsehole.'

'If you'd shut up and stop judging them, you might learn something.'

'All right. I'll give it a chance. This is all very new for me. I suppose that's where they grow their food?'

He was looking at what resembled a neglected vegetable allotment. Among the tall weeds there were several raised beds, some with squashes and root vegetables; most of the beds appeared to only contain nettles. Three adolescent lupans armed with traditional spades heaped soil onto a small mound.

He thought of mentioning that the lupans needed to hone their weeding skills, but decided to swallow the remark. Instead, he said, 'Who taught them to grow veggies?'

Before Sandria could respond, Zia who had been following, touched Scott's arm and pointed to a nearby plot where a toddler of barely five watched a male, who might be her father, dig over a bed.

Had she understood his question? Her eyes had a look as if she had. What about all his sarcasm about lupans? He felt oddly embarrassed at the thought that she had been quietly listening in.

'So they all learn from the older people,' Scott said to Zia. 'But who taught you – the first ones?'

Zia's eyes smiled. He sensed she wanted to answer him, but didn't know the words.

'I showed them some basics,' Sandria said. 'How to dig soil, make compost and how to sow, but they seem to learn even more from each other. They know a lot about gardening that they couldn't have learned from me. Like the way they handle weeds. I showed them how to pull weeds, but they refused to do it. Somehow their gardens manage without weeding. Look at those precious children with their spades. When Asra was that age I tried to teach her basic gardening but all she wanted was to play with wolves.'

'When did you last see her?'

Sandria's voice faltered. She looked away so he wouldn't see her eyes fill with tears. 'About a year ago.'

'Is there something I can do for you?'

'No, I'm all right. I don't know why I brought you here. We need to leave.'

She grasped him under the arm, almost dragged him back down the hill. Zia followed several steps behind; appeared thoughtful.

'Can you at all imagine what it must feel like to lose a child?' Sandria said. 'No man can understand it. I saw her last up there, chasing a wolf through the vegetables. She let me hold her. Her body was so hot against my skin. She brushed my face, kissed my eyes, and then said, 'Mother, Asra returns. Be not sad. Nothing is ever lost.'

'She can talk?'

'Yes.'

'Do any others talk?'

'They all recognize a few words, but Asra's different; you can have a conversation with her – if you ever find her.'

'I've never heard anything so strange. If Asra can talk, then they all have language abilities. Why don't they use them?'

'I wish I knew.'

Scott turned to Zia, 'You do understand us, don't you?'

Zia raised her eyebrows in a look that asked him to repeat his question.

'I don't think she does,' Sandria said. 'Eisa says that our language structure is too complicated for them. It's specific to our brains. Theirs are wired differently. Even when Asra speaks, she often makes no sense. Her thoughts and feelings are so different. She'll always be a stranger to me.'

She burst into tears. Scott took her by the shoulders and let her cradle her head against him. 'I'm also worried about the women in the village. Many of them are pregnant again; they're all scared for their babies. Every woman dreams of having a normal, human baby.'

Sandria pulled away from him, dried her tears with a coloured cloth. 'Nothing changes,' she whispered. 'I don't know why I stay up here waiting for her to appear.'

'You have me to take care of,' he said.

He thought the levity would help her, but she turned stiffly away.

'I want to go,' he said to Zia. 'To leave. Get it?'

She heard him. Straightening herself, she tried to stare him down, to let him know that he wasn't going anywhere.

'Why not?' he demanded.

Clearing her throat with a click, she said, 'Wolf.'

'Fine. So, what about the wolf?'

Zia pointed at the forest, nodded slowly and repeated, 'Wolf. Wolfborn.'

NINE

From her bedroom window Linella had a clear view of the summer sky. While entire constellations drifted by she watched restlessly. Her thoughts swirled in endless circles. She raged at Johnson for turning against her; regretted that she lost her cool, if for no other reason than it was not the way to win him over to her side. Still, things between them were so broken that she had nothing left to lose. That morning she'd have to tell the refugees she could no longer protect them. What words could she summon to deliver the message? She tried to compose a speech in her head but got no farther than a paltry opening before rage choked her. What was about to be destroyed was not a house but a community. People working with their bare hands had made the very bricks of their homes, their energy supply, vegetable gardens, orchards – an environment where children grew up protected from the horrors of war and squalor. They had nowhere to go. Soon after sunrise, exhausted and distraught, she fell asleep.

The sun was high in the sky when she dragged herself out of bed for an espresso. Despite the turbulent night her mind was quiet. All that remained was for her to march down to the village. Let the bad news spill out in whatever words it chose.

Over breakfast she decided to try out Eisa first. He might not agree with her on the Plague cure but he was steady and rational in a crisis. She left her dishes unwashed on the table and headed down the track to the village. She passed a stand of olive trees, their branches laden with clusters begging to be picked. Arjan planted them when he was a gangly overgrown kid, his pointed spade packing the earth enthusiastically around the root ball. A lump grew in her throat and she forced her eyes away; this wasn't the time to be tearful.

Even as she approached Eisa's house, the cold stovepipe protruding above his roof told her that he wasn't there. A quick look through his window revealed his unmade bed, stacks of unwashed dishes and papers scattered on his table, the look of a place that had been abandoned for days. Across the street two children tossed a beach ball to and fro. A year ago their family had moved there from Ethiopia. The father was so grateful to find a home that he had wept. Within a year he had planted a rice paddy in the waterlogged meadow near the brook, and was about to harvest the first crop. Clasping the ball the boy sauntered up to Linella. She scooped him up and gave him a peck on the cheek.

'How old are you Changri?'

His eyes shone. 'Six.'

'And when's your seventh birthday?'

The boy counted on his fingers. 'February six.'

'Then you come to my cottage on your birthday and we'll celebrate.'

With a heavy heart she set him down. Someone would have to explain to him that he might not see her cottage on February the sixth; that his world was going to end. His house bulldozed.

'Where is Eisa?' she asked.

'He's with Lina,' Changri said.

Lina lived at the far end of the main street. Every week Linella met her there for tea. Lina would share her deepest feelings. Lately it was her marriage that had gone cold. Arjan was never home, except to sleep and to say 'goodbye' when he left in the morning. She worried about the other women. Hana had withdrawn and was living with only alcohol for company. No one had seen her for days. Sandria only appeared in the village to load up on food. She never spoke to anyone. Lina bore the weight of

76

the community on her shoulders. The conversation over tea usually lifted her mood but only for a short while. Linella listened but offered only rare advice. A sympathetic ear was mostly what Lina needed. For her, life was to be endured, its pain accepted as inevitable, not to be wished away or healed. She couldn't understand why Linella didn't see it that way.

The village's main street was a motley assortment of buildings made of concrete blocks, cobb and timber, each one a different shape and colour. A chaotic array of mud and tin chimneys stuck out over the red tile rooftops. Electric wires strung across the street swung like spider webs. Several cars without wheels were rusting into the ground. Kids had decorated them in bright Arabic patterns. That morning many families sat out on their porches eating a late breakfast. The air felt breathless. The sun burned hotter than usual, so no one was in a hurry to go out and work.

Oli waved to her from his porch as he set out boxes of turnips, leeks and beets, then aubergines and peppers, vegetables that never used to grow in Scotland. People all over the glen traded for his vegetables, exchanging tools, building materials and clothes. His spread only reawakened her fear that this summer's harvest would be the last. After the eviction the seasons would continue, but the vegetable fields would lie fallow. Finally grass and heather would reclaim them.

'Beautiful aubergines,' she said picking one up.

'They're better every year.' He fanned his face. 'It's a hot one today. Another record-breaker.'

She didn't need weathermen to tell her that the world was getting warmer. The stream of lorries with refugees that landed on her doorstep was evidence enough of the climate disaster. She no longer wrung her hands despairingly at scientists' predictions that one day the rocks would boil. Why rail against the weather when you're about to be evicted?

She found Lina in her kitchen. Eisa and Arjan were sitting at a long wooden table, along with two newcomers whose names she didn't yet know. Their dark skin suggested they were from

Africa. Lina still wore the traditional black dress and hijab of her home country. She greeted Linella with a smile.

'My dear Linella. Come, join us.'

Linella eagerly accepted her second cup of chicory coffee, especially this cup, the way Lina made it by pouring boiling water over the grounds and letting them settle. Refugee coffee, she called it. While Linella sipped her cup she noticed that Eisa looked at her expectantly. He knew that something was wrong.

'What's happening up at the cottage?' Arjan said.

Linella took a deep breath. 'Johnson came by last night.'

In the ensuing silence Arjan folded his arms.

'And?' Arjan said, the word sounding foreign in the tense air.

'The army's headed this way.'

Arjan tilted back his bearded face and laughed nervously. 'Oh here we go again. More threats.'

'Johnson said that they wrote to you about their operation.'

'Maybe they did,' Arjan said with an indifferent hand wave. 'I got something a few days ago. I couldn't understand what it was all about.'

'It's a warrant.'

'Oh yes?'

'You need to tell us these things,' Eisa snapped.

Arjan lifted his hands defensively. 'They send me so much rubbish. What am I to do with it all? They use a lot of complicated words I don't understand. I've been throwing away these notes for months and nothing ever happens.'

'Maybe you should re-read the last one,' Eisa said.

In a halting voice, Linella related her conversation with Johnson. While she spoke Lina washed the dishes slowly and stacked them methodically into the wooden dish drainer. She listened intently to Linella but her graven face offered no clues to her thoughts.

Eisa let out a dry laugh. 'I told you this would happen.'

'Can't you persuade that Brigadier to call off the army or at least delay it?' Arjan said.

'I already tried. He said he can't do anything for us. I feel physically sick. I know, I've let you down.'

'None of us would be here but for you, Linella,' Lina said. 'You gave us a home.'

Arjan scratched his greying beard. 'Do you really believe him? Every year there's a new threat. Usually it just goes away on its own.'

Eisa said, 'If Johnson came out to tell Linella that the army's coming, it's coming.'

'We need to gather the village. Let the people decide what to do.'

'Democratically?' Eisa sneered. 'First we'd better decide what we want. It may save a lot of time.'

Arjan frowned. 'What do you suggest? That we pack up and go? Leave our houses?'

'We've all been thrown out of our homes before,' Eisa said. 'Why shouldn't it happen again? Leaving isn't the worst that can happen to us. I'd rather wander the hills than be locked up in a detention camp. They're such horrible places. Anything is better than that.'

Lina stepped up, her square face unyielding as a rock. 'This is our home. This is where we'll stay. You men work out the details.'

'Our life here is about to end,' Eisa said. 'They're going to evict us.'

'Your anxieties are none of my concern.'

The taller of the newcomers turned to his companion. 'It's what just happened to us in Inverness. This time we won't leave without a fight.'

Arjan placed his hand on the man's arm. 'Don't go for your gun so quickly, Elijah. We're not up against bounders. It's the Scottish army.'

Lina shrugged. 'I don't care who is coming. I won't leave my home to wander about in the woods. Neither will any of the women. Day by day we built those walls, the table where you sit, every chair and bed and the hearth. Our orchards and our gardens feed us; they're our life.' She stretched out her hands, heavily calloused and with cracked skin. 'These hands worked to build a life for you and for our children. They built this home.'

'You want to wait here for the army to evict us and drive us off to Aviemore Detention Centre?' Eisa said.

Lina's silence was stronger and more emphatic than her words. Arjan looked gingerly into her withered face. 'Don't you think something should be done?'

'Surely,' Lina said. 'The right thing must be done. I'm tired of all the talk and all your fears. If a tank comes down the main road, I'll be there in front of it. I have nothing to lose but my life. I will not run away to live like a bear in the woods.'

'Back off from that tank. The village's protection is the concern of the Elders,' Arjan said. 'There'll be no walking out in front of tanks.'

'Sort out what you want to do, but I'm staying.'

Eisa turned to Linella. 'Did Johnson say anything about the lupans?'

'He implied...' She struggled to find more words but her voice had died. She covered her eyes so the others wouldn't see her tears.

'They're going to take them away,' Eisa said.

She nodded.

'I was afraid of this.'

Elijah cleared his throat. 'When they bombed the Inverness colony, they shot the lupans who were trying to escape.'

'It was a terrible crime,' Lina said. 'I will not stand by and watch them shot.'

'Nor will I,' Linella said.

'So, we're going to wait here for the army,' Eisa said. 'Do we greet them with root vegetables?'

'Don't look at me,' Lina said. 'You already know what I think.'

'Fighting the Scottish army – is not a smart thing to do,' Eisa said. 'All we have are some sawed off shotguns. They have bigger guns. We could make them withdraw for a day or two but we can't win a war.'

'Then you need to build up your arms and ammunition,' Elijah said. 'I know where to get some cheap machine guns. I'll even find you a rocket launcher. If we show the government we mean business, they'll leave us alone.'

Arjan held up a warning finger. 'We've survived here for longer than most camps by avoiding confrontation. The neighbours know that we have no guns, and they value us for staying unarmed. We've many friends among them, friends we would immediately lose. Armed response is a bad idea. But we can't leave voluntarily either.'

'Well spoken, husband,' Lina said with a faint smile.

What about your discovery, Eisa?' Linella said. 'People would kill to know that there's a cure for the Plague. Can't you use it to negotiate with the government?'

'Yes, Eisa,' Arjan said. 'What about this miracle cure?'

'God, here we go again. Now you want me to work miracles. Right now, all I have are results on paper. Some ideas. My scraps of paper and figures aren't going to win a war. People negotiate over land, guns and money. Tangible things. Not over science.'

'It's worth trying,' Linella said. 'I could mention it to Johnson.'

Eisa's lips tightened. 'Don't do that.'

'It might save the lupans.'

'Or seal their fate.'

'It's the wolf-children I'm thinking of,' Linella said. 'We face eviction but they risk their lives. We can't just sit back and do nothing.'

'Give me a chance to think about it,' Eisa said.

'Then hurry up with your thinking,' Lina said. Her voice shook with emotion. 'You may want to forget them but they'll never forget you. If we face any danger, they will be here, protecting us. Enough. I won't speak any more now. Please, excuse me.'

She walked out of the room, leaving a deafening silence. Linella got up and followed her. She found Lina in a small bedroom leaning against the window frame. Linella wanted to take the woman in her arms and hold her but she sensed Lina's remoteness. Lina often became emotional whenever the lupans were mentioned.

'I know you're thinking of Rami,' Linella said.

Lina responded with a simple nod.

'I'll never know how you feel because I've never lost a child. But I'll fight alongside you as if I had. They're as much mine as they are yours.'

'Thank you,' Lina said. 'It means a lot to me. I try not to think about Rami, but just now, when I heard you say that they might be shot? ...I almost died.'

'I hope it won't come to that.'

'Of course. But it won't be good. I'm sure he doesn't miss me, that I'm totally irrelevant to his life, but he's my boy. What else can I say?'

'Do you want to see him?'

'As if I haven't tried. You forget how he used to come here regularly, drink tea with me. We would stare at each other across the table. All I wanted from him was to hear him speak – to say something to me. Anything. But he wouldn't. He sat there with his lips shut tight. I know he can speak. If Asra can talk, so can the others. But they won't. He won't.'

She shook her head. 'It's better for me to stay away. I can't pretend that we can have any relationship.'

'What did you mean when you said that the children won't forget us?'

Lina stared out of the window, as if afraid to reveal too much of her pain. 'I'm not sure what I meant. Last night I had this dream. I dreamed of him many times before but this time I can't ignore it. In the dream he told me that we don't need to be afraid, because the wolf-children will never desert us. They've pledged us their protection. I don't know what the dream means. It's like a message from God. We must stay in the village, that's all there is to it. We abandoned the children when they were small. To leave the village would be to abandon them again. We cannot break faith with them.'

'I can't imagine life without them. They're our children.'

Lina let out a wail and raised both hands to her face, her chest convulsed with sobs. She did not resist when Linella took her by the shoulders and pulled her in close.

TEN

Linella climbed the winding path up to the colony. She paused often to look back at the village. Smoke rising from several chimneys reminded her of the people who lived there, that she wasn't alone with her burden. Now that she had delivered her news, the villagers would sort out what to do about it. Her next task was to tell the lupans, a task that seemed impossible. The language-barrier was only part of the problem. Time was the main difficulty.

For lupans, the present moment was the only reality. *Thou art blest compared wi me, the present only touches thee*: Robert Burns might as well have been talking to a lupan instead of to a mouse. Lupans could sit for hours observing rain, wind or sunlight, with the intense stare of a wolf stalking its prey. She'd never noticed a trace of anxiety. They weren't anxious because for them, the future didn't exist. Living closely with natural cycles, they knew that day followed night, and spring followed winter, that you sowed when the Earth grew warm and took in the harvest before it cooled off. To tell them that the army was coming, at some unspecified future date, to wipe them out was like trying to tell them that the sun would one day darken at noon.

Could Maguire help her? He might not care what happened to lupans but he hated the Scottish army and was sympathetic to refugees. He might know a lawyer who could stop the operation. Perhaps a European human rights court that would intervene.

She found him outside the den where she had left him, sitting opposite Rami and Zia, trying to converse with them. He had removed his splint and was sitting with his bad leg under his chin, apparently pain free. What was going on? Several days ago the leg was broken. It couldn't have healed so quickly.

'I want – to see – Sandria. The woman,' he said slowly, accompanying each word with a hand gesture and facial expression.

Her eyes puckered, and wearing a deep frown, Zia said, 'Woman.'

'Fine. Where is the woman?'

Zia smiled and said, 'Woman.'

'Where? Where is the woman?'

Zia pointed at Linella and broke into a medley of noisy clicks that might be laughter.

'She understands!' Scott shouted. 'She understands one thing. Thank God for some human company.'

Linella nodded at his leg. 'You look like you're making progress.'

'I'm coming back to life but I don't know if I like it. Look at them. I've tried every sign language known to man. They understand less than my dog.'

'Maybe you shouldn't try so hard.'

'They intrigue me. I want to figure them out.'

'You'd better work fast.'

He peered at her. 'What's going on?'

Her voice choked, 'I spoke to Brigadier Johnson. An old friend. He said that the army's about to sweep the refugees out of the village; take them to internment camps and bulldoze their houses.'

Scott raised his eyebrows. He rubbed the white stubble on his chin. 'Did he say when?'

'No. He just advised them to pack up and leave as soon as possible.'

'And go where?'

'They're not going anywhere. They've lived here for almost thirty years. Do you know a lawyer? Anyone I can talk to?'

85

'Try President Christie.'

'Scott, I'm serious.'

'A while back I could have helped you. Now I'm a wanted man. What do you expect me to do?'

'Anything that'll make a difference.'

'The rules are changing, Linella. It's a different world out there. I'm tired of seeing good people locked up only because their country was flooded out or burnt up. I've fought the system for a long time. I don't want to be a part of it. Especially as a lawyer. It's all so damned corrupt.'

'That may be a fine elitist attitude for you to have but what about the refugees? What are they supposed to do?'

'Why ask me? I'm out of here.'

'You are so not out of here. You're living in this colony now and it's about to be destroyed. You'll be around to see the drones gun down the lupans.'

'They're coming here too?'

'Yes they are. They have orders to close the colony and shoot any lupans that try to escape. Shoot them like dogs.'

'I can't say I'm surprised. Lupans aren't exactly very popular, even with their mothers.'

'That's all you have to say?'

'When the army kills people like you and me, no one complains. They call it collateral damage. This is no different.'

'This is different, damnit!'

Scott adjusted his leg to find a more comfortable position.

'If I could walk, I'd help the refugees pack their stuff. I don't know what to do about the lupans. They don't have a future. This is their inevitable end.'

'How can you be so calculating?'

'It's the survival of the fittest. Whenever there's a conflict between two cultures, the one with the bigger guns wins. The lupans don't have any guns, which is why they're going to die. People hate them for what they are. Feel threatened by them. What else do you expect?'

'I expect people like you and me to do what we can to protect them. You've no idea what the wolf-children are. You can't just sit back and let them be murdered. They're our children. No alien gave birth to them. We did. We must stand by them; fight for them.'

Scott looked skyward, untroubled by her outburst. Rami and Zia watched her closely, frowning as if trying to understand.

'What do you want me to do?' he said faintly.

'I want you to protect them.'

'Against attack-helicopters and drones? You're crazy. You have a contact in the army. If you really want to protect them, get that brigadier to call this thing off.'

'He won't. He was able to warn us; that's as far as he'll go. We're on our own. Don't you see? If you or I don't protect the children, no one will.'

'We can't change anything. If the lupans want to live they'd best bugger out of here. Run off into the trees where they'll be harder to find. If you really want to help them, get them to understand that, and good luck.'

While she struggled to respond, she felt Zia's hand on her shoulder, a firm hold. Zia was offering her emotional support. Her arched eyes asked a question. She wanted Linella to tell her why she was so disturbed.

Linella looked back into Zia's golden eyes. 'If only you could grasp what's about to happen to you.'

The deep creases in Zia's brow hardly stirred. She uttered a series of clicks, nodded approvingly.

'What is she saying?' Scott said.

' I don't think she knows what we're talking about.'

'Can you draw a picture – something visual to help her out?'

'I'm not sure they understand drawings either.'

Zia placed her hand on Scott's shoulder, smiled at him inquiringly. 'Okay,' he said. 'You want me to talk to you?'

'Give it a try,' Linella said.

Scott shook his head. 'I've been trying all morning.'

'Hold her hands. That sometimes helps.'

Scott took Zia's hands gingerly as if afraid he'd catch a disease, swallowed, and said, 'You must gather your people and hide. Bad people are coming in flying machines. They want to take you away to a bad place. Kill you. You must protect yourselves.'

'They don't understand *bad*,' Linella muttered.

'Fine – then dark, evil, nasty men are coming. Whatever. You have to protect yourselves against them. They're going to kill you.' He gestured – a knife cutting his throat.

Rami and Zia studied Scott's face. Curiously their eyes moved synchronously as if a single will lay behind them. Even their brows had the identical look. The faces blended to where Linella couldn't tell which face belonged to whom. She'd been confused that way before. Lupans gathered in a group tended to disorient her. On one occasion she was searching among several lupans for Zia and didn't recognize her standing two feet away.

Scott moved uneasily, uncomfortable under the intense scrutiny. Then the lupans' faces separated and she saw Rami and Zia again as distinct persons. Zia smiled at Scott.

'Maybe she understood what I said,' he said.

'I'd be surprised. It was very complicated.'

'We will help you to escape,' Scott said to Rami.

Rami's arm swept down in a cutting movement. His hard eyes suggested he did not want to hear any more.

'I guess that means they don't want to move,' Scott said.

'Looks like it. I don't know what to do. I can't sit back and watch the army mow them down.'

'Do you think they understand how bad their situation is? They don't look all that smart.'

'They're more intelligent than you can imagine.'

'You'd never know it.'

'They're highly empathic. They can sense your mood, your feelings and your attitudes. I'm sure that they understood the sense of our conversation.'

'Without language?'

'Not having it, it doesn't get in the way.'

'If you say so. Anyway, I don't have time to figure them out. As soon as my leg's a bit better, I'm going to just…'

He broke off and looked away. Linella smiled at his nervousness. She'd half convinced him that lupans could read his mind. He didn't want to tip them off about his plans to escape.

'The swelling under your neck isn't looking so bad,' she said.

'Odd, isn't it?'

'Maybe if you stay here with the wolf-children you'll be cured of the Plague.'

'Yes, Sandria said something like that too.'

She hadn't planned to tell him about the cure, but now she had to. It was the only way to save his life. Eisa's warnings and doubts seemed absurd. If Sandria knew, then what was the harm in telling Scott? Wasn't he as much a local resident as the villagers? She told him.

When she finished, Scott sat quietly, his face an expressionless mask. 'I suppose I'd better stay.'

'You believe me?'

He shrugged. 'It makes as much sense as anything I've heard. But if what you say is true, why aren't you spreading the news? People are dying out there.'

'I don't want to let them die.'

'I'm confused.'

'Eisa feels that once the news gets out, the wolf-children will all become lab animals, to be disposed of once some vaccine is extracted from them. Telling the world could be the worst thing for the children.'

'I see. But we're talking about the survival of the human race at the cost of a few lupan lives.'

Linella turned away. All emotion seemed to freeze up inside her. Finally she blurted out, 'Your attitude is so typical. It's why we mustn't tell anyone. Until people treat the wolf-children with the respect that they deserve, they'll get what's coming to them.'

Scott glanced at Zia and Rami, who were closely following the exchange. He thought they had they frowned when Linella spoke about lupans becoming lab animals.

He shook his head. 'They'll destroy the lupans anyway. With or without your help, the lupans are history. Do you want them to die a meaningless death like slaughtered lambs, or do you want their death to mean something? In giving up their lives, they may save the human race.'

'What a shitty way to look at them. Slaughtering them to save our skins, and then calling it their *noble* sacrifice.'

'You want the Plague to claim more lives?'

'The price of the cure is too high.'

'Who says that experimenting on lupans will kill them?'

'Scott, they don't survive in captivity. If they're not in their natural environment, they die. I want to broadcast the cure. I'd tell the media about it today, but not if it means that our children will die.'

'Maybe this news will make people think again about lupans. People will recognize that they're not all bad. That they have a useful role to play. I already feel better about them. Enough to make me want to stay in this colony. I'm sure that many others will feel the same way. I'd go and break the story.'

'I'll think about it.'

'Don't wait too long. It might be the only way to save the colony.'

As she walked back down the path Linella met Sandria climbing the hill. Maybe Sandria hadn't heard about the impending attack, because she walked with a light skip. She was wearing a pale blue dress gathered about the waist. Her hair was tied up to emphasize her oval face. A necklace of moonstones hung about her neck.

'Hello, Linella,' Sandria said with a broad smile.

'You doing fine, Sandria?'

'Did you see Scott?'

'Yes.'

'Isn't his leg amazing? After only seven days?'

'Yes, he's doing well. Sorry, Sandria. I can't stop to talk.'

Linella continued on down the hill. Her heart hammered and an overwhelming feeling of jealousy arose from nowhere. She stopped to catch her breath and wondered why she felt so strongly about Sandria and Scott having sex. Sandria always wanted another baby to replace Asra. A human baby. Let her jump Scott in the night and fuck his brains out. Didn't she see his heart was closed? For Scott, lupans were sub-human and hardly worthy of life. Let her have him, Linella repeated under her breath.

She was about to pass Eisa's house when he appeared at the doorway and waved for her to come inside.

'Got a minute?' he said. 'I don't do well in large groups where everyone's talking at once. After you left, our Abyssinian friends kept on with their warmongering. It looks like they've convinced Arjan to buy us some guns. It's a very dangerous decision and will end badly for us. I don't want to have to open up a trauma centre for gunshot wounds. There has to be another way.'

'I'm very sorry about this. I don't know what to say.'

'You've survived in your cottage without any guns. Not even bounders bother you. Will you try and talk some sense into those men?'

'I don't think they'll listen to me.'

'Can you get the story out, that the government is about to send in army tanks to evict defenceless refugees?'

'Like start a blog?'

'To hell with blogs. I want a reputable station to cover the raid. No one wants to see people shot up. Not even the government.'

'My cousin works for Scottish Broadcasting. I'll talk to her, but do you really think publicity will help the wolf-children? People watch videos of helicopters chasing lupans for their evening entertainment.'

'I'm out of ideas. I don't know what else to do. Maybe that pilot has some suggestions. He's helped us before.'

'He told me to break the news.'

Eisa's eyes narrowed. 'What news?'

She had to come clean. If telling Scott about the phage was wrong, she needed to know.

'I told him about your Plague cure. I had to because he was about to leave the colony. I couldn't sit beside him, looking at his swollen neck and not tell him. He said he would stay in the colony to try out the cure.'

Eisa's face grew pale. He sucked air through his teeth. 'I hope he does.'

'What do you mean?'

'Linella Sienkiewicz, that was a bad call. Maguire could put all of us at risk. We have to hope that, if he spills, no one will believe him. There are so many quacks with home remedies for the Plague that it's an incoherent roar. Let's hope that the word of a lawyer on the lam won't carry any weight.'

'They would listen to you. You have the lab results. You could show them to the media. Is holding back that cure the right thing to do?'

'You don't sound too sure.'

'I can't ignore the victims.'

'I'm not ignoring them,' Eisa snapped, his face dark as thunder. 'Don't look at me as if I'm a monster without any feelings. I won't allow wolf-children to become lab animals. Trust me on this one. We mustn't speak until the world is ready to respect their right to life and freedom. So many have died in captivity, or have been shot like dogs.'

He paused, looking past her as if at something far away. 'I had one.'

Linella looked closely at his pained face. 'I never knew.'

'Ten years ago. I had a wolf-girl. She was shot dead by a farmer over by Aviemore.'

'I'm so sorry. It must have been terrible.'

Eisa nodded.

'What was she like?' Linella said after an awkward pause.

'Beautiful. Even if we never exchanged a word. She...' He paused to compose himself. 'She was about to talk. I swear she was.'

'Did you tell anyone here about her?'

Eisa shook his head. 'No. Don't ask me to. There are some things I can't visit again.'

ELEVEN

Scott sat with his back against the standing stone. It tingled when he touched it as if from static electricity. He massaged his shoulders against its surface to release the tension in his back. The combination of the tingling and the stone's roughness felt good. After a few minutes of rubbing he found that his body relaxed to where he could breathe easier. Painfree. Even his bad leg felt stronger. Crazy, but it's like I'm connected to some bloody battery.

He had limped up to the hilltop to find a place where he wouldn't be hemmed in by gawking lupans. Where he could think about what to do next. Linella's news of an impending attack came as no surprise. From his sailplane he'd already seen army columns on the move. But what she told him about a cure to the Plague left his head spinning. Lupans – the saviours of the human race? The absurdity of it all. Yet hadn't his Plague symptoms recently declined? He cleared his throat and swallowed. Painlessly. It could be coincidence, or nothing but a placebo effect, but he didn't believe it. Too many things Linella told him about the Plague made sense.

I might have to learn to love the lupies after all, he muttered.

If the cure was real he was stuck in the colony with the buggers. He'd have to let Zia whistle and click to him as she stroked him daily. Would there be enough time for a complete cure before the army sent in their drones? He hoped so. He'd be sorry to see the lupans chased out of their homes, but what could he do? He'd already explained to Linella that he was a non-person, a sick and wanted criminal. While the army columns moved into place, he was sidelined, sentenced to live among Neanderthals he couldn't communicate with. Submit to their wishes, if he wanted to live.

She's a good woman. I wish there were more people like that. A pity I can't help her this time, he repeated.

Looking back at the colony he noticed that Sandria had come back from the village. He waved to her. She had to be looking for him because she soon spotted him on the hilltop and headed his way. The afternoon sun shone on her dark hair. A gentle breeze caught her blue dress behind her to reveal her slender figure. Lately she'd been much friendlier. Smiled more often and responded to his conversation without being critical. She also liked to touch him flirtatiously when she squeezed past him. He hadn't been inclined to respond. Not that he didn't find her sexually attractive. Sandria wanted someone who could help her forget about Asra, a role that he didn't want.

'You're looking sunny,' he said when she reached him.

She smiled. 'You're not looking bad yourself. You've walked here without your splint.'

'Maybe this place is doing me some good, enough to consider staying a while longer.'

'I'd like that.'

'If it rids me of Plague.'

Her smile vanished. 'Who told you?'

'Linella.'

Sandria appeared to withdraw. 'You can stay here if it suits you.'

'Are you upset that she told me?'

'Not really. I just hoped that you'd want to stay here anyway. Regardless of the cure.'

'I'm sorry if I hurt your feelings. I do appreciate your company.'

'Thanks for the apology.'

'I have you to thank for my recovery. For being alive today. I guess I'm glad I didn't kill myself after all. I'm starting a new life in a very strange place, with strange people. It's all very different from anything I know. Thank God you're here to keep me company. Without you this place would be torture. How do you survive here alone?'

'This is my place. Since Asra's birth I felt drawn to help the wolf-children. They never had parents to teach them the basics, how to take care of themselves, use tools or cook their food. Wolves can teach them how to hunt, maybe even how to take care of their children. But they can't teach them everything. They still need human interaction. They're not wolves. The human part of them is starving for attention. They need someone like you to draw it out. I think that's why they want you here. You have so much to give them if you could only see it.'

'You'll have to help me understand them. I can't figure them out.'

She had drawn closer; her face only a foot away. She smiled, waiting for his response. He tried to turn away, pretend to ignore her, but realized the attempt was stupid. For days he had followed her every move, desired her whenever she touched him, argued with himself that he needed to maintain a distance. All the time he felt an intense thirst to touch her soft body and feel the rush of human emotion that would lift the weight on his heart, light the sleeping fire in his body and make him feel human again. She let him draw her against him, and kiss her on the cheek. Her body felt warm and pulsing with life. She rested her head on his shoulder, waiting for him to make the next move.

'When did you hear about the cure?' he said.

'A few weeks back, Eisa told me what he knew, but I always believed it. Last summer a woman and her child, both infected with Plague, wandered in from the woods. The villagers were too afraid to allow them into their houses so they ended up staying here with me. I expected them to die soon but instead of dying, their Plague symptoms disappeared. One cure would have been a miracle. But two?'

'You weren't afraid to touch them?'

Sandria's eyes flashed. 'I didn't care then if I lived or died. I'm a mother who lost her daughter. What can happen that's worse than that? I treated them; made them comfortable. After they were healed they left. I told Eisa about them. He started to work on the science behind the cure.'

She stroked him under his neck where it was still swollen and began to massage the area. He tensed, not wanting her to touch him. Wasn't she risking her life?

'I'm not afraid,' she said. 'Nothing will happen to me. We've touched before.' Her words softened his resistance. He let go, enjoyed her warm fingers against his skin.

'You should wash your hands when you're finished.'

'I don't need to.'

Before long they were back in the den, where she let him hold her close. They kissed. His heart hammered at the thought of taking her, but doubt also held sway. Could he risk giving her the Plague? Should he have sex with her if she wanted it anyway?

'I need to lie down a bit,' he said. 'My leg.'

She helped him onto the heather, undid his trousers and pulled them off. She massaged his thighs. Her eyes smiled at him, inviting him to participate with her in a secret conspiracy. Not as a patient. She undid her belt, let her dress fall about her feet and stood naked, facing him. She'd set her sights on him from the moment they met, knew that she could take down his last resistance and make their union inevitable.

As they came together, he thought no more about the threat of infection. He let her take him. Plague be damned.

After they separated, she lay still against him with her eyes closed. The stove was dead; a cold breeze seeped in through the doorway. He pressed himself against her for warmth, but he felt oddly alone. For now, sex had quelled his desire for a woman. He was glad she was there, but what did they have in common to sustain their relationship? What did she want from him? He felt he was missing something that he ought to know. Something she wasn't telling him.

In the shadow of evening Dream Woman summons Blue Sky and Beauty Woman to her house. Dream Woman is known for her love of solitude. She doesn't appear to need anyone. If she wants to see anyone she prefers a face-to-face meeting. She reserves merging for ceremonial work. Because of her delicate skin she never leaves her house while the sun is above the horizon.

No one knows why Dream Woman lives in the shell of a house built by Elder People instead of in a den. That was where she was found one day, having wandered in from the forest, with no memory of her past. The Earth's song is strong in her. She not only knows the world under the sun and moon, familiar to everyone, but is mistress of lesser-known dark pathways, where she often walks alone and communes with spirits. When people feel perplexed, sick, or lost, they sit down on her carpet and allow her to read them. Though she says very little, they find that being alone with her strengthens their spirit.

Upon entering her house Beauty Woman and Blue Sky find Dream Woman stirring her stew over hot coals set in a small pit. The smoke is so thick that they can barely see her. Blue Sky coughs, rubs his eyes and retreats to the doorway. Dream Woman beckons him back.

– Swallow the smoke and you'll feel better.

Blue Sky tries the remedy and finds that the smoke no longer stings his eyes.

She pours two bowls of stew for her guests. She watches them closely while they eat. There's little about them that she does not detect, no matter how intimate.

– And what of the Messenger? – Dream Woman asks, with a sharp look at Beauty Woman.

– His body is healing. Each day his spirit grows stronger.

Beauty Woman would rather not say more but Dream Woman's insistent eyes force her to continue.

– He's mysterious. Unknown. By touching his body you can approach his spirit, but not too closely. He holds himself alone, clothes himself with superficial thinking, and resents our attempts to penetrate his veils. Looking at him I sense his grief, the pain that arises from his loneliness. He doesn't see yet that his thinking and language are illusions. That they separate him from us and from the all.

– You would go deeper with him?

Beauty Woman inclines her head. – I've been close, close enough to know every part of his body, but cannot go deeper. He may not relate to us, or we to him. Not unless we walk the Dark Path together.

Dream Woman strokes her long hair with her fingers while she reflects on Beauty Woman's request. Outside the ceremonial circle she does not discuss the Dark Path.

– Can't you relate to him as he is?

– It's not enough.

– Because you want more? – Dream Woman's question comes across accusingly. Beauty Woman inclines her head.

– Why the Dark Path?

Beauty Woman is about to cry. Her feelings for the Messenger rise in her breast, so powerful they threaten to overwhelm her.

Dream Woman embraces her gently. – Show me why it must be the Dark Path.

– So that we can merge with him, see the world through his eyes. Be intimate with him. Doesn't the ability to merge appear in all when they take the Dark Path? Upon returning, they are no longer strangers but belong to the People.

Dream Woman's demeanour darkens. – Elder People cannot take the Dark Path.

– Aren't they people like us?

Dream Woman sighs. – Recall the man and woman who tried the Path. The man died and the woman lost her ability to speak. She ran off into the forest; not even the wolves know what became of her. Elder People's minds are not like ours. They are always alone.

– Chattering non-stop to themselves – Blue Sky adds.

Beauty Woman doesn't need to reply. The others see her

passion, her desire for intimacy with the Messenger.

– He's barely a newborn sapling, – Dream Woman says. – No one can part him from his isolation. It's all he has.

– If he doesn't take the Dark Path, nothing in him will change. His suffering: I feel it even as we reflect on him, cannot resolve itself. He may feel isolated but he is one of us. We've eaten together, spoken without words. Like us, he was born of a woman. Our bodies understand each other. Why should our minds be fundamentally different? Won't you open the doorway so that we can take the Path together?

– Then let it be, – Dream woman replies after a pause. She knows that Beauty Woman will persist until she has her way.

– Either he'll return with an awakened mind, or he'll die. All men die, some in a greater stupor than others. To die in a stupor is no loss.

– He will not die.

– Wolfborn may also be able to guide him – Blue Sky says. – She wants to meet him.

– Ah, Wolfborn and her pack. – Dream Woman makes a dismissive gesture. – Wolf-ways are not our ways. He doesn't need wolves. They'll only frighten him.

– Yet we learn much from them.

– Wolfborn speaks the Messenger's language – Beauty Woman adds. – She may be able to reach him in ways we cannot. We must take him to her when he is strong enough to walk.

Dream Woman looks back dubiously.

– Strong enough to run from the wolves to save himself – she replies.

– Very good, if after meeting the wolves, they haven't torn him apart, bring him to the gathering den. The women will open for him the doorway to the Path.

TWELVE

During the following weeks Sandria stayed close by. She brought a regular change of clothes, cooked whatever he asked for, walked him around the colony and made love to him at night. She allowed Zia to do her daily massage but looked on with a jealous eye. Initially he enjoyed Sandria's attention but he struggled to sustain a conversation with her. On their walks around the colony she talked incessantly about whatever trivia fell out of her head. He didn't know what to say that would interest her. The sex was great. But as the weeks passed he grew increasingly restless.

With each day he was able to walk farther. As he watched the small swellings vanish from his body he felt he was witnessing a miracle. For some incomprehensible reason he'd been selected to live again. Since his early teens he had ceased to believe in any divine agency; the world was a prosaic place run by blind laws, well explained by modern science. Lately he wondered if that was all there was. His healing appeared altogether mysterious no matter how he tried to explain it. Why should he be the one to be cured, when all he'd wanted was to kill himself?

Would he be the only one? What about the thousands of victims who crammed every hospital bed, all waiting for the miracle that had come to him? The more he thought about it, the more he realized that his enforced vacation with Sandria would have to end soon. The hardest part would be to tell her. However he explained it she would say that if he loved her he'd never consider leaving; that he was only running away from her. Perhaps he was.

His thoughts constellated as he bathed one morning in the small pool below the colony, the one place where she left him alone and where he had space to think. Talking about the cure to journalists would accomplish nothing. Com sites were so flooded with useless remedies, from drinking seawater to soaking in olive oil, that no one cared to read them. He might make the evening news if the police arrested him, but he'd have no credibility. A criminal who shouts out in a courtroom that the despicable lupans are the long sought cure, wouldn't convince anyone. Without scientific knowledge to back up his claims, his efforts would be useless.

Climbing out of the pool he quickly reached for his towel. He'd been so deep in thought he had not noticed how cold he had become. He sat on the bank shivering and waited for the sunlight to warm him. Two male lupans sweaty from hauling stones jumped into the water and splashed about, whistling cheerfully. Despite their higher body temperatures they enjoyed the frigid water. Even in a biting wind lupans never wore any clothes. Nature had endowed them with a superior thermostat.

Did they realize that their days of freedom were almost up? Poor souls. All they wanted was the right to breathe, to live their carefree lives, enjoy an afternoon swim and haul stones about – a right denied by people who were resentful because of environmental problems they'd brought upon themselves.

That evening he tried to tune into a local news channel for any information about what the army might be up to, but his wrist com only yielded static.

'Any news from the village about when the army will make a move?' he asked Sandria.

'I'd have told you if I knew.'

'Okay.'

'You're so agitated these days. Is anything the matter?'

'I need to get away from here, do something with my life.' He blurted out the words before he could recall them.

Sandria's face turned slowly toward him and she let out a sigh. She'd evidently expected the conversation.

'I'm sorry,' she said.

'Look, it's nothing personal. I like being with you. I wouldn't be alive except for you. But I have things to do out there.'

'And what's waiting for you out there?' Her tense voice sounded like a harp string about to break.

'I can't rest on my laurels while thousands of people are dying, their bodies covered by tumours.'

Sandria shrugged.

'How can you sit here and do nothing about it?' he said.

'The Plague is not my concern. I'm not a scientist. I've enough to keep me busy, helping the wolf-children.'

'Someone has to tell the world.'

She nodded, but he realized he hadn't convinced her. She still believed that he was making excuses; that he was fundamentally tired of her

'They won't let you go,' she said. 'Don't you see?'

'Look, I appreciate everything you've done for me. I'm only alive because of you, but this place has nothing more for me.'

Sandria's eyes brimmed with tears. 'Then go. I expected you to leave me once you got what you wanted.'

She waited for him say that he loved her. Unfortunately it was the one thing he couldn't tell her.

Soon after sunset Zia appeared and, with a familiar click, indicated that she wanted to treat his leg. While she massaged it, her clear eyes searched his face, not missing any detail. He made his mind a blank, fearing that she would detect his intention to escape. Perhaps she had, because the following morning he found two male lupans planted outside the den, apparently on guard. They followed him to the pool and sat nearby while he bathed. To test their intentions he took the path leading down the hill, but hadn't gone fifty paces before several lupans appeared ahead of him, barring his way. Their appearance was no coincidence. He wouldn't be allowed to leave without a fight, something he wasn't keen on, given his bad leg.

'I think I'll wait a couple of days,' he told Sandria that evening. 'They know I'm about to bunk it.'

'They're more perceptive than you think.'

'Why do they want me here? What earthly use am I?'

'You're important to them.'

'Why?'

'Maybe if you stayed long enough you'd find out.'

Sandria left the den saying that she needed the fresh air. After she disappeared Zia ambled in, her golden belt swinging in her hand. She smiled at Scott, whistled a greeting and looked into his eyes, her thin lips parted to form a question. Was she asking how he felt, or why he wanted to leave? She howled faintly like a wolf. Again her eyes asked something. Did he understand the call?

'What do you want? I don't understand,' he said.

'Wolf,' she said. 'Forest wolf.'

'What about it?' She knew the words but for some maddening reason couldn't form a sentence.

She placed his walking stick in his hand and closed his fingers about it. So, she wanted him to come with her. Why not? At least he might find out why they wanted to keep him.

They climbed the path to the monolith on the crest. Zia walked a few paces ahead, waiting for him when he fell behind. A cold wind crept under his jacket and made him shiver. The light of the full moon gave the hill an otherworldly appearance. The shadowy bushes and rocks that they passed all resembled crouching animals. At any moment he expected them to come alive. Not until he reached the standing stone did he see Rami sitting beside it. Rami arose, exchanged a look with Zia and then nodded at Scott.

'Where are you taking me?' Scott said.

Rami pointed at the forest where the glider had crashed. Grasping Scott's shoulder he gave him a firm push.

'Hey, just you wait a minute. I'm not going anywhere.'

With a nervous smile Zia uttered a faint howl. 'Wolf,' she said.

'What do wolves have to do with me? Are you going to feed me to them?'

Sensing his unease, she stroked his arm, a friendly touch meant to convey that things were as they should be and that she and Rami meant no harm. They stood a few feet away, waiting for him to decide whether to accompany them. He sensed that if he refused, they'd take him back to the den. He'd be safe there, but no nearer to understanding why they were keeping him prisoner.

'I'll go with you,' he finally said. Later he wondered why he hadn't been more afraid; why he trusted them when he knew nothing about lupans or their intentions.

Zia walked ahead along a narrow path that wound in and out among the slender birch trees. She adjusted her pace to his hobble, stopped often to take his arm when he stumbled. Rami followed several paces behind. They soon entered a pine thicket where the air was heavy with pine resin, and so dark he could barely see his way. Why did he feel like a prisoner being led to his execution? A knot tightened in the pit of his stomach; a deluge of questions assailed him. Where the hell were they going? What did the lupans really want from him? Zia said something about wolves. Each shadow in the darkness took on the shape of a beast ready to leap for his throat.

Zia led him by his free hand. With her other hand she brushed aside hanging branches. She had to have the night vision of a wolf because she never stumbled and was quick to move him past unseen obstacles. The pine scented air was difficult to breathe. If a wolf leapt at him from the darkness he wouldn't know where to run or how to defend himself. He picked up his step, moved as fast as Zia would let him toward a growing patch of light. Behind them, Rami walked so quietly that Scott was never sure he was there.

The thicket opened up, giving way to gnarly oaks and beeches. Now that he could see his way his panic eased. He decided that his fear was groundless. In any case, if he needed to run for it he had a clear path of escape.

They were crossing a large clearing where trees had been logged when he realized they were not alone. Beside Zia crept a large wolf. Its massive size made his breath falter. He'd seen wolves that played with the lupan children but they were puppies compared to this monster whose muscular forelegs reached up to his waist, the open jaws, powerful enough to snap a human leg in two. Its bright eyes bored a hole in him. He tried to look back but the wolf growled threateningly as if taking offence. This was the wolf's domain and Scott was only a guest. He tried to hold his stride as if nothing terrible was happening but his legs wouldn't stop shaking. One wrong move could be his last. Observing his discomfort, Zia reached out to the wolf and rubbed its head. In response to her whistle, it fell back to where Rami walked. Though Scott's terror eased, every few steps he looked back to check on the wolf.

From behind a small bush appeared a second wolf, smaller than the first, but with long black hair and a silver stripe on its brow. At first it shot ahead, looked back at Scott and Zia and dashed back to Rami, circling like a dog that wanted its morning walk. It stopped several feet ahead of Scott. The moonlight falling on its face allowed him to glimpse its eyes. Was he mistaken, or were they yellow with a circular pupil, like a lupan's? Before he could get a better look, the wolf moved aside so that its face disappeared into shadow. It circled him a few times at a distance and then faded into the trees.

The rising pain in his leg forced him to lean on his stick and drag himself along. Whenever he looked back, the large wolf had crept closer. He stared into its eyes – a bad mistake, because the wolf uttered an angry growl that stilled his blood. For an eternal moment they faced each other, the wolf's fur standing on end, its body tense as though ready to leap at his throat. His heart pounded with the thought that one of them had to die, but then the wolf turned aside and allowed him to walk on.

As he plodded after Zia, he searched again for an escape route. Had he totally misread the lupans? They'd brought him there to feed him to their wolves; to provide them with cheap entertainment. Wasn't that why they healed him and why they wanted him to stay in the camp? A healthy man would entertain wolves better than a wounded one. The thought gathered strength to where it overwhelmed all counter-arguments. Scanning the trees he saw pairs of gleaming eyes on all sides. He could try and run, but how far would he get, stumbling in the darkness with a bad leg, before a wolf sank its teeth into him?

Zia took hold of his hand. Her dilated eyes tried to console him but he grew impatient.

He pulled his hand away. 'I'm all right.' Nothing she did or said could allay his panic. 'Lead on. I want to get there.'

There was no one to respond. Zia had melted into the shadows.

'Zia!' He searched among the trees, but the forest had swallowed her. There was no sign that she'd ever been there. Rami had also disappeared, leaving Scott with only the wolf. It crept closer, a low growl growing in its throat. What had happened? Why hadn't he listened to his common sense, that he was no more than warm fodder for the beast? Why hadn't he run for it when he had the chance?

Lifting his stick he jabbed at the wolf, but it darted out of range. They faced-off, ten feet apart. Scott felt a palpable pressure to give way but he stood his ground. The wolf crept forward, his eyes on Scott's stick, his growl louder. Scott backed off. He poked at the animal, but it ignored the stick. If the beast sprang he was lost.

With his eyes fixed on the wolf, he retreated along the path; he no longer had a choice. The wolf decided where he must go and it pushed him deeper into the thicket. After what felt like hours he emerged into a moonlit clearing. That was when his leg collapsed under him, and he fell sideways onto the grass. Pain shot through his body. In final desperation he yelled out. His voice echoed among the trees, but there was no one to hear him or to come to his rescue. The wolves had him where they wanted and would slaughter him like a deer.

The panting of a large animal closed in from behind. The wolf stuck its head within a foot of his head, its mouth open and its large tongue lolling out. More curious than menacing, the yellow eyes locked into Scott's. If it wanted to look friendly it had chosen a bad time.

'What do you want?' It was all he could stammer. He was in the presence of something massive, an overwhelming power that could destroy him with one swipe of a paw. Already it had subdued his will so he could barely move.

Spreading out its muscular legs the wolf sank down on its belly. Scott's pounding heart began to calm down. The beast waited for him. What should he do? He was too tired and too afraid to move. The animal licked its jaws and slid closer, within Scott's reach. He'd been among enough dogs to understand the gesture. The wolf wanted to be stroked.

Inch by inch he moved his hand closer to the wolf, as if about to touch an electric fence; ready to withdraw if the animal snapped. The jaws shut; the wolf looked away but otherwise remained still. Scott's quivering fingers met the wolf's coarse fir and immediately pulled back. Nothing happened. It wanted to be touched again. This time he stroked the fur gently and allowed his fingers to massage it deeper. Touching the wolf felt like connecting with a source of raw power. A dark voice sounded inside him, 'By now I could have killed you.'

It lifted its head and uttered a series of calls, answered immediately by several others and then more until hundreds of forest voices were shouting at each other. Initially distant, the calls grew louder. Soon many pairs of eyes appeared among the trees. Grey shapes rushed into the clearing, yelling excitedly and bounded up to where Scott lay.

THIRTEEN

He would have fled but, as in a typical nightmare, his legs turned to putty. His heart hammered impotently, unable to summon an ounce of action. He waited for a wolf to sink its jaws into him. Amid deafening yelps the shadowy forms circled him, but despite their bared teeth they held back. What were they waiting for? Lifting his head he saw the large wolf he had met earlier, stationed a few feet away. He snapped at any other wolf that tried to advance. Two more ran up and down the line, pushing the beasts away from him.

A high-pitched call sounded from the trees. The moonlight revealed a long-legged figure, bare-breasted, that blitzed into the circle, half running, half leaping, with masses of hair flying behind her. She greeted the wolves with a melodic howl. Yelping and jockeying for attention the wolves surrounded her. In short bounding movements she reached the leader. Scott didn't have to look into her eyes to know from her spider-like limbs and stringy hair that she was lupan. The circle of wolves pressed against her, their snouts begging for attention. She patted several, but finally pushed them away and stepped out toward Scott.

'You.' She pointed at him. 'Why are you here?'

The rasping voice, reminiscent of the rustling of dry leaves, sounded so unexpectedly that he thought someone whom he hadn't noticed had spoken, but no one else was there. Though her body had the energy of an adolescent, her wrinkled face seemed older than the rocks. She had strong protruding cheekbones, a large mouth, her lips parted to show a row of jagged teeth. Her golden eyes had dilated pupils that appeared to take in the night. Several patches of white hair were woven into her matted black hair along with twigs and leaves. Responding to a hand gesture the wolves withdrew from him and they surrounded her. They paced restlessly. A few nuzzled close to her but respectful of her presence they stayed a few feet away while they waited for her command.

'Man, if you are the Messenger,' she said, 'give us the message.'

He tried to speak but couldn't. Surrounded by wolves, she had the power to obliterate him if she didn't like his response. He looked away, rather than try to wrestle with her stare. After a moment he felt her hand under his chin. Kneeling in front of him, her face a few inches away, she tried to make eye contact.

'Speak,' she said. 'They will not harm you. Who are you?'

His name was a label that could mean nothing to her. What did she want from him? He had a history as a lawyer, but that old life seemed more meaningless than his name.

'I came in a plane,' he said, deciding that she might want to hear about why he was in the forest. 'I crashed among your people. I've been with them since.'

'Yes, with mother.'

Sandria? Of course he should have guessed from her use of language that this was Asra, though she didn't resemble Sandria in any way. Her eyes in particular had a clear look that pierced all veils and any attempts to dissemble. He could hide nothing from her.

'What message does mother send?' Asra said.

'Message – I don't know any message. She misses you.'

Asra looked straight at him, thoughtfully. 'Long are the days while she waits.'

'She wants to see you.'

'Then she must come here. There is no other way to meet. Why have you come?'

'Rami and Zia brought me. I don't know why.'

'Yes.' She waited for him to tell her more. What did she want from him? While he struggled with the question the baleful wolves crept closer.

'Send them away,' he said.

'You are stronger than they. You have the power to order them. Do it.'

'Please.'

The closest wolf halted a couple of feet away, crouched low ready to leap at him; but respectful of Asra it made no further move.

Her face softened. She smiled like a parent explaining a simple matter to an undisciplined child. 'They're here to listen. To your message. Speak.'

'I don't have any message.'

'You do. It concerns our people. Speak to us.'

His teeth chattered so uncontrollably he couldn't assemble a coherent thought. Everything that had happened since the accident passed in front of his eyes: meeting the lupans, his entanglement with Sandria, Zia's daily treatments and his healing. What else? Linella's face swam into view. Her warning. Was that to be his message?

'Your people need to get out of the forest,' he said. 'Run for your lives.'

'Yes.'

'The army's on the way.' Observing her puzzled look, he asked, 'You know what an army is?'

'What's an army?'

'You'll wish you didn't know. They're people armed with tanks and guns. They want to take your people away. Kill them. Soon. In a few days. If you want to live you have to hide from them before they destroy you. There's my message.'

While he spoke she sat frowning, either not understanding or thinking about something else. Finally she said, 'Words are difficult for us. Speak again, who is coming?'

110

'I've already told you.'

'Say it again. We are wolves. Know the forest, how to hunt; how to feed pups. This thing – the army. It's coming?'

'Yes.'

'You are man?'

'Sure, I'm one.'

'You breathe air like men, those you call army?'

'I suppose so.'

'You speak like army?'

'Let's say I do,' he replied, wondering where she was leading him. If she understood what he'd said, why was she toying with him?

She pointed at him accusingly. 'You destroy us?'

'I don't. It's the army.'

Her eyes blazed with anger. The wolves paced restlessly in circles about her, waiting for her signal to attack. Responding to a wave of her hand they retreated. 'Is there a difference?'

'I'm not going to destroy you.'

Her extended finger jabbed at his heart. 'I? You? The army? It's all the same thing.'

Scott swore silently. If she didn't understand the difference between "I" and "You", he'd never get through to her. Evidently she believed that he – one man, spoke for the collective human race. When he told her that the army was about to attack, he might as well have said that he, Scott, had come to destroy her people.

'Why do you hate us?' she said.

He didn't answer. Why bother when they couldn't agree on the meaning of words? If he refused to talk, perhaps she'd leave him alone.

'You are the army. It's a fact.'

'I'm not but...'

Her steady eyes prevented him from saying more. In a perverse way she was right. He wasn't sure where his sympathies lay. He was grateful to the lupans for having healed him. He was intrigued by them; admitted that they might be a lot more intelligent than he'd previously thought. Did he like them enough to fight for them? To stand between them and the army? Asra not only understood him, but saw through his attempts to dissemble. She discerned his ambivalence – that he didn't care what happened to lupans as long as the human race survived.

'I'm not the army,' he said. 'I'm a separate person. We're all separate human beings. Is that so hard to understand? Throw me to your wolves if you want to, but if you kill me, you'll lose a friend. I don't want your people to die. You deserve to live, to take over our world. God knows, we did our best to fuck it up. Maybe you'll treat it better.'

'How can you help us when you're confused? You don't understand the simplest thing, that you are the army.'

'What do you want from me?'

'Nothing.'

'Suppose I want to help you?'

She appeared taken aback, 'You do?'

'Well, yes. I'd like you to survive. Maybe we can learn from each other.'

'First you must see the fact, that you are the army.'

'It makes no sense.'

'You must.'

'Fine. I'll rearrange my logic but that won't stop the army from attacking you. They have guns, weapons, helicopters and explosives.'

Asra laughed. 'One day all those will be gone.'

For some unexplained reason he believed her. The intelligence in her eyes told him that she was no fool. She knew that lupans would outlast the human race.

'Give them this message,' she said. After a pause she added. 'They'll die, if we die. Then all dies.'

'Say that again.'

Her eyes had the look of a patient teacher trying to get a point across. 'It's so simple when you see it. If we die, you die and all dies.'

112

He shook his head. Where had she wandered off to now? Was she talking about him or the human race? Again he faced the maddening problem that Asra didn't distinguish individual personalities from the collective.

She ripped a tuft of moss from a rock and handed it to him. 'Life. Look at it. Smell it.'

He took the tuft, not sure what to do next.

'It... speaks,' she said, slowly to emphasize each word. 'Sings ... of... death. You must listen to it – this voice... inside you.'

With fists clenched and fire in her eyes she waited for his response. She was fighting for her people's survival. She wanted his help but he held back. He wasn't about to start talking to moss, like so many tree-huggers and eco-terrorists. Where the environment was concerned, he put people's lives ahead of trees. He saw no reason to change that. The tuft of moss lay limp in his hands.

She placed her hand over his heart. Its heat seared him like a hot iron. 'If we die, you die, and all life dies.'

The ground under his feet appeared to give way. He clung onto rational objections that she was playing with words, that she was only a retarded lupan who ran with wolves. No different from tree-huggers. But she *was* different, belonged to a different species. The words were spoken with a power that tolerated no opposition. She had to be right. Her instincts and perceptions lay far beyond normal people's experience. Her awareness extended deep into the forest to the entrails of the Earth where it touched the core of life. If he didn't understand her, it was because he lacked the mental capacity. Not because she was mistaken or deluded.

To him as the representative of the human race she delivered a chilling ultimatum.

He struggled to breathe, gasped, tried to force air into his lungs but all strength drained from his body. Asra's craggy face shimmered and wavered. The wolves burst into a chorus of deafening howls, pawed and advanced on him, but he was too disoriented to be even afraid. He stumbled and fell to his knees. His stomach heaved and he vomited.

When he was able to look up he saw the wolves gathered around their leader with Asra in their midst. They nudged each other out of the way for a place next to her. Their calls intensified. Each wolf tried to make its voice heard. Other grey shapes emerged from the trees to join the pack. Once they were all gathered they ran off, first as an amorphous mass, and then spread out into a long line. They made several laps around the clearing, the chief wolf maintaining a clear lead. His massive legs swept through the air rhythmically and hardly appeared to touch the ground. No one dared draw even with him. Behind him ran Asra, half-crouched to resemble a wolf, her long hair flying in the wind and her high-pitched voice audible above the chorus. Her human legs were no match for the wolves and she soon she fell back to midway in the pack.

Then Scott lost her. One moment she was there, and the next she had melted into the forest, or so he thought at first. The pack circled again and when it passed close to him he noticed the black wolf he had met in the forest, running behind the leader. A cold shiver ran through him. He wanted to put Asra's name on the wolf. How was it possible when everything he knew spoke against it? People only changed into wolves in cheap horror movies. Yet when he saw the black wolf with the silver stripe he saw Asra.

They dashed off into the forest, their howls more distant till they faded into the sighing of the trees. He staggered to his feet. What had happened to him? Surely he'd only fainted and dreamed the rest. Asra – had he really spoken to her or imagined the entire episode? She'd delivered him a message. What did it mean?

He felt Zia's hand under his shoulder. She appeared as mysteriously as she'd vanished, with Rami next to her. What should he do next? He was so shaken he barely knew who he was – Scott or the army?

Her words reverberated inside him as if she were there

114

speaking them. If people destroyed lupans they would doom themselves and all life on the planet. Her assertion felt true in the forest clearing under a full moon but what could he do with the message? Who would believe him?

'Let's go back,' he said to Zia and Rami. Not waiting for them he picked up his stick and limped off toward the trees.

FOURTEEN

The wind had abated and a profound stillness settled among the trees. Scott heard only the crunch of grass beneath his feet and the occasional wolf-howl in the distance. Though he tried to keep up with Rami and Zia, his aching leg forced him to take frequent rests. Soon he lagged a few hundred feet behind them. At first they waited along the path for him to catch up, but then they carried on regardless until he lost sight of them. He was alone; free to go where he wanted. Should he return to the colony or head for the refugee village?

'If we die, you die and all dies.' He wanted to dismiss the words but he couldn't. His encounter with Asra left him with a sense of awe. Not only she had a total command of the wolves and ran like one. She had changed into one. *No, that's too crazy*, he muttered. It didn't really happen. Yet part of him believed that it had. Two months ago, stuck in an office and filing legal briefs, he could not have imagined that he'd be lost in a forest, conversing with lupans, growing mystical about them and feeling responsible for their survival. But he was no longer that lawyer. He didn't know what had happened or where he had lost his rational mind, but he had.

He had to communicate her message. In some ecological way whose workings he didn't understand, the survival of the human race depended on the survival of the lupans. Perhaps it had to do with the Plague cure, but he doubted it. She wouldn't know anything about the Plague or its cure. However, that argument might win over people who otherwise had no love of the Earth or its ecology. They'd look more kindly on lupans if they knew that lupans could cure the Plague.

He halted again to consider which way to go. If he wanted to reach the village, now was his chance. Rami and Zia were out of sight and wouldn't notice he was gone until he was far away. Would anyone in the village listen to him? Linella might. When she told him about the cure, he had sensed that she wanted to make it public, as long as releasing it wouldn't harm the lupans. She could be an important ally. She knew the doctor who had the scientific details necessary to convince sceptical researchers; she might persuade him to change his mind.

The village had to lie somewhere downhill to the left of the path, no farther than an hour's walk – if he didn't lose himself. Now was his chance. The trees parted that way suggesting an easy approach. Shuffling along on his bad leg he might not get far before the lupans found him, but he had to try. After crossing a small clearing he found a narrow track that led steeply downhill. Positioning himself sideways, he descended, step by step and using his stick to support his weaker leg.

After ten minutes, he had gone down a hundred feet toward a small gully, pausing only to scan the forest above him for any sign of activity. He was crossing a clearing exposed to the sky when a howl caused him to freeze. Wolf or lupan? He took several breaths to calm his agitation then crept on under the protection of a spreading oak. Two long-drawn howls answered the first calls and were followed by several short yelps. The first howls might be lupan; the second were definitely wolf. For a few minutes he waited under the oak canopy, trying not to breathe loudly, then decided to press on. He had to maintain his lead. He soon reached a thick pine forest. He stopped there to search the brightening skyline for any sign of pursuit, but saw nothing suspicious.

The sun had just risen above a distant hill when he emerged from the trees onto the gorse-covered slope that overlooked the village. He was far below the lupan colony. Upon reaching a small

117

hollow he sat down, closed his eyes and waited for his breathing to settle. Hopefully the lupans had decided to let him go; but he somehow doubted it. From the way they'd recently guarded him, they wouldn't rest until he was back under their control.

He started, awakened from a light sleep by somebody calling to him, 'Scott – is that you?' Fearing he'd been discovered he scrambled to his feet, only to find Sandria, a few feet away.

'I'm glad I found you,' she said.

'Is Rami out looking for me?'

'They came back without you. I was so worried. What are you doing?'

'I got lost in the woods.'

'Where are you going?' The hesitation in her voice told him that she knew he was trying to escape.

'Wait a minute. I've a lot to tell you.'

'Are you coming back?'

'I don't know. Don't look at me that way. This isn't personal.'

'I wouldn't think so.'

'I'm scared, Sandria. Confused. I need your help. I've spent the night with wolves. Asra was there.'

Sandria's coldness dissipated. She looked at him with a sudden longing.

'She's alive; seems to be well,' he said. 'Even if she's living with wolves. It's the life she wants. They have a great respect for her.'

He couldn't share with Sandria his last glimpse of Asra. She'd never believe him.

Sandria's eyes seemed to follow his thoughts. 'So, she's with wolves. I guess I'm supposed to be happy about that.'

'I don't know what to tell you.'

Sandria's eyes flashed. 'I want more than words. Do you understand? I want something that you can't give a mother – to know my child. Hearing about her through you, Rami or Zia isn't enough. I want to hold her. I want to hear her voice. It's what I must have.'

'I understand. She said she was sorry that you're waiting for her, but your separation can't be helped. She wishes it were otherwise.'

'So do I.'

'There's more, and this is where it gets difficult. She said that we – I guess she means the human race – must protect the lupans. That human life, in fact all life on the planet depends on their survival. If the children are destroyed, the human race will be next.'

Sandria let out a coarse laugh. 'The human race? What does she know of the human race?'

'We did have some trouble understanding each other. She thought I was speaking for all people. I couldn't get her to see the difference.'

'No, for her there wouldn't be.'

'Why do you say that?'

'Wolf-children don't have individual personalities. For thirty years I've lived with them. Sometimes you'll see two or three walking in step as if they were one person, their eyes moving like one set of eyes. They look alike because they are alike. They own nothing – not their own memories, not their thoughts or feelings. Not even their bodies.'

'How do you know all that?'

Sandria drew close speaking barely above a whisper. 'One day when I was alone with Zia, she let me look into her eyes, deeply, the way I look into your eyes. I lost myself; didn't know who I was. Then we switched bodies. I found myself sitting where she was, with a lupan body. In that instant I shared the mind of a wolf-child. It's nothing like ours. It reaches far beyond their body to places where you'd go mad. Places where you don't know who you are. After I returned to my body, I ran for my life. For days afterwards I couldn't look at a lupan.'

While she spoke to him her face appeared to change. Sometimes he saw Sandria's distraught face, and sometimes Asra's thoughtful eyes. He said, 'It's crazy. Do you expect me to believe that you switched bodies?'

'I don't care if you believe me or not. I hardly believe it myself, but it happened. I was so afraid of losing myself that I stayed away from here. I never wanted to see them or hear their voices again. But I can't forget Asra. Even though we'll never know each other, she is my baby.'

'Sandria, she's not yours or anyone's. She's gone far beyond us.'

'I guess she has.'

'She wants us to convince people to stop destroying lupans. That our survival depends on their survival.'

'So you're finally ready to fight for them.'

'I want that Plague cure to be shared. It's our only chance. Something has to change people's attitudes about the lupans.'

'That's up to Eisa.'

'We have to persuade him. Sandria, we can't hold back something so important. Millions of people are out there dying. Will you come with me to see Eisa?'

'Sure, to Eisa or to the moon.'

Hearing the edge in her voice he looked at her again and saw that her eyes were moist, about to break into tears. While he'd been lecturing her about saving the human race, she was waiting to tell him something much closer to her heart. She crossed her arms across her chest and stroked them, trying to stay warm. He wanted to give her a hug, but saw that she did not want to be touched.

'Did I say something that hurt you?'

She wiped a tear from her eye, looked away from him. Her lips were drawn tight, unwilling to speak.

'Is something wrong?'

'I'm pregnant.'

Her words sounded like a crack of thunder. For several seconds he wondered if he'd heard correctly. He had. A cold emptiness opened inside him. A child – the last thing he wanted. He tried to speak but couldn't string any words together.

'Please don't be cross with me.'

'What do you think? You're damn right that I'm angry.'

'Please don't hate me. I'm not an evil woman. It's just that I've lived such a lonely life. At least until I met you. I couldn't help myself. You don't realize how special you are. No one except you has ever been accepted by wolf-children. I fell in love with you. Not because I wanted a child, but because you are who you are.'

'Thanks for the news.'

'You have to believe me.'

'I don't know what to think.'

He wished he could feel tenderness toward her, but instead he felt outrage and a sense of violation. Betrayal. That she had manipulated him into this because she wanted a human child. The moment she saw him wounded in the den, she saw her chance, and she took it. He wanted to at least tell her that he was overjoyed that she was pregnant, but everything inside him had frozen up.

'Scott, please say something.'

'I don't have anything to say.'

'You don't want this baby, do you?'

'When I landed on that hill, I only wanted to die. If I had, I'd have fewer complications. You wouldn't have found a patient to bring back from the dead and yes, a father for your baby.'

'Scott – I want you. Don't you see that?'

'You want a human child and security for it. Apart from that, you don't really care much for me. Sandria, I don't know what to tell you. This is not a good idea. Now that I'm well, I have things to do. Raising a child isn't one of them; not in this nasty world. We need to first make sure there's even going to be a world around for any children.'

'So you want me to have an abortion. That's it isn't it?'

'Maybe.'

'Not on your life.' Her hard eyes meant the subject was beyond discussion.

'Then I don't know what to tell you.'

'Leave.'

'I'm not leaving.'

'I don't know why you should bother staying with me.'

'I'm not a bastard. I won't abandon you when you need me. If you decide to have this baby, I'll do everything for you and for the baby.'

She held out her hands. He took them then drew her in until her moist face was pressed against his chest. It was the only decent thing to do.

A high-pitched whistle sounded from the hillside. Sandria's body went taught. 'It's Rami.'

'Come on.' Grabbing his stick he limped down the path toward the village. Was there any use? His stiff legs would not move fast enough. On all sides shadows grew out of the scrub and materialized into lupans. Uttering shrill cries and waving their arms like windmills they rushed at him. Four appeared ahead of him, their stern faces not inclined to give way. He lifted his stick, hit the closest one and then turned to deal with another. Before he could strike again, someone grabbed the stick from behind and wrenched it from his grasp.

Rami's spider-like form appeared out of the air. He took Scott's shoulder in a vicelike grip. His eyes asked the question, 'Where do you think you're going?'

Scott shouted and struggled to free himself from the grasp. 'It's okay. I need to get down to the village. Fuck it – the village. Do you understand? I'm not running away.'

Rami's steady eyes hardened. He didn't appear to have understood.

'Sandria. You tell him.'

Sandria stood several paces to his right, surrounded by Zia and several female lupans.

'Please leave us alone,' she told Zia. 'We must go down to the village. We'll return soon.'

If Zia understood, her blank expression didn't show it.

'You can come with me,' Scott said to Rami. 'We want to see Eisa.'

A ring of male and female lupans tightened about Scott. Rami released his shoulder, nodded at the path that led up the hill toward the colony. His unyielding eyes made Scott stagger. He forced himself to resist Rami's crushing will.

'I'm doing this for you,' Scott said. 'I want to save you. Just get out of my way.'

A smile spread over Rami's face, as if to say, 'You don't know what you're talking about.'

Zia advanced until she stood barely a foot away. Her breasts had grown taut. What did she want? Her eyes glowed with an angry fire, like a woman confronting a wayward lover.

Sandria let out a shriek. 'No you don't, you bitch! Get away from him.'

Zia's growing smile only enraged Sandria further. She would have clawed out Zia's eyes except that Scott pulled her back. 'Sandria, leave her alone.'

He'd never suspected that Zia wanted any relationship. He assumed that she and Rami were monogamous – as far as lupans went. But her entire body appeared to call him to herself. Now that she had healed him, she wanted to grow closer, and was annoyed that he was trying to escape. Only a lupan might guess what sort of relationship she wanted.

'She wants to have sex with you,' Sandria said.

'She doesn't want anything of the kind. I don't know what she wants.' He looked around for a possible escape but the lupans maintained a tight ring. 'They want to keep me here. I can't fight them all. Do one thing. Go to your doctor. Better still, get Linella to go with you. Tell the doctor to release the cure.'

'I want to stay with you.'

'I'm all right. I won't be far. Go to Eisa.'

'What about her?' Sandria nodded at Zia.

'Leave her alone. She won't do anything to me.'

Sandria turned a dark look at Zia, tightened her lips then spat at Zia's feet. 'That's for you.'

She pushed through the lupans and strode rapidly down the path.

FIFTEEN

Linella opened her eyes. Her head pounded like a sledgehammer hitting a post. Someone was tapping at the window. Where the hell was she? She had no clothes on, wasn't in her own bed but in a room cluttered with old furniture and books and a ceiling made of rough hewn beams embedded in cobb; somewhere in the village.

A foot away Eisa's mop of grey hair rested on a pillow. She sat up quickly as if stung by a bee. Fuck – what have I done? After searching her foggy head she recalled she had walked down to Eisa's house to tell him that she'd contacted the media. No one wanted to cover the army's planned raid. The TV reps, polite but dismissive, said that if they interfered with a military mission, the government would pull their license. Eisa invited over Arjan and then plied everyone with dandelion wine. More people arrived, some with guitars. Several women struck up an impromptu chorus. At some stage she collapsed into Eisa's bed. She must have let him make love to her. That was why she was naked. She lay there feeling empty and alone. She thought she'd finished with their relationship years ago. Why had she done it? She didn't need anyone to complete her. Certainly not Eisa who'd never understand her no matter how hard he tried. Lately she felt that she was wasting her life. The refugees would soon be gone, the lupan dens emptied, and she'd be left making flower bunches. She couldn't talk to her sons about her loneliness. Last night she thought that Eisa would understand.

He turned toward her and presented his stubby chin, his eyes half closed. She kissed him lightly on the lips. His arm curled about her waist and pressed her hard against his body as if he owned her. She did not resist. The tapping on the window grew insistent.

'Someone's at the window,' she said.

Eisa groaned and turned over. His half closed eyes told her that he wouldn't be functional for at least another hour. She slid out of the bed, found her dress on the floor and slipped it over her head, leaving the back unbuttoned. Her headache raged, her vision was blurred but she stumbled over to the window, and cracked open the shutters. Sandria stood outside, breathing hard as if she'd been running. Seeing Linella she jerked back in surprise. Her anxious eyes indicated that something was wrong.

'What's happening?' Linella said.

'I need to talk to Eisa.'

'I'll get him up.'

While Sandria waited on the torn couch, Eisa sat sheepishly looking around for his clothes. 'This is all a bit early. Is the world falling apart?' He nodded at Sandria. 'Sorry about the way I look. I feel even worse.' He sank into a padded chair, tilted back his head and stared at the ceiling. 'Coffee!'

Linella lit a fire in the wood-burning stove and put on a pot of water for coffee. Sandria sat quietly, not responding to Linella's small talk. Something was bothering her, but Linella was too hung-over to ask. As she handed Eisa his coffee, he pulled her in closer to kiss her but she turned her face away. He needed to know that last night ended with last night. This was the morning.

'Sorry, Sandria. You deserve a better reception,' he said. 'What's happening?'

'Scott sent me here.'

'Ah yes. What about old Maguire?'

'It's about the Plague cure. Your discovery.'

'Oh that.' To Linella, 'Didn't I tell you Maguire would want to blab it?'

'You did. I still think it's a big mistake to hoard it.'

Sandria paced nervously. 'So do I. Scott says that revealing the cure will change people's attitudes to the wolf-children. It could save them.'

Eisa rolled his eyes. 'God, why does this happen so early in the morning? I can hardly see straight and you want to discuss the future of the lupans. Right, talk to me. What's going on with Maguire?'

'He tried to reach you, but they stopped him. Took him back to the colony. That's why he sent me.'

'I thought he was a bit of a racist. What made him see the light?'

'Rami took him to see Asra. I think she convinced him.'

'He saw Asra? Wow. Is she okay?'

'Apparently so.'

'And he made it back. Presumably the wolves didn't eat him.'

'Eisa, please listen to me. I didn't come here to listen to your sarcasm. Asra told Scott that if we destroy the lupans, the human race will also die. So will all life on Earth. I don't know what to do with this news. Scott wants it delivered to whoever will listen. Can you help us?'

'I'll try,' Eisa muttered.

'I wasn't there, but I know my daughter made a huge impression on him. He came away from her changed. With a new attitude. Now, he'll do anything he can to protect the children.'

'Man, what am I to do with all this?'

'Why did they stop him from coming here?' Linella said.

'They want him,' Sandria said. 'Zia can't seem to let him go.'

'Zia?'

'Look, can we drop it. It doesn't matter.'

Sandria's jittery voice matched by the anger in her eyes only made Linella more curious. Sandria didn't want to talk about Scott because something had happened between them. She sat with her head in her hands to conceal her feelings. If she could, she'd be running for the door.

She's pregnant. The thought came to Linella from nowhere. She knew she was right. Her first impression of Sandria at the window was of a panicked woman who had received news that she couldn't handle. Maybe she'd come down the hill for Eisa's advice. Why shouldn't Sandria and Scott have had sex? They spent many lonely nights together. Scott was the sort of guy who'd miss having a woman to hold. Sandria wanted another child before her biological clock chimed, a human child, and she'd caught Scott in her web. Poor bastard.

'I'm worried about what they're doing to the bloke,' Eisa said.

'Fucking Zia can't be all bad,' Linella said with a coarse laugh. She glanced over at Sandria to see if her words hurt, and they had; Sandria's eyes swelled with tears.

'Don't be a bitch,' Eisa said.

'Right.'

'You won't release the cure, will you?' Sandria said. 'I don't know why I bothered to come here.'

'Give me a chance. I've been listening, haven't I?'

'Then why don't you see that sharing your cure will save the lupans – our children?'

'If you tell prejudiced people that lupans, the object of their hatred have something people need, you'll only make them more resentful. They'll grab from the lupans what they can, but continue hating them.'

'How do you know that will happen?'

Eisa took a swig of coffee. 'God, my head hurts so bad I can barely see straight.'

Linella said, 'You don't know what you're talking about. The Plague has wiped out millions, and you have a cure. How do you reconcile that, Doctor Habash? Aren't you in the healing profession?'

'Don't try to guilt me about this, Linella.'

'This is about saving lives.'

'Sure. But we need to be smart about it.'

'If someone is about to drown, I'm not going to second-guess throwing them a lifeline. I'll do what needs to be done. It's instinct.'

'Stop shouting. You're making my headache worse. In the past ten years, two billion people died of starvation. Others are at our gates, begging to come here, or to Iceland. They'd be heading for Siberia, except that the Russians machine-gun refugees on sight. And now we have the Plague. There won't be many of us left. I can't feel guilty about people who are dying, just because I'm still alive. The carnage is a natural process. Gaia, if you like the metaphor, is reducing our numbers to a safe level where we won't kill off all life on the planet. In a convoluted way Asra may be right. The only thing left for us to do is to give birth to the lupans and make sure that they're safe. That's why I want to protect them.'

'You think you're so fucking smart,' Linella cried. 'No wait, you listen to me,' she added as Eisa tried to protest. 'Why can't you accept that the lupans can save the human race by giving us the cure to the Plague? You answer me that one.'

Eisa shook his head. 'I'm convinced that the Plague is a red herring. Nature didn't create an entire new race only to supply us with an antidote to a disease created by her to cull the old one. Biologically it makes no sense. The lupans are here because they're important in some other way. If they're immune to the Plague, it's because they have better survival qualities than us. They're not here to put us on life support. We are an evolutionary dead end, about to join the dinosaurs; an experiment that's run its course. A costly experiment, because we've almost wiped out all life on the planet. Somewhere back in time we took a wrong turn. We became very clever, built great cities and developed technology to fly to the Moon. It all came at a very high cost. The lupans are Gaia's answer to humanity's wrong turn. They're the next model – an improved one.'

'It's despicable to talk about people like they're disposable cars,' Linella said. 'You need to shut up about the human race, and see people – like me, like Sandria – we're made of flesh and bone, people you can touch. We're the people you'd as soon kill off. The human race is a fiction.'

'It's real enough.'

'Where? Point it out to me. If you can't then I will.' She jabbed her forefinger at him, and then at Sandria. 'You're talking about us. About killing us.'

'What about our children? Do they matter? I won't do anything that would endanger them. They're young, barely able to hang on and they need our protection. Once the news about the phage gets out, the lupans will all be rounded up for medical research, the way our medics use Rhesus monkeys. For two hundred years we've killed monkeys in the name of medical research, given them cancer, parasites, the Plague – you name it. No one gave a fuck as long as we were saving human lives. We'll do the same to lupans. Labs in Glasgow are already experimenting on them. It's only going to get worse. People will exploit them for as long as they can, then ditch the remains.'

'You're seeing things far too black. There are good people out there.'

'I haven't seen too many lately. Don't you see that people will make lupans into a commodity, to be bought and sold? Slaves to ward off the Plague? Neither you nor I can stop that. The best we can do now is to keep our traps shut about the cure.'

Linella stood up quickly. The discussion was heading nowhere. Nothing new had been said to persuade Eisa to change his mind.

'I have to go home.'

Bastard – what possessed me to sleep with him, Linella thought as she strode out of his house. We are so different. I cannot relate to his sarcasm, his scientific mumbo-jumbo or anything about him. And I gave myself to him, thinking he could love me? I am so stupid. Haven't learned a damn thing in fifty years.

Climbing the path up to the cottage she passed through an orchard of gnarly trees laden with peaches. She paused under them. The dappled sunlight under the trees brought her some comfort. Despite Eisa's gloomy view of the future the sun still shone and ripened the fruit. *If only we could focus on that instead of scrabbling among our anxieties? We have so much. Nature even brought the Plague cure to our doorstep, but we're too anxious to accept it.*

Lina was walking down the path toward her, a basket of peaches dangling from one arm.

'You're in a hurry,' Lina said.

'I have to get back and check on the boys. Oh, I am so angry with him.'

Lina smiled. 'Eisa? I thought that last night you two were having a good time together.'

'I was drunk.'

'Come have some tea with me.'

'Thanks but I can't stop.'

Lina picked out a few peaches. 'Take these. Try one now. This year they're very sweet.'

Linella wasn't inclined to eat a peach but, feeling she could not refuse, took one anyway. The peach proved so sweet that the fruity flesh melted in her mouth. She offered the other half to Lina but she declined.

'What will you do with so many?' Linella said.

'Make jam.'

Nothing ever bothered Lina. In the face of the impending raid, while the men gathered an arsenal of new guns, Lina gathered fruit, pruned the trees, prepared olives for pressing or stored vegetables in the sheds for the coming winter. She didn't ask whether the community would still be there. The question seemed unimportant.

'I need to do more to protect you,' Linella said. 'When I think of you, your trees, your homes or the children, I get restless to do something about it.'

'You've already done enough. We don't need protection, especially the sort that the men are planning. I don't know what they think they can do. Change the track of a storm? Shoot at it?

130

I've no time for such nonsense. I need to take care of our harvest, put food on the table and supply the house with wood for the winter. It's enough.'

'It's our life.'

Lina nodded slowly. 'The men don't see that without our work they would never survive.'

'I feel so useless. All I'm capable of is to cook and keep house. Meanwhile the glen is under attack. What am I doing about it?'

'The only thing you can.'

'What's that?'

'To cook and keep house, knead bread and lay the table. You give so many wanderers a home. What else should you do?'

'Something for people who are dying of Plague.'

Lina's eyes hardened. 'Only God can help them. You cannot. It's too big a matter for anyone. Linella, my dear.' Lina took her arm. 'We need you here. Don't try to save the world. It is too big a place for anyone to take care of.'

A horn-call cut her off, three shrill blasts that echoed from the hills. Linella felt a cold chill penetrate her. The Koppiemaul horn call was a sound she never wanted to hear. The next moment, she was running up the hill.

'Get Arjan and the men,' she shouted to Lina.

Two more blasts sounded, the second cut off in midstream. Had the blower been shot? The horn call could only mean that trouble had come to the cottage. Bounders, Corsican refugees or the army had been sighted. Her boys were sounding the alarm. In a blinding panic she raced up the hill.

Go burn my house; burn all my fields. Leave the kids alone.

SIXTEEN

The Messenger walks alone, climbing the rocky path to the colony. Accompanied by the People, he nevertheless doesn't want anyone to touch him or to even draw close. His head is bowed like a captured animal's. He doesn't look at anyone, certainly not at Beauty Woman. To return with her to the colony and to the People is not what he wants. If she could merge with him she would understand why he is so angry, but he chooses to remain aloof and mysterious. She must be satisfied in not knowing him.

Earlier that night when Beauty Woman discovered that the Messenger was lost in the forest, she felt unexplainably bereft, as if someone close to her had died. She wanted to find him immediately. At first Blue Sky refused to help, saying that the Messenger must be allowed to leave if he so wishes. She persuaded him that the Messenger might be mauled by a crazed wolf; that his encounter with Wolfborn had weakened his spirit to where it would shatter like a clay pot. Now that his body was healed, she couldn't abandon him. She had given him back his life. That gift already formed a bond between them that she could not be ignore.

He's still confused about what happened among the wolves. His encounter with Wolfborn left him so distraught that he fled from her like a flustered stag. She made him see his relationship to the People, and that he must protect them. Perhaps he wants to do something helpful, but he's still too muddled to see the situation clearly. Unless he takes the Dark Path, he'll never understand the people he's trying to help and whatever he attempts will unravel.

Beauty Woman places her arm about his neck and gently strokes his cheek. At first he resists, but her body's magnetism overcomes him, allowing him to put aside his reservations. Her caresses tell him that she desires to know him intimately. He's intrigued by her but frustrated that they don't have a common language. Will she forever remain silent, with a voice no more articulate than a wolf?

His eyes ask her, why he must return to the colony, away from his own people, to whom he needs to convey Wolfborn's message?

Beauty Woman doesn't know how to reply. She can't make him see, any more than she could make a blind man see. Even if her tongue could express his language, words alone wouldn't suffice. He'd find her explanation incomprehensible. Clasping his hand she reassures him that he's where he needs to be. Whatever lies ahead, she will not leave him. Tensing up he pulls away from her. He's afraid of an unspecified danger. Doesn't trust her not to lead him there.

They arrive at the gathering den. It has a vaulted roof of wood and cobb supported on long poles, leaving a large circle in the centre open to the sky. Upon entering, he senses the den's power; that he is not in control there. A weaker man might turn and flee back down the hill, but the Messenger stays. Meeting Wolfborn has already strengthened him. He knows that he is not an accidental visitor; that his life was spared so that he can accomplish a significant task.

Of course, the dome's ambiance disturbs him. The wall's plain whiteness forces him to look distractedly here and there for something he can cling to. The wall is a mirror in which people see their reflection, and it's not always a comfortable sight. Many, on looking at the wall, feel a sense of being alone and cast into an empty, stark place. Or they must face down fear in the form of a predatory bird that swoops down on them. The Messenger's panicked eyes suggest the latter vision. She clasps his hand; leads him to the centre.

Several saplings sit there playing a game with pebbles. Blue Sky tells them to scamper off into the woods. The den is needed for a gathering.

Dream Woman enters. Her body glows with vitality. Her long white hair, falling over her shoulders, sparkles with power. In her presence everyone falls silent; few can meet her eyes without flinching. The Messenger immediately recognizes her from a previous encounter. He knows that something important brought her there. He demands to know what she wants with him. Fixing him with her gaze she asks if he's ready. He shrugs, apparently resigned to whatever is about to happen.

With a cold smile she tells him – This will make your life worth living.

She orders the women to gather firewood and put it into the central pit. Once the fire is lit she sits next to it. From the basket under her arm she draws out herbs and crushes them in a small bowl. Several women join her in the circle. Wondering what it all means, he asks Beauty Woman. She assures him that he'll soon know but her response makes him impatient. He says that he's waited long enough. Unless the People physically restrain him he will leave. She replies that this is not possible. She touches his hand to her breast to indicate relationship, a simple gesture that everyone understands, but he snatches his hand away as if her breast scorched him. His darting eyes reveal his fear, of relationship, of the fire, the sweet smelling herbs and the stark walls with their disturbing images. He's mostly afraid of losing himself.

Dream Woman looks up at Beauty Woman. – He's not ready. Why haven't you prepared him?

– All saplings are afraid when they come here. He's no different.

Dream Woman points to the empty place next to her. Her gesture, simple yet imbued with power, calms the storm raging inside him; silences his fear and disperses his internal mists. Sitting next to Dream Woman he clasps Beauty Woman's hand. She is the only one he trusts. She tells him that he is important to her. Otherwise she'd never have led him there. If the vision comes, he will know everything. If it doesn't, her words and explanations will amount to nothing.

Dream Woman throws the introductory herbs into the glowing coals. With a fan woven from pine needles she spreads the scented smoke so that everyone can breathe it. The Messenger sniffs cautiously. His hand in Beauty Woman's feels limp. He hasn't slept all night, and the fumes make him so drowsy that he begins to dream. She strokes his face to wake him up. He must remain conscious. If he sleeps, he will miss everything. He opens his eyes and looks around. Now that the fumes have relaxed him, he allows himself to feel the power of her body. His arm curls about her waist and rests there.

With several strokes of her fan Dream Woman disperses the smoke and then throws a second handful of herbs onto the glowing embers, herbs that open the door to the place of visions. She intones the introductory note. Whenever Beauty Woman hears it she sees pale grass sprouting in springtime. The tone rises and falls, a lone chord in search of companion sounds. Two women respond, one in a lower and the other in a higher pitch, but it's the same song. Beauty Woman joins in. Her body resonates with the chord, desires to sing and dance and to follow the sound to its birth-place. The Messenger pulls her in closer. The voices awaken his anxious thoughts and his fears; he needs her reassuring presence next to him. Perhaps the opening herb has already unseated his daily awareness and brought him to the doorway. His confused eyes and twisted forehead mirror his stormy thoughts. He wants certainty, to know what is happening and, failing that, to escape from the circle. He doesn't flee, because the voice in his head tells him that, only cowards run from things they don't understand. She encourages him to hold her. Despite his anxiety he responds to her warmth, accepts her

135

protection and her strength. He wants to lose himself in her, feel her closeness and the chord that sings in her. His staring eyes meet hers, astonished but thirsting for more. What does he see? Wolves running circles around a moonlit clearing. Somewhere among them is Wolfborn. Beauty Woman strokes his face, his cheeks and then his lips to draw his attention away from his memories and back to her.

– Awaken, leave those visions. Look at me. Look with me.

He lets go of his visions, all his dreams, and so their minds merge. His body, weakened by the fumes, can no longer contain his mind, and so it crosses over to her body. The barriers between them crumble and she finds herself inside him, looking through his eyes at the body that she sometimes calls her own. She's in a place of swirling darkness filled with ghostly shapes and screaming winds. In the background a loud drum keeps a persistent beat, the pulse of blood surging through his body. Hundreds of voices all cry out, each one wanting to be heard, each commanding others to be silent. She hears his frightened voice screaming something about a disease. *We die, you die and all dies!* Those words, pounded repetitively on the great drum, have lost all meaning. Amidst swirling mists lie vast cities, smoking ruins with people's bodies piled high. For one horrible moment Beauty Woman sees them, then they are swept aside, leaving only Sandria – Dark Woman, though her name is more truly Woman of Pain. She's pregnant. Somewhere in the darkness she's about to give birth to a sapling. The image vanishes under a choppy sea of thoughts. How can anyone live in such confusion? Who can make sense of all the quarrelling voices?

Looking through his eyes at her body, she knows that the Messenger is merged with her. Her golden eyes stare back, so anxious. Well might they be. The Messenger has never encountered deep silence, a place where all human words must die, and all names cease to exist. For him it can only mean death. For a terrible moment he struggles to hold onto something familiar. Hold onto her body, but how can he when they have switched bodies? The golden eyes through which he peers glaze over and die. Where is he? He has stepped off into an abyss and is falling, with nothing to grab for support, nothing to name, least of all himself. He cannot stem his fall, nor has he the will to do so. The mystery will either awaken inside him, or it will destroy him. He hurtles down into emptiness where she can no longer reach him.

Her trembling lips cry out. Dream Woman breaks the chord. The other voices are also silenced. Blue Sky catches the Messenger's body before it hits the floor and then lays it down gently. Beauty Woman, still deafened by angry voices in the Messenger's head, can barely see her surroundings. What has happened? His white face is that of a dead man. His quivering lips move noiselessly, unable to speak. Dream Woman strokes his brow to awaken him but his eyes stare fixedly at the ceiling, unaware of anyone.

– He has fallen into darkness – Dream Woman says, as if she'd expected it all along.

– He must not die – Beauty Woman says. – Can't you do something for him?

Dream Woman arises and dusts off her body. For a moment her large eyes look into a faraway place that no one else sees. – You are his guide – she says. – You must go and find him.

SEVENTEEN

Linella sped up the hill but no matter how fast she sprinted, the cottage never seemed to grow closer. She cursed the long dress that prevented her from taking large steps, a retro flower-print she'd put on for Eisa. A good lesson, but would her sons have to pay the price? They wouldn't have sounded the horn casually. City gangs hadn't been spotted in the glen for over a year. She'd almost convinced herself that the glen was invisible to them. When she was within fifty feet of the cottage a shot went off like a crack of thunder. She screamed as if she'd been hit. Was someone aiming at her? Looking up she saw a shotgun barrel thrust through a skylight. Andrew – the fucking hothead was shooting at the bounders, trying to get himself and everyone else killed. Two more blasts went off from behind the house and then came rapid fire from an automatic. Too panicked to scream, she forced her legs on.

Upon reaching the driveway she found a large pickup, its rear raised up on thick tyres and graffiti on the sides that read, 'Scotland for the Scots.' In the back were several men clad in camouflage with rifles in their hands, Glasgow bounders, judging by their fair skin and shaved heads. Facing them was a line of Corsican men, brandishing firearms they weren't supposed to have.

Roberto waved a vintage machine gun at the men in the pickup. 'I'll aim better next time.' He motioned for Linella to stay away. 'We're handling this.'

What about the boys? Are they safe? She couldn't think straight for the blood pounding in her head. Glancing at the skylight she saw it had opened a crack to reveal Josh and Andrew's faces looking out. At least they were safe – for now.

Roberto stepped forward. 'Turn that thing around and beat it.'

'Fucking afros,' a tall stocky man in the pickup muttered. He pointed his rifle at Roberto. 'Go back to your own country.'

Roberto's gun didn't flinch. 'I warn you only once.'

'Put those guns down!' Linella cried. To Roberto, 'You too! On the ground with them.' She wished the Earth could swallow her. Her voice seemed so inadequate; her foreign accent only a hindrance. The men in the pickup turned their weapons on her but then lowered them as if in answer to someone else's command. A voice from the cottage screamed, 'Mum!'

'Nobody shoot!' she yelled. It'd be just like Andrew to take a pot-shot at the pickup and start a full blown battle.

For years she'd tried to get the message through their thick skulls that violence only causes more violence. They knew what had happened to Jane, but they still didn't understand a damned thing.

They hadn't been with Linella, the terrible night when she and Jane drove through a no-go area of Glasgow. A gang of gun-toting yobs, their heads blown out on ice, stopped their car at a barricade and dragged them out. A burly clean-shaven man with cold eyes pinned down Linella and mounted her. Linella let him do what he wanted, hoping that he'd leave her alive. Which he did. Jane wasn't so lucky. Linella found her body nearby in a pool of blood. For years afterward she tried to bring Jane's killers to justice. The police offered her no help, citing hundreds of victims in every city, and complaining about a lack of manpower. She stormed the offices of MPs, obtained promises but nothing else. She hung memorial pictures of Jane throughout the cottage and lit candles in front of them, but the pictures only stoked her rage. One morning while assisting at the birth of a child, who turned out to be another lupan, she was overwhelmed by a feeling of gratitude: that she was alive, that she had her women about her and their golden-eyed children. Jane who helped build the first houses and who took care of the pregnant women would have wanted to be there beside her. She wanted Linella to live, not to be consumed by a futile pursuit of justice. Despite Josh and George's objections, she turned her gun collection over to the police. 'I can't bring Jane back,' she told Josh and George. 'But, by getting rid of my guns, I might stop someone from being shot. There will be no killing in this glen.'

Later she wondered what she'd actually do if she met Jane's murderers. She hoped she could treat them as if they didn't exist.

The yobs in the pickup couldn't be Jane's killers, but were about the same age. They'd probably lived on benefits all their lives, as had their parents and grandparents. When they weren't looting the countryside for food they got high by trashing shops owned by foreigners, killing refugees or shooting wolf-children for sport. It was all part of feeling self-righteous and patriotic. They held their guns loosely. Didn't regard her as a threat. Thank God. Roberto's men also lowered their weapons.

'If you want food, there is plenty for everyone,' she said to the leader.

'They don't want food,' Roberto said.

A sarcastic smile showed below the leader's bushy moustache. 'So, you're in charge here. You don't sound Scottish. You're a filthy Pole.'

'I'm more Scottish than you'll ever be.'

'Bugger off, old woman. We're not after you.'

She stood her ground.

'I said, bugger off.'

'Mum!' Andrew shouted from the skylight. 'Get out of the fucking road.'

'Yes, do what he says,' the leader said.

'Shoot her now Bill,' said one if the men. 'We're wasting time.'

Bill lowered his rifle, jumped from the pickup and positioned himself so that Linella blocked him from Roberto's line of fire.' He shoved the muzzle against her head. 'Get out of the fucking way.'

'Go to hell,' she whispered through clenched teeth. She stared into the man's blue eyes. He'd killed before. Killing meant nothing to him. Her body wanted to escape but another force, one she could not understand, held her still.

She turned to Roberto. 'I want all of you back in your tents now.'

Roberto laughed coarsely. 'They'll shoot us in the back.'

'No one is shooting anyone.' She grabbed Bill's rifle. 'You don't belong here.' She tried to wrest it from him, but he tore it free and aimed the butt at her head. She flinched to avoid the blow.

'We're not after you,' Bill said, lowering the gun. He nodded grimly at the Corsicans. 'They need to go home. Scotland isn't for their kind.'

She knew she couldn't hold them back. But if she gave an inch, there would be a pitched battle with dead bodies. Her sons among them. She tried to summon up a reply, but found that she had nothing to say.

Something moved to her left, new arrivals from the village. Arjan was there with several others, all brandishing their shiny new guns. Great, this is where the shooting starts. Holding Bill with her eyes, she said, 'We have company. If you fight, everyone loses. Put away your guns and go. I don't want anyone to die. Leave now and you'll all be safe.'

Bill scanned the new faces, brown faces that almost gave him a stroke. If he hadn't had men to lose he would have gunned down the refugees, all in a day's work. He fidgeted with his rifle as if finding it uncomfortable. Finally he lowered it and nodded for his men to do likewise. The pickup's electric drive kicked in. He swung himself into the back. He spat at Linella. 'Fucking bitch, we'll be back. A lot more of us. See how you like our rocket launcher.'

The vehicle whined off in low gear. Linella watched the dust cloud recede down the access road. 'I'm collecting those guns,' she said to Roberto. 'Put them all there.'

'If we hadn't shown up here with our guns, your kids would have been dead,' he said.

'So would you, if you'd started shooting.' She wanted to say more, but a sudden weariness overcame her. She staggered, sat down on a bench. Arjan and Elijah approached her. Arjan patted his new machine gun and looked sorry not to have used it. 'Thanks for coming,' she said. 'Thank God no one's been killed. Oh, this world is so terrible.'

Arjan shook his head. 'You should not stay here alone.'

'Where are my boys?'

Looking around she saw Andrew in the doorway, shotgun in hand. 'Good God, you almost got yourself killed. Give me that gun.'

'Well, what was I to do?' Andrew demanded sheepishly.

'You never learn anything.' She nodded to Roberto. 'Neither do you.'

'What you did was stupid,' Roberto said, waving his hands like windmill blades. 'Those men would have killed you. Made your children orphans. They are completely evil. They only understand force.'

'Yes, they're evil, but this is my house, and here you obey my rules. You were supposed to leave *all* your guns with me.'

'What about them?' Roberto nodded at Arjan and Elijah. 'Do they keep theirs?'

She stared at the metal barrels, hanging like male appendages, ready to go erect and ejaculate some steel. And that's what they fucking are, the way men see it. To relieve the men of their guns would be to castrate them.

She shook her head. 'None of you understand. How can you? Don't you remember Jane?'

Arjan winced. 'Of course we remember her.'

'Then think of her before you fire your hardware. Her killing was one too many.'

142

Roberto called to his friends in Italian and left, unhappy that she hadn't shown him more gratitude for saving her house. Perhaps she should have. She resolved to make up with him later. As she got up to go back into the house, Josh appeared in the doorway. 'Mum, it's your phone.'

From his nervous expression, she knew that the caller had to be Johnson. And it was. She carried the phone into the toilet and closed the door.

Johnson's voice in the earpiece sounded indistinct. 'Are you all right?'

'Yes. Why shouldn't I be?'

He spoke slowly, slurring his words. 'We heard that bounders were headed your way. I wanted to check on you.'

'Thanks for the call. We sent them on.'

'You sound a bit upset.'

'I'm okay. How about yourself?'

'I don't have good news. I just found out that I'm infected. The doctor said that it's in an early stage. Probably treatable. But there it is.'

'Brian, I'm so sorry.'

Her words lapsed into silence. She thought of Eisa and about his cure. Scott's apparent recovery proved that it worked. Why should Johnson have to wait for Eisa to make up his mind?

'Brian, I don't want you to die.'

'Thanks, but this is not up to you. I want you to get checked out. It's been a few weeks since we were in contact. I don't know the Plague's incubation period but I might have passed it on to you. Go get checked out.'

'I don't need to, Brian. I'm immune.'

After a long silence, Johnson cleared his throat. 'What are you smoking?'

'There haven't been any casualties in this glen. I know why. I wanted to tell you about it when you were here, but you know. We got into a fight.'

Johnson's flat voice responded, 'Go ahead.'

'We're in constant contact with the lupans. Everyone knows they're immune to the Plague. Doctor Habash, down in the village, has discovered that lupans can transmit this immunity to us. That's why we haven't had any cases, even when we've been exposed.'

'Come on, Linella, that's like another quack remedy. I know them all.'

'Eisa has all the scientific research to back him up. You should talk to him.'

'Eisa Habash?'

'That's the man.'

'Yeah. I heard about him. Has he told anyone else about this?'

'I don't know.'

'I'm not sure about this.'

'Brian, if you settled here, you'd be cured. I know that for a fact.'

Johnson let out a dry laugh. 'That might not be a good idea. Things are moving fast, much faster than I thought. I'm afraid that no one can stop it now.'

The hard edge to his voice made her blood run cold. Closing her eyes she tried to stave off her mounting anxiety. 'What are you saying?'

'You've only got a few days left for whatever decisions you have to make.'

She waited for him to elaborate but he said nothing more. 'Are you saying the army's on its way?'

'I'm saying nothing of the kind.'

Of course he wasn't. The police regularly monitored her radio phone because she was a troublemaker. Johnson wouldn't say anything over the phone that might implicate him. Still, he tipped her off, hoping that she'd clear out before the shooting started.

'Thanks for asking about me,' she said. 'I'm really fine and I feel okay here. I wish you would come. It would do you good.'

The silence that followed was so flat she thought they'd been disconnected.

144

'Brian?'

'Yes, I'm here. You really need to get away before those bounders come back. Koppiemaul isn't safe these days.'

'I can't leave. My friends are all I have.'

'Linella, think about it.' The line went dead.

She put down the phone, stood quietly with eyes closed, thinking about the tidal wave headed for Koppiemaul, about to sweep away her life. *What do I do? Lina has her olives and peaches to harvest. That's her life. All I have are my dahlias.* The past few weeks she'd been too overwrought to make her flower rounds. The neighbours would be wondering if she was still alive. By now they'd have all heard about the bounders and would be video-phoning each other for the latest news.

Andrew met her in the sitting room. From his anxious look she knew he wanted to argue with her about his rifle but didn't know how to start. 'Not now, Andrew. I have to sort my head.'

Grabbing a pair of scissors she headed for the flower garden. The multicoloured heads bobbed in a light breeze, each with several bees nesting on it. Touching the flowers she felt a curious sense of peace steal over her. Despite Johnson's warning, her anxiety for the future of the colony appeared to lift from her breast. She felt connected to the land and its life; doing something real. The land had always supported her, protected her. Why should that change? No matter how dark the world outside the glen became, she was under the protection of a more powerful force than anyone could conceive, one that permeated the hills, the trees and the stones. Beside it, the threat of an outside force seemed unreal.

She was tying up a bunch when a dark face materialized among the dahlias. After a moment she realized it was Zia.

Zia's appearance at Koppiemaul meant that something was wrong. She clicked her tongue and held her hand out to Linella, begging for help. Her wrinkled face was dark with concern.

'It never ends,' Linella muttered, realizing that she had to go with Zia. Something had happened to Scott. What if he were dead

145

or badly hurt? She couldn't leave her sons alone in the house. Before nightfall the bounders might return in greater numbers. She'd humiliated them, and they weren't likely to forget it. Roberto's men still had their guns; she didn't trust them not to start shooting at the first sign of trouble.

'Kids!' she yelled. 'George, Andrew, Josh!'

Her panicked voice made them race out, George still wearing his video helmet. 'I'm going with Zia. Something's happened up at the colony. I don't want you up here alone. Pack your things and go down to Lina's. I'll meet you there when I can.'

'But Mum, we want to stay here,' George protested.

'Be down at Lina's in an hour. God only knows when those bastards will return. Do it for me, please.'

She took Zia's hand and followed her down the hill. Usually Zia's warm hand felt reassuring. Even at the darkest times Zia knew no fear, but not now. Zia's hand felt inexplicably still, like any normal human who knew what it was to be afraid.

EIGHTEEN

Darkness wraps its arms about you. It's a relief not to see anything, not to think, not to know. There's a name, Scott Maguire, but you can't place it. You're in a room with a sweet smelling fire, among lupans. They're humming a tune that worms its way into your head, jams any thought you can muster. Drowning like a fish on land you flop about, but the sea is far away. Inevitably you'll die. Rising to her knees she presses her thighs against yours; without reserve. Her eyes search you. Her dark pupils expand to swallow you. You give way to her desire because she's all there is, immerse yourself in her and pass through the doorway of her eyes only to find yourself looking down at your body.

Over there is Scott Maguire, the only man in the circle, the man you know. Is it you? Not really, because when you lift a hand to your face you find a wrinkled hand with leathery skin. Lupan. You're a smelly, naked lupan. Not human, not even a man because you have a woman's breasts and genitalia. You scream again but it's like trying to talk while someone is throttling you. Your lupan voice can't understand human language, let alone form any words. You can't even think a human thought, so what would you say? The encircling faces stand out in deep relief, so clear that you can map out each wrinkle: the curve of the lips while they articulate a song, a spot of dried blood below the cheek. Eyes, once dumb and inarticulate, now speak to you. You can feel a lupan's joy, sorrow or perplexity as if it were yours. Those feelings

147

don't end with you, your body, or with others in the circle but extend beyond the walls to the surrounding rocks and trees.

The albino watches you, knows what you see. Her hands sweep up and down keeping time to the music. You watch her thoughts: slow waves that plough an uncharted sea, each one rhythmic and well ordered.

Inside you a deep and immovable silence takes hold, so immense that you're no more than a raindrop that falls into an ocean. So this is what it's like to be dead, without hope, memories or anything familiar to hold onto. For a moment you teeter at the edge of your familiar world, looking at your body – at someone called Scott Maguire, and then you drop into a well. For a long time you fall. You don't care what lies at the bottom, or if there is a bottom.

You die. The bond connecting you to your body snaps. Your memories, your relationships and everything you've owned, float away. Ready or not it's total annihilation. One big nothing. You're left in a dark place where nothing human, nothing lupan, not even the whisper of thought exists.

Silence. Darkness. Silence and darkness. Darkness and silence. There's nothing to see in that emptiness, because there's nothing there. Nothing particular. It doesn't relate to you, because you don't exist. It belongs to itself: to nothingness and everything, to nothingness and fullness. One can't exist without the other. Whether emptiness or fullness, it's not dead but teems with life like the gurgling fluids in a womb about to give birth. You're not part of it because you're not there, except as an observer, both everywhere and nowhere. Really dead or is the brain in your old body firing its neurons at random, in a final gasp before it gives up? You're not quite finished with life. Who are you? When the question arises it doesn't make sense. Memories float about at random. You recall a sunny day when a mechanical bird fell from the sky. Among the wreckage you found a wounded man. Are you that man or are you the lupan who saw the bird fall? Whose body do you have? Whose memories? Yours or everyone's? Is there any body you can call your own?

Water's dripping a drip, drip over a rock into a pool. You listen to them as if your life depended on it, aware of every tone and every sound until you feel the water inside you. Is the water out there or are you the water? Is there any difference? You reach out, touch the rocky wall with your fingers, allow them to scrape against it, feel the cold slick stone. You rub harder until it hurts. The sensation tells you that you exist, but as what? Feeling your arms and legs you find you're naked except for a gold belt about the waist. The slit between your legs tells you that you're female. Long ago you made that belt. For now you might be female, but you could as easily be anything, even the water or the rock.

In the ethereal light you discern that water trickles down the rocky walls into a small pool, from where it flows into a narrow stream then disappears into darkness. You watch every drop, as it grows on a sharp rocky point, becomes an elongated globe, separates, falls and plops into the pool where it produces a few circular rings. Each drop is thought into existence and presented to you as a gift. You don't wonder about its purpose or whether it should mean something. In observing, you feel more alive and awake than ever.

The bite of a cool breeze makes you aware of your body. Of your breathing. You're not entirely alone because you share the space with another. Eventually you make out a dark shadow wrapped in flame, sitting by the pool. You recognize Wolfborn.

A forest presence respected by wolves and lupans, she runs clothed in a female body. Sometimes you'll find her wearing a wolf skin. You could merge or switch bodies with her to satisfy your curiosity, but don't see why you should. She greets you with a broad smile, showing a line of wolf teeth. When she speaks, her husky voice reverberates inside your chest.

– We are here together. Have you decided?

What's there to decide?

Her golden eyes erase all boundaries between you. She allows you a glimpse her world, the wind on your face while you run alongside the Protector. The joy of hunting with a well-disciplined pack. With your body transformed into wolf you can fully participate in the hunt. You can watch the nurse feed the newborn pups, even help with their upbringing. But though you run with the pack and resemble a wolf, the others look at you strangely. They know that you're different. Though you were raised on wolf-milk and know their ways you'll never be one of them. Because you aren't a wolf.

You ask, – What am I?

– Neither man nor wolf, but Earthborn.

The word awakens the image of swirling waters, bubbling gases and smoke from a cauldron set over volcanic fire in the ocean depths. Growing in its warmth are exotic plants with tentacles tall as a tree, giant snails, blind fish that swallow the hot gases. You're looking at the hearth of conception.

She's following your thoughts. – There's more to the story. Listen.

– Far away in a land destroyed by war, several women escape into a desert. Their homes are destroyed by fire, their husbands killed and their fields laid waste. After walking for days through a rocky land where nothing grows, and where it never rains they are about to collapse and die when they unexpectedly cross a small stream that issues from a forest of gnarly trees.

While she speaks she shows you the weary women, their faces immersed in the water, relieved to be alive for one more night. They gather berries from nearby bushes. Though bitter, the berries soothe their hunger pangs. A cold wind sweeping through the scrub blows sand in their faces. Retreating to a sheltered spot between two large rocks, the women pull their head coverings over their faces, and huddle together for warmth. Sand piles softly about them. They hear several long-drawn wolf howls borne on the wind, shiver in fear and pull closer together.

– At nightfall a large man emerges from the trees. He is a head taller than any normal man, with long white hair and a thick grey beard. Wordlessly he clears away several large rocks and scoops away the loose sand to create a hollow. Invites the women to take refuge

150

there. After they settle there he hauls in dry trees and branches and snaps them with his bare hands to make firewood. From his knotted fingers he produces a flame and thrusts it into the sticks. Soon the fire's warmth spreads throughout the hollow and gladdens their hearts. The women thank him but he does not reply. Perhaps he doesn't speak their language. He heats up a pot of water to which he adds various herbs and roots. He serves them the soup. While the women drink it, they stare at their host, but are too weary to ask him who or what he is. His wild eyes stir a deep longing in their hearts, awaken in their bodies a desire to dance with him and to feel his strong body against theirs. So grateful are they that he restored them to life, and so bewildered by his power, that they all lie with him and allow him to impregnate them. One by one they fall into a deep sleep, except for the youngest. She awakens unexpectedly to see her lover change shape from a man into a large grey wolf. She is so afraid that she screams. Hearing her, the wolf turns to her. His fiery gaze holds her motionless. In a deep grey voice, he tells her that he will one day return for his children. And so he departs.

– He returns?

Wolfborn bares her teeth. – When I was a child, a woman carried me to meet the wolves. They'd been waiting for me. For all of us. They fed us, shared in our upbringing and taught us the ways of the forest. We belong to two worlds: their world, and the world of those who gave birth to us. We don't know the language of our mothers. Forgetting that we are their children, they kill us for sport and dispose of us as they want. Often in their eyes we see a deep seated pain, loneliness and a fear of death.

– We need you. You're the first to have walked our path, the only one who knows us. As I speak your language, so you speak ours. You won't forget it when you awaken.

Who is she talking to? You clothed in the body of a female lupan, or someone else?

– You have the power to open up a world that has always been closed to us, – she says. – The world of your people. Our destiny lies with you. You are the Messenger.

Grasping your arm, she draws her face so close that you see yourself reflected in her eyes. – Isn't that what you are?

Her long finger points to a bearded dishevelled man lying on the ground whose twisted face is trying to scream. You scream.

'He's waking up.'

Linella held Scott's arm to stop him thrashing about and hitting himself in the face. His eyes flickered open, stared but did not appear to recognize her. He turned his head left and right, looking everywhere except at her.

'Messenger. That's what we are,' he said.

'Scott. Listen to me. Can you hear me?' she said.

Zia sat a few feet away on the den floor. Her face glowed suddenly and she let out a low whistle that appeared to express relief. Earlier, when she brought Linella to the den and showed her Scott's body, Linella was sure that he was dead. His face was white as stone and he wasn't breathing. His hands were cold and growing stiff. What could she do? She burst into tears at the sight of his lifeless body and at her helplessness. In death he had a gentler look. Gone was his cynical mask. Living among the lupans had changed him, but she'd never know how.

Zia held Linella's hand against Scott's face. That was when she felt a faint pulse, enough to tell her that he wasn't dead. She sponged his body with warm water, wrapped it in a blanket and waited with him through the night. Not until morning did he begin to stir.

'What did you do to him?' Linella demanded.

Zia disappeared from the dome, to return quickly with a bowl of dried herbs. Linella crushed them between her fingers, sniffed them. The smell made her feel so dizzy that she staggered. Their smoke might have a narcotic effect; could be hallucinogenic enough to push anyone over the edge.

'You let him smoke this shite. No wonder he's out of his mind.'

Zia stared back with a blank look as if she'd been caught doing something wrong.

Linella flung down the herbs. 'Don't you use that on him again. Do you understand?'

'Asra.' Scott was speaking. His eyes focused on Linella and smiled. He stroked her face gently. 'You're here?'

'I'm not Asra. I'm Linella – from the cottage.'

'Cottage Woman.'

He could see her, at least for now. She needed to keep talking so that he wouldn't drift off again. 'Scott – do you know where you are?'

He looked around at the ceiling, its thick tree-trunks cemented with cobb. 'It's home.'

'Close enough. Now lie still. I'll get you some water.'

He gripped her hand and pulled her toward him. 'I need to see you. I want to know who you are.'

'I'm Linella.'

He shrugged as if she'd said something irrelevant. 'It doesn't matter. Cottage Woman.' He took her hair, caressed it, brought it to his face to smell. 'You're beautiful. Your hair, it's my hair.'

Perhaps talking wasn't the best thing for him. In his delirium he was unsure who he was and who she was. He even called her Cottage Woman, a name that Zia used. Still holding his hand she sat where he could see her without turning his head. Like acid, the drug might have to run its course before he recognized her and came to his senses.

His eyes shone like a fanatic's. 'I know who you are. It's me – we're the same.' He looked around frantically. 'What am I doing here? I'm not supposed to be in this place. Don't keep me here.'

'Scott. You're safe with me. Linella.'

He sighed. 'I guess that was your name.'

It was a while before anything felt real. People changed shape before his eyes: Linella into Asra, to Cottage Woman. Rami into Zia. He'd change places with Linella to look through her eyes at a bedraggled man on the floor. She held his hand and tried to get him to talk, but the more she tried the more he resented her efforts. He wished she'd leave him alone. The den was a cold dark hole where he'd been cast, imprisoned in an arbitrary body. Gone was the silence of the cave, the place where he understood everything, felt kinship even with the walls, the dripping water, the air, Wolfborn, Beauty Woman and the others. Where he had no sense of being separate. His awareness moved with ease from person to person. Now he was alone in a defined body, in a wilderness where he didn't belong, separated from everyone, and tormented by screaming and anxious thoughts.

Why did she insist on being there, coaxing him to stay with her in that small prison, when all he wanted was to leave? But it was too late. The door back to the cave had been slammed in his face. Moment by moment her world drew him into its orbit. Whatever happened in the cave was fading as fast as a dream upon waking. Soon, it would feel no more real than a child's fantasy, gone beyond recall – something he wished might be real. He'd share the same prison as Linella, no longer able to exchange a word or thought with the wolf-children.

Death was a better option. Why hadn't he broken his neck when he crashed his glider into the hill? The result would have been the same. Either way he was stuck in what people called 'the real world', in truth, the place where nothing made sense, where he was alone, an exile with only rudimentary words for communication, hardly able to understand the natives.

Linella offered him a bowl of steaming broth. He pushed it away. 'Don't.' The last thing he wanted was food – something to yank him back to his prison cell.

She froze, feeling that she'd done something wrong.

'I don't need anything. God, why am I here?' The words sounded strange on his lips. He'd forgotten how to speak and was trying it for the first time. Words felt clumsy, weird sounds that attempted to translate thoughts, or to imprison them, steering them along established tracks. No wonder the lupans dispensed with all language. It only got in the way.

Zia knelt by him, placed her lips close to his. He stroked her lined face. Her breath felt warm. Comforting. Her golden eyes were gentle. They cared for him. She knew what he was thinking because she could at any time enter his mind as if it were hers. Earlier he'd have felt too vulnerable to allow her so close, but now he no longer cared that his inner world was no longer private. She kissed him lightly on the lips, smiled and got up to go.

'Don't,' Scott said, but Zia was already walking to the door. She swept the hanging reeds aside and was gone, leaving him with Cottage Woman. Sitting beside him she braided her long white hair. Her nervous fingers suggested that she was impatient with his slow recovery; she wanted to be somewhere else. When he first saw her there he'd begged her to go, but now that he'd been drawn back into her world, the thought that she might leave him, that he would be left alone in prison, sent him into a panic.

'Will you stay with me?' he said

'I'm not sure I can do anything for you.'

'Keep talking. I need to hear your voice. Please tell me that you'll stay.'

'I'll stay. Don't worry about that.'

'Tell me about the cottage.'

'It's all right.'

'You have children?'

'Three sons. They – they're well.'

Her words stumbled out as if spoken by a robot. Her nervous eyes told a different story, that something was wrong. So this was it – he'd come back from a place where everything made sense, to this place where stupid human beings scrabbled about in a confusing fog.

What did she most fear? The army. That word arose again in his mind. What was it but a tidal wave just out of sight and about to roll over them all? She hoped her children would be safe. He read all this in her expression, also she wished she could be anywhere in the world but here. But for whatever reason she didn't want to allow him to go mad. Alone.

NINETEEN

The Koppiemaul horn blasts awoke the village from its torpor. Men dropped their building and gardening tools, grabbed the closest knife or gun and sprinted up the hill. Eisa followed them. Within minutes Sandria found herself alone outside Eisa's cottage. Though the street was deserted the air felt so tense that she found herself pacing restlessly. She could do nothing other than wait for news and hope that no-one would be hurt. She didn't have a home to return to. The only home she knew was up at the lupan colony, now the last place she wanted to go.

She wished she could feel some concern for Linella's danger – for what might be happening at Koppiemaul. Instead she only heard Linella's hateful voice, talking about Scott and Zia having sex. Ridiculous, disgusting, but there it was. If that's what he wants, let him have sex with her. With a horse if that suits him. He obviously didn't want to have anything to do with her or with the child that he'd fathered. Of course, he mumbled the standard line about taking care of her if she wanted to keep the baby, but he'd as soon she had an abortion to save him the trouble of having to think about the baby. Or about her. An abortion – when the pregnancy was the answer to all her dreams, the one thing that could heal her suffering? If he didn't want the baby, so be it. She would take care of it herself.

While mulling over those thoughts she saw Lina walking toward her, down the street with her basket of peaches. Her lined

156

face was more careworn than ever. Her stoop suggested that she carried much more than peaches.

Sandria nodded a greeting. 'Any news from the cottage?'

Lina shivered. 'I'm afraid it's bounders. Will you come with me? I don't want to be on my own.'

For once, their roles were reversed and it was Lina who needed support. From early childhood Lina had bossed Sandria about; made sure she knew the rules and fell into line. During their wanderings in search of a home Sandria grew to depend on her older cousin who never flinched in the face of adversity. After settling in Scotland the dependent relationship was sealed. Sandria knew that she could not fight the self-styled matriarch. Removing herself first to River House, then to the colony, wasn't a bad choice. She defined her own role and didn't have Lina around to tell her what clothes to wear, how to comb her hair or how to live her life.

But things had changed. Scott had moved in on her and emotionally evicted her from the hill. She was pregnant and without a home, unless she wanted to return to the village, to live there under Lina's gaze. Not an ideal situation, but less complicated than living with Scott.

Before long they reached Lina's kitchen. Lina put the kettle on, washed a couple of stray bowls and arranged them neatly on a rack. Sandria sat at the table, uncomfortable and waiting for Lina to notice her. She needed to tell her about Scott; eventually about her pregnancy. Lina, who criticized sex outside of marriage, would be furious, but she'd eventually accept it. She stood by the stove, one hand resting on a simmering kettle, her lips drawn tight and too absorbed in her thoughts to talk.

'They should have reached the cottage by now,' Sandria said.

Lina flicked on her wrist-com and scanned rapidly through several channels. 'Still no news,' she sighed. 'The men have been gone for an hour. Praise God that there's been no shooting. I'm always afraid that one of them will fire their gun, and then everyone will be shooting. These days we have too many funerals.

I don't trust Elijah not to start trouble. All I want is for them to come home.' She flicked off the com.

'I hope Linella's boys are all right,' Sandria said.

'She needs to stay up there. Too often she leaves them alone while she flirts with Eisa. There is no future in that relationship. I don't understand what women find so interesting in that man. He's a good doctor – I'll say that.'

'She must feel lonely. I don't blame her wanting to be with Eisa.'

'We're all lonely. It's a fact we can't escape.'

'You have Arjan.'

'Yes, there's Arjan. At least we're still together. Don't mistake me. I love Arjan, but when I watched him run up the hill, I was afraid I was seeing him for the last time. But what can I say? All our lives we've lived with danger. With war. We have to be prepared for terrible things. I don't know where to find hope. I would never have the courage to live alone like Linella.'

'Me neither. I feel a lot safer up on the hill.'

'Yes, and with that pilot. How is he doing?'

'He's fine.'

'You enjoy taking care of him?'

'Well enough.'

Lina's eyes darkened. The tension behind Sandria's words had to be obvious. 'You want to talk about him?'

'I'm upset with Scott. I don't know if I want to go back to him. You see...' Words choked up inside her.

'Are you involved with him?'

'Well yes. I suppose a relationship was inevitable. I'm sorry. This is going to upset you but I have to tell you. I'm pregnant.'

Lina smiled. Sandria waited for more of a response, but all Lina did was to affect a smile that said – I didn't expect any better of you anyway.

Why did I have to tell her? I knew how she'd react.

Lina removed the boiling kettle from the hob. Her face displayed no emotion while she took two cups from a shelf, opened a jar of dried mint and spooned it into a chipped teapot. With several swift strokes she sliced up a lemon.

'You think I should marry him?' Sandria blurted out.

Lina hardly looked up. 'Of course. We would all be overjoyed for you.'

'It's not going to happen.'

'No, somehow I didn't think so.'

'Why is that?'

Lina's face hardly stirred in response. She set the teacups on the table and then sat down. 'We live in very difficult times, too difficult for most people to make that sort of commitment.'

'This is nothing to do with my commitment. I want Scott to be involved with the child, for him to be a good father, but he wants to leave, to go back to the outside world. I don't know what he thinks he can do there, because he's a wanted man. He'll immediately end up in jail.'

'Maybe he doesn't like the colony. It's not everyone's idea of a home. If you moved down here would he agree to stay with you?'

'I don't know. I don't think he wants me to have the baby.'

'Does he love you?'

'He said he does.'

Lina's cold stare said that she didn't believe it. She sipped her tea. 'Why didn't he come down with you today?'

'They wouldn't let him. We were on our way to see Eisa when they stopped us. The whole colony was there. They took Scott back up the hill so that Zia could take care of him. Zia! Do you know what I mean?'

Lina grimaced. 'Oh no. That would be dreadful. Ugh – I feel sick thinking of them trying to couple. It's bestiality.'

'That's how I feel. Part of me wants to run up there, grab Scott and bring him here. But I'm afraid of what I'll find. I don't trust Zia. She's had her eyes on him for a long time.'

'No doubt she has. It's you I'm worried about though.'

Worried, yet Lina's severe eyes looked down at Sandria as if she had done the unspeakable.

'You think I'm a whore,' Sandria said.

After a long silence Lina cleared her throat. 'No, but it's obvious to anyone why you did this. We both lost a child. It never gets easier. Maybe I'm more practised. For years I've kept up a wall, one that I built stone by stone. Otherwise I couldn't go on living with my grief. With you it's different. You always talked about having a normal child, one who might help you to forget Asra.'

'And if I have?' Sandria clenched her teacup. 'Isn't that normal?'

'Of course. It's what most women would do.'

'But you still disapprove.'

'You misunderstand me.'

'I don't think I do. Don't you have a heart in your body, Lina – one that feels what I'm going through? We're both mothers. The same horrible thing happened to us.'

Lina sighed. 'I don't need to be reminded of the past. It's best left alone and not disturbed. Please don't talk about our children. Long ago we agreed that we're different. We handle our grief in our own way.'

'This is not about the past. I'm going to have a baby. I'm terrified that it might be another wolf-child. Don't you see? I'm alone. Completely alone.'

Lina's lips parted in a fleeting smile. 'You may feel that way, but you don't have to. We're all here for you. We're your family. I think of you often, wishing you would live with us again. For things to be as they once were. I'd be overjoyed if you would come down from the hill. We will all take care of you and the baby. But you have to choose.'

She would have a home, security and friendship, but at what price? Many nights while she lay in the den, Sandria considered returning to the only family she knew. But she would have to accept the strictures, the order, the way that things are done and Lina's matriarchal authority.

'I have to think about Scott and find out what he wants. I left him with the wolf-children. Everything between us is unsettled. I'm afraid of what they might do to him.'

Lina shrugged. 'Surely you don't believe he loves you.'

'I don't know. I think he does.'

'How do you feel about him?'

'I want him to be a father, a real father; but if he won't, I'd rather not see him again.'

'Of course you'll eventually sort things out with him. Maybe this isn't the right time for it.'

'Can I stay here for a couple of days? I need to let things settle a bit.'

'Of course you can. This is your home. You mean a lot to me, Sandria. You know I'll do anything for you, and for your baby.'

Somehow Lina's welcome didn't ring true. Over the years nothing about Lina had changed. She wanted Sandria back in the village, indeed in her house, to keep an eye on her. Control her. But where else could she go?

When the men returned, Arjan described their confrontation with the bounders.

'That woman is totally crazy. They were all about to shoot her, yet she walked up to their gun barrels; talked them down. One day she'll get herself shot and wonder what happened to her.'

'But no one was killed,' Lina said. 'Maybe she knows what she's doing.'

Arjan shook his machine gun. 'You women will never understand that the only thing those bastards respect is power – and this is power.'

'Keep your power to yourself. Don't even try to convince me that your guns will do us any good.'

Arjan and Eisa sat at the table expecting food. Lina placed yesterday's corn on the cob in front of them. Arjan gnawed rapidly through one; wiped his mouth with his sleeve. He then paused as if suddenly remembering something. 'Zia even came to the cottage to see what was going on.'

161

'Oh yes?' In her confusion Sandria got up from the bench. 'What about her?'

'She looked agitated. Came looking for Linella. They left the cottage together.'

'Where did they go?'

'I didn't see. If they're not here they went back to the colony.'

'I saw them walking up the hill,' Eisa added.

Something had happened to Scott. Nothing else would have made Zia come looking for Linella. But why had she chosen Linella and not Sandria to help with Scott? Sandria felt tears start in her eyes. Who had taken care of Scott for so long? Fed him and kept him clean? Loved him? A chill feeling of loneliness crept into her. A door had been slammed in her face, and she was outside, in the cold.

TWENTY

Linella awakened from a disturbing dream. A voice was calling her name; a familiar voice but one she couldn't place, telling her she needed to be somewhere. Immediately. She tried to remember the dream but the more she grasped at it, the faster it faded. A few feet away Scott lay curled up under an old blanket, his knees drawn up against his chest. At least he was sleeping peacefully. In the middle of the night he had wakened up screaming. He had stared at her but did not seem to recognize her. While he thrashed around like an epileptic, she watched over him to make sure he didn't hurt himself, but otherwise left him alone. Exhausted, he finally collapsed into a fitful sleep.

Shouldn't she be with the boys? They were supposed to be down in the village with Lina and Arjan, but what if they'd decided to return to Koppiemaul, where no one could protect them? Her warnings meant nothing to George, or to Andrew for that matter, bullet-proof hotheads who thought they could single-handedly hold off the Scottish army. She put on her jeans and heavy boots. If something was about to happen, she needed to be down in the village with the kids.

Could she leave Scott here? The past two days he appeared to have recovered from the drug experience. He ate well, talked more and made frequent eye contact, but he was far from normal. Sometimes his eyes acquired a terrified look. He'd drift away from her, asking her who he was. His own name. She tried to talk him back to sanity but he only stared back, hardly listening to her.

Finally she shut up and held his hand until he settled down. Zia's presence no longer calmed him. Whenever she drew close he would shout at her until she left the den.

'Why don't you want her here?' Linella asked him. 'She can help you.'

'I'm not ready for her. Or others. They get into my head.'

What now? Her anxiety for her boys' safety agitated her so much that she paced around the den. She was about to leave when she noticed that his eyes were open.

'I have to go down to the village,' she said.

His blank expression suggested he hadn't understood. 'Scott, I don't want to leave you but I have to check on my kids.'

'I'll be fine.'

'I won't be away for long.'

'Take care of yourself.'

She wrapped her arms about him. He held her close, his bearded face pressed against hers. Perhaps he thought he was holding her for the last time. Gently she extricated herself from his embrace.

'In the village, you'll see her,' he said. 'Tell her...'

'Sandria?'

'Yes. I want her to know... that I remember her.'

The morning wind rustled among the bushes. She wrapped her arms about her chest for warmth. Embracing Scott had left her heart racing. Why was she so determined to take care of him? What did she see in him that left her breathless? The strength in his eyes, the intense way he looked at her, not missing any detail? Almost like a lupan. His visions? He didn't talk much about them but she knew that he was in touch with a mysterious world that she couldn't see. If he suffered, so did iron tempered on an anvil, but it would emerge harder and with an edge. She wished she could ease his suffering, but she wasn't Zia. Her healing power was limited.

On the horizon a thick cloud-bank hid the sun and cast the valley into grey shadow. She scanned the land for any moving

164

vehicles, Koppiemaul Cottage alone on its hill, the neighbour's fields and her access road. Though she saw nothing suspicious, the air felt tense, like a storm about to break. Something just over the hill was waking up.

Her heart aflutter, she ran down the path, crossed through the break in the wolf fence. A metallic scream stopped her short, forcing her to cover her ears. A fighter plane had appeared overhead, so low that she could almost make out the pilot. Banking left, it circled the colony then swooped down on the village. She held her breath, expecting to hear an explosion, or gunfire, but the fighter only skimmed the rooftops and the fields, then disappeared over Koppiemaul. It was barely out of sight before a second and third plane appeared and performed similar manoeuvres. She ran down the path, her legs racing with a life of their own. She had to reach the village immediately. Several more screams rent the skies but they no longer made her flinch. The thought of her boys drove her madly on.

From far off came the howling of wolves, their usual response to flying aircraft, but this time their cries were long and drawn. Painful. If they felt threatened they might just come out and attack. Kill anyone who happened to be there. Just what we need, she muttered as she ran. She reached the first house. That was when she heard rapid gunfire.

'It's begun!' she screamed.

The planes were nowhere in sight. The shots were coming from men in the street, sounding the alarm by shooting off their rifles. Before long there was another sound, the low growl of heavy machinery. Tanks were moving into position. Here was the fucking show of force – aircraft and tanks to terrorize the people and make them too afraid to resist. It would not work, not if she knew Arjan, Elijah and the others. Even Lina who never picked up a gun was a force to be reckoned with.

The village street was soon swarming with armed men. Standing on a rusty car Arjan shot his gun in the air and yelled for everyone to join him. Where were the kids? She called out to

Elijah but he was moving too quickly to take notice of her. Gathered in a motley mass, the men sped up the hill toward Koppiemaul. She headed for Lina's house. Where are they? What if they're on the front line?

She opened Lina's door, leapt up the rough wooden staircase, three at a time, and arrived in the kitchen where she found Lina and Sandria, white-faced, by the kitchen stove. No one else was in the room.

'Where are my kids?'

Lina's scared eyes turned to Linella. 'Josh is upstairs. George and Andrew are gone.'

'Where?'

'With the men.' Lina shook her head, appeared on the verge of tears. 'Please stay with us. We're frightened.'

'I have to find them.'

'And then what will you do?'

Linella's trembling legs finally gave way. She collapsed onto the bench and put her head on the table. 'Nothing. Nothing.'

'Please stay here here. We need you.'

A sense of futility soaked into her. Her boys were out of her reach. She could no longer protect them. This was not Koppiemaul, where she could call them for dinner or badger them to tidy up their stuff. They'd chosen to be with the men. Did she expect anything else, now that she was no longer relevant to their lives? At most she was the mother that they grudgingly put up with.

Josh appeared in the doorway, waved to Linella and sat down at a separate table. At least he was safe. She wanted to go up to him and hug him, but he sat stiffly. Withdrawn. Always the dreamer, he never liked action movies or video games. If he had his way he'd be sitting under a tree and writing a poem.

'I'm so glad you're here,' she said.

'I wanted to go but figured I'd wait here for you.' He spoke without making eye contact; perhaps he felt embarrassed at staying behind.

'Thank you, Josh. That means a lot to me.'

'If you don't mind, I want to go out.'

'Why?'

'I'm not going to fight, but I can't sit around this kitchen. I'm only going as far as the orchard to see what's going on.'

Closing her eyes, she nodded. She didn't have the heart to stop him. At least he wouldn't be on the front line.

Sandria sat like a statue opposite her, her eyes staring in the distance. She avoided looking at Linella or talking to her. Linella cast about for something to say that wouldn't be banal. Finally she said, 'Scott is doing well.'

Sandria raised a brow. 'How are they treating him?'

'As always. He asked about you.'

'What did he say?'

'That he remembers you.'

Sandria shot back a cold look. 'I'm glad he's not suffering from amnesia.'

Linella decided not to reply. She couldn't handle Sandria, not now when the village was under attack.

George could never explain to himself why he'd gone with Andrew and the village men. Unarmed, he wasn't likely to be of any help. In fact he was more in the way. Unless he could pick up a stray weapon, one he knew how to point and fire. This time he wouldn't be fighting aliens on a screen. His legs felt wobbly; his insides churned. If he could have run for it without being noticed, he would have. Andrew walked steadily beside him and didn't appear afraid of what lay ahead, but then he had mother's hunting-rifle to empower him. The men carried sawn-off shotguns. A few had newly-acquired machine guns on their shoulders, weapons they'd barely tried out.

The track passed through a meadow with two unfinished stone circles. Its golden grass, two feet tall, still waited for the women's scythes. When they reached the meadow the village men sighted a large tank on the crest, its six-inch muzzle pointed at them. Marching toward them were several camouflaged figures, helmeted and with protruding antennas, their rifles ready for action. George shrank behind Andrew. *Too late to run now.* If only the ground would swallow him up, or he could duck into the tall grass. Arjan stiffened at the sight of the column. His machine gun lowered, he muttered something in Arabic to Elijah. The other men all had nervous expressions. Like George, they'd rather be anywhere else in the world.

A tall stocky soldier walked several paces ahead of the others. He waved his arms up and down suggesting he wanted to parley.

'What happens now?' George muttered.

'Hold tight, man,' Andrew said.

'Should we shoot them now or shoot them later?' Arjan grumbled to Elijah.

Standing with his automatic rifle against his shoulder, Elijah said, 'God knows. Give him a chance.'

Raising his gun Arjan said, 'That's far enough.'

The soldier pointed to a spot in the track. 'Those weapons all go in a pile, there. Do it now.'

Nobody moved. In response to a hidden command the soldiers all went down on one knee, their rifles pointed at the village men.

'Do it,' the soldier repeated.

'Not so fast,' Arjan said.

'Where's Arjan Almagheri?'

'That's me.'

'You're an illegal settlement and are subject to deportation. Put down your weapons or we will open fire.'

'And who are you?'

Arjan's cold stance made the soldier turn crimson. 'I'm Major Gordon. You have one fucking chance, you brownie scum. We don't want any trouble. We don't want anyone to get hurt. We're here to execute evacuation orders.'

From an inside pocket he produced a large envelope, made a movement to hand the envelope to Arjan, but Arjan raised his weapon.

Gordon flung the envelope on the ground. He retreated a couple of paces. 'It's all there.'

Arjan's response was cut off by the roar of two fighter jets that skimmed the village roofs, climbed over the lupan colony and vanished over the forest. As the echoes died away George heard the baying of wolves, clearer and closer than before. 'You hear that?' he said to Andrew.

Not showing any emotion, Andrew said, 'They're coming.'

Arjan nodded at the envelope. 'What's it about?'

'You have an hour to gather your belongings and report to the lorries on the hill. No harm will come to you if you put down your weapons and co-operate.'

Arjan handed his machine gun to George, stepped forward and picked up the envelope. Gordon stood several paces away, his hands on his hips.

'What are you waiting for chief?' said the closest soldier.

'Shut up,' Gordon said.

Arjan tapped the envelope on the palm of his hand. 'We're not leaving. We've lived here for thirty years and the government never complained. We pay our taxes like everyone else.'

Gordon's flat expression suggested he wasn't listening. 'I've no authority to discuss your individual situation,' he said. 'We want to do this peacefully. Will you help me, so that no one gets hurt? There are women and children down there.'

'Don't talk to me about my people,' Arjan cried out. 'We will never leave our homes. We stand ready to defend them. Even our women will fight.'

Gordon nodded at the men behind him and the tank on the hill. 'You're so fucking stupid.'

'We're ready for you. If you attack, we will defend our homes. Leave and do not trouble us again.'

'Be reasonable, man. Put down your guns.'

Gordon's words sounded so overwhelming that George was convinced Arjan would back down; but he showed no intention to move. His flushed face suggested a fanatical determination to

169

make a stand, whatever the cost. The soldiers were no more important to him than a few stray wasps.

Gordon picked up his rifle and returned to the army line. Even as he reached it, the turret of the tank swung around. Its gun belched smoke. A loud report sounded, the air whistled and the earth exploded, throwing soil and rocks into the air. The cloud barely cleared before a second shell struck in the middle of the olive grove and left a larger crater. A cry of dismay echoed from the village men. Frozen, they watched a missile land on the trees and leave raw earth and splintered wood. One shell struck an outlying steading and reduced half of it to rubble; the second shell finished the job.

Arjan's screams awakened his men from their torpor. They turned their weapons on the army men, only to find that they had disappeared into the long grass, or behind standing stones. Arjan fired his machine gun into the grass. Elijah joined him until there was a deafening chatter of gunfire. Response from the grass was immediate.

A bullet whistled by George's ear. Jerking sideways he fell flat into the long grass. With one hand he dragged Andrew down with him. 'Hold still,' he said. They covered their heads with their hands and pressed up against the earth. Bullets whistled overhead; agonized cries sounded from the men.

A few feet away Arjan collapsed onto one knee, his face twisted in pain. The gun fell from his hands. Elijah was also hit and forced to drop his weapon. After several minutes the gunfire ceased. The village men had disappeared from view. Were they all dead, or lying low?

The baying of wolves sounded louder.

Grass rustled and the soldiers arose out of the field as if by magic. Gordon shouted for everyone to put down their arms. Arjan staggered to his feet, raised both hands to show that he was surrendering.

'Don't shoot.'

The soldiers quickly encircled the villagers, a thicket of rifles pointed at them.

'I want all weapons on a pile right here. Move it,' Gordon barked.

Arjan looked around, appeared uncertain what to do. His men lay hidden and weren't about to show themselves.

Gordon shouted another order, but then his voice faltered. He let out a panicked yell. The soldiers lifted their weapons to fire but appeared to freeze.

The air was filled with wolf voices, hundreds of yelps and snarls approaching rapidly. The waving grass came alive with bounding grey shapes: a massive tide that bore down on the soldiers. Several fired at the beasts but most scattered in every direction.

George and Andrew lay still, too afraid to breathe. A huge grey shape leapt at a nearby soldier, sank his teeth into the soldier's arm and brought him down. The wolf let go, dove at another soldier who was fool enough to point his gun at him. He caught the soldier by the throat. Far up the hill the tank disgorged a few missiles, but the diversion had little effect except to enrage the animals. With military precision they formed a ring about the soldiers and closed in tight. A sickly stench of blood and spilled entrails permeated the air. As he watched the slaughter, George felt a disconnected exhilaration at the sight of untameable power set against human technology. No guns or armour could protect anyone who opposed it. Those caught inside the ring were as good as dead.

Andrew cried out, 'They'll kill the bastards. We have to stop them.'

'We can do fuck all,' George said. 'This is bigger than any of us.'

Standing by the window the women watched the wolves rush like a turbulent flood down the street. They'd heard the gunfire. Whenever a shell went off Linella screamed as if she'd been hit. Lina wailed hysterically, convinced that the men were already dead. Then the wolves swept through, their angry jaws bared, ready to take down their prey. Lina's lips moved in a quiet prayer. Placing her hand on Linella's arm she said. 'God be praised. We can only submit to his will.'

Faced by a tsunami, what can you do but wait and watch? There's no high ground to run to. Nothing left to be done. Nature doesn't ask permission before its wave obliterates you.

'We can't stay here,' Linella said. 'We have to help.'

'Out there?' Lina said.

'Yes, out there.'

'You can't help them. We need to wait here, take care of them when they come back.'

Lina's smooth words only stoked Linella's simmering fire. She cried out, 'Fuck it, I'm going to find my kids.'

TWENTY-ONE

Soon after Linella's abrupt departure Scott got up. The Earth trembled as if preparing for a volcanic eruption. He felt that something momentous was about to happen and didn't want to be caught unprepared in bed. Outside the den he found several lupans looking around distractedly, in anticipation of something but unsure how to react. Others, gathered on the hilltop, looked out over the valley. Rami and Zia were probably there. He needed to be with them when the crisis came.

He had barely walked since his vision in the cave, and his legs felt unfamiliar, unwilling to move. Step by step he forced them up the hill. He was halfway there when the first plane roared overhead. Earlier he would have run for cover, but this time he only smiled. Compared to the force the Earth was about to unleash, the fighter planes resembled a boy's plastic toys, about to be crushed by a giant hand.

When the tank began to shell the village, the Earth responded. He felt it shift under his feet, like a sleeping giant stirring to swat a bothersome fly. With a chorus of angry howls the wolves issued from the forest, tore down the hill, then up into the grassy field. Their echoing voices created the impression of hundreds, though in reality there were no more than about thirty. Gunfire erupted with renewed fervour. Some soldiers tried to face down the animals, but they found themselves dragged down. The luckier ones escaped from the meadow and ran for Koppiemaul with wolves snapping at their heels.

This was no computer game where imitation blood was spilled and the dead revived at the click of a button. This blood was real. His people were being torn apart: fools who sleepwalked into their own trap to find themselves pitted against a primal power they could not fight. Rami and Zia stood beside him and took in the massacre, shocked to see their brothers erupt with such violence. The soldiers puzzled them. They hoped that Scott would be able to explain why the soldiers had come and what they wanted. Inside his mind he sensed Zia's presence, looking through his eyes and reading his mind.

– What is this? – She asked.

– They're killing our people – he responded. – It's a disaster for everyone.

– Disaster? When attacked the wolves do what they must. Elder People are family.

He had to find Asra. She commanded the wolves; had ordered them to protect the refugees. She could not possibly know that such a response would result in a counter-attack that would obliterate everyone.

Zia read his thought as if she had authored it.

– Why must you go?

– Because I must.

The lupans found his resolve incomprehensible, but they didn't try to stop him. Barely able to see past his anger, he staggered down the forest path he'd taken a few nights earlier. He was certain that he'd eventually find her, or she would come to him. She knew that he wanted her. No doubt she was out there with the wolves, sinking her teeth into an unfortunate soldier, but she'd be back. He would make her answer for what had happened. He shoved aside birch branches and staggered on, pausing only to catch his breath.

'Asra!' he shouted whenever he stopped. His voice didn't appear to carry farther than the closest trees. He waited for a response but there was none.

He picked up a narrow track that led into a thicket of gangly oak trees interspersed with pines that didn't look familiar; but he continued. The forest felt tense, as if brooding over a hurt. He felt strangely separated from the trees, unable to merge with them as before. The land had been violated. But what about the massacre of the soldiers? Didn't that count for something?

He stumbled into a clearing that contained a half-eaten deer. Clouds of flies hovered over its exposed skeleton and its bloodied head. Death, slaughter – that was the way of the land, of wolves, only it was too real down in the meadow where wolves were killing people as if they were deer. People like himself, who had left home that morning not expecting to be mauled by wild animals.

A muffled howl sounded far away, then another. He heard several other voices, all headed his way, fresh from battle, wolves with bloodied jaws and angry enough to kill him on sight. He would put up a good fight. He'd rather not die, at least not before he confronted Asra, but he'd take what was coming to him. Scott Maguire had already died back in the cave. What would another death mean? He was no more than a container of memories called by some, Maguire. Zia and Rami flitted in and out of him as if his body belonged to them. Sometimes he found himself looking through their eyes. If the wolves ate him, they'd be eating a body with a name.

Their cries grew louder. Before long he made out grey shapes that darted among the trees. Several broke free of the pack and bounded up to sniff him over. The bloodstained jaws and dark patches of human blood on their fur evoked in him an uncontrollable hatred. He kicked at the closest maw; his foot struck the side of the wolf's head. Snarling, the wolf dodged a second swing then dove forward to bite. Scott's shoe struck it in the throat. The wolf drew out of kicking range but a second one leapt at him. Curiously unafraid, Scott waited until the beast was within reach and kicked again. He missed. The wolf withdrew to a safe distance along with the others. They looked too tired to want to bother him any more. He was about give chase when he heard someone behind him take in a deep breath. Asra stood a few paces away, watching him through a curtain of tangled hair. In daylight she appeared ethereal, her wan skin covered in irregular dark patches – a weak and mortal creature without any supernatural aura. She'd been crying, but her clenched fists suggested she could recover her strength in a moment.

Before he could speak she thrust out an arm, the open palm of her hand in a gesture of rejection. 'There is nothing to discuss.'

She stepped closer, her legs and arms moving with a flow reminiscent of a wolf. The fire smouldering in her eyes was ready to burst into a blaze.

'You ordered the pack to attack?'

'Ordered? Yes, you saw order. The way things are, the way things must be. Is that too difficult to understand?'

'You killed people. My people. How dare you!' He struggled to find words to express his horror but his rage stifled him. In any case he didn't have to tell her; she knew how he felt.

'Man, we killed you. The order demands that you must die.'

'You have no right.'

'There's the order. Everything happens because it must.'

'You've just dug your own grave. The people you attacked have the power to destroy you, to burn your forest and kill all the children. They won't forget this slaughter.'

Her golden eyes, so similar to a wolf's, followed him closely but showed no understanding. 'If you attack us, we respond as we must. The pack kills sick wolves that cannot run with it. Those who threaten us die. It's the way things are.'

'Keep your wolves away. God, you have no idea what you've done. The soldiers will be back. They'll find you if they have to burn the entire forest.'

Asra stared back, more interested in his fury than in anything he said. After he paused, she replied. 'You'll burn the forest?'

'I didn't say that.'

'You still don't see it. Long ago, when you were given fire, you turned it against the forest.'

'I did not.'

'You burned it. You'll do it again.'

Her steady look silenced his response. In a perverse sense she was right. He was not separate from his race, those who for millennia had been setting fire to forests. Or those who recently destroyed the Earth's tropical forests and left a changed world, one that barely supported human life. She'd demolish his every attempt to build a barrier between himself and his people.

'Walk with me,' she said. She reached out to take his hand but he drew it away.

'I've said what I came to say. I'm going back.'

She moved swiftly to cut him off. 'Not yet.'

'Oh?'

'There's something you must see.'

He told himself that he didn't need to see anything, but as he turned to go he knew that he could not leave her. A stronger will held him there, not necessarily hers but rather his desire to understand the mystery that she embodied. His sojourn in the cave left him alive but unable to return to his former life – to what people called the real world. He belonged to another, where lupans merged and exchanged personalities, didn't see themselves as separate from rocks or trees, a world he could barely navigate. Certainly not without her help.

'I'll come,' he said.

She nodded at a dark woodland. 'Closer to the heart.' Her bony fingers gripped his hand, scalded him to where he almost pulled it away. He set his teeth, fighting the urge to withdraw. Her hand connected him to a power that moved through the forest, whose breath could lift up or destroy mountains.

'Where are we going?'

She pulled him into a dense stand of fir trees. Shadows closed around them from all directions. 'Will you always be asking questions? What do you see?'

'Trees, trees and more trees.'

'Does moss grow under your feet?'

'I suppose so.'

'Its roots grew long ago, when forest covered every hill, when trees were taller. Touch the moss, and it will speak to you. It has a very long memory.'

He drew away from her. Nothing about Asra was as it appeared. If he wanted to survive as a person and not be annihilated, he would have to resist her. Refuse to cooperate.

Her sharp teeth flashed. 'What do you see?'

She appeared to fall, become indistinct and fade into the shadows. When he looked again he saw the black wolf with a white stripe on its head, jaws open, its small golden eyes studying him. He scanned the undergrowth, thinking his eyes deceived him, or that she'd crouched down to appear like a wolf; but there was only the wolf. He touched the animal's side, felt its short fur. The wolf twisted under his touch, moved away and then collapsed onto its belly among the thick roots of a large oak. Its form melted into the shadows to become a woman again. Not Asra but an old naked woman with withered skin and dried out breasts, sitting cross legged. Thin wispy hair covered her head. A pair of tired eyes studied him. She gasped for breath. Sweat rolled from her brow; she shivered as if she were fighting off a fever.

'Who are you?' he said.

She opened her mouth to reveal only a few brown teeth. 'Don't you know?' she said in a weak voice, Asra's voice.

'What's going on?'

She held out a withered arm for him to take it but he stepped away as if she were offering a snake.

'You want to speak with me?'

All breath left his body. He could only stare at the woman and hope that the nightmare would soon end. 'Tell me who you are.'

'I am the all, everything that lives. I am what is outside you and inside you. I am very old, and very sick. You're one of my creatures, a foolish attempt to embody intelligence. When I was young, the wolf was your partner. You learned from each other, even fed each other. The wolf taught you how to hunt; how to live as a family. It was a beautiful relationship. Something went wrong.'

'What happened?'

The old woman beckoned him, thrust her face close enough for him to smell her rancid breath. Her dry voice whispered, 'A catastrophe.'

'What catastrophe?'

'Don't you remember? You left me?'

'What... what are you talking about?'

'You abandoned me for another.'

'Who?'

'A flock of stupid sheep.'

With a strength that surprised him, she grasped his arm and pressed her withered breasts against his chest. She closed her dry lips against his. The world spun, all light faded and he felt himself falling into darkness.

TWENTY-TWO

They were lying together on a carpet of furs. Moonlight filtering through an opening in the hut's roof shone on her skin, revealing the curve of her breast, her oval face and the dark eyes that had enchanted him for so long. Once unattainable beyond hope, she had given herself to him without reservation. He could feel her beating heart; the pulse of her blood. Her body moved rhythmically with his, driving him to greater heights of ecstasy.

Then it was over. She collapsed by his side exhausted, her head nestled in his shoulder, her sweaty body against his, holding him so tightly that he wondered if she would ever let him go. After a while he felt the cold wind on his back, an uncomfortable reminder of the outside world. Now that he'd won his prize he found himself thinking, what next?

He had been away from Coldhill for two days. With the approach of the southern horde he couldn't stay away much longer. Scouts reported a tide of people, horses, livestock and loaded carts, all headed northward. They set fire to houses, raped women, and stole food supplies. In several days they might be at his doorstep.

Her eyes appeared to follow his thoughts. 'You want to leave?'

'I must. We'll be overrun unless we complete our fortifications. We barely have enough time.'

'Nothing stops the horde. Your wall will not stop them.'

'We must do what we can.'

'Bring your people down here. As you and I are one, so are

our people. No more can we be separated. Here in the forest your people will be safe from the Horde.'

'I don't want to leave you, but I must return to Coldhill. That's where we've built our lives. Our houses, barns, our fields and our sheep are there. I can't abandon them. Won't you come with me? We've ample room for your people. Behind our new wall we'll all be safe.'

'I thank you, but we will not leave the forest. This is where we belong. We're strongest where the power of the Earth sustains us.'

Her head held high, she waited for his reply. He did not know how to respond. He sensed that the real reason behind her refusal was that in Coldhill she would lose her status as leader of her people.

'You come here like a thief,' she said. 'To take what you want. Like a thief you crawl away before dawn. Didn't I give you everything?'

'Would you have me break faith with my family?'

Arising she walked over to the doorway where she stood silhouetted against the silvery night, looking out at the moon. The frosty air made her breath visible, but though she was naked, the cold did not bother her. Her regal bearing left him speechless. Why did he have to leave her so soon? Wasn't there another way that would not mean a final parting? From deep in the forest came several wolf howls. She was listening to them. The calls always awoke in him a deep disquiet. Wolves meant danger to the tribe. Respecting no fences they slaughtered sheep and lambs; even stole away newborn babies. When the wolf howled at night, people reached for firebrands to drive off the beasts.

He threw on his fleece, passed his hands through the arm holes, and then sat down to pull on his skin shoes. All the time he was aware of her disdainful look. Though naked she still maintained a commanding presence.

'If you must leave,' she said, 'won't you stay with me at least until sunrise?'

'I would stay with you for a year.'

'You give conditionally. That is the way of your kind.'

'I'll stay until sunrise.'

She donned a fur coat with the image of the sun painted on the chest; after pulling it tight, she fastened an embroidered belt about her waist and then slipped on two golden arm rings, a necklace of glittering stones and her gold earrings. Only when she'd arranged her jewellery did she acknowledge his presence.

Her head held high she led him to the fire pit, now reduced to a few glowing embers. Everyone had gone inside except for two women on fire duty. They were arguing in loud voices about who should stay on duty. She snapped her fingers to get their attention.

'We'll guard the fire,' she said. 'You can both go inside.'

From a woodpile she drew out a few sticks and stacked them on the coals. In the rising flames he made out a circle of trees with thick sweeping branches. She held her hands over the fire to warm them. Sitting apart from her on a rough bench, he felt cold and alone. Though their bodies had just mingled as one, the distance between then was never greater.

At their first meeting she bewitched him.

Her people's arrival in the forest created a stir on Coldhill. Most nomadic tribes appeared in springtime, stayed for the summer months to hunt deer or to fish and when the food supply dwindled they moved on. Because they rarely infringed on Coldhill, he left them alone. Her people arrived in the middle of winter and brought wolves with them. Either the wolves followed her tribe, or she attracted them with her witchcraft, but no sooner had her people arrived than wolves manifested where there had been none. Each night they killed a sheep or two. After several attacks he marched down to her settlement along with a contingent of armed men to demand that the newcomers leave. If they would not go willingly they'd be forced out. When she emerged from her hut to greet him, he stood as if turned to stone. All strength drained from him, and he forgot why he had come. She ordered benches for the guests, meat and mead. The respect she commanded astonished him as much as her beauty. She spoke his language, which she had learned from his cousins whom she'd met in the north. While they ate she told him that her people had come in search of warmer lands, and would stay for a few summers. 'So that we may grow close to the land.'

After they had eaten, he complained to her about the wolves and of the damage they caused.

'You keep sheep?' Her laugh rang like the clear voice of a bell. 'They're such foolish animals. Why do you keep them?'

'For meat; for their fleece.'

'The forest can give you everything. Look at us. We're well clothed, well fed and well housed.' She nodded at the huts, circular buildings made of skins stretched over a wooden framework. She fingered her glittering necklace. 'Look at the gifts of the land. And you complain about wolves? It's you and your sheep who have caused the conflict; not the wolf.'

'Nevertheless we will keep our sheep. We will protect them.'

'They'll be safe. I give you my word.'

'Do you speak for the wolves?'

'While we're here, no wolf will harm your sheep.'

She spoke with such assurance that he believed her. To question her would be to disrespect her in front of her people.

On the way home his men whispered about him. They saw how the nomadic leader had smitten him. He walked silently in a dream and did not speak to anyone. The following days he found pretexts to visit her and eat meat with her. Always gracious, she set out her best cuts and shared stories with him. She asked him whether any wolf had harmed his sheep; he had to reply that none had.

She soon responded to his invitation to visit Coldhill. One morning his scouts reported the approach of several forest women. She was decked out in jewellery and furs embroidered with sparkling stones. Her companions, following a step behind her, carried gifts of bear pelts. He greeted her halfway up the hill then led her into the settlement. She was curious about the sheep pens, barns, and grain storage bins. Though she smiled graciously at everything she saw, she appeared ill at ease. Perhaps the biting wind discomfited her because she asked an attendant for an extra skin.

'Why are your houses square?' she asked.

'Because that's how houses are built,' he replied, thinking her question strange.

'Such odd shapes, with sharp edges.'

He didn't know how to respond. Bemused, she followed him while he showed her a roof to gather rainwater, the slaughter-houses and the mill. She asked about the encircling wall. Twice the height of a man and made of roughly hewn stones, the wall protected Coldhill on the forest side, the only way to access to the settlement. Against the wall people had piled stacks of tree trunks. He explained to her that on a day when the wind was from the north, they would set fire to the wood. The intense heat from the blaze would melt the rocks, to form a glassy wall that no human might could break. The settlement would be, for ever, safe from attack.

When he asked her what she thought of it, she said, 'It's all wrong. It's not our way.'

'What is your way?'

'The way of life, of living things. Of passion.'

The moment he heard those words, nothing mattered to him except to possess her; take her in his arms, whether or not she was willing.

The wolf voices brought him back from his dreams. She nestled up to him for warmth, her arms wrapped about his waist. An impregnable fortress by day, she was needy by night. He did not know how to start a conversation. They lived such different lives. He could not conceive of abandoning Coldhill and everything he had built to live in the forest with only wolves for company.

They'd been sitting for a while when he noticed several pairs of eyes among the trees. Releasing her hold on him she stood up. 'They're hungry tonight.'

'What does that mean?'

'It's been a hard winter. We must feed them.'

She led him to the kitchen hut where the remains of a butchered deer lay on a table. He helped her gather up several joints and carry them back to the campfire. Soon a large wolf emerged from the forest, padded in a circle around the fire, lifted its head and uttered several howls, each one successively louder. The calls were immediately answered by a chorus of yapping. Three wolves bounded up to her. She stroked their faces and greeted them with a mock wolf howl.

Frozen by fear, he watched her stroke their faces, then put her hand into their open jaws only to pull it out unscathed. Luckily the wolves ignored him. After a while he breathed more easily, seeing that she commanded such respect that no wolf could possibly harm her. She tendered a meat joint to the largest wolf. He tried to tear it away but she uttered a low wolf growl and pulled the joint back. He snatched at it again but then submitted to her and gnawed the meat off while she held it. After he'd had a few bites she chased him off. The next wolf came up for his portion, and then the next. Finally she tossed the remaining chops into the tall grass where smaller wolves fought over them.

'Do you have more meat back there?' he asked.

'No.'

'You gave away your last joint – to feed them?'

'As you saw me.'

'What will your people eat?'

She sat calmly, stroking the side of a great wolf. 'We won't starve. Living in partnership with the wolves, we take care of each other. Tonight was our turn to share our kill with them. The next night, they'll kill an animal for us. It's the way we live.'

'And if the wolves don't feed you?'

'Then, we'll all face hard days. But we'll not face them alone.'

'Those hard days will be here soon. The horde is on its way, and will kill you all.'

'Unlike you, we don't need a wall.'

'What will you do?'

'Look around you. We live with wolves. They're our protectors, as we are theirs. No enemy will dare approach us if they want to live. Many tribes that attacked us did not return home.'

'We don't need wolves. Once our wall is fired, Coldhill will be impregnable.'

'And your people? How will they live inside that wall, unable to leave your home? Surrounded by enemies?'

'As we've always lived.'

He spoke the words easily. He often told his people that with hard work and clear thinking, all obstacles would be overcome. But her words awakened in him a sleeping disquiet. How would his people survive in a sea of enemies?

Well satiated, the wolves crept off into the forest. She piled a few sticks onto the fire. A fresh wind fanned the flames, making them dance madly. As he watched them, he suddenly realized that for the first time in months the wind was blowing from the north.

She sensed his restlessness. 'You want to leave?'

'I must. By dawn, if the wind is still from the north, I must command our people to fire the walls. This may be our last chance before the horde is upon us.'

'I asked for only one thing, that you remain with me until sunrise.' Her eyes grew moist as she tried to hold back her tears. 'One thing only.'

'I can't. If I stay, who knows what will happen to us?'

'You're no leader. The leader of your people is fear. It holds you captive and makes a shadow of you. To think that I gave you my body; that I may one day bear a child to the son of fear? If I'm pregnant, I'll abort that child before it's born. Go back to Coldhill.'

A sob broke from her but she choked it back. She walked back to her hut, her head held high.

Alone he returned through the forest. Now that her spell over him was broken he felt bereaved. He wished their parting had

186

been different, but accepted that what happened had to have happened. Their ways were too different. To survive, he had to rely on his strength, his ingenuity and what he knew to be true. He could not give up everything he'd built to live with wolves, howl like a wolf and rely on them to bring him food. Not even with the most beautiful woman in the world at his side.

At Coldhill he found everyone awake. The men were already laying the kindling beneath the wood stacks. Everyone cheered his return. He'd been away for several days, too long for his wives. He wished he wasn't returning empty-handed but it could not be helped. After a quick breakfast of oats and mutton, he climbed onto the lookout tower. The horde was already halfway across the plain. He could make out men with spears followed by lumbering carts. They had already sighted the settlement on the flat-topped hill, because their largest contingent was heading that way. The wind still blew strongly from the north, bent tree saplings and swept the yellow grass in long waves. Burning the walls might also set fire to the field, but the temporary loss of grazing land could not be helped.

To the sound of loud cheering, he set the first torch to the kindling. Others lit their torches from his fire and stuck them into woodpiles. Smoke poured out, soon followed by small flames. Before long the large tree trunks caught fire and the flames grew tall as houses. A deafening crackle filled the air. The wind fanned the blaze into a gigantic sea of fire. Sparks exploded, rich as stars on a clear night. People stood on their roofs with wet pelts and buckets of water to douse any fire that spread to the houses. So far the wind kept the blaze away. From the lookout tower he watched the fire's progress. The heat grew so intense that it scalded his face, making him turn away. In their pens the sheep bleated painfully. Many were so agitated that they jumped over each other or rammed the pen walls. Their bleating was soon lost in the deafening crackle. The heat had to be already strong enough to melt the walls. He'd seen it happen in their previous settlement where his father directed the firing. As long as the wind didn't change direction, the fire wouldn't harm the village.

Through smoke clouds he saw the fire spread downhill. He'd expected the grassy pastures to scorch, and they did. What he hadn't expected was that sparks carried on the brisk wind would reach outlying trees and set them alight. Before long, an entire line of trees was consumed. Fanned by the strengthening wind the trees became fiery brands that kindled their neighbours. Clouds of sparks showered down on the forest canopy and wherever they landed they gave birth to more fire and smoke. Soon a great wall of flame engulfed the trees as far as he could see. The roar and intense crackling was deafening.

Where was she? In sudden panic he realized that the clearing where she lived was in the path of the advancing fire. It would soon be there, spare no-one who remained. If only she and her people had already left their camp, taking nothing with them. Even if they had, the fiery line moved so rapidly that he feared only deer and wolves could outrun it. A scream rose inside him. His clenched fists pounded the tower; it was all he could do. The thickening smoke prevented him from discerning the fire's extent. He could only wait until the red fury spent its anger.

Later that morning, when the smoky curtain lifted, it revealed a wasteland of glowing ashes, scorched trees and naked hills.

After the heat subsided, the people left their houses to find that the stone wall had melted into a glassy mass, so hot that it scorched the hand. They danced, broke open mead casks and celebrated the fruitful end to a long labour. On all sides he heard cheering from cousins and brothers praising him for his achievement. Their voices sounded like the jabbering of witless animals. Inside him something had died.

He stayed for long enough to kiss his wives and to toast he project's success, after which he left the hill. Alone he had to search for her in the wasteland of ashes and smoking embers. He walked slowly and with a heavy heart. Upon reaching her encampment he found half burnt wooden skeletons of the huts.

Thankfully no human remains. In trepidation he continued his search. Farther in the forest he came upon several burned bodies, so disfigured he could not tell if they were male or female. At nightfall he found the charred body of a woman who wore two golden rings on her arms. Three blackened wolves lay around her. They'd been trapped in a hollow where they had taken refuge.

He removed the golden rings. Lifting up his hands to the sky he cried out in anguish. After the echoes of his voice died away he noticed that the deepest silence permeated the air. No birds, animals or human voices responded to his cries. None ever would.

TWENTY-THREE

When she arrived in the meadow, Linella's gaze was immediately drawn to the wolves. Perched on rocks and hillocks the grey beasts scanned the grass, their muscular bodies ready to obliterate anyone who stirred threateningly. She was barely able to move her shaking legs forward. A line of wolves guarded the track below the tank; snapped at any soldier who tried to escape that way.

Bodies lay everywhere, soldiers and refugees side by side. To her left a kneeling man with a mangled hand tried to stand up and then collapsed in agony; another with a trouser leg soaked in blood was trying to crawl. She soon found George and Andrew, running through the grass and carrying boxes of what looked like medical supplies. At the sight of them she erupted into tears.

A few feet away Eisa knelt over Elijah and squeezed his upper arm to cut off a stream of blood gushing from his wrist.

He yelled to her. 'Your bra.'

Without thinking she tore off her top and ripped the bra from her breasts. Eisa slipped it around Elijah's arm and worked it into a tourniquet. 'The army must take away their wounded. I can't handle them all.'

'What do you want me to do?'

'Go up to the tank and get some help.'

'What about the wolves?'

'Kick them. Kick them if they get in your way. You've got to go. You're the only one who might get through.'

Two soldiers were trying to crawl toward the track only to find a wolf staring them down. The soldier with the gnawed off hand tried to stand up again but the pain was too great. He cried out painfully. She grabbed a couple of bandages, stepped toward him.

'You've no time for that,' Eisa said. 'You have to go.'

A cold horror arose in her along with a feeling of futility.

Squeezing her hand, Josh awoke her from her torpor. 'Mum, don't go. They'll kill you.'

The soldier was looking up at her with a pleading look. His fair-skinned face still had remnants of teenage acne on his chin; he couldn't be much older than Andrew. She pulled her hand free from Josh. 'George, take care of that man. I have to get past the wolves. It has to be me.'

'Mum!' Josh screamed.

'Wait here. I'll be back. Don't worry.'

Andrew picked up a fallen rifle. 'I'm coming,'

'Not with that gun you're not.'

'You're not going alone.'

'I know how to handle wolves. You don't.'

'Mum, you'll get shot,' Josh pleaded.

'You have to trust me. I know what I'm doing.'

Andrew took a deep breath. 'I'm coming with you, Mum.'

'No you're not.'

Andrew's firm look told her that he had made up his mind. She didn't have time to argue. Of all the kids he had the steadiest nerves. Besides, she could use his support.

She nodded to him. 'Okay. But put down that fucking gun.'

Andrew handed the gun to Josh who took it gingerly, as if unsure of which end to point. Andrew pulled out a switchblade. 'I've got this.'

'Keep it handy, but you won't need it. Josh, you stay with George.' Seeing Josh's distressed look she added, 'We'll be fine. The wolves know me.'

She quickly picked out Alpha Male. Larger and more muscular than the others, he stood on a small rise from where he surveyed the field. Before any wolf moved it always glanced to him for approval. 'That way. Walk steadily. Just don't show him you're afraid.'

She had approached wolves many times, but not when they were possessed by such bloodlust. Were they so rabid that they'd attack her? They might. To calm her nerves she breathed with deliberation, her eyes fixed on Alpha Male. Beside her, Andrew looked as relaxed as if on a Sunday hike. Either he didn't understand the situation, or his bravado masked his fear.

The wolf fixed her with his gaze. His large paws clenched the ground. The leg muscles bulging from his sides testified to a power that could crush her instantly. Emitting a low growl he warned her not to come closer. She walked on; she had to, her head held low so he wouldn't regard her as a threat. When she reached him, he sniffed her over then circled her. Fire smouldered in his eyes; froth dripped from his jaw. She squeezed Andrew's hand so tightly that he protested, 'Mum. I'm all right.' Tears welled up in her eyes, but she kept them back. This was not the time to show weakness.

The wolf's growl intensified. She screamed, 'Get out of the way.' Like a tangible force his will wrestled with hers, trying to push her back, but she stood her ground. Unexpectedly he gave way, grudgingly, and moved aside to let them walk on. His angry glare was fixed on her back. Two wolves followed several feet behind, either to check that she and Andrew didn't stray or to protect them from soldiers. She shouted back at her escorts, 'Go back. Go!' For all the effect her words had, she might as well have been shouting at the wind.

When they reached the tank they found a line of soldiers, rifles in hand. *Stupid fools.* A single shot would send the escorts into an uncontrollable rage in which they'd maul anyone in sight. Already they crouched low, growling menacingly. Holding Andrew's hand for support she found it strong, with barely a tremor unless from excitement.

'Don't shoot,' she shouted. 'Put down the guns.'

The men looked quizzically to their commander, standing

behind them. With a flick of his finger he made them lower their weapons.

'They'll spring if you fire.'

'Talk fast,' Gordon said in a low voice that didn't conceal his anger.

'You need to rescue your men.'

'What do you mean?'

'Those boys are wounded. They're bleeding to death.'

Gordon's face remained solid as a rock. 'We'll get them soon. Once we have air support.'

'They won't last that long. Look, I can handle the wolves. Give me four men and I'll bring your wounded up here.'

Gordon raised his brows. Another time he might have ignored her but he was too shattered to argue. Nothing in his training had prepared him for an attack by rabid wolves.

He nodded to the soldiers next to him. 'You four.'

'They're to come unarmed.'

Gordon shook his head. 'Can't do. They take their weapons.'

'You've no idea what you're up against. They have to go unarmed.'

'They can't do that.'

'Miss Linella, we'll help you,' shouted a voice from behind the soldiers. Roberto stood there along with several Corsican men.

'Let my friends through.'

Roberto swaggered forward. 'It's all right. I'm a veteran. I've done this sort of thing before. We'll bring your wounded.'

Gordon scowled. 'Move fast. Once the helicopters come, I can't answer for your safety.'

'Then call them off,' Linella said. 'We're bringing you your men.'

'I'll do my best.'

Do my best, she muttered while she led the Corsicans down to the meadow. Gordon was scared; he couldn't be rational after the wolf attack. Was he crazy enough to place her in danger while she rescued his men? In the heat of battle people did insane things.

Her wolf escorts had vanished. There was no sign of other wolves in the field either but she still felt their presence. At the first sign of trouble they'd be back.

Eisa eyed her helpers suspiciously. 'We've no spare stretchers. We need them for our men.'

'No problem,' Roberto said. 'We know how to move people.'

Two Corsicans lifted the man with the severed hand. Others supported those who could almost walk, whom they could easily carry, but the most critically wounded were left for the promised helicopters. Luckily the soldiers on the hill, surmising that wolves were no longer an immediate threat, abandoned their protected position and marched down to help.

She was dragging a wounded man uphill when two helicopters swooped down on the field, gun barrels extended. A cold sweat broke from her. Here was the army come to machine-gun the wolves from the air. She couldn't run, not when the soldier she carried weighed on her. Around her everyone dove into the grass. The Corsicans also mysteriously disappeared. Skimming twenty feet above the ground the helicopters circled the field. A sudden burst of gunfire kicked up a cloud of dust in the field. 'Call them off!' she yelled at the tank. 'There are children down there.' Her voice was lost in the helicopters' clatter.

Her heart hammering and scarcely able to see, she struggled up the track. She could not drop her load or take cover; she had to hope the helicopters would recognize she was carrying one of their own.

When she reached the tank she found Gordon there with Andrew. Gordon nodded at her. 'It's all right. They'll hold their fire.'

Her legs felt suddenly too weak to support her. She staggered, caught hold of the tank but ended up splayed on its metal surface. Andrew stepped up. 'Mum, let me take you home.'

'Where are the others?'

George and Josh popped into view. 'We're all okay.'

But nothing was okay. Following the assault the world had changed. Not only soldiers and refugees had died, but a dream had died. Now the refugees would be bundled away, their village razed. The forest would be burned. As for the wolf-children? Thinking about them filled her with panic.

'I want to go home now,' she said.

The cottage wouldn't be safe, but then nowhere was safe. She needed to be close to her kitchen and her table where she was in control.

Leaning on George, she put one foot in front of the other and let him lead her away from the tank, the field and its bloodied grass.

They entered the cottage. Andrew ran to the living room and turned on the wall-screen. Linella collapsed on the couch; stared at the flickering images. Always faithful, her collie snuggled close to her, wanting to be stroked. The Koppiemaul attack was on every channel with footage of snapping wolves played over and over again. The camera swivelled to a well-dressed commentator who interviewed a clean-cut expert on 'the lupan problem.' The expert spouted off that the troubles with lupans had gone far enough. Something needed to be done. 'I am deeply sympathetic to any mother who gives birth to a lupan; however, biologically, lupans are not people – *homo sapiens*. They're not capable of human emotions or intelligence. They must be contained; destroyed if necessary.'

Pictures of soldiers who had been killed flashed by, along with family shots. An opposition politician, standing behind his lectern in the Scottish Assembly said, 'This tragedy happened because the President has soft-pedalled the refugee issue. Every day a thousand more refugees pour into the country. In the face of this disaster, the President has no option but to resign.'

'This is so stupid,' Josh cried out. 'The wolfies had nothing to do with this attack.'

'Try telling him that,' Linella said, lying with her eyes closed. The high-pitched voices coming from the screen said everything.

Once a refuge for illegals, Koppiemaul was in the path of the storm.

She was shivering as if working up a fever. Her heart was about to burst. What's happened to me? Am I about to die? She looked at her familiar walls, the pillar candles in the picture window, the bookcase jammed with fifty-year-old cookbooks and vases of fresh-cut flowers. This was her place. Through the archway was the tiled floor of the kitchen, the stove and the antique oak table where so many stories had come together.

Harsh voices from the outside world invaded her living room. People holding placards that read, 'Scotland for the Scots' screamed that the government was sitting on its arse, and had allowed refugees and lupans to walk all over them. 'They're killing our sons and daughters!' screamed a white-haired woman.

'There'll be no wolf-people in my house after I'm dead,' said a man loaded with shopping bags. 'My dad and his dad worked to make a life for me, not for lupans.'

She could hardly listen through her tears. *You're killing my children, my sons and daughters. You are the murderers. Nobody will touch my children.*

'Shut off that noise,' she said.

'Mum, we need to know what's going on,' George said.

'Watch it on wrist-com. Bring me my phone.'

In her nervousness, she misdialled Johnson's number three times before she reached his voice message. He was probably stationed with his military boys, and overseeing the attack on Koppiemaul. But he'd check his messages. She stammered into the phone, 'You bastards have really made a mess of things. I want you to call me. There's something you need to know.' She threw the phone across the living room. It smashed against the wall. The dial flew off in pieces, but she didn't care. For several minutes she could only feel rage and a sense of violation. Sure, Johnson told her the army was coming, but they had shelled the village, destroyed orchards and terrorized women. No wonder the wolves attacked to protect the village, and the lupans. They'd do it again. Johnson and his gang were so thick-skulled they believed their firepower could solve every problem.

'Mum, can I get you a drink?' Josh stood in front of her, a worried look on his face.

'Water.'

He sat beside her while she sipped the water. He looked shattered. Since coming home he had been on the verge of tears. He'd seen one horror too many. Across the room Andrew sat like a statue. He had the cold look of a soldier trained to kill when necessary. Since morning he appeared to have grown taller. His determined expression told her that he wanted to go back to the village to be with the men.

Andrew cleared his throat. 'What do you want to do now?'

'Wait a minute. I need to catch my breath.'

From the kitchen came sounds of George moving about and cooking something. Remarkably he was taking care of them. Usually he was lying on the couch and shooting aliens. He wouldn't be shooting aliens any more now that he'd stood shoulder to shoulder with Andrew and the village men, and tended the critically wounded. She wasn't ready for this day. She had never wanted the boys to hold a gun, but keeping guns away from them had made no difference. War had come to their doorstep, a conflict which, like all others, would solve nothing.

'I need to stay here for a few days. I'm not ready to abandon our home.'

Andrew let out a sigh. 'Mum, there's a war going on. The guys down at the village need me and George. That's where we belong.'

'There's nothing for me to do down there. I have to wait here in case Johnson calls.'

'Yeah, Johnson will help us.' Andrew didn't try to hide his sarcasm.

'Any better suggestion? How about President Christie? Do you have his phone number? Hello Mr. President, I am totally shocked that your army shelled my house! Try that.'

'What are you saying?'

'I've asked Johnson to come here. I have to talk him out of another attack. There's a chance that he'll listen.'

Andrew looked away.

'Stay with me. At least a day or two.'

'Sure Mum, we'll take care of you,' George's voice sounded from the kitchen door. 'We've enough ammo to hold off the buggers.'

'We'll all be safer down in the village,' Andrew said.

'There are no safe places. Up here at least we're out of the line of fire.'

Andrew frowned. 'I still think this is a time for everyone to stick together. Anyone who can carry a gun should be in the village. I want to go.'

'I do too, but I know in my soul that, in the long run, we're needed here. Can you trust me on that one?'

Andrew shrugged. 'Sure, Mum.'

'Pasta anyone?' George held out a couple of steaming bowls.

Josh jumped up to help. He at any rate was relieved not to have to abandon the cottage to the winds. Andrew turned on the wall-screen and began to rapidly flip through channels. When Josh brought him a bowl of pasta he turned it away, saying, 'You eat it.'

TWENTY-FOUR

The following morning Linella set off for the colony. During the night she worried about Scott. Since the army's attack a lot could have changed on the hill. The lupans might have run off into the forest, taking Scott with them, or his mind might have wandered off into the netherworld. Any number of things. He needed to be taken away from the lupans and their influence. Once in her cottage environment he would find himself. If Rami wanted to keep Scott up on the hill, she was ready to do battle with him. This time she wouldn't stand aside.

Josh insisted on going with her. Even as a child he had a better understanding of lupans than Andrew or George. He still liked to visit the colony and watch lupans at work; occasionally he dug over a garden bed side by side with them, but that morning he was coming to keep an eye on her. Aware of her impulsive nature, he didn't trust her not to abruptly decide to stay there.

They found Scott's bed empty. He wasn't in the nearby dens either. The lupans all appeared too bewildered to articulate any response to her questioning, other than in their incomprehensible clicks. Zia and Rami had to know what had happened to him but they were nowhere to be seen.

'Run up the hill and look around,' she told Josh.

'What's he like?'

'He's a man. Walks with a limp. Any bearded man with wild eyes will do.'

A futile search through more dens revealed that the hill was partially deserted. The males had all disappeared. Several female lupans were hauling baskets of vegetables from a den onto a small cart. Moving with an uncharacteristic haste they hardly looked at Linella when she whistled at them. She stopped a young female, no older than fifteen, walking down the hill with a basket of potatoes on her head.

'The Man?' Linella asked her in a heated voice. 'Where is he?'

'Man' was a word most lupans understood but the girl returned a blank stare. Perhaps she knew Scott's whereabouts, but didn't know how to respond.

'Where's Rami?'

The question flustered the lupan to where she almost dropped her load. Linella decided not to bother her further. Josh returned from the hilltop with no news about Scott, but reported that all male lupans were down in the quarry. When they arrived there they found Rami and several others splitting a stone from an outcrop.

Rami looked thoughtfully into the distance while she told him about Scott's disappearance.

'You have to find him.' she shouted, hoping that her loud voice would put a fire under Rami. 'He might be stuck in the woods with a broken leg, bleeding to death!'

He stroked her shoulder, to try and calm her, but otherwise wasn't moved by her outburst.

Rami's reassuring looks did nothing to quell her anxiety, but she realized she could do no more unless she wanted to single-handedly comb the forest. Besides, she had to be in her cottage in case Johnson called.

She returned home, grabbed her worn broom and embarked on housecleaning. She jerked the broom under the kitchen table and threw the chairs about, but she couldn't stop thinking about Scott. They'd been together for only several days, not long enough to know anything about each other, yet his presence dominated her thoughts. Since his drug experience something mysterious had awakened in him, something she'd thirsted for all her life.

Not religion. She hadn't been to church since she was ten. Her table was her church, the people who shared it and her children, the congregation. She accepted that life was mysterious; that she'd never know if life after death was real. Yet she knew beyond all rational counter-arguments that the supernatural world existed.

She had first encountered it thirty years earlier, on the night she and the newborn Asra first encountered the wolves. Sitting on a log she had clutched the baby to her breast, determined to protect it from the encircling beasts.

A large shadow left the forest eaves and padded up to her. The bright eyes fixed on her. The wolf's pendulous abdomen told her that this was a lactating nurse. Her arms tensed and drew the baby close to her chest, but the tighter she pulled, the more the baby squirmed. Asra cried out in a voice resembling a wolf's howl, adding her characteristic clicks. The nurse halted a few feet from Linella and walked around her. *Please God, don't harm the child.* She tried to breathe but air suffocated inside her. The wolf's warm rancid breath played on her neck. She examined her from behind, came around to her front, poked her nuzzle into her chest and let out a warning growl.

She wanted the baby.

Linella gave her the baby. A power she did not understand forced her to hold out the baby so that it could latch onto the wolf's teats, and feed there. It suppressed her instinct to protect the baby from harm. Despite all rational thoughts, she knew that the baby would be safe. And it was.

Often when she looked into the children's golden eyes she felt the presence of something beautiful that she couldn't put into words, an overwhelming peace that surpassed all human attempts to mimic it: the same mystery that she had encountered, the night with the wolves. It was often there when she sat close to Scott, listening to his rambling. She'd find herself attentive to him, even if she couldn't follow his labyrinthine thoughts, and not notice the passing of time.

Perhaps he represented a new hope; an end to her loneliness. What if he had been mauled by angry wolves? Surely Rami and Zia cared enough about Scott that they wouldn't allow that to happen. Still, he might have wandered off into the forest, his mind unhinged, unable to find the way back. She grew so anxious that she put on her boots, resolved to search the forest single-handedly. Then she recalled that she had to wait for Johnson in the cottage. It was where she belonged.

Every hour a plane roared overhead. Higher up against the clouds, small surveillance drones circled like vultures and evoked the feeling of an impending attack. The tank hadn't moved from its post at the head of the track but a dim light that shone from its hatch showed that it was occupied. Soldiers guarded it at all times. Let them march in circles around it day and night, as long as they weren't shooting anyone.

George and Andrew were away in the Corsican camp, but they promised to return if anyone drove up to the cottage. They lived in a world of guns and conflict, guy stuff she never wanted to know about. She wondered what she had in common with them. Was she no more than the mother who had brought them into the world? Now no longer relevant? They'd turned out differently to how she imagined or wanted. At dinner-time they ate quietly, not saying much. Since the attack, their faces looked hard. Implacable. Though she'd stewed coq au vin for them, using her last bottle of English wine, the speed with which they shovelled the dish away told her that they'd as soon snack on corned beef.

'What's happening with Roberto's family?' she asked, trying to break the silence.

'They're all right,' Andrew said.

'Just, all right?'

'Mum, you've got to stop worrying about us. We can take care of ourselves.'

A loud tap at the window made Linella sit up in her bed. Her darkest fear awoke that bounders had returned in greater numbers. This time she was finished. She was about to cry out to Andrew and George when she heard a familiar voice say, 'Linella?'

It was Scott.

He was leaning on the windowsill, his face pale, a large bruise on one cheek, his arms scored by briars and his shirt torn open. Despite the mild night he shivered from the cold.

She flung open the window. 'Are you okay?'

He nodded slowly.

'Come to the back door.'

She unlocked it. He staggered into the kitchen; slumped into a chair. His hair and beard were entwined with sticks and leaves. Leaning back limp, he let his arms dangle lifelessly. He was panting as if he'd run all the way from the forest. Perhaps he had.

'Thank God you're here,' he said when he was able to speak.

'You're all bruised. Let me clean you up.'

'It can wait.'

His intense look made her feel awkward. Gone was the erratic shifting of his eyes and the lack of focus that had so worried her. He was studying her with the gaze of a lupan, not missing a single detail.

'I was so worried about you,' she said. 'I went looking for you.'

'I know.'

'Where have you been?'

'Wait a minute. Do you have some coffee? I'm about to fall asleep.'

She loaded an espresso pot with chicory-coffee and set it on the stove, all the time aware that he followed her every move.

'You startled me at the window.'

'Sorry about that. I came because I need your help. It'll take a while to explain.'

The coffee pot began to bubble. She shifted it to the cool part of the plate.

'Where do I start? The day the army attacked,' he said. 'When the wolves came out to defend us. I went looking for Asra. She controls the pack. Is the only one who can stop the slaughter. I found her, too late to make any difference. She and her wolves were already returning from the field.'

Scott related his meeting with Asra. She'd told him that the wolves' attack was inevitable, part of the order of things. He tried to recall her exact words. How much should he tell Linella? Intensely domestic, she was not subject to mystical flights. If he told her that in the space of a few minutes, he had lived the entire life of another man from a vanished age, she'd dismiss him as crazy. But he had to say something about Coldhill, about the fire that had destroyed the forest, along with the woman he loved and her wolves. Linella had to know the tragic events that happened long ago and how those events changed the course of human history.

'She told me a story of something that happened in that forest long ago.'

Linella sat opposite him, her head propped up on her hands, listening closely.

He related the story the way he had seen it unfold, only in third person: how the man and woman met, of their passion and their parting, his return to Coldhill, the approaching horde, and finally about the fire that destroyed the forest.

She poured him coffee and then set out a few stale biscuits. The wild look in his eyes troubled her. What was he going through? Another nightmare that he was somehow persuaded was real?

'Did Asra make up that story?'

'Let me finish. Fire destroyed the world, but it didn't stop the horde. Our wall was able to hold them off. For a short while. The woman with the wolves told me that Coldhill couldn't survive a long siege, and it didn't. We had to abandon it. The horde was a horrible sight; thousands of starving people eating the bark off the trees. We ended up in the wasteland, among the ashes, with no living animal except for a few sheep. Things would have been different if we had joined her people, and the wolves. The forest would have been our home and not a field of ashes. We wouldn't have lost our understanding with the wolf. That's what changed us deeply. We became adversaries; have been ever since. The old partnership died. Since then we've imposed our will on the land, burned it to suit us, threw it aside like a whore we've paid and no longer want. Am I making sense?'

'I think so.'

He stopped, realizing he was narrating in first person. If she thought he was crazy so be it. 'That same story is playing out today. It's not something I can explain to you. Not rationally. Human behaviour is the same, no matter the country or place. If the army destroys this colony, another army will be doing the same in the States, another one in China and so on. There are no isolated incidents. What we do here, we do everywhere, because we are all one people, with one nature. That's what happened long ago when the forests were burned. It didn't only happen at Coldhill. It happened everywhere.'

'It must have been terrible.'

'Yes. The worst part of the story is about me. I was the man who started it.'

'What do you mean?'

'I was there. I lit the fire.' He closed his eyes, winced as if feeling a wave of pain. The air in the kitchen tingled as if an electric storm was about to break. It became so tense that she struggled to respond.

'You lived long ago? Is this like reincarnation?'

'No it's not. I don't know how to explain it to you but it is real. Personality is a fuzzy thing. I'm convinced it is an illusion. Often I can't tell what separates you or me; me, and that man who lived long ago. You and the woman?'

'I was that woman? I'm not understanding.'

'It's difficult.'

When he awoke to find himself alone in the forest, he

wondered who the unnamed woman really was. The vision faded so quickly that her features shifted and moved, depending on the woman he thought about. At first he saw Asra. The deep lines in the wolf woman's face and her dark hair had the primordial quality of Asra. Hadn't she also told him that he – Scott – had left her for another long ago? But then the woman's face changed. At first he saw Sandria, but then he recognized Linella's features, the sweep of her long hair and the fire in her eyes. Looking at him across the table, she slipped from her own form into that of the unknown woman. Back again.

Linella sat as if in shock, not knowing what to make of him. 'You have to help me understand.'

'It makes sense, at least to a lupan. Lupans see things differently. Imagine what it feels to actually be someone else – to be so lost that you don't know if you're you, if you're me, or that post holding up the roof? I know what it's like because I've been dragged through hell, a place so painful that I lost myself. Except for a bundle of memories, all sense of who I am was stripped from me. Lupans aren't attached to this or that body. Not even their names mean anything. They make them up and change them when they feel like it. Their egos are so diffuse that they can merge with each other; lose themselves in another. When lupans decide to do something, they all decide together. They can work as one person. They don't experience time the way we do. For them, there's no reason why you couldn't be a woman who lived long ago.'

'That's fine, but I'm not a lupan.'

'I'm not either, but I know their mind. It's a terrible place for anyone to experience.'

'Yes, I have to wonder, or…'

'If I'm crazy? I'm not. What I'm trying to explain is that our common experience, of being separate individuals, is an illusion. The lupans don't see it that way, and they're right.'

'Scott, I'm having a hard time with all this. I'm not you, or Rami or Lina. Thank God I'm not. What am I missing?'

'Long ago we were different; more like lupans than the way we are today. When we burned the forest, something fundamental in us changed. For the first time we felt alone; separated from nature. Having lost our partnership with the land we were compelled to conquer it. Subdue it, exploit it or die. We developed as individuals, people alienated from each other and who compete with each other for scarce resources. It made us capable of killing each other. Since then it's been a long and lonely journey, a journey that brought us here, to the brink of our own destruction.'

She was following him. Her eyes showed that finally she understood, or that at least she wanted to.

'We must stop the next attack. It must not happen,' he said.

'What do you want me to do?'

'It there anyone who can stop it?'

'There's Brigadier Johnson. I've been trying to reach him for days but I'm not sure he wants to help. People want blood. Ten soldiers were mauled to death; dozens bitten. People want justice. They won't stop until the lupan colony is burned and all our children dead. Even if we stopped the army, irregulars would come out and finish the job.'

'They aren't here yet.'

'They will be.'

'There's a lot at stake. The survival of the human race.'

'Scott, I can't think about it, not when I have attack-drones circling overhead. What can you or I do? All I have is you, the boys and the people down in the village. Also Rami, Zia and the children. If I stop to think for a minute about the human race, that everyone's going to die of the Plague, or starve to death, I'd be so paralyzed that I couldn't take a step. I can't do anything about millions of starving people. I can't stop the hatred on Union Street. All I can think of is the people around me. My relationships.'

'You're not alone. The lupans are closer to you than you know. They've become part of me. I feel them inside me, their warmth and their presence. It's something beautiful. If they die, then I die.

It's that simple. I wish you could see it – but I can't take you there. It's a very painful road to walk.'

They had been sitting in silence for a few minutes before Linella noticed that Josh was standing in the doorway. He looked as if he had been there for a while listening into their conversation.

'Mum, there's a new car over by the tank.'

'Another one?'

'I think it's Johnson's. I figured you'd want to know.'

TWENTY-FIVE

Johnson arrived soon after sunrise. He noticed that the cottage's kitchen lights were on; Linella often rose early and might already be about, but hopefully, with the army's constant coming and going, she hadn't noticed his truck drive by. After parking next to the tank, he checked his machine-gun and spare magazine. Slowly he swung his legs out of the car. The extra weight of his armoured jacket made him stagger. Leaning on the car he breathed slowly to recover his strength. The swelling under his chin felt raw, a constant reminder that he was on borrowed time. This might be his last mission before the disease claimed him. He waited. The surveillance helicopter he expected had just appeared from behind the forest, and moved in to sweep the field for wolves, snipers and other surprises.

A cloud of drones circled above him like swallows gathering to migrate, but they were more a deterrent than an attack force. Once he set foot in the field he'd be on his own. Minutes went by. He listened to his breathing, grateful that his body was still alive; resentful that his time would be up sooner than he wanted. Finally he heard the pilot's rasping voice in his earpiece, 'You have an all clear.'

'Any animals?'

'Negative.'

'You're too close. Withdraw 2-k to the north and maintain position.'

He waited until the helicopter drifted out of sight and then he crept down the track, scanning the long grass and ready to shoot anything that moved. Wolves blended into the grass; aerial recon could have missed one or two. You wouldn't know for certain until it leapt for your throat. Footage of the wolves' attack was still raw in his mind. Each time the grass rustled he swung around, his finger on the trigger. Nothing would please him more than to gun down a brute or two.

His superiors hadn't wanted him to come alone, but he convinced them that this was the last chance to secure the refugees' co-operation, and avoid more casualties. Before the next military operation he needed to find out if the refugees were really sitting on a cure for the Plague. If so, extract the details. Aware of his infection, the bosses suggested other people for the mission, but he convinced them that he had to go. This mission was personal.

Not far from the track several lupans were excavating a hole. How they resembled spiders, with their bony bodies and stringy hair. As their picks swung to and fro, soil spilled out of the hole as if a large mole was at work. Nearby lay a four-foot long stone, propped up on wooden poles, waiting to be inserted. He held his rifle ready. Lupans rarely attacked people, but following the assault they might be capable of anything. However, they didn't even glance in his direction.

He headed toward the remains of an orchard: a mass of craters and splintered trees. Thirty years of toil and growth obliterated in a split second. Why had Gordon brought the tank when he'd been warned of the disastrous consequences? Because, as always, Gordon was determined to do it his way.

The refugees kept a good lookout because, by the time he reached the orchard, a line of armed men assembled on the path to block his advance. He slung his gun over his shoulder and raised both hands, signalling that he wanted to talk. The nervous way they pointed their guns at him, told him that they'd as soon shoot him to get even for the attack. Oddly, he didn't care if they did.

A lean man in a white tunic stepped forward, his automatic rifle pointed at Johnson's chest. Johnson guessed that this was Almagheri, the refugees' self-styled leader.

'I'm Brigadier Brian Johnson,' he said. 'Can we put down our guns and talk?'

Arjan scarcely moved. 'What do you want?'

'I'm alone. You've nothing to be afraid of.'

The gun barrels shifted away. Johnson took several laboured breaths; broke into a wheeze. His chest tightened as if a metal band was squeezing it.

'Are you infected?' Arjan said.

'Yes, I am.' He waited to catch his breath. 'I'm looking for a doctor, Eisa Habash. I want to talk to him.'

'What about?'

'Maybe I want him to treat me. He knows who I am. Can you call him over?'

Arjan raised his wrist-com to his lips. 'Eisa – where are you? Come to the apricot orchard. We have a soldier, Brigadier Johnson, who wants to talk to you. I think he's infected.'

Johnson sat down on a flat rock, laid the machine-gun against his feet and closed his eyes. Lately he'd been sleeping sixteen hours a day; he could drop off at any moment. How much longer did he have? Much depended on what happened next. If there really was a cure. If he could pry it loose.

A few minutes later a lanky man in jeans and a ragged t-shirt popped into view. His long grey hair was tied in a pony tail; his nervous demeanour and intellectual eyes suggested an idealistic type with no military training and who kept his cards in full view. He should be easy to handle. Eisa nodded for Johnson to speak.

'We need to talk. In private,' Johnson said.

'I don't want you in the village, infecting us.'

'Very well, we'll talk here.' With one foot he slid his machine-gun toward Eisa. 'Add my gun to your arsenal. Ask your friends to give us some space?'

'What you say can be said in front of everybody.'

'This is personal. Just give us fifty feet, so that you and I may have a private conversation.'

'Arjan, can you and the guys back off a bit?' Eisa said.

'You sure about this?'

'I think we're okay.'

'Fine, but we'll be watching.'

Arjan collected Johnson's gun and retreated with the men to the crest of a small hill. Johnson pointed to a space on the ground. 'We might be here a while. I suggest you sit down and make yourself comfortable.'

Eisa remained standing. He looked away as if afraid to meet Johnson's eyes. 'What's this all about?'

'I'm here for two reasons. One has to do with the disaster that happened in this field. We lost some good men. So did you. There's no way to bring back the dead. To repair what happened.'

'I appreciate the sympathy. But we were attacked.'

'I'm not here to discuss who fired first. What happened was a tragedy that must not happen again.'

'Your call.'

Johnson took several deep breaths.

'Can we work on it together, to make sure that no one else dies?'

'You want us to walk away from here like sheep?'

Johnson shook his head. 'Never said that. I want to find a way for you to be able to live here for as long as you want. But I need your help. As you see, I'm infected. I don't have long to live.'

'I'm sorry to see that. I can do nothing for you.'

'Maybe you can, and not only for me. I suspect that you have a cure for the Plague; that you've known about it for a long time.'

Eisa looked away, an obvious attempt to conceal his thoughts. Johnson smiled to himself, knowing that he'd scored.

'What are you talking about?' Eisa said.

'Don't try my patience, doctor. I don't have time for your denials. We'll start with Linclla Sienkiewicz. She told me about your discovery.'

212

'Did she?'

'Everything.'

'How interesting.'

'What are you hiding?'

'I'm not hiding anything?'

'You're hiding a cure that involves daily contact with the lupans. I'd like to discuss that cure with you now.'

Eisa forced a laugh. 'Linella's crazy. I don't know where she gets her ideas.'

'You don't understand the seriousness of your situation, doctor. You have a village of illegal refugees, people who need your help badly. This is your only chance to avert some planned air-strikes. We can come to an arrangement, so that you can stay here.'

'You want to broker a deal?'

'You don't have a choice but to hear me out. People on the street are boiling over. They want you and your lupans wiped out. Eliminated. They don't care how. If we bombed you all out of existence, there would be very few tears shed. That's the present reality. Luckily for you, you have one last chance to save yourselves. If you happened to come up with a cure for the Plague, your situation could change. Dramatically change. The government would get off your back and forget that you're here illegally. We'd even provide you with protection from irregular paramilitaries.'

'And the lupans? What about them?'

Johnson let out a dry laugh. 'We can't save them. No one can. Too much happened in this field. The lupans and their wolves will have to pay the price. I wouldn't be too concerned for them.'

Eisa hesitated before replying. He'd known that one day when the situation became critical, his information might secure the refugees' safety. That day had come. He would have to choose between his family and the lupans. While Johnson waited for him to speak, Eisa thought of Sharma; of her large golden eyes. He'd tried to forget her but whenever he saw a lupan he wondered what Sharma might look like had she lived. What their relationship might be. Younger than Zia, she had lighter skin; fair hair untypical for a lupan. She'd even begun to babble like a human baby. The dream of growing close to her died, ended by a gunshot from a moving pickup.

'You don't know what you're asking,' Eisa said.

'Cooperate and everyone wins. What's there to decide?'

'There's a lot more at stake than you can imagine.'

'We can come to an agreement. How long are you going to wait while people die of Plague?'

'I need an official commitment that our village will be kept safe. Protected by the government.'

'You have it.'

'Where?'

'You want me to write it down? Get me a piece of paper and I'll put it in writing.'

'You?'

'There's no one else here. I'm not trying to cheat you. I've been given full authority to negotiate with you. I won't promise what I can't deliver.'

'I want the lupan colony included. For it to be protected along with our village, and for the government to keep their hands off the lupans.'

'You want me to guarantee that some bounders won't set fire to the colony?'

'You know what I'm talking about.'

Johnson shook his head. 'As I said, I deal only with humans. Don't get me wrong, I'd like to protect the lupans, but I have no authority to discuss their situation.'

'Then I'm sorry, I can't help you, Brigadier. You've wasted your time coming here. The lupans are our children. We gave birth to them and we'll fight to protect them.'

Johnson stood up quickly, his face dark as thunder. He towered over Eisa, blotting out the sun. 'I don't know why I bother with you. How can anyone withhold an important cure for the Plague, especially you, who call yourself a doctor? The inhumanity of it all. Every hospital bed contains a Plague victim. Have you seen the stacks of coffins? Have you talked to families of the victims?'

'I understand the medical situation, Brigadier. Better than you. You don't know what you're talking about. Every day someone comes up with a new idea for a vaccine. So far nothing has checked out. I'm not sure if I've discovered anything. All I have are some observations and ideas. Don't expect me to hand them over at gunpoint. Or at the cost of our lives. It may surprise you but we believe that our children deserve basic human rights. The moment this cure is verified, the lupans will become lab animals, kept alive only to supply a vaccine. I won't let that happen.'

'I can't discuss the lupan question. I have no such authority.'

'Then find someone who has. You may not have too long.'

Johnson's eyes narrowed. 'Don't threaten me, doctor. I know enough to deal with my own situation. I don't need your help. But you need mine. If we don't come to an arrangement, on my signal the Air Force will attack. In moments we'll secure you and all your documents, and there's nothing you'll do about it. You'll end up losing both your supposed discovery and your village. I'd advise you not to overplay your hand.'

Johnson pointed at two large helicopters that hovered above the hill. Eisa had no doubt that Johnson was not bluffing. Now that Johnson knew for certain that the cure was in the village, he would stop at nothing to secure it. Certainly he wouldn't flinch at killing more people.

Johnson shrugged. 'Do we have an agreement? I'd rather avoid a military strike.'

'Why should you care?'

'So that's your thanks. For years I protected you from government edicts. That lupan colony wouldn't be out there except for my intervention. Your village would have been dismantled long ago. I think I've done my bit.'

215

'And now?'

'Times have changed. Today, some things aren't possible. After this attack, with ten soldiers dead, people understandably want to wipe out the lupans. It can't be stopped. Everyone has to decide which side they're on. I can't believe that you, doctor, will allow people to die, so that you can protect lupans. For God's sake man, do the right thing.'

Eisa was looking at the hill surmounted by standing stones, the circular dens silhouetted against the sky. Whether they'd still be there a year from now, with a thriving colony, depended on how skilfully he dealt with Johnson in the next hour.

He stood up, dusted himself off. 'I think we should continue this discussion in my house.'

Johnson's lips curled into a sneer. 'You're not afraid that I'll infect you?'

'You've done enough damage. We lost five men in your attack, five men with wives and children, and who are now grieving. Don't talk to me about loss.'

TWENTY-SIX

'We've no information,' the soldier by the tank told Linella when she asked him where Johnson had gone.

She tapped the car's windshield. 'This is his car, isn't it?'

'We've no such information,' the soldier repeated.

'He's down in the village,' Scott said.

'He has no business going there. Why didn't he come see me?' she demanded as if Scott were to blame. 'Let's go.'

At the apricot orchard they met Arjan along with several companions. 'Johnson's with Eisa,' Arjan told her. 'They talked for a long time.'

'About what?'

'I don't know. It was private.'

'You've absolutely no idea what they were talking about?'

Arjan shook his head. 'None, but the Brigadier didn't look all that good. He is infected.'

'Thanks,' Linella said and hurried on.

Why instead of talking to her had he gone to see Eisa? Something was wrong. After waiting several days for Johnson to show up, she didn't know if she wanted to talk to him after all.

'Is he on our side?' Scott asked.

'I don't know. Maybe.'

Her hope died when she opened Eisa's door to find him sitting at his table and handing a stack of papers to Johnson. Upon her appearance Eisa pulled away from Johnson, like an unfaithful lover caught in a compromising position.

217

Johnson's smiled at her, an affected smile that sent blood rushing to her head. 'Well look who's here. How good of you to join us.'

'Thanks for nothing,' she said.

'And your friend is?'

'This is Scott.'

Johnson shuffled his stack of papers. 'Maguire? Yes, I know about you. There's a civil warrant out for your arrest.'

'Are you here to serve it?' Scott said.

Johnson shrugged.

'We're in the middle of something,' Eisa said to Linella. 'What do you need?'

His wavering voice revealed more than his words. Linella suddenly felt small, useless; that she'd been cast aside. But the feeling was immediately replaced by a sense of outrage, that Eisa was about to cut her out of an important decision, one she deserved to know about.

'I want to know what's going on,' she said.

The men exchanged looks, but neither spoke.

'Brian, talk to me.'

Johnson said, 'Wait for me up at the cottage. I'll be there soon.'

'I want to know now.'

'All in good time.'

'You're talking about the Plague. About his cure.'

Johnson nodded. 'Nothing more than you already told me. I want to check out the story. Find out if there's anything to it.'

'I'm passing on my work,' Eisa said. 'All my notes.'

It was what she'd wanted. For days she'd begged Eisa to release the cure, but his abrupt announcement made her feel that she had been handed a fake coin. Eisa would never have changed his mind unless something important had forced his hand.

'So, you're passing on the cure. Nice,' she said.

'It's the right thing to do,' Eisa said.

'What changed your mind?'

'I can't withhold a discovery that may save so many lives. You were right. In the long run this will also help our children.'

'Where does all this leave us? Brian – I want some answers. We were attacked; our people were shot without provocation. Our orchards destroyed.'

'What do you want me to do?'

Tears of rage overwhelmed her. 'What do I want you to do? You bastard, are you listening? Am I talking about the weather?'

He waited for her to continue, his face an immovable rock.

'I talk about a crime such as Scotland has never seen, about the government killing its people, and you just stand there? How dare you?'

'Everyone suffered casualties.'

'You deserved it.'

Johnson's fist clenched. She fully expected him to hit her, but instead he let out a long breath. 'Tell me what you want.'

'To stop the slaughter. You must.'

'We're working on the problem.'

'Yes, you would be. How hard are you working on it?'

'I think we're close.'

'What does that mean?'

'There isn't going to be another attack. The government will probably leave you alone. I'm not the President, so I can't promise it. However, I think another attack is unlikely.'

The mechanical tone of his voice left her feeling queasy. Why didn't he look her in the face?

'I don't know if I can believe you.'

'It's the best you have.'

'What about the lupans?'

'I've no idea. I'm only here to find out about this cure. Thanks to Doctor Habash, I have material for medical researchers.'

'You think they'll find a cure in time for you?' Scott said.

Johnson shrugged. 'I don't know.'

'Why wait for a vaccine? There's a better way,' Linella said.

'Oh? And what's that?'

'I told you before. Go live with the lupans.'

Johnson smiled sardonically. 'How close do I have to get to them?'

She turned away as if she'd been slapped. 'You don't have to touch any of them. It's your life and your disease. Do what you fucking want.'

'Yes, shag a lupan to be cured. I'd much rather have it off with a sheep.'

'You must want to die.'

Johnson stepped up to her. 'This is not about me. If I have to shag a lupan, I'll shag a lupan.' He shook the pile of papers, 'This, is about saving lives. They're dying because you sat on a cure that might have saved them. You and your lupan pals have had your day, more time than you deserve. If you think for a minute that people will respect you for what you did, think again.'

'Wait a minute,' Eisa said. 'We have a written agreement to guarantee…'

'To guarantee nothing. Yes, doctor, we signed the piece of paper, but if you believe that anything you and I sign has any value, you're more stupid than I took you for. No one can change what's happening. Anyone who thinks they can is a fool. Don't look at me as if I'm from the moon. When news gets out about this cure – and that you sat on it, watch out for fireworks. I won't be able to protect you even if I wanted to. If I were you, I'd start packing.'

'In that case I'll have my papers back.'

Johnson held out the pile. 'You want them back? Here they are. Come on doctor. I'd like to see you change your mind. Except that I know you, and what you really want. A vaccine will be developed, doctor – with or without your help. Get over your delusions of grandeur. You're not that important.'

He set the papers on the table, took out a cigarette and stuck it between his lips. 'Yes, I didn't think you'd take them back.'

'You believe that a vaccine will save your life?' Eisa said. 'You're crazy.'

Johnson lit the cigarette. 'I don't care if I die in a month or in a year. Someday we'll all snuff it. There's nothing anyone can do about it.'

'Aren't you about to destroy your last hope?' Scott said.

'What are you talking about?'

'The lupan colony.'

'I don't comment about military operations.'

'You'd better think very carefully about this. Because if you attack this colony, you'll wipe out the cure.'

Johnson barely stirred. 'We already have enough lupans in captivity to supply us with a vaccine. This colony is irrelevant.'

'You are about to attack.'

Johnson took a drag of his cigarette and slowly blew out a cloud of smoke. 'As I said, I'd pack up and get out while you can.'

'Stop the operation. You don't know what you're doing.'

'Don't talk to me. I don't make government policy. I'm a soldier, and I follow orders. Try President Christie.'

'That's rubbish. You were able to intervene before. You're part of the chain of command. If you tell them not to attack, they'll listen to you.'

'There would have to be a very good reason for me to intervene.'

'If they die, we die,' Scott said. 'It's that simple. If we destroy the lupans, we'll destroy ourselves. Our survival depends on their survival.'

'Yes, I thought you'd say something of the kind. I don't know about you, Maguire. You've gone native. You'd better come up with a better argument to halt the operation other than repeating the same old line that we're all going to die. I'm a soldier. I can't change global warming. No one can change it.'

'This time, you can make a big difference.'

'You're crazy. The only difference I can make is to hand over those papers to researchers at Edinburgh University, and then prepare to die. No one can save your lupans. Your colony's finished. We lost ten soldiers in your field – all mauled to death by wolves. Twenty more were seriously wounded. Someone's got to pay for it.'

'Don't you want to live?' Scott said.

Johnson shrugged. 'I don't think about it.'

'There is a cure. I was infected. A month ago I had your symptoms. Today my infection's gone. All it took was day to day contact with the lupans, living with them and eating their food. Try it out.'

'I don't have time for this.'

'Johnson, we're talking about the human race. Doing one thing that will make a difference.'

'The human race?' Johnson laughed sarcastically. 'I'm glad to hear you use the words – that you still regard yourself as one of us and haven't written us off. Sure, I'll do what I can for the "human race." To hell with you people. Suddenly you're concerned for the "human race", after you kept the cure from "the human race." Or maybe, you don't give a damn, never did give a damn for anyone. Only for bloody lupans. At least we understand each other really well. We know whose side we're on.'

'Brian,' Linella said. 'Can't you use one ounce of your brain to see that we're not the enemy. Or is that beyond you? Are you so determined to be stubborn that you'll throw away *your* last chance?'

Johnson picked up the pile of papers. 'Here's my chance to live – not only for me but for everyone else. Don't lecture me, Linella. You've messed things up badly. I regret the day I got involved with you and your lupans. And now, unless you have something you haven't already said, I have things to do.'

He walked out, letting the door slam behind him.

'What do you think?' Linella said after a minute during which no one spoke. Tears streamed from her face, tears of anger and a feeling of betrayal. She'd hoped that Johnson would show an ember of feeling for her. Clearly she meant no more to him than a stranger. Standing by the window, Eisa drew on his cigarette and looked out at the street. He had to be deeply troubled, wondering if handing over his papers had been a mistake.

Eisa took a last draw at his cigarette, tossed the stub out of the window. 'Well, that's that. I need to confer with the others about what happens next.'

'You'll be safe,' Scott said. 'He'll protect you even if he hates what you did.'

'He wasn't very reassuring. I'm sorry I gave him all that material. I don't think that we're any safer for it. The best I can say is that some Plague victims may benefit from it. As for the wolf-children...' His voice trailed off. He shook his head. 'They need to get out of the way. Can either of you get through to them?'

'They already know what's going on,' Scott said.

Eisa raised his brows. 'So, what will they do about it?'

Throughout the exchange with Johnson, Scott felt lupan presences inside him, looking through his eyes, listening and asking questions. For a short while he allowed them to listen in; then he shut down his mind. Paying attention to the presences disoriented him. He had to stay focused on his goal, to persuade Johnson to stop the attack.

'What will they do? Probably nothing.'

'Don't they realize they're about to be obliterated?'

'They know. It's just that....' Scott paused, looking for words to express a vision that arose in him, of standing stones and a music that emanated from them and spread over the hills. 'They have other plans.'

The door opened quickly. Sandria stood framed against the morning sun. Her dark eyes immediately found Scott. 'I need to talk to you.'

Before replying he glanced at Linella for her reaction. Linella shrugged.

'Why are you looking at her?' Sandria said. 'This is nothing to do with her. Have you forgotten who I am? That I do still exist.' She tightened her head scarf. 'I'll wait for you outside.'

TWENTY-SEVEN

Since the morning of the battle, when he'd fled into the forest, Scott hadn't thought of Sandria. But there she was on the doorstep, resentful, nursing her bruised feelings and demanding attention. He wondered if she cared about more significant issues: the clouds of army drones that every hour of the day circled above, or the dead. While villagers waited for the hammer to fall at any moment, she attended to her miasma of emotions.

She waited across the street, her back bent under an invisible load; her eyes downcast. He sensed that she felt little more than contempt toward him. Gone was the kindness and understanding she displayed the afternoon she first seduced him. He still wondered why he'd let her. No doubt because he'd been lonely; because she made him feel that someone cared for him.

She barely met his eyes. 'Can we walk around the pond?'

She was hurting. He saw it in the stiff way she carried herself. He couldn't blame her for feeling abandoned; for hating him. But there were worse tragedies than emotional abandonment. Death was one. Every house they passed was in mourning; either someone there had died or had been wounded. A few people sat on their porches but under an awning where they were shielded from the aerial drones. Conversations were in subdued voices.

Leaving the village, they walked down to a small pond in a swampy corner of the meadow, now populated by ducks and several ill-tempered geese.

Not until they reached the pond did she speak again, 'This is about my baby – our baby.' Tears welled up in her eyes and choked off her voice. Seeing that she needed comforting, he felt moved to hold her, but he resisted the urge. She wanted something else from him.

'Before the attack, I went to see Eisa. I couldn't wait to find out.'

'What did Eisa tell you?' he said.

She wiped her tears on her head scarf and stared at him as if expecting him to read her mind. 'He did a genetic test on the foetus. It is lupan. We're going to have a lupan.'

Of course you wanted a human child. That was the entire point of our relationship. He suppressed the impulse to laugh at the irony of the situation. *A lupan child! Extraordinary.*

'I see.'

'Scott – is that all you can say? This is your child too.'

'I know.'

'Our baby is a lupan. How do you feel about that? Anything?'

'I feel honoured. Life has chosen us to give birth to something new. Something beautiful.'

Sandria's lips tightened. 'Beautiful, yes, that's what it is. At least you've finally said that.'

'I'm sorry you don't see it that way.'

'What about me? Can't you at least pretend to care about me? I already gave birth to a lupan. I was raped. My sisters were raped. We all had lupans. Are you so thick that you can't see what it did to us? I had to abandon Asra to the care of wild animals. She joined the wolves.'

'Sandria, I know about Asra.'

Her flushed eyes turned on him. 'Then you must know that I can't possibly go through the same hell again. I will not carry a lupan to term, only to later abandon it. Never to see it again.'

'This time it will be different.'

'Different?' She shook her head.

'You won't have to abandon it. Don't you see that?'

A curious sensation came across him that he and Sandria were not alone. A third, and a fourth presence had joined them, listening in on the conversation. Zia was there. He could almost smell her pungent sweat. The sensation so disoriented him that he glanced at his hands to make sure they were his and not a lupan's.

'Are you listening to me?' Sandria's shrill voice brought him back to the pond.

'Of course,' he said.

'Well?'

'Don't you see, this isn't only about us? We, the human race, are giving birth to lupans. It's what has to happen.'

'Scott, I'm not the human race. I'm the woman in front of you, someone you can touch, someone you can hold. Flesh and bones. Can you look at me? I'm talking about our baby.'

'So am I. You're a mother, no different from thousands of others. They're all going through the same thing. They're pregnant, scared and they're giving birth to lupans. Like it or not, you are the human race.'

'I don't know what nonsense you're talking about.'

'I'm doing my best to explain.'

'I don't want your explanations or your philosophy. I want you. I went through this before, gave birth to Asra only to be forced to dump her in the forest. I'll never do it again.'

'You want an abortion?'

Silently she looked into the distance.

'I thought you were against abortion.'

'Human abortion? Yes.'

'Of course, lupans aren't human.'

Sandria's eyes lit up. 'Don't give me that rubbish. For months I put up with your racism – calling lupans Neanderthals or subhuman apes. There was a time you had no use for them.'

'I was stupid then.'

'And now you're so smart. Don't lecture me about the value of lupan life. The thing growing inside me is no more than a cancer. If I choose to get rid of it, that's my decision and mine alone.'

'What about me? Do I have a say?'

'I've been waiting for that; for you to take an interest in our baby. The last time we spoke, you wanted an abortion. Looks like you've changed your mind.'

'People change.'

'And pigs fly.'

Scott picked up a stone and flung it into the pond where it disappeared with a loud plop. He followed with a second and then a third stone until the pond was filled with ripples. Now she would play her trump card. If you care enough about me to bring up the baby and provide a home for us, I'll keep it.

'Scott, will you stop throwing those stones.'

'I don't know what else to say. It's your body. I won't tell you what to do with it.'

'Do you want me to give birth to it only to carry it up to the colony and drop it in some lupan nursemaid's arms? Is that what you want?'

'Sandria, I never wanted to be a father. Three months ago I was in a plane trying to kill myself. If I'm alive today, it's thanks to you. Also, because there's something important I have to do – to save lupans from being massacred by stupid people. I want the child to be born. I'm sorry you don't feel that way too.'

'I'm barely five weeks along. I'd hardly call it a child.'

'Yet that's what you call it.'

'Let's not split hairs.'

'I'll put it another way. I want our baby to be born; I want every woman who can bear children to have a lupan baby, and to take care of it. To be a mother, a real mother. That's the only thing that will save us. We're facing disaster because of women who abandoned their lupan babies and who no longer care what happens to them. They'd as soon the children all vanished one day. It'd make them easier to forget. That has got to change.'

'If this thing inside me means so much to you, then come down from the hill and live with me. Take care of me, and our baby.'

'I can't.'

Sandria turned a cold eye on him. 'It's because of Linella, isn't it? As soon as you found out that I was pregnant you dumped me for that whore. She's a regular one. Sleeps with whoever is free.'

Ordinarily her stab would make him feel defensive, but he let it go. He didn't care what Sandria thought about Linella. Also, he was aware that Zia, still merged with him, was listening in. Though she didn't understand the exchange, she found human relationships endlessly entertaining.

'Go away,' he whispered. 'Not now.'

Sandria peered at him closely. 'Are you talking to me?'

In response to his request, Zia's presence faded into the background. 'Never mind,' he said. 'We're talking about Linella.'

'I don't want to hear about her.'

'She's part of my life. Our life. You can wish all you want to have me to yourself but it's not going to happen.'

'You just want me around, to give birth to your lupan.'

'I want it to be born, and I'll take care of it. We'll all take care of it.'

'Who's the "we"?'

'More people than you can imagine.'

Sandria's face stiffened. 'So, you want a surrogate mother to give birth to your child, only to give away – to her? Don't think that I'll ever share my flesh with that whore. If you want me to bear your child, you know exactly what to do. I will not be a surrogate mother.'

'We're all surrogate parents. We were never anything else. Nature chose us to bring them into the world, then let them go as soon as they're viable. Wolf-children never belonged to us. But that doesn't mean that we can't have a relationship with them. We can. We can also learn a lot from them.'

He walked several paces away from her. A breeze stirred the pond water, making it glitter in the morning sun. He studied the moving surface; each wave that emerged from the water for a brief moment, only to fade and reappear elsewhere. The waves didn't have any permanent form; each rose into existence for a brief moment before it returned to the lake. Not unlike lupan personalities, rooted in an unknowable ocean. Lupans would identify with this wave or that, whichever pleased them, but they regarded the ocean as the only reality, more real than its surface waves.

'I'm going to have an abortion,' Sandria said.

Her words lashed out like the crack of a whip. For a moment he could not summon any adequate response. Sandria would have the abortion, to get back at him. Even at the cost of her unborn baby.

'Other wolf-children will be born. There are other mothers,' he finally said.

He turned away from her, walked alone back to the village.

Beauty Woman returns to the grassy field to watch the men complete the stone circle. The meadow still carries the pungent smell of wolves and spilled blood. The sun might warm the grass but it cannot heat the dark air or dispel an oppressive feeling of fear and hatred.

With levers and rollers, the men lift the last stone from the cart. In their hands the stone's mass is lightened so that it is no heavier than wood. It slides effortlessly into the waiting hole. The men adjust its tilt while listening to the earth's hum, now faint, now growing to a roar depending on the stone's placement. After finding the position that yields the strongest sound the men wedge it in with small stones.

She feels an overwhelming joy not unlike the elation of a mother whose newborn takes its first breath. Following a long and painful separation Earth and Sky are locked in a close embrace, so complete they can no longer be separated. The earth's hum, once barely perceptible, has become a scream, complete with deep bear-like growls, the high-pitched twittering of small birds, wind whistling among tree branches, volcanic eruptions and raging floods. Bolts of jagged lightning crack open the sky and reach into the earth's entrails. Each sound awakens in her sorrow, fear or joy, feelings so powerful that if she allowed them to permeate her, her body might splinter. Unable to contain them in her body she finds herself dancing. She gyrates on one spot, leaps from foot to foot, dances several rounds of the stone circle and then hurls herself high into the air and over the central stone. Others watch her, initially amazed, not understanding what has happened to her, but when they hear the same song in every cell of their bodies, they join her in the dance.

Scott had barely left Sandria when he heard Zia calling to him from the meadow. There she was dancing on the stones with a wild abandon as if she had taken a narcotic. He let himself merge for long enough to sense a cocktail of emotions with the destructive power of a hurricane. Fearing that they would sweep him over a destructive waterfall, he broke off contact. He'd been lost before and was determined not to let it happen again. He'd have to be content to only watch her dance. She hurled herself into the air to land with her hands on the central stone and legs in the air, and then flipped over to sail like a bird without any sense of weight. Others in the circle joined in, singing, their voices creating a melody without words that blended with the hum of the stones. The lupans, who rarely made any sound other than whistling, had found their voices. Not allowing his mind to drift for an instant, he listened to each sound as it formed and then faded to be taken up by the next. The sounds lived only for a moment, and they'd never be repeated except in memory.

He was still humming a few stray notes when he returned to Eisa's house, hoping to find Linella there. Instead he discovered Eisa alone at his desk, sorting through a pile of papers.

'She's over with Lina and Arjan,' Eisa said, barely looking up.

Eisa's preoccupied look indicated that he did not want to talk. He was too distraught to do anything other than shuffle his papers.

While Scott waited for an explanation, Eisa said, 'I don't want to sound ungrateful, but please leave the village. Take Linella with you. I've made a bad mess of things. I need to be alone to repair the damage.'

'Is there something I can do?'

'Nothing you can do here. Go back to the lupans. They're the ones who really need your help. God save all of us if they're bombed again.'

TWENTY-EIGHT

Lina wasn't home, and so Linella decided to return to her cottage. If Scott wanted her, he knew where to find her. Sandria's appearance had put her into a tailspin from which she couldn't pull out. Yes, Scott and Sandria had unfinished business to settle, but it wouldn't end there. No doubt Scott preferred Sandria because she was younger, thinner, with a better body and offered him good sex. She had shown up for no other reason than to win him back, so that he would take care of her and their baby. Why wouldn't he fall for it? He was a guy, with primal instincts no different than other men.

It would be all wrong, she said. Sandria's pregnant because she seduced him for her own selfish purposes. He doesn't belong with her any more than with a one night stand. She can't mean anything to him. Can't he see that?

Something in her had changed when he told her the story of Coldhill, of the unnamed man and woman in the ancient forest. After her initial disbelief she turned the story over several times, unable to let it go. As if it was part of her history, something she had personally experienced. She could still see the wolves that fed from the woman's hand. Clearly, as if they were standing a foot away. She smelled their rancid breath when they opened their jaws to snap up the scraps. The smoke from the fire burned her eyes. She'd cried out to him: 'Leave me then. Go back to your sheep.'

So, call me stupid, deluded or whatever, but if you were there,

I was there too. If you were the master of Coldhill, I was the woman with the wolves. You fell in love with me. I didn't want to let you go that night but you left me for your security, your wives, your castle and your sheep. And when you set fire to your walls, your fire engulfed me. It's happening again; the forest's about to be burned. Unless we stay together and prevent the fire, my wolves and my children will be burned alive. It's not going to happen. This time, Scott, you will not leave me.

A loud buzzing made her quickly look up. A drone no larger than a hand was hovering ten feet away. It had the long segmented body of a dragon-fly with wings that beat so fast they were a blur. A single blue eye gleamed at her. With a scream she flung herself under the branches of a nearby oak tree and pressed herself up against its gnarled trunk. Drones usually kept away from trees to avoid getting tangled up in branches. What did it want? Its protruding needle indicated that it was armed with a laser. Could sting her badly. Rising several feet it circled above the tree, waiting for her to come out. She held her breath. Tears started in her eyes. Why the sudden interest? Now that Johnson had no further use for her, were the authorities about to arrest her? People were often placed under drone surveillance just before the police showed up.

'Had a good look, Brian?' she shouted. 'Now piss off.' Not reacting, the drone continued to circle. At least it wasn't firing; not yet.

Her hands clawed the bark of the tree. If only she could disappear among the branches, but they were too weak to support her. She would have to wait, until the thing finished with her.

A loud crack stopped the buzzing. The drone wobbled and crashed into the ground. The stone missile that had brought it down bounced on the path. Twenty feet away, Scott crouched motionless.

'Don't move. It still might be alive.'

She remained pressed against the tree while the drone's wings twitched in death throes. After all movement ceased he sprinted up to it and sank his boot into it.

'Come.' He held out his hand. 'We have to get under cover. They'll send more, and this time they'll be cross.'

She wanted to thank him, but couldn't find the words. What did 'Thanks' mean anyway? He knew that she was grateful; didn't need to be told. Holding hands they headed for the cottage. She tried to run but he held her back. 'They're watching. Walk like nothing's going on or they'll be all over us.'

'What do they want?'

'To keep track of the key players. You're important to them.'

'What do you mean?'

'Your friend Johnson wants to know where you are at all times.'

Not until they had entered the cottage, and she had slammed the oak door, did she let him hold her. For several minutes he clasped her against him in an embrace that brought tears to her eyes. He had really returned and would not casually leave her again.

Though they'd been gone for only a few hours the living room air felt musty and uninhabited. There was no sign of the kids. She guessed that they had run off to the village where they always wanted to be. She whistled for Lisa. Hearing no response she surmised that the kids had taken her too.

She called up Andrew on his wrist com.

'We're down with the guys,' Andrew said. Anticipating her question he added. 'Mum, there's nothing for us to do at the cottage. The guys need us here. Please come and join us.'

'I need to stay here.'

She cracked open the picture window and stood by it inhaling the fragrant morning air, but its freshness couldn't dispel her fear of the impending attack. Her doubts about Scott resurfaced unexpectedly. He walked around the room, barely looking at her. Finally he sat down in the two-hundred-year-old rocking chair and stared into space as if he'd taken a hit of cannabis.

'What did Sandria want?'

'Do you really want to talk about her?'

'I'm curious.'

'She found out that her baby – our baby, will be lupan. She wants to have an abortion.'

'She does? Oh no.'

'You don't like it any more than I.'

'Did... did you tell her that I would take care of the baby?'

'That's not the point.'

'Then – what is her point?'

'She wants a human baby. It's what she's lived for. And now that her dream has died, she'd as soon the baby died too.'

Linella shook her head. She looked Scott full in the eyes. 'If I was able to conceive – I'd have a lupan child today. Ten of them.'

Scott's grey eyes softened. 'I know you would. You wouldn't abandon them the way all the mothers did.'

'No, I wouldn't. But I'm not the one who's pregnant; neither can I conceive, so let's drop it.'

'Okay.'

'Make yourself at home.'

'I could use a bath.'

'First door on the right.'

'That's fine.'

While he soaked in the tub Linella walked in with a clean change of clothes, glanced at him keenly and left without a word. He could tell that she wanted him: the firm clasp of her hand as she led him to the cottage, the way she let him hold her. She was passionate enough to make love to him but he wasn't sure he wanted her to. They were in a war zone where anything could happen. Death could come to either of them. Besides he needed to keep a clear head to be able to help the lupans.

Not that they wanted his help. Zia appeared unflustered by Johnson's warning. He sensed that she was busy with 'more important matters'. What important matters? Dancing on stones? The lupans were certainly in a jolly mood, singing and dancing in and out of stone circles. Even Asra emerged from the forest to join in the festivities. If they knew about the approaching danger, they didn't appear to be concerned enough to take any action. He doubted he could change that.

He found Linella in the kitchen. She had changed out of her jeans into a long black dress. Standing barefoot she looked tall and strong, the mistress of her home. She dumped a bowl of root vegetables into a steaming pot, slammed on the lid then turned to him with a smile. He sensed she had resolved her doubts about Sandria.

'You're looking civilized,' she said.

'I feel human again.'

'I thought you were part lupan.'

'That too.'

'Are you in touch with them?'

'Sometimes. Not at the moment.'

'Good. I don't particularly want to share you.'

'We may have a few days before the army makes its move. Johnson won't give the go-ahead until he finds out what's inside Eisa's papers.'

Linella shrugged. 'Why should Eisa's papers make any difference? Johnson doesn't give a damn for the wolf-children. He already told us that there are enough of them in captivity to develop a vaccine.'

'I know, but he's very ill. Sometimes people change when they're faced with death. I think he'll hold back the army until he knows something for certain about the cure.'

'I hope you're right.'

She drained the steamed vegetables, added a herbal mix and served them onto plates of boiled rice. After weeks of eating lupan stew, each bite felt so mouth-watering that he took time to savour it. Sitting across the table she watched him closely as if she'd slipped him a drug and was waiting for it to take effect.

'I'm coming back to life,' he said.

'That was the idea.'

After they finished eating, she walked with him around the

flower garden, telling him the Latin name of each plant and its history. He'd never kept more than a symbolic patio garden. He was overwhelmed by the profusion of colours and names. Soon he found his attention wandering back to the hill. Various lupan personalities merged in and out of him, curious about what he was doing. Looking through their eyes he saw that the celebrations were over. People were running between dens, gathering tools, cooking gear and other belongings into the meeting den, all in response to an overarching order. There was a sense of expectancy, the need to prepare for an event, as yet unnamed. The earth's heartbeat still pulsed in the background, along with echoes of the lupan song he had heard by the stone circle.

'Wake up there,' Linella said all of a sudden. 'Don't you like these dahlias?'

The colony faded and he found himself with her among a sea of bobbing heads with long spiked petals.

'They're beautiful. A lot of work. Why do you raise them?'

'What else would I be doing? The boys don't need me except to cook for them. They're out of this house. The village women don't need my interference. There's nothing for me down there. The wolf-children are growing up; they're happy on their own. What do I have left except for my flowers? It's what I know. I wanted to show them to you. Now that I've done that we can talk about other things. What should we do next?'

'You're annoyed with me.'

She shrugged. 'I shouldn't be. Flowers are my thing. I don't expect you or anyone else to be interested in them. In the middle of all the mayhem and destruction, why should anyone care about flowers?'

'You've been growing them for years. You sound as if you're tired of them and would rather do something else.'

'It's what I know. Cottage Woman – isn't that what they call me up there?'

She would have said more but appeared to choke up. She shook her head, took a deep breath.

'Do you want to go back to the colony?' she said quickly to change the subject. 'Maybe we should help them prepare for the next disaster.'

'No. They don't need me there.'

'Me neither.'

While she walked about the living room straightening furniture, he let himself merge again with the lupans. It felt like sinking into a dream. He sensed their warm presences, their sensitivity to the rocks and trees and their unbridled wildness, untamed by civilizing strictures. When they ate venison he tasted their meat. He shared the exhilaration of two males who chased a deer through the wood, so focused on their quarry that their minds did not admit any stray thought. Soon many personalities in him vied for attention, and he switched from one to another, so rapidly that he forgot where he was or who he was. He was drowning in a whirlpool of multiple eyes and ears. Linella brought him back by shaking his shoulders.

'Don't do that again,' she said once the room stopped swaying and he was again aware of her. 'Promise me that you won't.'

He was back, confined to his body and his spinning thoughts, a closet from which he couldn't escape. He breathed hard; his heart raced as if he'd run for miles.

'I have to stay in touch with them. It's the least I can do.'

'Then tell me before you go off.'

Sitting opposite him she rolled a cigarette. 'Want one?'

'No.'

'You're cross with me. I can tell that you are. Is it something I said?'

Was it the cigarette that made her appear so earthy? So ordinary and rooted in a world that appeared so paltry. He had travelled through the cave with Asra, gained access to the lupan mind and had lived an entire life with a goddess. He thought he was still with her, until that cigarette.

'I'm thinking that I can't stay here,' he said. 'I don't belong here.'

'Is it me or my cottage?'

'You've no idea of what's happening to me. What I've gone through. Sometimes I don't think you want to know, because it may uproot you. Destroy everything you think you know.'

Linella took a long drag, held the smoke then let it out through her nostrils. 'Wow, there's a presumption.'

'It's not true?'

She shook her head. 'You're wrong. I want to understand you, Scott. You've no idea how much. But you need my help. You're about to step off a cliff. We were never made to see things like lupans. That's why we're not lupans. I will not let go of you, allow you to wander off into your world of visions. If I have to stay potted like a plant to keep you sane, I'll do it. That's how much I care for you.'

'You want to shackle me?'

'No.' She closed her eyes. 'I want to keep you alive.'

'In your garden? With your flowers? You'd as soon forget about them. You need to get away.'

'You're right. I've been stuck here in this cottage ever since Stan left. With my table. People still like to come over. So do lupans, but they don't really need me. My kids certainly don't. I've often dreamed of a way out, but I don't know where I would go. Or where I belong. I'm no visionary. All I can do is cook.'

'You're capable of much more. If you wanted to, you could walk out of here today.'

'If you say so.'

'What's stopping you?'

'This is my world, the table, the kitchen, the children that come around. It's what I do. I can't imagine life without my cottage.'

'You weren't always planted in the ground.'

'What do you mean?'

'I'm talking about your story. Our story – what happened long ago in that forest, when we met, when you tried to convince me to join you in your nomadic life, with only wolves to protect us.

You were the leader of your people, the one they depended on for their livelihood. That's the life that awaits you, one you have to reclaim. We both have to take the path that we didn't take long ago.'

Linella reached out and clasped his hand. She wept. He could almost see the cottage walls crack and crumble into dust, leaving them exposed to the evening sky. She drew him close to herself and kissed him. 'I'll go with you.'

For several minutes she held him against her. He heard her racing heartbeat. Then she pulled away, looked quizzically into his eyes. 'Are we really alone?'

There were no stray voices. For the first time that day all the lupan presences had withdrawn, perhaps as a courtesy, so he could be intimate with her.

'There's no one else,' he said.

Before he could resist she wrapped her arms about his waist and pressed him to her chest. He felt her breasts grow taut. Her dress rode up to her waist, her warm legs mingled with his and pulled him in closer. His heart hammered with excitement. If she wanted to take on his journey he would help her. Her back arched, responding to his caresses; her body stiffened. She swept back her mop of curly hair so he could see her oval head and her blue eyes. When he entered her, his heart shattered into a thousand fragments of light.

Exhausted from their lovemaking they lay still in each others embrace. Her quiet eyes searched him, trying to read his thoughts.

'I don't want to say "good-bye" to you again,' she said.

The following morning she left him sleeping on the bedcovers, pulled on her jeans and a t-shirt, and then went to the kitchen to brew some coffee. A morning fog had crept overnight into the valley and drew a thick veil over the lupan colony. Since waking up and finding Scott next to her, she felt an overwhelming peace; that things were as they should be. Despite Johnson's warning, she wasn't anxious about what might happen. The most intractable problem could be solved. Her life was about to change. She'd leave to the world she'd built over many years, walk out of her cottage to take an uncertain road. The thought of it used to scare her but now it evoked a sense of excitement.

She was waiting for the coffee to brew when Scott came in. He was humming an odd tune that seemed to be stuck in his head. He held her close, his head against hers. On the stove the pot hissed and spluttered for attention but she ignored it. After releasing her he gazed out at the foggy landscape. His faraway look told her that he'd wandered off again and was looking through another's eyes. She wished she could share that closeness with him, be able to look through his eyes, but she knew that Scott needed her the way she was. Firmly rooted.

'Something's going on up there,' he said. 'Do fogs like this come around often?'

'Not at this time of year. More in the spring.'

'It's not a normal fog; it has something to do with the sound. Can you hear it?'

'Hear what?'

He hummed the tune again, a series of high notes his voice could barely reach. 'Recognize it?'

'Yes, from you. All the time.'

'I'll shut up. Listen carefully.'

After a moment she became aware of a hum, not unlike the tinnitus that perpetually plagued her, but deeper in tone, reminiscent of a beehive of many voices engaged in a common task.

'I think so. What is it?'

'The Earth's heartbeat.'

'What?'

'It's the sound of life in the Earth, only much louder now that the stone-work is finished. Those standing stones work like a giant amplifier.'

'Thank you for that explanation.'

241

'Thanks for not being more flippant.'

'Scott, you're not explaining it at all.'

'I'm trying, but it's like trying to describe colour to a blind man. The Earth's not a dead lump, Linella. It's alive, changing and intelligent. Most people see only grass, heather, moss, worms and trees. They don't see roots, rocks, the air, the rivers, and that they're all connected the way our blood-vessels are connected in our bodies. And just as our bodies are intelligent and conscious, so is the Earth. It's a living entity, only much vaster than us. Aware. And it sings. What you're hearing is its voice.'

TWENTY-NINE

During the following days Scott and Linella stayed in the cottage while forecasters puzzled over the fog's persistence in the highland glens, when the rest of the country was soaked in glorious sunshine. None of their explanations made sense. Each day they promised that the fog would burn off by noon, but it appeared determined to confound their models. Thicker than any in recent memory, it spilled over the peaks of all but the tallest mountains. Nothing but featureless grey was visible from the cottage windows. At least the clouds of buzzing drones gave up and went away. In the intense silence not even a bird's voice sounded. Linella had never felt such an intense isolation; as if the hills and even the outside world had ceased to exist.

But it hadn't. Television news assured her that not only the world of cities and people was still there; Koppiemaul hadn't been forgotten either.

Lupans and wolves featured in most news programs. The political debate on what should be done about them only intensified, with each party trying to outbid the other as the party that would take decisive action to solve the problem. The news kept her in a constant state of agitation. She would pace the room, her head in turmoil, feeling that she was trapped in the cottage. Unable to act.

Scott didn't watch the television. He complained that it gave him a headache. The very images appeared to puzzle him. He'd stare at them with a look that didn't understand what he was supposed to see. 'I can't make them out,' he finally said. 'They're like so many flickering blobs. They don't speak to me like they used to. I can't make sense of all that confusion.'

'For how long will we sit here? Don't we need to be doing something?' she asked Scott one morning.

'We're where we need to be. We have to wait for the lupans. They have a plan.'

'What plan? Is it to move out under cover of fog?'

'No, but the fog will give them extra time. There won't be any attack while it hangs around.'

'I like being with you here, Scott, but I have to get out or I'll go insane. I need to go down to the village or to Dufftown. It's not my nature to sit around when things are this critical.'

'They are critical.'

'Then why are we sitting here?'

Scott returned a blank look.

'I know,' she continued. 'You came here looking for me. You want us to reclaim our lives. I'm ready.'

'Everything up on the hill has gone quiet. I'm trying to figure out what they're doing. What they need.'

'Maybe you've stopped hearing things.'

He shook his head. 'The voices are still there, but I can't tell what they're saying. All I can make out are wolf-voices.'

'Like this?' She cupped her lips and let out a piercing howl.

'What does that one say?'

'Come to Koppiemaul. It's dinner time. I use it in the evenings to call the wolf-children. I often wish they'd spend the night here. I could take care of a dozen.'

'They prefer each other's company. They don't need us.'

'What about their mothers? Don't they feel something toward them, even if it's a feeling of abandonment?'

'Their mothers? When I'm merged with Zia or Rami, I sometimes glimpse an empty place, a place of yearning. If a lupan is capable of any anxiety, that empty place would be it. Asra asked me about her mother, but I sense that long ago she gave up any hope of having a relationship with her.'

'But she must care. When we were attacked, the children came to our defence. At least they sent the wolves in to protect us. Even at the cost of their lives. They must still care about their mothers.'

While she was speaking Scott's eyes glazed over to where he appeared to ignore her. She was inclined to shrug him off, then realized that he had actually drifted off to wander down one of his labyrinthine paths. 'Are you here? Scott! Talk to me.'

His eyes met hers. 'I'm all right. Listen, can we bring the village together? There's something we have to tell everyone.'

'What is it?'

'The mothers must return to their children. It's the only way to save their lives. The army will never dare bomb the colony as long as our people are up there, with women in the font line. We have to convince them to go back.'

'There's nothing I want more, but it's impossible. It won't happen.'

'Why not?'

She shook her head. 'The wounding is too great.'

'I don't understand.'

'Scott, you're not a woman. You have to see it from a mother's point of view, a mother who abandoned her child. Maybe she had to. Or maybe the child ran away, but abandonment is what it feels like. For years the mothers have been trying to forget their children even exist. They never visit them. They don't even want to see them a mile away.'

'Eisa cares. Enough to withhold the cure to the Plague from the rest of the world.'

'You're trying to be rational. It isn't rational. At some level, Lina, Gharam, Hana and the others still care about their children. They'd be destroyed if anything happened to the lupans. But that doesn't mean that they're ready to include them in their lives. They're too overwhelmed by shame; of having abandoned them.'

245

'We can't sit back and let the army destroy them. I'll be on that hill in full view when the helicopters attack. I'll go alone if I can't persuade the women to come with me.'

'You can't get rid of me so easily. I'll be beside you.'

'We stand more of a chance if we have a crowd around us. More than the pair of us waving flags. We have to convince the women to join us.'

'I don't know how to even start that conversation.'

Linella poured the coffee, now lukewarm, and pushed a cup toward him. She folded her arms. 'I suppose I'd better try. They'll never listen to you. They don't open up to people they don't know well. I'll start with Lina.'

'Why Lina?'

'She's the matriarch. If she decides to go, the others will follow her. It won't be easy. Whenever I mention Rami she becomes very angry and ends the conversation. Maybe she'll see it differently if she realizes that she can save their lives.'

'If she's the best chance we have, we need to see her right now.' He downed the coffee in one gulp.

They left the cottage. Linella locked the door and hung the key about her neck. Was she coming back, or would the storm sweep everything away? She looked longingly at the stands of dahlias and lilies. Years of work; so many memories associated with their cultivation. She turned away. *Why am I thinking of my fucking flowers when our children are about to be killed?*

Scott waited beside her, his eyes with an unresponsive look, no doubt exploring dark pathways of the lupan world – places from which she was excluded. Though their bodies mingled as one and she felt closer to him than ever, what she wanted most, to share his thoughts and mind the way he shared it with lupans – was still denied.

From deep in the white morass of the fog came assorted sounds of men shouting, a lorry backing into place and loads thrown down on a hard surface: sounds that brought a lump to her throat. The Corsicans were breaking camp and moving out while the fog concealed them. Maybe she had expected too much from Roberto. In his place wouldn't she pack up her family and ship out before more shooting began? Why should he fight for lupans he didn't know and couldn't care less about? Nevertheless he owed her something. Why, at the very least, hadn't he come over and told her he was leaving? Given her the chance to beg him to stay, or to thank him for rescuing her?

They passed through her outer fence, walking in silence through a mist so impenetrable that they could barely see three feet. Holding her hand Scott picked out a way down the stony track. There came the sound of several shots fired in succession, then the rapid burst of gunfire. Linella's blood ran cold. Had a new military assault had begun? After a moment she realized that the muffled gunshots were coming from too far off to be in the village. The men might be training at their target range, deep in the forest.

They arrived at the meadow where she was startled to see several tall figures loom out of the mist and lurch toward her. She was about to cry out when she realized they were part of a stone circle, recently completed. The skin on her face tingled. The air crackled as around transmission pylons She felt inexplicably tense as if lightning was about to strike. Scott also felt it because he grasped her hand tight and pulled her away from the stones.

'What's going on?' she said.

'You feel it, don't you? It's power. Raw power. Don't think the lupans are defenceless. I wouldn't want to be hit by one of their lightning bolts.'

'They'll fire on attack helicopters?'

Scott's voice was happily delirious. 'Maybe. We'll find out soon.'

'Yes, more disasters.'

When they came to Lina's house they found it empty. The old man living next door said Lina had gone out with a pot of soup to feed the wounded. After a couple more inquiries they found her in Oli's house, sitting by his bed. Oli had been shot in the leg. He waved to Linella from his bed. 'I'm sorry to have to greet you from this position.'

Lina was hunched over, her face grey. She appeared to have aged twenty years since Linella last saw her. She smiled at Linella but the smile didn't appear genuine. She was annoyed at having been interrupted at her work. She didn't acknowledge Scott's presence.

'What brings you down here?' she asked Linella.

'Lina, I have to talk to you. It's important.'

Lina raised her eyebrows. 'Can it wait a minute? I have to call on Jordan while the soup is still hot.'

'We'll wait in your kitchen.'

'I'm not sure about this,' Scott said after they exited the house. 'My presence isn't going to help you. Maybe you and Lina need to talk this over one on one. You women have a private language that I don't understand.'

'Scott, I need you. I can't do this without you.'

They returned to Lina's house, still unoccupied. A pot of water simmered on the stove. Someone had left a half-finished cup of warm chicory on the kitchen table. Linella suspected that it was Sandria's.

They had just finished their tea when Lina appeared. Businesslike, she walked up to the stove, opened the fire hatch and stoked the coals rapidly. She asked if they had eaten breakfast.

'We're fine,' Linella said.

Lina sat opposite, supported her head on her hands and nodded for Linella to speak.

'How is Oli doing?'

'Each day he takes a few more steps but he's in a lot of pain. I'm worried that some shrapnel is stuck in his stomach. We need to get him to a real hospital. Don't talk to me about the patients.'

'I want to know.'

Lina's stern face softened. 'I'll tell you later. I'm very tired. These days I hardly get any sleep.' She shook her head. 'This fog drives me crazy. I keep imagining that when it lifts we will find ourselves surrounded by tanks. But I do my best. It's all I can do. There's no one else to care for the wounded, to wash their laundry or change their dressings.'

'What about Eisa?'

Lina shrugged. 'What about him? He keeps to his house and his papers. Sometimes he checks on the patients. I can't worry about Eisa, Johnson and all that business.'

'And Arjan?'

Lina let out a dry laugh. 'He's walking again. Praise God his wounds are not serious. You'll find him with the men, up in the forest trying out their new guns. As if they can change anything. They pulled out their guns before, and you saw what happened. They never learn. But I'm telling you nothing new. What about you, what did you want to talk about? You said it was important.'

'It's about Rami,' Linella blurted out, not knowing how else to open the conversation. She had expected Lina to freeze upon mention of the name, and she did.

Now she's going to walk out.

However Lina didn't stir. She looked past Linella into empty space. 'Did something happen to him?'

'No.'

'So, why bring up his name?'

'It's not only about Rami,' Scott interjected. 'It's about all the children. Johnson told us that the government will try to remove them from the hill. I'm afraid they may be killed. We have to do something to prevent it.'

'And what do you propose? Another battle?'

'We have a different plan.'

Lina scarcely stirred. The cloud that descended on her brow upon the mention of Rami only deepened.

'I'm not saying anything,' she said. 'You can keep talking.'

'The women can stop the attack if they all return to their children. The army won't dare to bomb the colony while you are up there.'

'They fired on us before. Why should our presence on the hill change anything?'

'They were facing armed resistance. Believe me, they won't want any pictures of wounded women to hit the news channels. They'll put off their attack, at least long enough for us to negotiate with them.'

'Negotiate. Yes.'

'It doesn't seem like much, but it means a delay – maybe enough to make a difference.'

'You want us – to all – go up there?' Lina spoke the words slowly and appeared to choke on each one. 'Do you know what you're asking?'

'I'm asking for the mothers to return to their children; to recognize them as their own. The world must see that the lupans are your children; not some alien, apelike species, but people with feelings who must be protected at all costs. If you save their lives you might save a hell of a lot more – like the human race.'

Tears rolled down Lina's face. Her arms shook. 'It's impossible. Don't you see that?'

Linella clasped Lina's hands and held them close. 'Why is it impossible, Lina my dearest?'

Lina's lips tightened. She turned away.

'You can talk to me.'

'Not about this. Please don't ask.'

'Can you at least think about it?' Scott said.

Lina's cold eyes flashed at him. 'For you it's so simple, so clear. All we have to do is to march up that hill to embrace those – yes, those children. First we must sort through them. Today I don't think I'd recognize Rami. Then when the helicopters attack, we hold hands and show the whole world just how much we love our little golden-eyed babies. It is so simple to you.' Tears ran down her face and she sobbed uncontrollably.

Linella had expected the conversation wouldn't be easy, but she wasn't prepared for Lina's bitter tears.

Lina turned coldly to Scott. 'I don't expect you to understand because this all happened long ago. But she knows. Those children are our shame.'

Shame – the word lashed out unexpectedly. Of course. The mass rape that had left the women pregnant. The tragedy of that day had never been forgotten. With the birth of each child, the mother re-lived the violence of that dreadful night. The squalling child was regarded not as a child sent by God but the spawn of Satan; the fruit of violence. Such mutterings were common among refugee women in back rooms. Every lupan birth brought predictable looks of disapproval. Even outside the community, religious zealots voiced sentiments that wolf-children were a divine curse, brought on to chastise the human race for its atheism. Among the women the feeling of shame was so pervasive that they were unable to bond with their children. After trying unsuccessfully to mother them, they handed their wolf-children back to nature.

How could the mothers revive a relationship that never existed?

'Unless we intervene, they will die,' Linella said.

Lina nodded.

'Are you content to watch it on television?'

'We can't stop it.'

'Can't – or won't? I for one will not let it happen.'

'You're so perfect. As if you're the only one who cares. We gave birth to them, not you. We stayed awake night after night with the howling things, terrified that they'd kill us.' She held up her right hand, whose forefinger was crooked. 'This finger was almost bitten off when I tried to feed him. Not even dogs treated us the way those children did. You have no idea what you're asking.'

'Do they mean absolutely nothing to you?'

Lina let out a loud sob. 'I've already told you. We have a bond with them. A painful bond. We fought for them, for them to have their home. We gave them everything, until we had nothing left to give. They left us for their wolves. Let them live separately from us. We wish them well.'

'What are you most afraid of?'

Lina wiped the tears from her eyes. 'That I'll lose myself. Everything I've fought for. For years I've kept that door shut. If I should open it, my grief and my shame will tear me apart.' Embarrassed, she glanced at Scott. 'Excuse me for talking like this.'

'Maybe you don't know how special they are,' he said.

Lina's lips tightened. 'It's something I'd rather not know. The less I know about them, the better.'

'I won't abandon them,' Linella said. 'Scott and I will go up to the colony to be human shields. My boys will come too. We'll lead anyone who wants to join us.'

Lina grabbed Linella's arm. 'It's suicide. They'll kill you. I don't want you to go. Why are you doing this?'

'Because no one else will stick up for them.'

'Linella, I have lost so much. Please don't leave me. I can't bear the thought of you up there alone. Please.'

'It's where I belong. I never gave birth to a lupan, but they are my children: Rami, Zia, Leila, Tahani and so many others. For thirty years I've lived with them. They come to my table. I feed them. I feel that I understand them deeply though we've never exchanged a word. I can't let them die alone while we sit safe in our houses watching television. It would be a terrible betrayal.'

'You don't have to do this.'

'I do. And so should you. By now we'd all be dead or stuck in a detention centre, but for our children. They sent in the wolves to protect us, even at the cost of their lives. We have to stand by them. Even if it seems useless.'

Linella rose from the table. 'Come with us.'

Lina stared back. 'Don't ask me to.'

As Linella turned to go, Lina caught her arm and said, 'I'll come, but only because of you. I won't let you die alone. I don't want you to die.'

They fell into each other's arms, both weeping.

'Won't you convince other women to come with us?' Linella

said. 'We need a crowd up there if this is going to work.'

Lina sighed. 'Hana will come with us – her child, what is her name?'

'Zia.'

'Yes, Zia. If I convince Gharam and Hana, the others will follow. They're not deeply wounded, as I.'

THIRTY

– They're coming.

Merged with the Messenger, Beauty Woman watches his thoughts swirl like a babbling stream seeking its way amid endless chaos. One thought rises above the morass, surprising her with its clarity.

– They want their children – she tells Blue Sky.

Through the Messenger's eyes she sees a large room filled with village women. Many are weeping. One of them is her mother, but which one? Beauty Woman hadn't recently thought of her, a small woman named Hana who shouted "Zia" to her. She was never happy no matter what "Zia" did. Mother's shouting conveyed only that she was angry, and that something was wrong. When she was too tired to shout she threw books, dishes or whatever was close at hand. "Zia" quickly learned to find good hiding places. Finally mother became uncommunicative and no longer responded when her child cried.

One morning mother took her to the hut outside the village and left her there with other saplings. From that day, Cottage Woman and Dark Woman took care of her. She never saw her mother again. For days she hid in a cupboard lest the sun in the sky see her. She'd been cast aside because of her unusual eyes, because she didn't use words when she wanted something, and because she preferred wolf-milk to her mother's milk. Mother was so angry that she deprived "Zia" of the security and warmth of her body. So did many others leaving their saplings with each other for protection. They knew that they were different; that their mothers would not and could not do anything for them. Only the spirit that gave birth to them could nurture them.

Among the women in the room Beauty Woman recognizes only the Messenger and Cottage Woman. Cottage Woman speaks to the assembly but her gaze turns often to the Messenger. Her eyes glow with a new passion. Though their bodies are separate, their souls burn like indistinguishable fires.

Near Cottage Woman sits a small stocky woman dressed in black with a stern, unsmiling face marked by time. Strong Woman would be her name. Whenever she speaks others fall silent out of respect. Long ago she had a lithe body that danced, laughed and could even sing. After she gave birth, sorrow silenced her song. She tells the mothers that they must all return to their children. Protect them from the fire.

Where is mother? Beauty Woman scans the faces and finds a tall, thin woman who hesitates whether to join the others. Time has wrinkled her face and withered her hands. Her body seems little more than an empty shell. Is this frail woman the terrifying Hana who threw books at "Zia"? Her eyes have a lonely look; a hunger that no nourishment can satisfy. For many years Hana hasn't thought about her child and isn't sure she wants to. The Messenger tells her that unless she accompanies the others, she may not see her daughter again. Hana replies that she is too tired, and doesn't have the strength to climb the hill.

– Tell her to come – Beauty Woman says. – I want to see her.

Their meeting may not satisfy mother's hunger, but it may help her spirit to find its way home.

Later that day, while gathering mushrooms, Beauty Woman encounters Dream Woman, dancing in a forest clearing. On the foggy days when the sun is hidden, Dream Woman is often seen walking alone, wrapped in a bear-skin to keep warm. She speaks with trees and rocks, tends not to respond when people address her. When Beauty Woman appears, Dream Woman pauses in her dance. Not wanting to disturb her, Beauty Woman tries to leave, but something makes her stop. A power appears in the clearing, one that requires her to speak to Dream Woman.

Dream Woman is alone. She has withdrawn into a place where no one can merge with her. The cloud of death envelops her.

– You're leaving us? – Beauty Woman asks.

Dream Woman picks up a leaf, examines it as if she sees the entire world contained there.

– No more than tree-leaves wither and fall. That's what we are. Merge with the leaf and you'll find the entire tree. It lives only for a season. Like us. After I leave, you must guide the People. Their springtime is over. They are in full summer. Autumn lies ahead and like this leaf, they fly off in the wind, swirling and dancing.

She spreads her arms and twirls in a circle so fast that she must be dizzy.

Dream Woman's utterances are often mysterious, but now she appears determined not to be understood.

– Why is everyone gathering food? – Dream Woman mutters, after she stops spinning. – Everyone is hauling pots of potatoes, burying them. Burying all their food supplies as if the world is about to end. Tell me because I don't understand anything. What is all this activity about?

– A fire is coming. We have to protect our food lest it burn.

– By trees and hills and sky, what do your preparations matter?

– Shouldn't we save our food?

– Nothing that you own can burn. Can a dream burn? Can your vision?

Dream Woman peers closely at Beauty Woman, a look that penetrates her to the core.

– It's a great mystery, if you can only see it: the whole that is in us and outside of us is immortal. Fires come and go but they cannot touch place from where we come and where we return.

– Then we must do nothing?

– There's nothing to do.

After a long silence, Dream Woman lapses back into a dream. She no longer responds to further questions.

Returning to Blue Sky, Beauty Woman relates her encounter with Dream Woman, but he shrugs off her enigmatic utterances. He's more concerned about the village women's intention to march up to the colony.

– They must not come here – he says. – The fire may destroy them.

– They feel that they can hold it back.

– They don't understand fire. How can they expect to control it?

– They belong here. Don't you see that their coming here is important? They must be with us when the firestorm awakens.

After she lies down for the night she feels Wolfborn's presence in the den: Wolfborn in whom the spirit burns strongly, who taught her how to hunt with the pack, commune with wolves, gather edible plants and to heal wounds. She was Beauty Woman's mother in ways that Hana never could be.

The mothers' imminent return troubles Wolfborn, because she is unusually silent. Finally she tells Beauty Woman, – As you gain one mother, so you lose another.

– Why do I lose you? – The thought screams through Beauty Woman.

Wolfborn presents the image of a destructive fire. Wolves, who smell approaching danger when it is days away, know that fire is coming. She must face it along with them and die by their side if necessary.

– What can we do for you? – Beauty Woman asks.

– Take care of the People. Of your mothers.

Beauty Woman weeps. Her exchange with Wolfborn awakens in her a cold sense of loss, the thought that the voice that has been her constant companion may one day fall silent. The thought doesn't feel real. Yet death is real, the ending of the familiar. Each breath she takes connects her with death. She sees it whenever a sapling or a deer dies. Loss, emptiness and an ending. She consoles herself with the vision of Dream Woman, dancing in the forest, her insight – *Nothing you own can die.*

At daybreak she awakens. The intense light and warmth penetrating her body tell her that the fog has lifted. There's no need to wear skins that day. Starlet is whimpering for her milk. She places the baby to her breast. With a soft kick, she wakes up Blue Sky.

– We must greet the women – she tells him.

The village women appear near the foot of the hill. They wear sombre clothes; many support themselves with sticks. After many foggy days, the sun has reappeared, but the Earth's breath has also grown strong, kicking up clouds of dust and shaking the dry bushes. It tears at the women's clothes and pushes them against the hill. Younger women support the older ones; help them over stone steps. Despite the wind and the frequent boulders that block the path, the women persist, step by step, determined to reach the colony.

Leading are Cottage Woman, the Messenger and Strong Woman. Beauty Woman recognizes a few others but Hana is not among them. Neither is she in a second column, one comprised of men who carry boxes and sacks of provisions. She locates Hana far behind the others, walking with three stooped women. They move slowly, leaning on their sticks and looking longingly back at the village. The wind saps their strength; the stony ground hurts their feet. Mother's companions stop to rest. They sit with their backs to the hill and appear despondent. Will she continue? She talks to her companions. It's clear that they want to turn back.

Beauty Woman feels an overwhelming urge to take action. She tightens the scarf that holds Starlet to her back. She runs down the path with the swiftness of a deer, squeezes past the first group, and then the men with the loads. Driven by a passion she doesn't understand she lets her body find its speed. Mother must come. She must not turn back before they have met.

Mother hides her face in her scarf. Her long grey hair released from its confinement flutters freely. Struggling against the persistent wind, she cries out that she can't go on. She doesn't want to see her daughter. Her taller companion takes her by the arm and leads her back down the path, the way they had come. Then she catches sight of Beauty Woman running toward her and cries out, 'Zia.'

Despite the distance of intervening years, mother has no doubt that this is her 'Zia.' A smile breaks over her face, a look of wonder. But as Zia draws close, mother's smile fades and she pulls away. 'Zia's' nakedness disturbs her. Hana quickly removes her shawl and drapes it about Beauty Woman's waist. Then she's astonished to see Starlet's small face looking out from her perch. She hadn't imagined that her daughter might also be a mother. Beauty Woman wishes she could speak human words, but all she can do is weep. She takes her mother's head and cradles it. She kisses mother's cheeks.

'Talk to me,' Hana says. 'I want to hear you speak.'

Hana's words sound little different than the chattering of a stream. Articulate sounds that communicate feelings. She wants to be understood, for her daughter to know her. The words also stir a dark memory inside Beauty Woman, one left behind in a dark cave where it was shut in by burdensome sorrow. Looking into her mother's hollow eyes she recalls a painful day when she hid from mother's anger. What had "Zia" then withheld from mother? She'd withheld all hope of communication between them. Language.

Without knowing how or why, Beauty Woman speaks, 'I thank you. That you come.'

Mother stares back. 'You can talk?' she says. 'Not only you're here, but you can really talk to me.'

'We talk. Yes, we talk. We thank you.'

I? We? You? Beauty Woman isn't sure how to use or place the words or what they're supposed to mean. If Hana understands them, then they presumably mean something.

Supporting mother under one arm, Beauty Woman helps her climb over a stone step, and then up the path to the colony. Upon approaching the others, she hears more voices. Not only the mothers are speaking, but so are the People, using long forgotten words. They speak simple greetings of recognition. The mothers are astonished to hear their children's voices. Strong Woman asks Blue Sky to speak, and so he does – stringing together random words like stones on a necklace.

Why had words been hidden so deeply and for so long, not used by anyone except Wolfborn? No one understood them, but that hadn't always been so. When the mothers abandoned their children, the children deprived their mothers of words. They fell silent because they did not want anyone to know them or to understand them. Only in silence did they feel safe. The children did not need language to communicate with each other; only with their mothers. They found language troublesome, difficult to use because it chopped up thoughts into unrelated fragments. After the final parting, any attempt to speak with their mothers evoked only pain and frustration.

They invite the mothers into their den where they share a simple meal. Beauty Woman sits opposite Mother and offers her a bowl of deer stew. At first her mother declines the bowl.

'Eat,' Beauty Woman says.

With her long fingers Mother picks out a piece of meat, chews it slowly, but then spits it out. Her teeth aren't used to tough meat. Beauty Woman pre-chews the piece, as she would for a child, and offers it again but Hana turns away. Other mothers are having the same difficulty with the stew. They end up only drinking the broth and eating oat cakes.

Blue Sky talks with his mother, Strong Woman. She doesn't want to eat; only to listen to him. He slows down his thoughts so they can be separated into their constituents and presented to Strong Woman as sounds, but what emerge are half-formed distortions. A tree uprooted from the ground that contains it. A bird plucked from the sky.

'Do you eat this stew every day?' she asks him.

'Every day eats the stew,' he replies.

260

Strong Woman says she doesn't understand, so he tries again: 'The stew is swallowed by the day.'

After several such exchanges she falls silent. Perhaps the recovered language doesn't bring them any closer. The differences between them are deeper, rooted in the unique ways they think; the ways they perceive each other. For Strong Woman, he will always remain a sapling, separate from her. Blue Sky however sees a mother, no different from others; no different from Earth or Sky.

She smiles at him kindly. 'You were a beautiful baby.'

'The baby's beautiful,' he acknowledges.

Beauty Woman serves tea in small clay cups.

'We drink it,' she tells Hana. 'Do we like it?'

Hana sips the tea and smiles. 'It's wonderful.'

She talks at length to Beauty Woman, tells her why she has come – that helicopters, drones – words that Beauty woman doesn't yet understand, are on the way. A terrible danger faces the People.

'We came here to protect you.'

'Fire coming,' Beauty Woman says. 'As it must. We're together in its face.'

'You're not afraid?'

Beauty Woman doesn't know how to reply. Mother's trembling eyes reveal that she is overwhelmed by dark thoughts, a deer cornered by wolves and barely able to move. Now that she has found her daughter, she is afraid that the meeting is only for a few hours, and that they will lose each other again.

'This moment, we are here,' Beauty Woman says. 'Look – can you see? That we are. No differenting. Just us here. Now.'

She struggles to find the right words to express to her mother that nothing matters but the two of them taking shelter in the den, two who have found each other and who are no longer separate; but when she tries to say it, the words pull her away from Hana. They are like a blunt knife, only able to cut and divide.

The mothers' return attracts the attention of mechanical insects. All afternoon they swarm above the dens, in unusually thick clouds. Whenever the villagers venture outside, the buzzing insects follow them, chasing them right up to the door.

By twilight the wind is so strong that everyone remains indoors. Even the insect clouds are gone. The trees twist and bend, their branches waving madly, stirred into the great dance. Dark clouds race across the sky, waves that seek an unseen shore. The Elder People take refuge in the gathering den. It's well provisioned for them and contains comfortable beds. Though they're happy to have found their children, they still prefer the company of their own kind.

Blue Sky leans into the stone on the hill, and surveys the darkening world. Trees are bent horizontal with all their branches waving. Yet through the wind he still hears the Earth's resonant hum. Far in the forest Wolfborn and her pack take shelter in a hollow while they await the fire. It will come as surely as morning. The mothers' return to the hill has brought comfort and security to the People, but it has not helped the plight of the wolves, or of Wolfborn. Is the Earth strong enough to protect them? Blue Sky asks the question, and allows it to reverberate inside him but he hears no answer.

He returns to the den where he finds Cottage Woman by the stove, heating up a pot of water. She stirs in a heap of nettle leaves, shakes the pot. The stove's heat makes her arms and face sweat. Her slow movements carry a beautiful rhythm. If she didn't wear so many clothes she would feel better. Her beauty would glow even brighter. On a nearby bed the Messenger lies with his eyes closed, pre-occupied with his thoughts, talking to himself about events that have not yet happened: giant insects, bloodshed and death. He doesn't need the food that Cottage Woman prepares, but wants her presence beside him, so she might draw him away from his dreams. Blue Sky takes the ladle out of her hand and leads her over to the Messenger's bed.

That night they all lie together, the Messenger against Cottage

Woman, who embraces Beauty Woman and who holds Blue Sky. Luxuriating in the warmth, softness and scent of their bodies they fall asleep. Blue Sky stays awake longest, recalling the day the Messenger's bird crashed in the forest. When he saw it fall, he knew that the Messenger's arrival meant more than the fall of a random leaf. Earth had drawn him out of Sky's embrace and presented him as a gift to the People.

THIRTY-ONE

Sandria pressed herself against Eisa's door for shelter against the wind. She grasped the door-handle but did not turn it. The past few days she had thought obsessively about what she had to do, going over it from every angle until she exhausted herself. She needed to expel the thing growing inside her, a life-form as alien as her first child. End of discussion. When she asked Eisa for an abortion, he took a long draw at his cigarette, and looked away. He'd terminated a few lupan pregnancies but did not like doing it. Abortion was not part of village culture. Most women carried their lupans to term and then they went through the inevitable parting when the child was a few years old. The baby immediately latched onto the alien breast and drank greedily. The parting was only the first blow in a protracted grieving process. Those who terminated their pregnancies recovered from their loss sooner.

Lina begged her to join the women on their pilgrimage to the lupan colony. Sandria told her 'no' knowing that refusal could result in her ostracism. But she couldn't bend to Lina's will. She didn't need to return to the colony for an ephemeral sighting of Asra. Neither did she want to risk meeting Scott only for him to, once again, try to change her mind about removing the foetus. By staying behind she could take care of the pregnancy, without his or Lina's interference.

The wind buffeted her face. It whipped her skirt against her legs. She pulled her shawl over her head to keep out the flying dust. Her hand tightened on the door handle. In or out – she had to choose. She went in and slammed the door behind her. An acrid smell hit her nostrils, cold smoky air with an aftertaste of stale whisky. In the dim air she could barely see a few feet in any direction. She covered her face, afraid to breathe the rancid air. She called into the dim room: 'Eisa!' Her voice sounded hollow. Something was wrong.

She struggled over to the window, tore down the rag that hung over it and pushed open the windows. A shaft of outside light shone into the smoky room, onto his table heaped with paper, books, and empty whisky-bottles. The wind sent a flock of papers flying in circles. Only when the smoke lifted did she find him, lying face-down behind the stove.

Shaking his shoulder felt like massaging a lifeless lump of clay. Was he dead? She placed her cheek by his parted lips, barely detected any breath, then felt under his neck for a pulse. If he had one it was weak. He might not be dead. Not yet, but with each passing second he was closer to death. An empty medicine bottle lay a few feet away. He'd overdosed. Who could she call? The women were all gone, and so were most men. Of Linella's boys only Josh remained in the village. She'd left him sleeping in Lina's attic room. Protesting loudly he'd agreed to help women and kids who stayed behind.

With her scarf pulled tightly over her face she stepped outside. She couldn't see more than a few feet in any direction. Flying sand stung her eyes. The boarded-up houses reminded her that she was alone. She yelled out, 'Josh!' but her voice didn't carry above the screaming gale. She'd almost reached Lina's when she glimpsed his curly mop emerge from the doorway.

'It's Eisa!' she yelled. 'Call an ambulance.'

Luckily Josh didn't debate her. Pressing his wrist-com against his lips he shouted, 'Nine nine nine. Ambulance. Koppiemaul Camp – the refugee camp.' Frowning he clapped the com to his ear. 'They say they'll send someone. What's happened?'

'He's overdosed. Come with me. Can't wait here.' She grabbed Josh's arm and dragged him back down the street.

They found Eisa where she had left him. A slight quiver in his lip was the only indication that he wasn't dead yet.

'What do we do?' she said.

'You think mouth to mouth will help?'

She pressed her lips tightly against his, blew; once, twice, three times. When she could blow no more she pulled away only to watch the room spin. 'I can't,' she gasped.

Josh touched her shoulder. 'Let me try. I've done this before.'

He moved in enthusiastically as if he'd just finished his first-aid class, gave Eisa a few breaths, pumped with both hands on his chest, breath, chest and so on. After what felt like an eternity, Eisa began to breathe.

Josh sat back, wheezed while he tried to catch his breath. 'Man, that's hard work,' he shouted above the wind. 'At least he's alive. What did he do?'

Sandria picked up the medicine bottle. It was labelled with Eisa's indecipherable scrawl. 'I guess he took those, whatever they are, and chased them down with whisky. Where's that ambulance?'

Josh flipped on his wrist-com and spoke into it. Even through the whistling wind Sandria could hear the roar of static. Josh punched in some numbers. He shouted into the com, 'George – come in, guy.' He shook his head. 'There's nothing but static. Man, this storm is unreal.'

'What about the ambulance?'

'I can't get through.'

'Try again.'

While Josh struggled with his com she searched Eisa's desk for a suicide note. She rummaged through scientific reprints, a writing pad covered with Eisa's indecipherable scrawl, mostly in scientific jargon. In the middle of the desk lay an art-pad which she picked up and leafed through. She'd no idea that Eisa could draw. The charcoal sketches, mostly of lupan nudes, were very lifelike. One page showed the same female child, about six years old, viewed from various angles. Her endearing expression suggested this was someone that Eisa cared about. The final sketch was of a baby with wrinkled skin and large eyes; definitely lupan. A name scrawled in the corner read, "Sharma." She'd heard it before but wasn't sure where.

Looking around the room she noticed a large picture frame on the wall with several photographs of young lupans in a forest setting. The large girth of the pine trees was uncharacteristic of the young forests near Koppiemaul. A lupan baby set against a tree looked remarkably like the one in the final sketch. Its pose was identical.

Josh waited nervously beside her. 'We need to do something else. Like pump his stomach.'

'Where's that ambulance?'

'Stuck down the main road. I heard something about a military convoy.'

So that was it. The army was moving into place. No ambulance would get through, not until they had finished their job. Here she was, alone in the village with the tanks about to roll in.

She knelt beside Eisa, shook his shoulder desperately and called his name but he didn't respond. She could barely tell that he was breathing.

'My Mum's a pretty good nurse,' Josh said. 'I'm going to call her.'

Linella was the last person Sandria wanted to see but she was too flustered to to tell Josh not to call her. If Linella came she'd inevitably bring Scott. He'd guess why Sandria had come that morning to Eisa's house. Another confrontation would follow.

Josh punched various codes into his com, texted, and listened with his ear plugs. 'It's all static. I can't hear a thing. I'll be faster running up there.'

Before Sandria was able to protest, he was at the door. 'I'll bring her.'

She covered up Eisa with a blanket, placed a couple of pillows under his head. Unable to sit still she paced the floor, occasionally looking out at the dust storm. Would Eisa last long enough for Josh to return with some help? She was in a bad dream from which she longed to awaken. She'd come that morning for an abortion, to rid herself of a mistake, and now she was forced to keep vigil by his dying body. What had driven him to try to take his life? Hardly anyone had seen him since he handed his work to Johnson. Locking himself in his house he had refused to open his door when she banged on it. She'd glimpsed him sitting motionless on his sofa. People had stopped calling on him, even if they needed him. They assumed he was having one of his well-known bouts with depression. Not surprising. After the disastrous battle everyone in the village was depressed. People had to deal with their loss in their own way.

An hour or more passed before she noticed Linella standing beside her, white hair tangled, and breathing hard from running down the hill. Josh followed her in and heaved the door shut.

'Get him onto the bed,' Linella said. 'Jesus, what has he done?'

After they'd lifted him onto the bed, Linella rummaged through several cupboards. The first was full of medicine bottles; the next was crammed with machinery parts and surgical tools. She grabbed a small circular machine.

'Here's the pump. Where are the tubes?' Rummaging in a carton she found two thin translucent tubes, held them up to the light to check them out.

'Have you pumped a stomach before?' Sandria asked.

Linella glared back. 'Get me a light so I can see what I'm doing. I've no idea if this will help but we have to try it.'

While Sandria held up a battery-powered head-light, Linella plugged in the pump. She greased the thin tube, tilted back his head and inserted the tube in his nose, slowly manoeuvred it back and forth. Her confident manner suggested she had done it before. After a few minutes the pump whirred. Mucus and fluid appeared in the tube. Eisa coughed and spluttered, about to choke. Linella tilted his head back to open an airway. She gave him mouth to mouth. His chest rose and fell, even after she released his lips, indicating he was breathing on his own.

'Is he going to make it?' Sandria said.

'If he wants to. God, why did he do this?'

After the mucus had stopped flowing, Linella pulled out the tube and laid Eisa on his side where he was more comfortable. He was breathing regularly. He cleared his throat a few times, spluttered, opened his eyes briefly and then closed them. She searched his face for any flicker of consciousness but he appeared to be sleeping. Had she done everything right? Long ago she'd helped Eisa rescue a mother who overdosed after giving birth to a lupan. The pump procedure appeared simple. Whatever she'd done, Eisa looked no worse for her efforts.

'Did he leave anything like a note?' Linella said.

'No.'

'When did you find him?'

'Two hours ago. Maybe longer.'

With nervous fingers Linella stroked Eisa's face. When would he open his eyes? He breathed spasmodically, but appeared to sink into deeper sleep.

'He left these.' Sandria flipped though several sketches for Linella. 'Did you know he could draw?'

'Let me see that one – the baby.'

'Sharma?'

Looking at the sketch brought a lump to Linella's throat. She'd seen many pictures of lupan babies but this one inexplicably made her tearful.

'It was his girl,' Linella said. 'He told me about her – that she was dead.'

'He had a lupan girl?'

'Killed by farmers near Aviemore. Look at the poor thing. He never got over her murder. For him it was yesterday. That's why he was so fanatical about saving the children. Even if it meant that people would die from Plague.' She shook her head. 'I didn't realize what I was asking of him. Parting with his work, handing it over to Johnson must have been a terrible blow. He must have felt that he'd betrayed her.'

'That's rubbish.'

'It's not rubbish. He put Sharma's face on every lupan. Then he had to decide between saving people's lives or lupans. He had no choice. He couldn't live with himself after what he had done. I wish he'd trusted me enough to talk to me. He was so sure that the children were finished; and that he was to blame for it.'

'Poor guy.'

'If only he could see them now. Sandria, an extraordinary thing happened when they met their mothers. They began to talk.'

'That's impossible. What are you saying?'

'Go up there and you'll hear them. They're not as clear as Asra. They're trying to use words but it comes out all mixed up. Doesn't always make sense. But it's an amazing first step. They have such musical voices. I sense a new relationship with them. Things are going to be different.'

Sandria looked away, cold and unwilling to engage. Linella regretted her euphoria, realizing that it wasn't what Sandria needed at that moment. She was still wrestling with that to do next.

'You came for an abortion?' Linella said.

'Yes.'

'I'm sorry you feel that way.'

Sandria shrugged. 'This pregnancy wasn't supposed to happen.'

'I know. You wanted a normal baby.'

'And if I did? I gave birth to a lupan. I won't do it again. Never. You say you understand? You can't possibly understand.'

'I was with you when Asra was born. I took her to the wolves. Together you and I cared for the children in River House. I was always there for you when you needed my shoulder. I've kept so close to you, Sandria. Don't tell me I don't understand. I deserve better.'

'What do you want of me, Linella?'

'You already know. You came here to end one life, and ended up saving another – Eisa's. Wolf-children are life. If I could, I'd have a dozen of them. It's too late for me, but not for you. I wish you could see that something beautiful is about to be born. If you'll allow it.'

'I can't. Don't ask me to.'

'Sandria, as we speak the army is advancing. Our colony is about to be wiped out. Our children. In all your self-pity have you forgotten them, how you've always loved them? You dedicated your life to them. The colony wouldn't be there without your help. Think about what you're carrying. It's hope – the only hope we have.'

Sandria closed her eyes. She felt an avalanche inside her start to move and then gain speed, to sweep away her fear. She took Linella's hand and squeezed it. She knew she would keep the baby; allow it to be born, even if she didn't understand why.

A scream shook the walls, the kind that stopped the heart, all thoughts and every breath. The shadow of a fighter plane fell on the window.

'My God – it's here,' Linella whispered. 'I have to go.'

Two black helicopters with double propellers hovered over hill. Evidently the gusting wind made no difference to military planners. They would start their offensive when they wanted to. Even from the bottom of the hill she could see the cloud of dark drones that swarmed above the colony. Those weren't tame, surveillance drones. Sparks flashed from them, deadly lightning bursts that rained onto the hilltop. Where were the women? Surely the drones wouldn't dare to fire at them.

She sped up the hill. Josh was already several paces ahead of her. Above the dens rose a pillar of black smoke. She couldn't stop the disaster. Neither could she influence what happened to the lupans, but she had to be there.

THIRTY-TWO

'We're going in.'

Gordon turned from the wall-screen to check Johnson's reaction. They were sitting side-by-side in the cottage commandeered for a command centre. Couches and armchairs had been pushed against the walls to make room for metal tables and folding chairs. Soldiers sat in front of small screens, virtual helmets on their heads. The farmer's wife walked among the tables with a tray of teacups and biscuits, asking who wanted sugar and who wanted milk.

Johnson's only response to Gordon was to shrug. He'd already told him that gale-force winds made the operation too risky to initiate. If soldiers' lives were lost there would be a serious public backlash. The presence of refugee women in the lupan camp complicated the operation further. Gordon needed a plan to protect them. No-one wanted to see defenceless women being blown up. Gordon replied with his usual bluster that he had thought of everything. Though the wind was stronger than ideal for helicopters, the weathermen said that it would let up by noon. Besides, it was blowing from the west, right where he wanted it. Despite new developments, Operation Sudden Fire was still uncomplicated; with a 95% chance of success.

For several days the fog had delayed the operation. While troops and politicians waited for a clearing, tabloids demanded immediate and decisive action to avenge the army's humiliation. 'Can They Do Anything?' read one headline. 'Are the Wolves in

Charge?' read another. President Christie, whose approval ratings plummeted after the earlier raid, promised a TV spectacle of wolves being shot up to the music of 'The Ride of the Valkyries.' Then all lupans would be incarcerated. That morning, Gordon assured Christie that if anything went wrong, a broadcasting time lapse would allow him to edit out embarrassing footage before it hit the screens.

Johnson pushed himself laboriously out of his chair, breathing heavily through his surgical screen. He shuffled closer to a wall that contained two LED screens. One showed the first helicopter's camera, poised above the lupan colony. The second camera was pointed at the tree canopy, its waving branches no more than a blur. The swaying images testified to the gusting winds that battered the helicopters. With gloved hands he held onto a chair back for support. For a moment the room faded, before returning to focus. He wiped his brow; steadied himself. He ought to be in hospital taking intravenous antibiotics, but had decided he could not stay away. Too much was at stake.

When would he hear back from the Edinburgh lab? The researcher he spoke to sounded excited when he saw Habash's papers. Two geneticists on his research team were apparently already working along similar lines. Habash's research might provide missing information. What about a vaccine – say within a month? The researcher almost laughed, but said that anything was possible. He would rush through a new treatment protocol as soon as a vaccine was ready for trial. At the time, Johnson was hopeful. Now he wasn't so sure. Looking at close-up shots of the lupan dens, he felt that an irrevocable step was about to be taken. What if Linella was right – that the cure was out there? That his only chance to live would be gone in an hour?

When he stormed out of Eisa's house, he was still convinced that he'd survive. Whatever his symptoms, he'd be luckier than others. The new antibiotics would work on him; researchers would confirm Habash's discoveries and they'd develop an effective vaccine. He certainly wouldn't have to live among lupans to be cured. That was then. The cottage walls appeared to close in on him. Each painful breath told him that he was no different from other Plague victims. He was dying. He had put his hopes in researchers who could never agree among themselves, and who took forever to do anything.

Standing beside him, Gordon followed the wall-screens, unconcerned by the rocking images; his craggy face showed no flicker of emotion. Johnson wanted to tell him, *Hold off. We're about to cut off the branch we're sitting on. If they die, we die.* Maguire's words didn't sound so outrageous any more. The swelling beneath his chin seemed to say the same thing. Even Linella's assertion, that living among lupans would cure him, began to make sense.

'Gordon,' he said in a hoarse voice.

The Major's shaven head turned toward him. He frowned. 'You okay, Brigadier?'

Johnson nodded. Gordon had his orders; he had no choice but to proceed.

The camera zoomed in on a cluster of dens, then on the standing stone where several lupans were gathered. Farther down the hill two lupans were running for cover. At least they were smart enough to get out of the way. Where was Linella? The refugee women were all gathered outside a large den. He couldn't imagine her to be anywhere else, but he did not see her among the women. His jaw clenched and his heart raced at the thought that she might soon be trapped on the hill; so close to the forest fire and the bombing. Gordon's plan called for surgical strikes to destroy stray wolves, and then an air landing. Troops would surround the colony and use tear gas to extract lupans from their dens, a plan that should minimize collateral damage. But in any operation things could go wrong. They often did.

A nearby desk monitor displayed an infrared image of trees with embedded hot spots. Animal life; most likely wolves. Cross hairs locked onto the hot spots; followed them while they meandered. The wolves may have sensed they were under observation, because the hot spots suddenly scattered. Several headed toward the lupan colony.

'Fire when ready,' Gordon said into his headset.

The forest image retreated as 'Helicopter A' climbed to its firing altitude. Moments later several rockets streaked into view and vanished into the canopy leaving thin vapour trails. The trees shuddered; smoke billowed out where the rockets struck, followed immediately by fiery tongues. The soaring flames raced from tree to tree and within minutes formed a wall of fire. The wind fanned it, pushing it toward the colony. Tree after tree became a fiery torch. Sparks rained down on the canopy to ignite new fires. The smoke soon grew so thick that trees and flames both vanished into a grey morass. The camera slewed to the clearing between the forest and the colony: a patch of dry grass and scrubby bushes barely visible through the glowing clouds. The images turned orange, wavered and appeared to lose focus.

One by one the wolves raced into the clearing. At first only a few, but soon a vast tide stampeded in, some with smoking fur. That was where Gordon wanted them. Mini-drones swooped in. Hundreds of fiery beams flickered through the smoke and seared whatever they touched. As soon as a wolf left the shelter of the trees, it stumbled and fell, not to rise again. Cameras zoomed in on individual animals, caught them in their death throes, and then zoomed out to show piles of lifeless wolves. It was the footage that Christie asked for. Wagner's music kicked in. The command room broke out in cheers. Soldiers removed their helmets and crowded round a TV screen where an excited television commentator yelled as if a football goal had been scored: 'This is the moment of reckoning. There they go, boys!'

Johnson shook his head. So this was payback for the army's humiliation – dozens of stupid beasts shot up in front of cameras. It might go over well with the public, but wouldn't comfort a widow who had lost a soldier. More than this would be required. Punishing lupans wouldn't be enough either. He massaged the lump under his chin. 'We don't know what the hell we're doing,' he muttered.

Destroying a species was nothing new. The world contained only a hundredth of the plant or animal species that thrived fifty years earlier. Most had been destroyed through ignorance or as a result of global warming. But this action was deliberate; inspired by the view that humanity was at war with sub-human beasts. That lupans were no more than Neanderthals. No-one knew what they really were; no-one cared.

The fire line crept up to the clearing's edge. Trees flared briefly before toppling in a shower of sparks. As Johnson watched, an unexplainable dread took hold of him that something horrible was about to happen. Only grass and scrub lay between the conflagration and the first dens. Something Gordon hadn't thought of was that the blaze would leapfrog across the meadow to the dens where it would trap the women and lupans before anyone could rescue them.

'Major, that fire's not going to stop,' he said but his voice barely carried above the room's cheering.

'Gordon!'

Gordon turned to him with a condescending smile. 'Relax, Brigadier.'

'There are women down there.'

'I know.'

Why am I here watching this? Johnson whispered to himself. Someone needs to stop this madness. But he could do nothing except stand there and watch the disaster unfold.

From the hilltop Scott watched the wolves fall, their voices ever weaker and more anguished, no longer hunting-calls, but despairing howls; warning others to stay away. Blinded by smoke he could only make out light-flashes from the drone clouds; and the spreading fire. Where was Asra? Searching inside himself for her voice he found only an eerie silence. She might already be among the dead wolves, killed in her wolf-form.

Standing beside him Rami was an immovable rock. Far from despondent at the sight of the slaughter, his eyes grew harder. He appeared to be listening for a hidden cue. The Earth's hum had grown so loud that it overwhelmed the crackling fire and the thudding helicopters. Zia held onto Rami for support. Her eyes had a faraway look, engaged elsewhere. She was out there with the wolves; dying with them.

Where was Linella? Time stopped when he thought of her. She'd disappeared two hours earlier to answer Josh's distress call that the doctor had overdosed. If only she was safe in the village, but what if she wasn't? At the first sign of trouble she'd surely be running up the hill to make sure her women were out of harm's way.

So far they were unharmed, but for how long? The meadow was catching fire and the flames crept toward the colony; and the women. They still had time to run down to the village but he doubted they would. Now that they had rediscovered their children they wouldn't abandon them to face the fire alone. They were there to be a human shield. This was their time.

What was Rami waiting for? Despite his ability to merge with Rami, Scott couldn't understand why he wasn't leading everyone away from the doomed colony. Rami's stony face indicated that he wasn't about to move. He had other plans; escaping was not among them.

Suddenly Scott noticed smoke clouds rising from the direction of the village. Had the fire already encircled the hilltop? It had. Through the dense pall he made out a line of rising smoke spreading downhill along a small canyon that extended toward the village. At the foot of the hill the fire found ample gorse and heather fuel. A brisk wind sent the flames toward the village, and the path leading there. If Linella was heading uphill she could already be surrounded by fire.

'I'm going to find her,' he said to Rami and Zia. He tore down the hill, past the empty dens and on, to where the smoke was thickest.

The wind pushed him against the hill, blowing smoke and ashes in his face. He closed his eyes to avoid being blinded. Yellow clouds hid the village from view and appeared to thicken in every direction. Wherever he turned he saw glowing arcs of flame devouring the bushes. High above the smoke stood the wind-generators, their blades whirling madly. Choking and spluttering he stumbled down the track, pausing only to peer into the smoke for anything that moved – a person or even an animal.

It had happened before. From the tower on Coldhill he'd watched a fire consume the forest, and along with it the woman with the wolves. Asra or Linella? Both faced the same fire. Would they also succumb to it, like the unnamed woman? His legs carried him on. The heat scalded his face and arms; his hands blistered. What would he do when he could go no further? When the smoke overwhelmed him? He might end up burning up along with the hill, but he had to try and find her. He'd let her die before; it would not happen again. With his eyes stinging, streaming with tears, he couldn't make out where he was going. His feet swept through hot ashes. The stench of burning rubber from his shoes reached his nostrils. The flames from passing bushes scorched his hand.

Then the wind shifted direction. He felt a sudden lull before it resumed, this time at his back, blowing the smoke and heat away from him. Suddenly he could see the hill again. He was about to walk into a fire line. But the line of flames twisted around in a wild dance, and then retreated from him. Louder than the crackling flames was the high-pitched sound of the Earth's song, no longer a melody but an anguished scream.

That was when he heard the first explosion.

Johnson heard the panicked cry from the helicopter pilot. He had steered the machine above the burning trees for a dramatic shot. The trees spun madly in a circle. The pilot yelled that he was losing control. The screen images swam as if seasick. When they steadied again, it was to show the approaching ground – a

278

wasteland of ashes and smoke about to swallow the camera.

The blast echoed across the glen. It shook the cottage windows. The soldiers held their breath. No one wanted to believe that the helicopter had crashed, along with twenty on board. A mechanical malfunction? A backdraught – or something else? Johnson licked his dry lips. The wall-screen remained featureless grey. Its neighbouring screen showed burning trees. The helicopter pilot was screaming, something about the wind, about not being able to see. He wanted to investigate the first helicopter's crash. The screen shifted to the smoking meadow with the wolf carcases, several blackened tree-stumps still standing, and now the burning shell of the first helicopter, its tail blown halfway across the clearing.

The meadow suddenly spun around in an unrehearsed about-turn and then tilted sideways. Johnson heart stopped. He shouted out, 'Get that chopper out of there.'

Even as he spoke, the image wavered like a photograph about to catch fire and then a yellow curtain drew over the image leaving it blank.

Again the cottage windows rattled from the explosion. A pane shattered. Everyone cried out. Gordon stared at the blank screen, his whitened face turned to stone. The soldiers removed their headsets. For a full minute no one spoke. Finally Johnson cleared his throat.

'Major, put out that fucking fire. Then order medical helicopters. I want to be on the first one that lands.'

He staggered over to his desk where he slumped into his chair. He tore off his surgical screen. Removed his latex gloves. So much had been lost. Stupidly lost. He knew what he had to do, and it wasn't what he'd decided earlier.

When the smoke in his eyes cleared Scott looked out over the blackened hill, heather, bushes and trees reduced to stumps in a field of white ash. The ebbing wind pushed the flames back down the hill. The thudding pulse of the helicopter blades was gone.

The explosions still echoed in his head. Somehow he wasn't surprised by what had happened.

His eyes still stinging, he scanned the ash piles for any sign of Linella. In earlier days, he'd come across the woman's body in a hollow. A cold dread settled on his heart, that he had come too late. He would only find her charred body, unless by some miracle the wind had changed direction in time to save her, or she was safe in the village. He picked his way through charred bushes, stepping where the ashes weren't smoking. Heat from glowing embers seared his face but he pressed on regardless. At any time the wind could change direction and send the fire after him.

Something inside him moved, as if a door had opened. A husky voice called out to him. He stopped, shook his head to make sure he wasn't imagining it. He could not mistake Asra's voice, 'Stay. Wait for us to come to you.'

Without moving he searched the hill. Somewhere in the wasteland Asra was alive. Not until the smoke cleared did he see her gaunt figure emerge from a hollow, her face seared with fire and her hair burned off. Following her were Linella, Josh and several wolves with singed fur. Linella stumbled through the ashes. Her grimy face was smeared from frequent wiping and from tears, her arms blistered and her hair tangled with ashes. Seeing him she allowed a wry smile to emerge.

'I'm sorry,' she muttered. 'I must look terrible.'

THIRTY-THREE

Blue Sky stands in the meadow, or what had once been a stretch of waving grass, now an expanse of warm ashes. His awareness touches the smoking tree stumps, a sea of ash with the burning shells of the Insects, to the distant hill where flame tongues still consume the trees. Tired flames, they're almost satiated. Around him are piles of smouldering bodies, what remain of Insect People and wolves. Death is the new reality. Grey voices that spoke to him since he was a sapling are silenced. The land doesn't feel like a place that can sustain life, but one that wishes to sleep. The People's dens no longer make sense. Incongruous objects, they don't belong in the dead landscape.

It's no longer the place where seasons proceed in an orderly way, crops growing in the spring and dying in winter, where saplings are born, are fed on their mothers' or wolf-milk. The partnership with the wolf has ended. Not only have the wolves died but the wolf inside him has died. An arm has been wrested from his body and left a bloodied stump.

He cries out. His anguished voice echoes in the grey emptiness. There's no response. Even the Earth's voice, previously so vibrant, has faded to a whisper, no louder than the rustling of phantom birches. What is it saying? Something about sleep and a grievous wound; that a bleak winter must cover the land before any promise of spring. The People must take care of themselves. They'll draw no nourishment from ashes. They must rely on their supplies and on assistance from their mothers until the next spring.

Why did so many wolves have to die? The question appears inside him, but there's no answer. Nothing can explain the piles of wolf corpses. Not even the hatred of the Insect People, an absurdity in itself, can be seen as a cause. Since when can absurdity cause anything? The wolves knew the fire was coming, but they decided not to escape from it. Why not? While watching them emerge from the burning forest, he sensed that they had chosen to submit to the fire's inevitability, rather than to resist it.

Awakening from those thoughts, he finds that his feet are leading him toward Dream Woman's house. He needs her guidance. Her vision is strong. Where he sees only loss, perhaps she can find hope. If she is alive. Her house stands alone next to a stand of smouldering stumps. The fire burned off its roof and blackened the stone walls. Any normal person left inside would have been burned alive but Dream Woman is not normal. People saw her lift hot coals from a fire and swallow them. Perhaps her mastery over fire has saved her.

Halting in the doorway he looks in. An unwholesome stench of cold ashes emanates from the darkened room. The fire has swept through. His entire body tenses in anticipation of what he may discover. And so he finds her body on the stone floor, her white arms stretched above her head, eyes staring at the open roof, and a smile on her pale lips. The fire scorched her loincloth but did not mark her body. From the still look on her face he knows that she did not die in pain. He stands over her, more perplexed than grieving. He had come there seeking her support, only to find that she alone, of all People, had given her life to the fire. She had to have done it deliberately. Fire could not have touched her unless she allowed it. She'd told Beauty Woman that she was ready to leave the People, and she did. As mysteriously as the day she appeared from the forest.

Closing his eyes he senses a rich silence so palpable that he can almost touch or taste it. In its presence all his doubts and questions about the catastrophe fade. As he draws the deep stillness of the room into himself he understands that he no longer needs to know anything. Or hear her comforting words. Her spirit has merged with him, stronger than when she was alive.

The sun has moved over the walls and is shining on her face, when he senses he is not alone. An unfamiliar man stands close to him, also looking at Dream Woman's body. He wears the clothes of Insect People, is bareheaded and carries no weapon but he leans on a metal stick. His laboured breathing shows that he's very ill, like an old wolf about to creep off into the woods to find his final resting place. His pale eyes search the body. Nervous, he's not used to being among People.

'I'm sorry that she's dead,' the stranger says. His scowl indicates that he's not sorry at all. He'd come to search the house, and then move on.

'She gave herself,' Blue Sky says.

The stranger is astonished to hear his own language. 'What? You're talking.'

'Yes. We did talk.'

'I'll be damned. Now we have talking lupans.'

With the end of his stick her touches her body, pokes at the loincloth. 'She's not burned, not even her hair, but everything about her is burned. What's that about?'

'About death. She doesn't speak.'

'I can see she's dead. But why isn't she burned?'

'She speaks nothing,' Blue Sky repeats. The words come to him clearly yet they appear inadequate, unable to calm the man's fluster.

'Okay, she's dead. I know that she's dead.'

'Not dead,' Blue Sky says, trying to communicate a sublime vision. 'She speaks *nothing*.'

But the stranger doesn't understand the meaning of *nothing*. He doesn't see or sense it, even though *nothing* surrounds him and permeates the air.

He takes a couple of steps toward the door, but then collapses against the wall. He struggles to lift himself, using his stick as a prop. 'Can you help me?'

Beauty Woman watches two giant insects clattering overhead. They skim the distant treetops where trees are still burning, and release a pink liquid into the smoke. After vanishing over the hills they return to repeat the manoeuvre. Elder Peoples' wisdom tends to awaken too late, after the destruction is done. She's standing with Hana and other village women near the shattered insects, still smoking and so hot that no one can touch them. Hana is so shaken by the sight and smell of death that she weeps. A smell of burned flesh permeates the air. The clearing is littered with charred and severed arms, legs or heads. Beauty Woman is more distraught by her mother's pain than by the devastation and death. She cannot summon any empathy for the Insect People. They died because of their blindness. In attacking the forest they challenged too great a power. They may as well have tried to seize a lightning bolt. *Order. The way things are*; so Wolfborn would say.

On a blackened mound she discovers the body of a large wolf whose half-burned head reveals a row of powerful teeth. This was once the Protector, the voice of the forest. The wolf challenged her when she was wrong, forced her to face her illusions and taught her to walk with her feet rooted in the land. He submitted to death; knew that it was coming. When the fire broke out he was first to leave the forest, and first to fall under insect-fire.

She is still standing by the carcases when she sees Wolfborn walking toward her. Wolfborn's hair is burned off; her eyes darkened and hollow. One arm hangs limp. Her erratic breathing indicates that she is struggling to hold onto life, but greater than physical pain is her sorrow. Beauty Woman only wants to embrace her; to cling to her, but Wolfborn moves swiftly to where the Protector lies. She wraps her arms about his body, kisses the bloodied snout and lets her head rest against his. This is their final parting, her thanks for the life he gave her. For the gift of her wolf-skin.

By the time Scott and Linella reached the colony the smoke and fire had already cleared. He found the grey land more stark and empty than he had feared. The dusty smell of death permeated the air. The village women, huddled and afraid, by the den where he'd had left them. They greeted Linella, hugged her but were unable to kindle any ember of joy.

Beyond the burnt land, helicopters circled and dropped fire retardant on smoking trees. The slow chop of their blades suggested resignation; that they were tired of the conflict and no longer interested in the colony. A transporter-helicopter with a red cross painted on its side settled on the far side of the field. Figures in heavy, white suits and air tanks on their backs dropped to the ground. They sprayed chemicals into the burning helicopter shells. Other soldiers followed, searching for body-fragments of their companions. The entire exercise appeared futile. The fire and carnage had achieved nothing, other than a spasmodic release of human rage. There would be more bereaved families, all asking why it had happened. Did they feel better for the massacre of some wolves?

Two figures approached, coming from the direction of Dream Woman's house. The first was Rami. Leaning on him for support was Johnson. His feeble steps disarmed Scott's simmering anger. The man looked a step away from death.

'Bastard!' Linella's voice rang out. Before she could claw out Johnson's eyes, Scott pulled her back. 'Easy now. He's sick.'

'Look what he did.'

'Linella, stop.'

'I'm glad you're alive,' Johnson said, unperturbed by her scarlet face.

'Small thanks to you.'

'Give me a minute.' Turning to a nearby soldier he said, 'George, tell them I'll be there in a moment. You all know what to do.'

'I came to check on you,' Johnson said in a faint voice. 'I couldn't stop thinking about you, down here. I was afraid that the fire might burn everyone.'

'A bit late for that.' She coughed, spat grime from her mouth and wiped her face with her sleeve. 'Did you come to finish your job, or have you had enough?'

Johnson tried to swallow, winced and took several deep breaths before replying. 'I hate this as much as you.'

'Fuck you.'

'I'll go if you want, but don't ask me to. The men are here to clean up, take away the victims. After they're gone, you won't see them again. Not for a long time.'

'Look around you!'

'Linella,' Scott said. 'Let him finish. He has something important to say.'

'Fifty people in those helicopters aren't coming home,' Johnson said. 'They were all good people who did their job well. Unfortunately we sent them here to die. None of this should have happened; not those deaths. Not the fire. I even feel sorry for the poor wolves. Maybe the buggers saved you again. Can you help me understand what brought those choppers down?'

'Helicopters go down in bad weather,' Scott said.

'It wasn't only the weather. Maybe it looked like it, but there was something else.'

'I tried to warn you. If you pick a fight with forces than can flatten you, you take the consequences.'

'I know. I passed on your warning. What did you expect? No one backs down while they have a choice; only when there's no other way. This operation's over. I'll make sure that it never happens again.'

'You can't make that promise.'

Johnson's granite face appeared to soften. 'No I can't. But believe me, you and your lupans are the last on anyone's mind. We're all grieving for the men and women we lost. The brass have their careers to worry about. I have my life. What's left of it.'

'You've decided?' Scott said.

'I want to stay here.'

'You what?' Linella said.

'I'm dying. They won't come up with a vaccine. Not soon enough for me. I'm afraid of what they'll do to lupans when they find it. Watching the firebombs go off, I was sure that we'd fired the last salvo, one that would kill the whole fucking lot of us.' He paused to catch his breath, then added in a weak voice. 'As long as I stay here I can prevent another attack. But you'll have to keep me alive.' He smiled at Rami. 'I think I'm convinced.'

'Staying here?' Rami said.

'Yes. I want you to tell me about the woman who died in the house.'

'Dream Woman?'

'She had to be something special. Albino.'

As Johnson threatened to topple, Scott took him under one arm. 'Take it easy.'

'Help me down to the dens.'

Leaning on Scott and Linella, Johnson staggered downhill toward the large den where the women and lupans were standing. His face had turned grey. Scott wondered if he would die before they reached the dens. Linella kept up talking to him. 'Keep walking, we're almost there. Don't give up. We'll have you cured. You're going to live.'

He would live; he wouldn't be the first Plague victim to be cured in the colony. Soon a flood of ailing people would be climbing up the hill; to other lupan colonies too. As long as the lupans survived and were left alone. Johnson would have to see to that.

Two soldiers intercepted them. They saluted Johnson. The first said, 'Brigadier, three men still have life-signs. We need them flown out.'

'Call Gordon. He's in charge.'

'With due respect, sir, you need to be flown out too.'

'Follow your orders. Tell Gordon to open the letter on my desk. It will explain everything.'

They came to the meeting den. Johnson sank into a wicker chair that was pushed out for him. Bewildered, the women stared at him as if they were seeing a space alien. He avoided eye contact with them.

After a pause, he said, 'You can all stop looking at me. We're going to see a lot of each other.' With a smile he turned to Linella. 'Get me something to eat. I'm starving.'